Leave Me Home

fight for me

Kim—
read with love
[signature]

A.L. JACKSON

Copyright © 2018 A.L. Jackson Books Inc.
First Edition

All rights reserved. Except as permitted under the U.S. Copyright Act of 1976, no part of this publication may be reproduced, distributed, transmitted in any form or by any means, or stored in a database or retrieval system, without prior permission of the publisher. Please protect this art form by not pirating.

A.L. Jackson
www.aljacksonauthor.com
Cover Design by RBA Designs
Photo by **Wander Aguiar Photography.**
Editing by AW Editing and Susan Staudinger
Formatting by Mesquite Business Services

The characters and events in this book are fictitious. Names, characters, places, and plots are a product of the author's imagination. Any similarity to real persons, living or dead, is coincidental and not intended by the author.

Print ISBN: 978-1-946420-13-8
eBook ISBN: 978-1-946420-14-5

Lead Me Home

More From A.L. Jackson

<u>Confessions of the Heart</u> – NEW SERIES COMING SOON
More of You
All of Me
Pieces of Us

<u>Fight for Me</u>
Show Me the Way
Hunt Me Down
Lead Me Home – Spring 2018

<u>Bleeding Stars</u>
A Stone in the Sea
Drowning to Breathe
Where Lightning Strikes
Wait
Stay
Stand

<u>The Regret Series</u>
Lost to You
Take This Regret
If Forever Comes

<u>The Closer to You Series</u>
Come to Me Quietly
Come to Me Softly
Come to Me Recklessly

<u>Stand-Alone Novels</u>
Pulled
When We Collide

A.L. Jackson

Hollywood Chronicles, a collaboration with USA Today Bestselling Author, Rebecca Shea —
One Wild Night
One Wild Ride — *Coming Soon*

prologue

I'd always wondered why people set themselves up for disaster.

Why they put their heart on the line when they knew it would only be crushed. Why they led themselves toward the slaughter like blind, ignorant lambs.

Willingly.

I hurried down the short hall of my apartment toward the pounding at my front door. Somehow, I knew that was exactly what I was doing. Yet, there was absolutely nothing I could do to stop myself.

A storm battered the walls, and the windows rattled with a low rumble of thunder.

The door clattered with a fresh round of banging.

The knocking felt a partner to the storm—violent and unyielding—yet so utterly distinct.

My heart rose higher in my throat with every pound on the wood. It was as if an accelerant had been poured directly into my blood.

It was close to two in the morning.

Someone showing up at this time of night—in the middle of a downpour, no less—should make me cautious.

If I searched myself, I guessed a little part of me was afraid, but only because I was sure of who was on the other side of the door.

He'd always been dangerous.

Dangerous to my sanity.

Dangerous to my heart.

Obviously, none of that mattered. I was drawn to him anyway.

Tied.

Nothing more than an offering.

I hoisted up on my tiptoes to peer through the peephole, and I sucked in a breath when I saw the tortured face pleading back.

So gorgeous in its hardened, chiseled way. Wind gusted through the longer pieces of his dark-blond hair, his shirt soaked and clinging to his massive body from having to make his way through the deluge that pummeled at the roof.

Quickly, I worked through the lock and yanked open the door.

Chills flashed.

A shockwave.

All brought on by the sight of him.

"Ollie," I whispered, my spirit in an uproar.

Neither of us would ever forget this date.

It was the anniversary of the day his sister Sydney had gone missing.

That was thirteen years ago, and in all that time, he had never come to me. As desperately as I'd needed him . . . as desperately as I'd known he needed me . . . he never came.

He staggered in with a half-drained bottle of scotch clutched in his hand and kicked the door shut behind him.

He dropped the bottle to the carpeted floor, and there was no time to contemplate the *thud* before he was stalking my way.

Body massive.

A burly, beautiful, beast of a man.

I took a startled step back, sucking for the air his presence had stolen. Energy streaked through the room. Those big hands darted out and captured my face in the same second his mouth captured mine.

Lips and tongue and searing heat.

Liquor kisses.

My head spun and need blistered across my skin.

He groaned in misery and released the words between the manic scourge of his mouth. "I need you, Nikki. Need you in a way I haven't needed anything in all my life. Take it away. Fuck . . . please take it away."

If I could, I would.

It was all I'd ever wanted to do.

"Ollie." His name was grief.

Love.

Regret.

"I need you, too. I've always needed you," I told him, the confession striking the air between us with the force of a bomb. Blowing through my tiny apartment. "Why did you wait so long?"

It was a question that had him swooping me into the overwhelming strength of his arms.

He kissed me as he carried me the few steps down the hall. He kissed me when he laid me down on my bed. And he kissed me when he murmured, "You are everything I ever wished I could have."

Desire blossomed in my body.

Full bloom.

So compelling it became its own beat, a thunder in my veins that rumbled as loudly as the storm that raged overhead.

The scariest part was the way my heart sang with the hope of it.

Because I had always belonged to Oliver Preston.

The problem was, he'd never fully belonged to me.

I owned his gazes. His protection. His regret.

But he'd never allow me to possess his broken spirit.

I knew it when he tore the clothes from my body and fumbled with his belt.

I knew it when his pants and underwear hit the floor.

I knew it most when he wedged himself between my thighs

and his body met with mine.

I gasped, and he cursed, and for a moment, it was only the two of us. For a moment, we weren't just another casualty of that horrible, horrible day.

Holding me, he moved in me. With me. He panted and touched and whispered, "You take it away. You take it away. You feel so good. So good."

His fucks were deep.

Possessive.

And somehow, painfully tender.

Tears filled my eyes when he pressed his forehead to mine, and a confession fell from his mouth on a low moan, "I miss her. I miss her so much. When will it stop? When will this feeling ever go away?"

I clung to him.

Gave him my body.

If I could, I would have given him everything.

But I guessed maybe I knew better when his body went rigid and he grunted when he came, one moment behind me as he drew out my pleasure perfectly.

Knew better when he slumped to the bed and wrapped me in his muscled arms that were covered in weeping ink.

Knew it when I fell into a dreamless sleep.

When I woke in the morning and he was gone, I realized I'd known it all along.

one

Nikki
One Year Later

"Miss Nikki?" The timid voice hit me from behind.

I stilled where I was refilling my disposable coffee cup at the table. It was set up at the back of the large meeting room in the basement of an office building we rented out every Tuesday night.

I gave myself a moment to gather my composure after the intense session before I turned around with a soft smile on my face.

Brenna.

She stood there, nervously twisting her fingers together, the bruise around her eye finally beginning to fade. She hadn't said a thing the entire session, but the fact that she had even shown up at all had felt like a victory.

"Hey," I told her gently. My heart suddenly felt as if it were too big to fit in my chest. "What did you think of the meeting tonight?"

She chewed at the inside of her lip. "It was good. Everyone is really nice."

"That's good to hear. We want you to be comfortable. It's a safe place."

"I feel safe here." She almost blanched when she said it. As if she never truly felt it or maybe she was scared to. She hesitated and then said, "I wanted to tell you something."

I set my coffee cup aside and fully turned to her. "Of course. You can tell me anything."

There was something about this young girl that got to me. Something that made me want to wrap her up and protect her. Hold her and keep her safe forever.

At barely eighteen with a two-year-old little boy, she'd already been through enough to last her a lifetime. Most of her turmoil was thanks to the piece of garbage who was supposed to be her boyfriend.

"I left him."

Relief.

Sometimes I wondered how it could be so intense.

"I'm so proud of you," I told her, not even trying to keep the emotion out of my voice. "Where are you staying?"

"My momma's. She said Kyle and I could stay with her a bit until I get on my feet."

"That's good. So good. Do you need any money? Anything from me?"

I knew I was making myself too available. Offering too much. But with her, I couldn't help it. All I wanted was to make a difference; although, I was pretty sure Kathy, the doctored psychologist who oversaw the group and mentored me, would tell me I was being a little too overeager.

Or maybe tell me I was straight up breaking the rules.

Call it a pitfall of my personality, I didn't care. I just wanted to do . . . something.

More than something.

Truth was, I'd give absolutely everything I could.

Brenna pursed her lips. "Just you bein' there for me that night meant everything. I don't think I would have had the courage to call anyone else. I've never been so scared—for myself or for my son. You were there when we needed you most. I don't know how to repay you for that."

I gave a tight shake of my head, unable to hold back the moisture that rushed to my eyes. "You don't need to repay me. The only thing I need is to know the two of you are safe. You keep my number close, okay? If you need anything, anything at all, I want you to call me."

"I will," she promised. Her gaze turned to the ground before she looked back up at me. Expression loaded with trust. "I just wanted to let you know."

"I'm glad you did."

Her nod was slight, and I gave her a small smile before she turned and climbed the steps leading from the basement floor meeting room.

Joy filled me full, and I turned back to the table and pressed my palms to it, head dropping as I pulled in a deep breath.

Two years ago, I'd taken the plunge and started accelerated online courses to get my psychology degree. Quietly at first, because I hadn't quite put my finger on why I felt compelled to start down this path. Unsure of where I was going or if I'd stay the course.

Mostly I'd been uncertain of *why* I was doing it.

My purpose.

I'd finally realized I'd just wanted to make a difference.

If I could make one person's life better, help them see the beauty of the world in the midst of so much cruelty and sorrow, it would be worth it.

Maybe I was doing it because of Sydney.

That was okay.

The only thing I knew was I wanted to pour something positive and good into the world after experiencing such a great loss.

That didn't mean the last two years hadn't been rough. It'd been difficult balancing all the online classes and now interning here with Dr. Kathy's women's program while I was still working at Pepper's Pies, the diner my friend Rynna owned.

But after tonight?

I knew it was all going to be worth it.

With a smile on my face, I finished cleaning up the refreshment area while Kathy stacked the folding chairs.

"Are you ready?" she asked.

I grabbed my bag and slung it over my shoulder. "I am."

We flipped off the lights and headed up the stairs. The darkness was thick as we made our way to the ground floor and let ourselves out the front door and down the steps that led to the sidewalk.

The Alabama air was muggy and thick, the summer night sagging with humidity.

The area was pretty much deserted this time of night, the street flanked by two and three-story office buildings that had been around since the beginning of Gingham Lakes.

The drone of cars echoed in the distance, and Kathy's heels clicked on the sidewalk as she headed for her car parked at the curb in front of mine. "Good night," she called.

"Good night. I'll see you next week," I hollered over my shoulder as I rounded the front of my old car to the driver's side.

She paused at hers. "You did well tonight, Nikki. Really well. The women feel comfortable with you."

I looked back at her.

It was funny how I was always the first to laugh. My first instinct to tease and play. But when it came to this, there was nothing but somberness on my face. "I hope so."

A soft smile graced her face. "They are. It's clear you're doing this for all the right reasons. Because you want to be here."

As soon as she said it, she slipped into the front seat of her car and started it. Her headlights cut through the darkness.

I was grinning as I opened my car door and started to slip behind the wheel, only to pause when my attention caught on a small, folded piece of paper tucked under the windshield wiper.

I snagged it, jumped inside, and started my car, only then unfolding what I expected to be a coupon or announcement or sale.

My heart stuttered in my chest.

Deep dents were made in the paper in scratchy letters.

Don't forget about me. I'm coming for you.

Dropping the note, I grabbed on to the steering wheel. My attention darted all around, eyes squinting as I searched the shadows.

There was nothing.

No sign of life other than the brake lights illuminated at the back of Kathy's car as she waited for me to follow.

Dread settled in my gut, and the tiny sheet felt as if it weighed a million pounds as Brenna and Kyle's faces filled my mind.

That little punk.

He thought he could scare me.

He thought wrong.

two

Ollie

What the fuck was I doing? I knew better than this. So much better than this. But I couldn't help it. Couldn't stop myself.

Not when it came to her.

Call it a sickness.

I didn't care.

It was after ten at night when I inched my car up behind her, and that pissed me off, too.

The girl traipsed across the deserted parking lot.

Alone.

Wading through this shithole like a sitting duck.

A tremor of anger ridged down my spine when my gaze moved over the area.

The lot was hidden at the back of the run-down apartment building, like it'd been designed that way specifically for some lowlife to take advantage of the defenseless and vulnerable.

Space nothing but a blanket of darkness except for a couple of dingy, dull streetlamps that barely leaked light in small pools onto the pitted pavement.

Two dumpsters lined the far end, motherfucking shadows

dancing out from behind them and across the asphalt like they were restless, eager to become a player in a horror story.

With her head down, she walked toward the exterior stairs of her apartment. She didn't even notice me since she had her attention all wrapped up in her phone that she was staring at in her hand.

Didn't know which was worse.

That, or her other hand being clutched around the handles of this huge-ass bag, just swinging it along at her side like she was begging for it to be stolen.

My chest clenched.

Reckless girl.

Reckless girl who was wearing these tight red pants and some flowery, flowy blouse that I'd expect to see some grandma wear.

How the hell it still managed to get me hard, I didn't know, but there I was, shifting in my damned seat.

Light brown, honeyed locks tumbled a few inches below her shoulders, her hair messy and wild and untamed.

Just like her personality.

As eager as her heart and as bright as her spirit.

Motherfucking sunshine.

The girl was tall and so goddammed skinny. All sharp edges and waif-thin lines. I had to remind myself I liked curves and big tits and handfuls of ass.

Nikki. Fucking. Walters.

The bane of my existence.

Hands gripping the steering wheel, I angled my car right behind her. The spray of my headlights struck her like a spotlight, making her jump about two feet off the ground. She spun around, hand with her phone going up to cover her heart.

Her mouth gaped open in shock.

Well, at least she noticed me.

I rammed the gear of my old Mustang into park and threw open the door, feeling all kinds of pissed off that this girl didn't seem to have a defensive bone in her body.

Self-preservation nonexistent.

She just stood there like a deer caught in the headlights, two seconds from being run down and unable to move to do anything about it.

Hankering for a confrontation, I jumped out.

The fear in her expression transformed the second she realized it was me.

Her eyes were an indigo-blue, like a cracked-open amethyst crystal.

Her own brand of indignant anger burned through the center of them.

Hurt and a fucked-up sense of loyalty.

God damn it . . . I knew better than this.

But with her, I didn't know how to stop myself.

three

Nikki

"Ollie." I rasped his name, trying to steady my wobbling knees. To steady my feet. "You scared the crap out of me."

He'd almost gotten himself a face-full of mace, which would not have been pretty.

And man, oh man, was the boy pretty.

It really would have sucked to muck up that view, even if he would have deserved it. Especially after the note I'd found tonight.

"You should be scared," he gritted.

Beneath the hazy glow of the streetlamps, my heart drummed an erratic beat, and I struggled to slow my ragged breaths that jetted from my lungs. Panic and angered surprise was a blaze that beat through my veins.

My nerves were already set to high-alert, every faint sound enough to have me looking over my shoulder, worried that little asshole would follow me. Threaten me as if I'd just give up and send Brenna back to him. Or maybe he'd go as far to hurt me the way he'd hurt her. Or worse.

"And what exactly am I supposed to be scared of, Oliver?"

He scoffed. "I could have been any asshole out hunting for prey. Some disgusting prick looking for an easy target."

The thing with Ollie? I *was* afraid. But not for my physical wellbeing. When it came to him, the only thing in danger was my heart.

He was always sneaking into my life when I didn't have the mental fortitude to resist him. Tonight, I was feeling fragile, and the sight of him just about dropped me to my knees.

I thought I'd made it plenty clear he wasn't welcome. Not anymore. Not after that night a year ago.

Giving comfort did not mean making myself a doormat.

And that was what he'd made me.

Nothing but a place to stomp the dirt off his big shoe.

My head shook. "Yet, you're the only asshole standing there."

A harsh breath of air left his gorgeous mouth. I tried to pretend I didn't notice. "Call me an asshole. Fine. I deserve it. But that doesn't change the fact that you were out here alone. Vulnerable. Someone could hurt you."

With the last, I saw the worry flash across his magnificent features. Maybe the hardest part was how genuine it was.

Which was precisely the reason I couldn't tell him what had happened tonight.

He'd demand I quit. He'd insist I was putting myself in danger and what I was doing was stupid.

Careless.

When I'd never been so full of *care* in all my life.

He stared me down.

Attraction trembled around us like a magnified force. Like the world still spun while we stood still.

The two of us no longer in orbit, and instead, we were strung up in an endless oblivion.

Shivers rolled, and it didn't have a thing to do with the tremble of fear I'd felt a few moments ago.

It was the potent energy that was this man blasting across my flesh like the warmth from a furnace on a cold winter's day.

My attraction to him was so intense I wondered how he didn't taste it in the air.

Bristling and brimming and begging.

Chemistry.

As much as I didn't want it to, it banged between us.

Painfully.

I didn't mean for my smile to come across as sad. There were just some things a person couldn't help. Not when we'd planned for things to turn out so differently between us.

"I don't exactly have someone I'm coming home to who can watch out for me, now, do I?"

He lifted his chin in some sort of defense, and a flash of severity and regret and things I didn't want to read struck through his eyes. "Why do you think I'm here, Nikki. To look after you."

My eyes squeezed shut, and I tried to pretend I didn't want to welcome it. His safety and his protection and his care. But it was right there, surging and spinning like a tease.

It was all compounded by the tight ball of hatred I held for him. He'd used me, and I'd let him.

"You're here to look out for me?" My words were incredulous.

"Yup."

Ollie, who was all rigid anger and glowering scowl where he clung to the top of the doorframe of the black muscle car that was almost as pretty as he was.

He looked like a savage beast with the long pieces of his dark, sandy hair pushed back on his head, the sides cropped short, beard on his face trimmed but full.

The man was this hulking tower of muscle and brawn and intricately drawn ink.

A haunting rendition of the lake had been imprinted on the entirety of his left arm, and a field of the same purple blazing star flowers we'd run through as children swayed from his wrist and up his forearm on the right, those massive, bulging muscles flexed in restraint as he gripped the door.

The position harshly exposed the words etched on his knuckles.

Lost on the left and *Soul* on the right.

It was as if they'd been purposefully tattooed there to punch me in the gut every time I saw them, the permanent reminder of what he'd lost.

Of what *we'd* lost.

My lips pursed. "Maybe I don't want you here."

"Too bad."

Cocky bastard.

I pointed at my apartment behind me. "I don't need this right now, Ollie. It's been a long night, and I just want to go upstairs, pour myself a glass of wine, and crawl into bed."

He stepped away from his car and slammed the door shut.

"Where were you tonight?" he demanded. As if I'd done something wrong.

Every inch of him was rugged and rough and commanding, his body dripping sex from behind a closed-off exterior.

It was all mixed up with this troubled kindness that weighed heavily in the depths of his sapphire eyes, his soft lips always quick to tip into a gentle smile.

He was an enigma.

A veiled mystery.

A cliffhanger waiting to be written.

Who was I kidding?

He was a goddamned mindfuck, that was what he was.

And he'd broken my heart one too many times for me to fall into that trap again.

A resigned sigh pilfered free. "I was at the women's support group. Remember? The internship I have. You know . . . to finish my courses to graduate?"

I didn't mean for the sarcasm to drip out with it, but it did. Ollie had this way of getting under my skin.

"Of course, I remember. I just didn't think that'd mean you'd be running around at all hours of the night." His return came out just as harsh.

"People have lives, Ollie. Jobs and families. It only makes sense for these types of meetings to happen after normal work hours, don't you think?"

"Suppose so. Guess that just means I'll have to drive you."

Lead Me Home

He said it as if it made perfect sense.

Why did he have to constantly do this to me? Pulling and pulling and pulling me closer.

And every time we collided, I only crashed into a brick wall.

"No, thank you."

"I wasn't asking." His voice was gruff.

Hard and demanding.

An extension of the man.

I exhaled heavily. "You have a bar to run. And I'm not a little girl, in case you hadn't noticed. You don't need to worry about me."

"You know that's impossible."

The jab of a knife.

That was what it felt like when he said things like that. A million little cuts over the years that left me continuously bleeding out.

"You haven't shown up here for a year. Why now?"

He flinched, a streak of vulnerability flashing through his face. "Lillith came into Olive's earlier. She said you bailed on her for drinks the other night, and you haven't been to the bar for like a week. Texted you to check up, and you didn't text back. Like I said, I got worried."

Shit.

The last thing I needed was this man melting me.

"I rescheduled on Lily because I had a test I needed to study for. She knew that. I turn my phone off during the meetings so it doesn't cause a distraction, and I barely just turned it back on in the car. And it's been three days since I've been in the bar. *Three days*."

Exasperation filled the last.

And there he was showing up as if he missed me.

But the way that he was looking at me had me wondering if he might. And those were dangerous thoughts I had no business entertaining.

"I'm a big girl, Ollie. I'm home. Safe. You can go on your way."

That intense gaze flashed, and his mouth pinched into some

kind of unfound resentment.

"Yeah. You're safe. This time. Thank God, considering you were walking around at this time of night with your face buried in your phone, paying zero attention to your surroundings. You should know better than that. Which is why I will drive you next week."

Annoyance blew out on my breath. He was impossible. "I was paying attention. I already had my phone programmed to 9-1-1 and mace in my hand. You think I didn't notice someone driving like a creeper into the lot?"

"Paying attention? Hardly. You could have been gagged and shoved in my trunk before you even realized what was happening."

I cocked my head. "The gagging I might be up for . . . not so sure about the trunk."

Sometimes I couldn't help but toss his nonsense right back.

Ollie growled. Actually freaking growled, and chills were flashing across my flesh, a whirlwind of energy that skated my skin like a rough, demanding caress.

"Not a joking matter, Nikki," he grated, taking a jolting step forward and getting right in my face.

No.

He was right.

It wasn't. Not after Sydney had gone missing fourteen years ago.

She'd left a chasm right in the center of us.

A black hole in our bright, shining sky.

Gaping and bleeding and pleading.

She'd wandered out into the night and disappeared without a trace.

That night, I'd lost both of them. Sydney was gone and Ollie had all but turned to stone.

Yeah. We still ran in the same circle. A circle that was tight. As close as family, the bonds forged between us just as important. Maybe more so.

The thing was, Ollie and I were on the opposite sides of that circle, keeping each other at arm's length and a world away.

Yet, somehow, after all this time, he continued to remain possessive of me. Keeping me under his guarded watch. As if I were a child he needed to protect. As if he'd forgotten everything we'd been through together.

What we'd almost been to each other.

I'd made the mistake of falling for him a long, long time ago.

When I was little more than a kid.

The problem was, he would never allow himself to fall for me.

Oliver Preston was armor and stone.

Bitterness and venom.

Broken fragments.

Shrapnel waiting to burst.

What made it harder was that there was no missing that huge, giving heart that he kept stunted. Hidden in the darkest kind of shadows.

That made him dangerous to my sanity. Poison to my heart. Yet, I always found myself back in his bar with my friends as if it didn't mean a thing, pasting on a smile and a tease while the man was slowly killing me.

But tonight? It all felt like too much.

"Seriously, Ollie. Don't burden yourself by worrying about me."

He hesitated, throat bobbing. "But I do. Can't change that. No matter how hard I try."

Emotion rushed. So tight. I felt the prickle of the tear blurring my eye before I even realized it was streaking down my cheek.

"Shit," he whispered. One of those big hands darted for my cheek.

I jerked back. "Don't touch me."

His hand dropped like a rock.

"Shit," he whispered again, this time a hiss of frustration. "I'm sorry."

My head shook. I searched his expression, my own frustration bleeding out. "You tell me it's impossible for you not to worry about me, but as far as I'm concerned, I shouldn't even cross your mind."

He flinched, and beneath his beard, his thick throat rolled with his swallow. I got the feeling the man was swallowing a torrent of things he couldn't allow himself to say.

Guard up.

Shields on.

"You're always on my mind," he admitted, voice low, scraping with the admission.

It was so unexpected it knocked the breath from me.

"You don't get to show up here, sayin' things like that to me. You don't get to yank me around, Ollie. I won't let you do that to me. Not anymore."

He swore quietly under his breath before he slowly brought that penetrating gaze up to meet with mine again.

Eyes tangled.

Spirits tied.

Hostages to the intensity that tightened my chest and filled my lungs.

How the hell was I ever supposed to get over him?

"I won't apologize for caring about you. For worrying about you. But the last thing I intended was to show up here acting like an overbearing asshole. I just wanted to check on you."

Tingles raced my throat. Damn him.

I gathered myself and pasted on one of those smiles.

Fake and brittle.

"Don't worry about me. I'm just fine. See." I lifted my hands out to my sides. "All in one piece. So you can leave, go on back to whatever or whoever it is you usually do on a Tuesday night."

Bitterness oozed out with the words.

I didn't mean for it to. Human emotions were such tricky little things. They could be fleeting and fast.

Forgotten before we gave ourselves time to ponder them.

Or they wiggled their way in, so deep that it was impossible to imagine they hadn't been part of us all along.

They came and they went.

They skipped out before they took hold or they lasted a lifetime.

Anger. Joy. Hate. Hope. Fear.

Attractions and crushes and obsessions.

The people who knew me best could say I suffered from any one of those emotions when it came to Oliver Preston. Lillith teased me relentlessly, and I let her, played it off as if it really didn't mean all that much.

He was the one thing I didn't fully let her in on. She believed my feelings for him amounted to nothing more than a mad crush.

The problem was?

I just . . . loved him.

I did, and I had for too many years, and it hurt too much that he didn't love me back.

I took a step back. "I need to go."

I turned on my heel and headed for the exterior steps of my run-down apartment. Even though Gingham Lakes had seen a major rejuvenation over the last decade, this area had not.

I couldn't afford anything else. I wasn't exactly raking in the dough managing Pepper's Pies.

But it was enough.

Enough to get by on until I finished school.

As I mounted the second-floor landing, I peeked over my shoulder.

I shouldn't have.

My heart stuttered at the sight of him. At the fact he kept looking at me in that way I wished he wouldn't. In a way that made hope and need glow hot.

His presence solid as he stared up at me from where he stood beside his car.

So thick I couldn't do anything but breathe him in.

Intoxicating.

The man was a drug.

I jerked my attention away and rushed for my apartment door, only to stumble in my tracks.

A harsh gasp sucked into my lungs.

Shocked.

Stunned.

Then my heart took off racing in a panic of fear.

Horror beating a path through my veins.

Dread took me whole.

My hand went over my mouth, and I choked out, "Oh my God."

I could feel Ollie pounding up the steps. Two seconds later, he was in front of me and pushing me back.

His stance protective when he ordered, "Don't move."

four
Ollie

Bitch.

It was spray painted in red across her door, and pieces of wood were splintered where a sharp object had been rammed against the door.

Probably an axe.

My heart raced like a motherfucker, anger and protectiveness and fear this blistering heat that churned a thousand tons of adrenaline through my veins.

My chest cinched tighter with every step as I inched forward.

It made it harder and harder to breathe.

Hit with the overpowering urge to make sure she was close, I reached back for Nikki.

Not sure whether to wrap her up and run with her or rush the fuck inside and take out any asshole stupid enough to still be in there.

Take out any piece of shit who might threaten her.

A fucking landslide of jagged rocks scraped at my throat, and I looked back at Nikki who was watching the whole scene through wide, horrified eyes.

Totally shocked.

My insides curled. Every worry I'd ever had surfaced. A surprise attack.

"You still got 9-1-1 up on your dial?" I gritted through clenched teeth, inclining my ear toward the door, trying to listen for any movement inside.

The frame was splintered. Lock knocked loose. Door hanging open an inch.

"Yes," she whispered, voice choked.

"Call it. Tell them to hurry," I urged, nudging the door open with the toe of my boot and taking a quick peek in to look around her tiny apartment.

Stillness echoed back.

But the place . . . it was trashed.

Pictures had been torn from the walls. Lamp knocked to the floor. Couch flipped, ripped apart. In the kitchen, which ran along the far back wall, boxes and cans of food were strewn across the floor.

Ransacked and ravaged.

I roughed a shaking hand over my face, trying to see through the red blaze of hate that clouded my vision.

I could feel my control slipping.

My sanity shifting.

Fuck. It'd been *shifting* all along—since the night my sister had gone missing and I'd become an entirely different man.

My cool had been nothing but a front as I waited.

As I watched.

As I forced myself to hang back, feign patience, until a debt came due.

It was what kept me moving every day. Hunting for my sister.

It was the singular focus of my life. What I'd devoted myself to.

Could feel a splinter of that focus breaking off as my hands curled with the crushing need to chase down any fucker who would even think about hurting Nikki.

Nikki.

Nikki. Fucking. Walters.

This girl threatened to be my undoing.

From behind, I listened to one side of Nikki's conversation with the 9-1-1 operator. "Yes, that's the correct address. The door is busted in, and it has been spray painted."

"It looks like it was splintered with a sharp object."

"Second floor apartment."

I cringed with every detail she reiterated.

Like I was having to see it for the first time.

"No, I don't think anyone is inside."

"No one is hurt. There's no need for an ambulance."

At least not until I found them.

"I'm not sure," she said.

Nikki nodded and whispered at me, "She said to wait outside and not touch anything."

I gave a restrained nod.

It was painful.

I wanted to charge inside. Do a little of that hunting I was made to do.

Protect her.

Just like I'd had the overwhelming need to do earlier, running over here to check on her since she hadn't returned my text.

I was the dumbass who'd showed up here unannounced.

But what if I hadn't?

Dread spiraled through me. A slow stir of something that had simmered forever.

Heat igniting beneath it.

All of two minutes passed before we could hear sirens approaching.

My eyes remained on that indigo gaze, refusing to lose sight, wanting to sink deeper.

Search for the secrets I could so clearly see hiding there.

I forced myself to stand still.

Her lips moved slowly as she spoke into her cell. "Yes, thank you, they're here."

She ended the call and pulled the phone from her ear.

"Who did this?" The question was nothing but shards of hatred from my tongue.

Slowly, she shook her head, blinked in a confused, agitated fear.

Didn't matter. I was certain I saw a moment of clarity doused with worry flit through her expression.

Her own intuition meeting with mine.

"I don't know," she whispered.

I wanted to grab her by the shoulders, shake her, demand more, but two officers were climbing from the cruiser that had just pulled into the parking lot below, their lights spinning through the desolate night.

Couldn't help but feel grateful when I saw the face of the man who started climbing the steps.

Seth Long.

He was an old friend from high school who'd gone into the academy right after graduation. A good guy. A good cop.

Surprise had him faltering a step when he realized who was standing in front of him. "Nikki . . . Ollie . . . God. The last thing I expected was to roll up here and find you two. Are you okay?"

The obvious answer was no.

But true to form, Nikki turned and plastered on one of her smiles. "Yeah. Thank God. We're fine."

Bright, blinding light.

Motherfucking sunshine.

A taste of sweet, sweet lemonade.

That was what Nikki was. Felt myself itching to lean forward and glean some of it. To swim in her calm and her belief.

They said sunshine chases away the dark. I swore, all it did was deepen mine. Amplify why I couldn't take her. Have her.

I was a bastard.

A sinner.

God knew what I was responsible for.

He also knew what I'd be willing to do—vengeance a greed I carried in the palm of my hands.

But that girl? She was a sin I'd never again commit.

Seth and his partner stepped around us, their guns drawn as Seth nudged the broken door open with the toe of his boot.

They edged in, quick to scour before Seth was back in the

doorway. "Whoever was here is gone."

"Thank God," Nikki whispered, releasing a huge breath.

Relief.

Wasn't even sure that I felt it.

The only thing it meant was the person who'd done this was still running the streets.

"I need you two to hang out for a bit while we take some pictures and dust for prints."

He swung his gaze to Nikki. "If you're up for it, afterward I'd like you to come inside to see if you see anything missing. I have to warn you, the place is torn up. It's not pretty."

Nikki crossed her arms over her chest. Hugging herself.

My sight snagged on the dragonfly tattoo on the inside of her right wrist. Every time I saw it, it felt like my guts were being shredded.

The way she wore her ghosts the same way I wore mine.

"It never was," she attempted like it was going to lighten the mood.

I wasn't fucking laughing.

The second Seth disappeared, I spun back around.

This girl was so fucking pretty it hurt to look at her. I bit back all those old feelings I couldn't feel. "I need you to go through every single person who might have done this to you."

She sucked her lip into her mouth. "I can't think of anyone."

I wondered if she knew I could see straight through her.

"Don't do this, Nikki. Don't protect someone who doesn't deserve protecting. What is it you're trying to hide?"

Seth popped his head back through the door, interrupting all the demands I wanted to make. "We're ready for you."

"Thank you," she said, sidestepping me and entering her apartment.

I followed right behind.

Nikki started moving through the place, cringing, clearly worrying as she took in the tornado that had ripped through her home.

A storm.

That was exactly what it felt like had hit.

It was the same feeling that had been gathering strength for a while.

Rising and lifting.

The nightmares I couldn't escape coming more often and more intense than ever.

That gut-deep intuition that something was coming.

Something wicked.

I paced her crummy little apartment, yanking at my hair, feeling like I might go out of my damned mind.

Seth was finishing getting her statement where they'd ended up in her bedroom while I stewed and raged in the living room.

I could hear her voice floating from her room. "There was this box my grandma just left me. She said there were some mementoes and keepsakes in there that she wanted me to go through and share with my sister. I only picked it up a couple days ago. I hadn't had the chance to go through it, yet. It was right up there . . . at the top of my closet."

"You're sure?"

"Yeah. It was definitely there."

"You don't know what was in there?" Seth asked.

I peeked down the short hall, watching him scribble something in his notebook.

"No. But it had a little lock. It probably looked like the only thing in the whole place that was of any value. Whoever it was is going to be sorely disappointed when they crack it open and find it's probably nothing but a bunch of pictures I painted my grandma when I was a little girl. The only other thing I can see is missing is a silver ring I'd left next to my bathroom sink."

Yeah, someone was going to be sorely, sorely disappointed.

Surely they didn't have the first clue that coming in here and messing with Nikki meant they were fucking with me.

Sometimes lessons had to be learned the hard way. I was going to be all-too happy to teach it.

The three of them moved back out into the living room, Seth talking while they did. "My guess is this is another case of punk kids running the streets and causing trouble."

Seth said it almost casually.

"They probably took off running when your neighbor came out to see what the commotion was. It happens more than I would like to admit. They're looking for anything easy to unload for a little cash, and if they don't find anything, they don't think twice about ruining people's belongings, out of spite or fun, I'm not sure. Either way, it sucks that you have to deal with the aftermath."

She nodded but looked unconvinced.

"Are you sure you can't think of anyone who would have done this?" he asked for the third time.

Nikki's gaze dropped to the floor, off to the side as she ran her hands over her arms and gnawed at that plump bottom lip.

She wasn't saying something. I knew it. *Knew* it.

She accused me of not knowing her.

What bullshit.

I knew her better than anyone.

She went back to hugging herself. "I can't think of anyone. I mean . . . I'm Nikki. Who could hate me?"

She gave a wide grin.

Honestly, it looked a whole lot more like a grimace than anything. Kind of pathetic and awkward and desperate.

She wasn't fooling anyone.

"What about at school or the diner?"

Her head shook. "My classes are all online, and everyone's wonderful at the diner. Who wouldn't be after Rynna feeds them those breakfast pastry pies. Happiest people in the world. I'm sure you're right, and it was just kids," she continued with a resolute nod. "There are packs of them roaming the area all the time. It was bound to happen."

Bound to happen.

I was *bound* to kick someone's ass.

"Luckily, if that's the case, they usually move on once they figure out there isn't anything of value for them to take."

Although Seth's words were obviously delivered to offer her some comfort, he kept shooting me glances on the sly.

Nikki laughed a self-deprecating sound. "Well, then, I'm sure that ring was worth a mint, and unless they were after the VHS player my grandma gave me for my tenth birthday, then they are straight out of luck."

Seth chuckled while he scribbled something onto a fresh sheet in his notepad. "You probably made yourself a prime target with that one."

"I knew I should have gotten a security system with all my valuables. Oh God, what if they'd found my Discman?" Her eyes went wide with feigned horror. "Living the high life is dangerous."

I would have laughed if I wasn't so pissed. Only this girl would make light of the situation.

She'd also be the one to hang on to all those pieces of her childhood.

My insides clutched as I thought about her hopping into her grandmother's car every Saturday morning.

Tagging along to yard sales and thrift stores like it was some sort of epic trip to Chanel.

Couldn't count the number of times the girl had busted into our house with pride in her eyes to show off the latest gadget she'd picked up with her grandma. Half the time, it'd already be obsolete or missing pieces or just plain ugly, but she never cared.

She'd go on about why it'd called out to her. Why it was supposed to have belonged to her all along.

Sentimental to the skinny bone.

Hell, I wouldn't have put it past her to be carrying a beeper in that huge-ass purse of hers, too.

"You should have been born in the seventies," Seth teased.

"I know, I was robbed. Think of all the awesome music I missed out on in the eighties."

He laughed. "Robbed. Vandalized. You really are a target."

Anger soured on my tongue. Knew he was being cool. Setting her at ease. But her safety wasn't a damned joke.

"All right, I think that's all I need for now," Seth said, ripping out the sheet and flipping the notepad closed. "You know where to get in touch with me if you think of anything else. Sometimes things become clearer after the shock wears off. We lifted a couple of prints, so I'll let you know what we find, and I'll send someone over first thing in the morning to get your door fixed."

Nikki sent him a wobbly smile. "Thank you, Seth. I really do appreciate it."

"Just doing my job, though, I have to admit, wasn't a fan of doing it here. You need to be careful, Nikki."

"I know."

He hesitated. "Are you sure you're fine?"

She nodded and pasted on one of those smiles. One of the ones that promised Nikki Walters was just fine.

Having a blast.

Even when the world tossed her shit and problems and trials, she chose to live life large and to its fullest.

"Yeah, I'm totally fine. No need to worry. I knew what I was signing up for when I moved in here."

Seth shook his head. "All right then, I'm going to get out of your hair. Take care of yourself," he told her.

He walked toward me and reached out to shake my hand. With the other, he slipped me the sheet he'd ripped out of the notebook.

Unease rumbled in my gut.

I gave him a tight jut of my chin. "See ya, man."

"Yup," he said before he and his partner slipped out.

Nikki followed them and did her best to wedge the door shut. While her back was to me, I peeked at the note.

None of this sits right. Call me.

Nikki grunted, trying to get it shut but the wood was too mangled and disfigured.

What if she'd been there? Alone?

What would have happened then?

What had the intruder's intention been in the first place?

Fear tumbled through me like a slow, excruciating burn.

Lava that sprouted from my soul.

Singeing my insides.

It was doubled by a bolt of that rage. A stake through my spirit.

It landed right in the midst of the rest of that bubbling fury, leaving me to barely hang on.

Sometimes I looked in the mirror and was terrified of myself, having no clue who I was gonna be when it happened.

When it all came to a head.

Where she stood facing away from me, I watched a tremble roll through her body. The girl refused to let on that she was shaken up by the incident.

She thought I didn't see her.

Problem was, I could see her too well.

"You knew what you were signing up for when you moved in here." There was no question behind it. Just an accusation.

A frustrated laugh jolted from her mouth, and from behind, she shook her head. "Sometimes there aren't any other options, Ollie."

She slowly turned to face me, and she lifted her chin a fraction.

Defiantly.

Proudly.

That was my girl.

Proud and way too brave and far too sweet.

A dangerously reckless combination.

"We work hard. We make do. We accept that sometimes our lives aren't as pretty as we might like them to be. We accept that our lives don't look the same as we once imagined they would."

Regret tumbled through me at that.

I was the holder of so many of the dreams she'd whispered about.

Dreams she'd trusted me with.

I was the image that no longer looked the same.

"It wasn't like I was going to continue to live with my sister once she got married and became a mom. So here I am."

She lifted her arms out to the sides like her reasoning was going to deter me. "Home sweet home."

She started for the kitchen that was only separated from the living room by a change from old, worn carpet to dinged-to-shit linoleum.

I surveyed the disaster again. Unease knocked at my ribs. My voice was low when I spoke. "Looks personal to me. You sure there isn't anything you want to tell me?"

She kept walking, dipping to grab three boxes of cereal that had been pulled from the pantry and dumped onto the floor.

But I saw it.

The misstep.

The way her spine went rigid in fear.

Hiding.

She was all too quick to cover the ripple of disquiet.

Her words shifted into an overcompensating rant that rode on her breath, "Little punks need someone to teach them a lesson. I mean, seriously, how uncool. Breaking shit for the fun of it. I just never have gotten that mentality. Making life harder for someone . . . because what? They're bored?"

She sucked in a saddened breath. "And my grandma's stuff . . . she's gonna be so heartbroken that I don't have it. It's hard enough that she's fallen sick. People don't even realize the things they do really hurt. Or maybe that's exactly what they want."

There was an undertone to all of it as she tossed the boxes back onto the shelf. Like she was processing.

Like she knew exactly who'd done this.

"Do you have a bat?" she asked, whirling around to face me.

Her expression had turned eager.

Actually fuckin' serious as she looked back at me like she just stumbled on the solution to all the world's problems.

Or at least hers.

Unreal.

She had to be insane.

Or driving me there.

"You're coming home with me." The words were out before I could stop them.

Yeah, it was a bad idea.

But there was no chance in hell I was gonna leave her by herself. Not with the lock on the door broken.

Like a lock made a difference anyway.

"What?" Her brows lifted so high they disappeared beneath

the long, wispy bangs that framed her face.

Her goddamned striking face.

Eyes wide and sincere and true. Color that shouldn't be possible.

High, carved cheeks. Smooth, olive skin. Plump, pink-tinted lips.

That smattering of brown freckles that crested the bridge of her nose and dusted beneath her eyes made her appear so damned young and innocent.

But it was that body that bristled with an undercurrent of energy and fire that sent streaks of light radiating from her like the breaking day.

Couldn't stand the thought of her energy fading away. This crazy energy that emanated from her skin like the glow of neon colors.

Couldn't stand the thought of someone touching it.

Snuffing it out.

Dimming that light until it was cast into darkness.

"I said you're coming home with me. You can't stay here by yourself."

Her mouth dropped open in offense, and she propped her hands on her narrow waist, trying to come off as valiant and strong when I saw the panic quiver through her veins.

Yeah.

I was fucking panicked, too.

"Excuse me, but I'm not sure when you decided you got to make decisions for me."

"When some asshole busted in your door, that's when."

She shook her head. "I'm not going to your place."

"No?"

"Nope."

I dug out my cell phone. "Fine, I'll call Lillith, and I'll drop you off there."

Horror crested those pink lips. "Don't you dare, Oliver Preston. It's almost midnight. You're going to freak her out. This is Lily we're talking about, and you know the last thing I need is for her to get all worried over me. She'll have Brody trying to build me my own sky-rise apartment or something."

Sounded like a good plan. I knew there was a reason I liked the guy.

"Rex and Rynna, then. Or maybe your sister Sammie. I'm sure she has a cozy couch."

So what if I was goading her.

"Are you crazy? And wake up their kids?" she screeched as she pointed at me. "And don't you dare say Hope and Kale. Chances are, we'd catch those two right in the middle of something they don't want us to interrupt. They can't keep their hands off each other. I think that was one of my best matches to date."

Her voice got all dreamy on the last. The girl thought she was some kind of arrow-shooting cupid, responsible for every relationship each of our friends had fallen into.

It was cute and eccentric and ridiculous.

Crazy talk.

That's exactly what this was.

What *I* was.

Crazy.

Crazy for even considering this. Crazier for insisting on it. Because I knew she was gonna refuse every single one of my suggestions and the only thing she'd be left with was me.

"Looks to me like your *options* are running out."

She stamped her little foot in defiance. "I'll go to a motel."

I spun on my heel and headed into her bedroom, dragging the duffle bag from the top shelf of her closet. I tossed it onto her bed, doing my best to suppress the images of the last time I had been there.

But they came fast.

An assault of greed and lust.

The girl under me. Skin so soft. Body so warm. Wrapping me in all that comfort.

Sunshine.

Had to grit my teeth to force out the words. "You're coming with me, Nikki. Don't fight me on this because you aren't gonna win."

"Why do you even care?" She was in the doorway, her pretty face pinching. I saw it, her eyes on the bed, picturing the same damned thing as I was.

Hurt hit her, wave after wave.

My stomach knotted.

Regret and need.

I turned away.

Ignoring it, that feeling that struck in the space between us. Something that'd always been there.

Always.

As we'd grown, it'd just transformed and gotten bigger and become something we shouldn't have let it be.

None of it mattered—not the mistakes I'd made, not the way I felt, not what I wanted.

I'd rather die than let something bad happen to her.

"Pack your shit, Nikki, or I'll do it for you."

And the last thing I needed was to be rummaging around through her underwear.

five

Ollie
Six Years Old

His mom knelt in front of him and squeezed him by the upper arms. "You're such a big boy. I'm so proud of you."

He looked up at the big yellow bus that rumbled at the curb, his belly full of something that felt like wings and his chest bigger than it'd ever been.

"Now, do you remember what I told you?" his mom asked as she adjusted the straps of his backpack on his shoulders.

He tightened his hold on his little sister's hand. "I've got to take care of my little sister. Always and always."

His mom smiled and it made his chest tighten more. "That's right. You're the biggest and the bravest, so you always watch out for your little sister. She's going to be scared going to school all by herself, but she doesn't have to be because she has you right there to protect her."

Pride swelled inside him. "I'll watch her the best, Momma. Just like Daddy said."

She leaned in and pressed a kiss to his forehead. "I know you will, brave boy."

"Beast Man," he corrected.

His momma laughed a soft sound and brushed her fingers through his hair. "That's right, you're The Beast now."

He proudly held up his *The Beast* lunchbox that his dad had given him yesterday when he'd gotten home from work. His dad told him he was a beast, destined to be a linebacker, bigger than any of the other boys.

Last night, his daddy had come into his room to tuck him in and told him he needed to watch out for his little sister.

Just like his momma was doing right then.

Their momma looked at his little sister, who was swaying in her pretty dress that she had picked out especially for this day. Ollie was worried it was gonna get messy if she played in the dirt, but their momma said that was okay. "You stay close to your brother, okay? He'll help you get to your classroom until you know your way around."

Sydney looked up at Ollie and beamed. "Okay, Momma."

"All right, you two, you'd better get on that bus."

She pressed a long kiss to Sydney's cheek, like the way she did when she was sad.

"It's okay, Momma," he said, "I've got her. I won't let nothin' bad ever happen to her."

She nodded at him and wiped a tear from under her eye. "I'm just sad my babies are getting so big. I know you've got her. Now go on and have a great day. I'll be right here waiting when you get finished."

"We will!" Sydney said, grinning wide and then even wider when she saw another little girl walking up to the bus with her hand in her mother's.

The girl's eyes were so wide and so blue they were almost purple. Like one of those purple flowers that grew thick in the fields and filled their momma's garden.

Though somehow, they were shiny and iridescent.

Like a big bubble floatin' in the sky and getting caught up in the rays of sunlight.

The girl's mom hugged her before she nudged her toward the bus. "Go on."

The girl's feet dragged on the dirt as she looked behind her.

"You wanna sit with us?" Sydney called out, not the least bit shy.

The girl's mouth tipped in a small smile. "Okay."

Sydney struggled to look around Ollie as they climbed up the bus steps and moved down the narrow aisle between the rows of seats, his little sister trying to get a good peek at the girl. "What's your name?"

"Nikki."

"Hi, Nikki! My name's Sydney. This is my Ollie. You wanna be our best friend?"

"I don't have a best friend," Nikki said.

Nikki looked a little bit scared. Like the way Ollie's dad said Sydney might be because she didn't know her way around.

Ollie puffed out his chest. "Well, you got two now."

Six

Nikki

The powerful engine of Ollie's car roared as we sped down the road. Night passed us by in a blur of city lights that poured in from above, and the silence had its own distinct vibe as it filled the cab of his car.

Hot and heavy and confused with a dash of anger thrown in for good measure.

Seemed fitting considering that was the way this boy always made me feel.

Angry and hot and on edge.

What the hell had I agreed to? I knew so much better than to bend to his will. So much better than giving in.

But how could I not? The truth was, I was scared.

Terrified, really.

I could feel the note I'd stuffed in my bag burning a hole in the bottom of it, flames of fear and worry and dread. They'd ignited the second we'd mounted the steps at my apartment, sure it had to be Caleb who was responsible for it all.

Should I just say it? Put my theory out there without an ounce of proof?

The hardest part was I didn't know if that would be betraying Brenna's trust. Disrespecting everything she'd offered me in her fragile state.

God . . . I just, couldn't do it. Not with the way Ollie was vibrating beside me like a lunatic.

I'd seen it in his eyes. Felt it radiating from his body.

He wanted to hunt and destroy.

I blew out a relieved breath when my phone finally buzzed with a return text.

Brenna: I'm fine. Is something wrong?

Me: No. I just wanted to check on you to make sure he was leaving you alone. Please text me if you need anything. I'll be there.

I wondered if my demeanor came across as some kind of dirty confession as I tapped out the reply.

Or maybe it was just the way Ollie was looking at me as if he wanted all my secrets. Because the daggers he was shooting were so intense, I could feel them penetrating the side of my face.

Fiery darts.

I thought he might have the power to flay me wide open with the pass of one. See everything hidden inside.

Brenna: Thank you so much for being here for me.

I hugged my phone to my chest as if it might send her a hedge of protection. Send her my hope and belief in her. For her.

Maybe I really had gotten in too deep.

"Who is that?" Ollie finally demanded, shaking me from my thoughts.

I turned to him, taking him in. He barely fit in the space of the seat, his long legs bent and tucked up under the wheel, seat pushed so far back he might as well have been sitting in the back seat.

Bigger than life.

Always, always filling my sight, eyes unable to look anywhere but at him.

He was squeezing the wheel with those massive hands, the muscles in his arms bulging and flexing with uncontainable strength.

I squirmed, and my tongue suddenly felt thick where it stuck to the roof of my mouth.

I didn't know if it was from looking at him or from the fact my gut told me not to let him in on the note. Not to tell him about the day Brenna had called me right after she'd called the police, and I'd run there to support her.

Caleb had called me the very thing that was painted on my door as he was being hauled away.

Bitch.

"No one," I told him.

His eyes darted to my phone. "No one? It's after midnight, Nikki. Don't tell me that's no one. And you refused to call any of our friends. That a guy?"

I almost laughed.

Was he serious? He was jealous I might be texting a man?

That was exactly what I should have been doing.

Texting a guy.

Someone who was totally Ollie's opposite.

Sweet and stable and harmless.

Not a man who could rip me to shreds with nothing but a glance. Not a man who would use me up and toss me aside then turn around and act as if I owed him something.

"What if it is?" I defended, not even trying to keep the outrage out of my words. He deserved it. "Why do you think it's any concern of yours?"

"Everything you do is my concern. I thought we already established that earlier."

"Right." It dripped with sarcasm, and I jerked my attention forward, my jaw working hard, propelled by a surge of fury.

I stared out the windshield. "You've sidelined every single one of my relationships. Convinced me they weren't good *enough* or you decided it for me and took it upon yourself to scare them away. I told you, you don't get to do that anymore."

Not after last year.

Over the years, I'd dated.

Never seriously. I'd never fully allowed myself to fall because I'd been waiting on him to come to his senses. To see me. To *feel* me the way I felt him.

Or maybe it'd just been *impossible* to fall because I already belonged to him.

My heart too tangled and wrapped up in him to recognize anyone or anything else.

"If that's a guy, then I need a name." His voice came hard, as sharp as a wielded knife. No question, a threat to cut without hesitation.

My laugh was one of disbelief. I gave a short shake of my head. "No, Ollie, you don't."

For the last fourteen years, I'd had to watch him with an endless string of girls.

Painfully pretending as if it didn't matter. I'd done it after he'd broken me when I was sixteen because I'd wanted to give him the space and the time to heal. But when he'd done it again, as if he didn't think it wouldn't destroy me? I was done.

I would no longer allow Oliver Preston to trample all over me. I was moving on, the best I could, the only way I knew how.

"Told you earlier you need someone looking after you. Should be clear enough after that shit went down at your apartment." His voice was gruff like he was scolding a child.

"Um, no, I don't. I'm a grown woman. And yeah, I appreciate you being there for me tonight. That's what *friends* do, but I don't need someone else to approve who I see or who I am with. I've never tried to do it with you, and it's high time I stopped allowing you to do it to me."

Veins bulged in his arms from the pressure he was exerting on the steering wheel, and that energy flared.

Friction and gravity.

Barbed spikes penetrated my skin.

I shuddered around it.

"Just didn't think you were the boyfriend type." It was basically a grunt from his sexy mouth.

Was he for real?

"Since when?" I challenged.

Ollie's jaw clenched in discomfort. Good. Maybe for once he would understand what it felt like.

He didn't care.

He didn't care.

I had to keep telling myself that.

What made it worse was the thought of inflicting even an ounce of pain on him made me sick.

He'd always thought he was the one who needed to stand up and protect me, but it was me who ached to protect him. Shield him and hold him, wishing he'd find that solace in me.

"Just tell me who you're texting," he demanded instead of answering my question.

For a flash, he turned that potent gaze on me.

Black sapphire.

Angry and hard.

"There are parts of my life you don't get, Ollie. Some things are private, like the relationships I have with the women who come to sessions. They're trusting in me, and there is no way I can allow you to get in the middle of that. And you know what? If I am dating someone . . . you don't get that, either. It's none of your business. You gave up that right a long time ago. You either need to respect that or accept that I can no longer be in your life."

A breath left him on a hard exhale, and his entire being flinched.

He looked as if he'd taken a swift kick to the gut.

Shocked.

Maybe I should have laid it out between us long ago.

Boundaries and rules.

God knew, I'd been following his for too long.

"Is that what you want . . . me out of your life?" He kneaded the wheel as he said it, agitation coming off him in powerful waves.

I stared across at him.

At his face.

His cheeks and his lips and the profile of his beard.

My beast.

"No," I said quietly. It was the honesty that came out behind it that made it ring in the air.

Slowly, he nodded. "Don't mean to be an asshole every day of my life."

"Are you sure about that?" I said, my voice cracking with the strain as I let myself tease.

A gruff laugh left his sexy mouth. I tried to still the tremor the sound evoked in the depths of me.

There was nothing I loved more than the sound of Ollie happy.

Pathetic, wasn't it? He'd hurt me over and over again, and the only thing in the world I wanted was for him to be happy.

The thing was that I knew the real man. The man hidden by layers of hatred and anger and sorrow. I knew the real heart. The heart concealed by the most devastating kind of grief.

He eased his fingers through his hair and blew out a sigh. "Yeah, I'm pretty sure about that."

"So, you just can't help it?" I ribbed. It was so much easier than being mad at him.

He cracked a wry grin and peeked over at me. "Just comes naturally, I guess."

"Bear," I taunted.

"Brat," he returned.

"Beast."

My heart fisted as we sparred, affection pulling free and spilling into the air.

"Sunshine."

The second he called me that, tears pricked in my eyes.

I beat them back, swallowed the lump that bobbed in my throat, and smiled over at him as if he was my oldest friend.

Because he was.

"Thank you for rescuing me tonight," I told him honestly. "I would have been terrified if I had walked up on that by myself."

"No worries . . . rescuing damsels is kind of my thing." The smirk he gave me was only half forced.

"Well, aren't you just the savage savior?"

He smiled over at me, and I smiled back.

"Saving you was always my job."

My insides shook.

It was so easy to fall back into rhythm with him.

He looked over at me, his expression softening. "Guess I should have known that wasn't a guy."

"Why's that?"

I shouldn't have let him bait me. Not when the subject was such a thin, shaky line.

He tacked on a dangerous smile. "Because if you were my girl, I'd be right there, protecting you. Not texting you like some pussy who doesn't want to get his hands messy."

There was some kind of censure in there.

Possession and a warning.

Yet, here you are, protecting me.

So badly, I wanted to say it, but I bit it back and let a smirk ride to my own mouth. "Um . . . this might be news to you, but being a bossy, overbearing asshole does not make you a man."

The brute grinned wide, his big body overflowing in the seat, hands squeezing down on that wheel as if he knew exactly what it was doing to me. "You sure about that?"

"Positive."

Ollie looked over at me.

The easiness was gone.

Obliterated.

In its place was a desperate man. The one who'd shown up at my doorstep for seemingly no purpose at all but to check on me but had been there the exact moment I needed him.

"Who did you piss off, Nikki? Need to know . . . don't care what it is you've gotten yourself into . . . won't be a dick about it. I just . . . need to know."

My chest squeezed, and I had to force out the response. "You heard Seth. It was probably just some kids."

He turned back to the road.

Lead Me Home

His big body was slung back deliciously in the seat. Everything about him was wholly overwhelming.

Utterly overpowering.

"Is that what you want me to believe?" He slid the question from between his lips like a low accusation.

That was the thing. Oliver Preston did know me. In all the ways that mattered most.

But even if I wanted to tell him, it wasn't my right. I couldn't break Brenna's confidence.

God knew what Ollie would do if he even *thought* someone was trying to hurt me.

I couldn't risk that.

Contemplating, I stared out the windshield, before I murmured, "I haven't done anything wrong, Ollie."

I didn't know if it was an admission or a defense.

"Never said you did, but sometimes doing the right thing puts us in a bad place."

A huff of air blew through my nose.

Wasn't that the truth.

"If I'm in trouble, I'll let you know. I promise, okay?"

His eyes darted across at me, his lips thinning as he pressed them together. "Thing I'm worried about is you're already there."

Two minutes later, Ollie made a quick left turn onto Macaber Street.

Strands of lights twinkled where they crisscrossed over the street, strung between the old renovated buildings to create a cozy vibe.

The area was a destination in and of itself.

The renovated buildings boasted restaurants and bars and cafés on the bottom floors, and trendy loft apartments with views of the city and the river took up the upper floors.

Even though it was after midnight on a weeknight, the sidewalks were dotted with couples that strolled along the storefront windows, wrapped up in each other as if they had nowhere to go, and groups of friends hopped from hot spot to hot spot to drink the night away.

I wasn't surprised to see Olive's, Ollie's bar, was still packed.

Curtis, the head bouncer, guarded the door, and a row of taxis waited to carry the revelers home after a night of indulging.

Ollie made the next left turn and whipped around to the back of the building.

He pressed a button, and a large garage door rolled up at one end of the building. He eased his car inside where his collection of restored cars sat in the private garage that took up a small section at the back of the first floor. He pulled the car into one of the open spots, killed the engine, and hopped out without a word.

Almost warily, I unbuckled and climbed out of the car as he grabbed my duffle from the back seat.

Raucous voices carried through the walls from the bar.

Sydney's soft voice floated to me as if she were standing right at my side, whispering it in my ear.

Insightful and real.

My best friend who'd understood the world before any of us could.

I could almost see her with her face tilted toward the summer sky, her legs dangling over the side of the dock, her toes in the cool water.

"I think it's the things that hurt the worst that mean the most, don't you?" she mused, her hair flying around her face as if she'd stirred a new concept that'd been waiting to be revealed. "Good or bad. That's what's gonna shape us. Make us into who we are. Guide us on the path to what we want the most."

She glanced over at me. "I think we'll know it when there's no other direction we can go. And I'm not going to be afraid of walking it anymore."

She wasn't wrong.

I gravitated toward this man.

But what she was wrong about was not being afraid of walking that path.

I knew first hand it was wrought with peril.

Just spending the night here, being in his space, felt as if he was going to break my heart all over again.

I also somehow understood there was no other place I could go tonight.

He'd found me exactly when I needed him before I'd even realized that need myself.

Maybe Ollie had been following his own path.

All I knew was he'd been there.

For me.

I had to be grateful for that.

He tossed me a look over his shoulder as he strode toward the building.

The man so gorgeous. Big boots eating up the ground with every mind-altering step.

So confident and brash and commanding.

"Comin', Sunshine?"

That was Ollie's way.

Reeling me closer, filling me up, and then cutting me free. Leaving me floating with no safe place to land.

I just prayed this time I landed on my own two feet.

seven

Ollie

Footsteps pounded on the damp earth.

Desperate.
Frantic.
Trees rose on all sides, sentries and witnesses, and branches tore into my skin as I ran through the oppressive night.
Searching.
My eyes blurred in the darkness. Muddied by despair. I stumbled through the forest. Gnarled roots twisted, like spindly fingers that had clawed out of hell to hold me back.
Tears burned my cheeks as the wind blasted my face.
Cruel like the laughter I swore I heard before it was swallowed by a gust of air.
I screamed in the middle of it. "Sydney!"
Voice hoarse, throat bleeding with the pain. "Sydney!"
Sydney. Sydney. Sydney.
I dropped to my knees.
Sydney.

My eyes flew open, and my breaths jutted from my lungs in a

panicked rhythm.

Pain lanced through my body.

Physical.

Rending.

Pain.

I deserved it, but sometimes I wished for one goddamned night of peace. I sat up on the side of my bed. With trembling hands, I raked back my hair that clung to my face, matted and sticky with sweat.

Blowing out a breath, I pushed to standing.

Through the faint light that bled into my darkened room, my gaze moved to the corkboard against the far wall. Like all of a sudden it might be pointing to the answer of a twisted, intricate mystery.

Revealing a secret.

Directing me to the missing piece.

All these years, that was what I'd done.

Dug.

Watched.

Waited.

Searching for . . . something.

Someday . . . someday I would find it.

Pushing out a strained breath, I shook off the memories.

Nothing but decay, eating away at my insides. Wondered when there would be nothing left.

I trudged for the door, needing to get out of this room where the nightmares always reigned.

Throat dry and desperate for something to cool the hell living in my belly, I stepped out of my room and headed down the hall.

At the end of it, I stopped dead in my tracks.

Motherfucker.

Motherfucker.

I scrubbed both hands over my face, wondering if I was hallucinating. If I'd thought my throat was dry before, I'd just landed myself in Death Valley.

All the lights in my place were off, except for the one inside the refrigerator. The door was wide open, the stark, white light illuminating the tight, round ass that peeked out.

White underwear covered only half of her cheeks, and those long, long legs were bare.

Greed tumbled through me like a landslide.

I fisted my hands. "What in God's name are you doing up?" I grated. My voice was so hoarse from sleep, making the words little more than a grunt. It wasn't like I'd forgotten Nikki had slept in the guest room at the very end of the hall.

Just hadn't anticipated finding her like this.

Gasping, she whirled around. Big, shocked eyes met mine like she hadn't expected me any more than I'd expected her.

"Ollie, you scared the crap out of me," she rasped.

That seemed to be the theme.

Her trembling hand flew to her throat like she was trying to ward off the shock. To reassure herself she wasn't in any danger.

Standing there, I wondered if that was actually true. Because right then, I was feeling dangerous.

Volatile.

Liable to make all kinds of stupid decisions. Like that night close to a year ago, a night I could barely even remember. All I remembered was pulling that bottle from the shelf and trying to drown the grief.

Then I'd woken in her bed.

Her naked body against mine, the smell of her on my skin.

So fucking perfect in my arms.

It was etched and seared and woven with the faint flashes and taunts of memories.

Her sweet, sweet touch, and my desperate greed.

A permanent scar to remind me I couldn't be trusted.

Especially with her.

The only thing she'd paired with those underwear was a thin, white tank top, her tiny tits exposed by the skin-tight fabric, nipples just barely peeking through.

My damned mouth watered.

Those stunning eyes sparked. Purple flames in my kitchen, burning me through as they went skating down my chest and abdomen.

The girl was drinking me in like she was just as thirsty as I was.

Not helping things, Sunshine. Not fucking helping things.

Clenching my fists, I did my best to convince my dick this girl was nothing but a skinny, bony stick and so not my type. Hardest part was convincing my traitor heart I hadn't wanted her for my whole life.

No matter how much shit was piled on top of why I couldn't have her, there was no way I could ever forget her touch. Her smile and her laugh and the way she made me feel like I was a damn king.

Her guardian and shield.

I doubted there'd ever be a time when I looked at her and didn't think she was the best damned thing I'd ever seen.

"Not sure what you expect when you're sneaking around my place in the middle of the night," I finally managed to say, breaking from the spell the girl had me under.

Magic in her fingertips.

And there I was, imagining sucking every single one of them into my mouth.

One by one.

Wondering if she'd groan and go wild or if she'd melt. Didn't know which way I wanted her most.

Sucking in a deep breath, she seemed to gather herself. Her brow lifted in speculation as she set the carton of milk on the island like she'd rummaged through my kitchen a million times before.

Guess there was no need to invite her to make herself at home.

"Middle of night?"

She spun away and hiked up onto her toes to grab a bowl from the cabinet, giving me another flash of that sweet ass.

Little tease.

She spun back around, and there were those tits.

Didn't know which view I liked better.

She really was trying to kill me.

"I have to be to work in thirty minutes."

My attention immediately shot to the huge, curved bay of windows that overlooked the city. Darkness still hugged the buildings, but the promise of something to come was baited in the sky.

"Just because you sleep half the day away, it doesn't mean I get to," she started to ramble, moving to dig through my pantry and my selection of cereals. "Early bird gets the worm—or rather, the breakfast pastry pie. Whatever you want to call it. And I have to be the one to make sure those pies are ready."

Right.

Work.

At an ungodly hour.

"And do you have to do it half naked?"

Couldn't help but bring attention to her state.

It was like only then the girl noticed what she was wearing.

Or lack thereof.

Her full, pink lips stretched into a lust-inducing O, and the shock was punctuated by a tiny sound.

A rash of fantasies rapid-fired through my brain.

Closing the distance.

Taking that mouth.

Devouring that body.

Olive skin and slender curves and cupid mouth.

Fuck.

I wanted her.

Wanted her propped on my counter and spread out on my bed.

She made an offended sound and angled to the side like that might cover her up. She pointed my direction with one hand while she wrapped her other arm over her tits. "Oh, you think this is funny, do you? Sneaking up on me this way?"

I was about to respond, but she didn't let me. That gaze narrowed. "Maybe you really were trying to take advantage of me while I'm here. How the hell a mountain of a man like you sneaks up like some kind of ninja is beyond me."

A chuckle rumbled free, half-pained, half-amused. "This from the girl who decided to parade around my kitchen half naked.

Just who is the one who isn't playing fair?"

"You were just asleep. I heard you."

Affection and regret pulsed through her expression the second she realized what she said. With what she'd let on.

She'd heard me.

Fuck. She'd heard me calling out for Sydney.

Shame rumbled through my spirit. It was a feeling she only managed to intensify.

The girl's magic at work again.

Thought she might be the only one who could really understand. Brutal, considering she was the one I couldn't let see.

My life was devoted to finding my sister. Whatever it took. Whatever the cost.

What made it worse was I couldn't look at Nikki without seeing Sydney at her side. Without my mind going to what Nikki and I had done.

I couldn't let her light be dimmed—tainted by that vacant, ugly space that roiled inside of me.

In a moment of weakness, she'd gotten in there once, and look how that'd turned out.

I roughed a palm over my face and down my beard. "You didn't hear anything," I told her. Any amusement in my voice had been extinguished.

That face transformed, and the easy playfulness she normally exuded shifted into some sort of a plea. Because when it was just the two of us together?

The space between us rippled and danced.

Begged to be erased.

That awareness between us became its own, thriving entity.

Rising from the depths.

The girl a crashing wave that was going to take me under.

"Ollie." Her voice was a petition.

Pure understanding.

Come to me.

Too soft and too kind and too full of all the things she couldn't make me feel.

Dropping my head, I lifted a hand. "Don't. Just . . . get dressed. I'll drop you at work. We'll pick up your car after you get off so you have it over here. God knows, I don't need to be getting up before the ass crack of dawn to drive you every day."

She blinked back at me. "You're crazy if you think I'm coming back over here."

"I think we already established that."

Crazy was my goddamned middle name.

Those lips pursed in that wild, impassioned way.

The girl who saw too much.

Too clearly. "I'm not coming back here after work. I only agreed to one night. You know I can't stay here, Ollie."

I didn't ask why. Both of us knew the answer to that. It still didn't mean I was relenting.

Hot air puffed from my nostrils, the same anger from last night slithering beneath the surface of my skin. "It's not safe out there, Nikki."

Didn't matter that she was all the way across the room. I could still feel the weight of her eyes searching me.

I itched beneath it. Tried to shield myself from that feeling that slammed and pulsed and moved.

"What are you going to do, Ollie? Keep me here so you can keep me safe from all the horrible things that happen in this world? Why now? What changed?"

"Are you joking? Some asshole broke into your house. That changed."

"It wasn't a big deal."

"Wasn't it?"

That storm rumbled in the depth of me. A warning. The quake of an omen that ran the length of my spine.

Maybe it was because of the anniversary of Sydney disappearing was inching closer.

But the dreams had become almost unbearable.

Intense.

Vivid.

Every morning, it left me with this gut-deep intuition that something was coming.

Something wicked.

"Just . . . have this bad feeling, okay?" I admitted, nothing but a fool.

I needed to keep my mouth shut.

Put a padlock on what I was feeling.

She took a step forward like she could reach me from across the space. "It's been fourteen years, Ollie."

I stepped back.

Away.

Headed for my room because I couldn't look at her for a second longer without completely losing it. I shouted over my shoulder as I banged into my room, "Be ready in fifteen. This isn't up for discussion."

eight
Ollie
Ten Years Old

"This is a bad idea," Ollie whispered.

If their daddy found out about this, he'd have Ollie's hide.

Sydney grinned. "Are you scared, Ollie Jollie?"

"Course, I'm not scared. This is just stupid."

A frown pinched his sister's brow. "What do you mean, stupid? This is a pact. And a pact means forever. There isn't anything stupid about that."

Nikki shifted beside him where the three of them sat at the back of their yard, their knees touching where they sat in the moonlight beneath the pour of the moon.

He looked that way.

She smiled. Softly. With a tip of her head.

Something tightened in is chest. Tightened in his stomach. She looked like a fairy with those big purple eyes.

Unreal.

So perfect she had to be fake.

"It's a pact, Ollie. Forever," Nikki said, like she was trying to get him to understand.

Forever.

He swallowed hard and picked up the knife Sydney had sneaked out of the kitchen. He turned his hand over to reveal his palm, pushing the tip into his skin.

He sliced a shallow cut into his flesh.

He bit his tongue, trying to pretend it didn't sting.

"Does it hurt?" Sydney asked, scrambling to get closer to watch the droplets of red bead in his palm, interest and awe in her expression.

"Not much." He glanced between the two of them. "You sure you want to do this?"

"Yes!" Sydney giggled, biting her bottom lip, always too excited for her own good. She was always racing off, getting them in trouble because she refused to listen.

Never being bad, but never following the rules, either.

And Ollie had promised his mom and dad that he would make sure she did.

He was pretty sure this was breaking that promise in a bad way.

Sydney took the knife and held out her hand, counting under her breath, "One, two, three." She squeezed her eyes shut when she made the slice. Then she giggled wildly. "I did it!"

She held up her hand as proof.

"Your turn," she said, handing the knife off to Nikki.

Nikki's teeth grabbed on her bottom lip. Ollie could feel her getting nervous next to him.

He always could.

Knew she was gonna be scared before she even knew it herself.

"You don't have to do this," he encouraged her, barely tapping her knobby knee with the pads of his fingers.

"I want to," she whispered back, but her words shook. She looked at him, a plea on her face. "Do it for me?"

"I won't know if it hurts."

"Yes, you will. You'd never hurt me."

He hesitated before he took the knife. She was right. He'd never hurt her.

Sydney took Nikki's opposite hand while Ollie took the other, holding the tip of the knife to her palm.

Nikki sucked in a shaky breath, and Sydney squeezed her hand. "Fly, fly dragonfly."

Nikki's lips moved silently when she repeated Sydney's words. "Fly, fly dragonfly."

Ollie slipped the knife across her palm.

Nikki flinched then smiled, holding up her hand in her own kind of awe as she watched the tiny line of red bubble up.

Sydney pushed her hand out to Nikki. "We are three. Forever and ever, you and me."

Nikki smashed her palm to Sydney's. "We are three. Forever and ever, you and me."

Ollie did the same with Sydney, and his sister beamed at him when they chanted the oath Sydney had made them swear back when he was in second grade.

He didn't know why his stomach felt different when he turned to Nikki, but something shivered through him when he pressed his palm against hers.

Their eyes met, and they whispered at the same time, "We are three. Forever and ever. You and me."

Forever.

nine

Nikki

He didn't say a single word to me on the ride to Pepper's Pies.

The infuriating, brooding, fuming asshole who I wanted to wrap up and hold and keep was completely closed off.

As if I was putting him out.

Like he couldn't be bothered.

After he'd been the one making all those overbearing demands.

His dumb, gorgeous face was held rigid, and those sexy, muscled arms rippled with tension, making the field of purple blazing stars shiver across his skin.

I thought maybe if I reached out and traced them, they'd be real. That the small touch would take me back to the days when we'd run through their fields.

Free.

Fly, fly, dragonfly.

Old grief tremored deep in my chest. Thrumming and pulsing out. I swore that I could see it clash with that furious, provocative sort of energy held in every inch of Ollie's delicious body.

As if he rode a fine line between past and present.

Never fully surviving on one side or the other.

I wanted to reach out.

Be his lifeline. His savior when he'd forever been the one saving me.

Ruining me.

Keeping me.

Alienating me.

Push, pull, taunt, tease, take, leave.

My head spun.

Wanting him so desperately and still praying for a way to finally break free of his chains.

I was beginning to think that was impossible.

Not with the way I'd felt looking at him this morning.

The man standing at the end of his hall.

Wearing nothing but his boxer briefs.

Body big and thick.

Burly and intimidating.

His need evident where his cock had pressed so massively against the fabric.

Almost as evident as the power that had blazed between us.

Electricity that spun in sharp, spindly barbs. Stakes to my skin. A hook in my soul.

My wicked savior.

My beast.

Too bad he had to be such a jerk.

He whipped into an angled parking spot in front of the diner.

I yanked at the handle and pushed open the heavy door, fumbling out from the low car and onto the pavement.

Day was just beginning to dawn on the horizon, a gray glow breaking above the mountains in the distance.

I slammed the door shut, freezing when he finally spoke to me through the open window. "Pick you up at three."

"That won't be necessary."

He whipped his face toward me as fast as he'd whipped his car into the parking spot. "Yeah, it is."

"You can't tell me what to do."

So maybe he had me feeling petulant.

Off-kilter.

Could anyone blame me?

"Ah . . . ten-year-old Nikki. My favorite." Mischief moved through those glittering eyes. "Feisty and stubborn. Don't make me throw you over my shoulder the way I used to do."

I shot him a glare while my tummy did a backflip. "You wouldn't dare."

"Wouldn't I? Think you've forgotten who you're talking to."

"You're impossible."

"If you want to call being right impossible, go right ahead."

Ugh. Of all the overconfident, presumptuous, cocky—

"That's what I thought," he said with a smirk, cutting off my internal tirade.

My mouth dropped open, tongue at the ready to protest, but he tossed me a grin, threw the gear into reverse, and revved the engine.

The sound had me stumbling back, and he jerked out of the spot.

Without a glance, he shifted into drive and gunned it.

The man just left me there, staring behind him, wanting to stomp my feet and throw a fit or maybe just scream.

Arrogant asshole.

"What on earth?"

I whirled around when I heard the voice coming from down the sidewalk.

What had I done to anger the gods?

Only a curse could explain this string of bad luck.

When it rains it pours and all of that.

Because there was Lillith with her hands on her hips, wearing one of her fitted pant-suits and heels that made her look like some kind of vixen who'd rolled around in a billion bucks.

Rynna, the owner of Pepper's Pies, was at her side.

"Tell me you didn't have a one-nighter with Oliver Preston." Lillith went all power-attorney lecturer on me.

That's what I got for picking a BFF who was gonna turn out to be a lawyer.

"I mean, I know you're infatuated with him, but seriously, Nikki? That isn't healthy. That man is liable to break your heart."

I had to hold back the dubious laugh.

Too late.

He'd done that a long, long time ago. Had been doing it all along.

Guilt swept through me. I hated that I kept it from her.

She was my closest friend.

Still, the sad thing was, she'd taken Sydney's place. And Sydney hadn't known the full truth either, so how could I tell Lillith? Maybe it was stupid, but that felt like another betrayal.

I forced a playful scowl on to my face. "Oh, stop it. You know full well I didn't have a one-nighter with Ollie. He may star in a fantasy or two, but that's where it ends. I think I'm a little too hot for him to handle."

More like he'd burn me to ashes.

Lillith narrowed her eyes in suspicion. Forever searching for the truth. But I'd played this one off for so long, she wouldn't recognize the lie. "Then why is he driving you to work?"

Rynna gave me an I-second-that look as we turned and headed up the sidewalk toward Pepper's.

I crossed my arms over my chest. "I think the real question is, what are you doing here before five in the morning, Lily? Shouldn't you be back home snuggled up in bed with that hot husband of yours, getting yourself more of those orgasms I was so kind to set up for you? Rynna and I have work to do."

Loosely translated? I knew Rynna wouldn't give me such a hard time.

At Pepper's front door, Rynna turned the key in the lock and widened the door for us to enter.

Pepper's fronted Fairview Street. It was another area that had undergone a massive rejuvenation over the last handful of years, including the luxury hotel Lillith's husband, Broderick, and his company had developed directly across the street.

The entire area buzzed with possibility.

Pepper's served sweet pies and pot pies and breakfast pies.

You know, basically heaven.

Rynna had inherited the little diner from her grandmother and brought it back to life. Her grandmother's unique recipes were the staple that brought patrons in droves every single morning.

Lillith gave a casual shrug. "I thought I'd help set up this morning."

I shot her a dry look. "Dressed like that?"

Another shrug. "So maybe I woke up starving and wanted the first slice of pie this morning."

"Are you pregnant?"

Nothing like a little deflection.

She gasped a horrified sound. "Shut your mouth. You know Brody and I aren't ready for that."

"Yeah, yeah, you have empires to build." I waved my hand dramatically.

Lily's husband, Broderick Wolfe, was the CEO of Wolfe Industries. His company had been responsible for a bunch of the revitalization projects that had been taking place in Gingham Lakes over the last several years.

She scoffed. "Hardly. We're just . . . focusing on us for a while."

"And all those orgasms I earned you. I have to say, my matchmaking skills are on point."

She playfully rolled her eyes Rynna's direction. "She really thinks she set us up with Brody and Rex, doesn't she?"

Rynna smiled. The woman was one of the kindest people I'd ever met. "You know there's no rationalizing with her madness. Let the poor girl have her delusions," she teased.

"Delusions?" I gestured to myself with both hands. "This is the stark, glorious reality. I'm responsible for all your happiness. I think you should give me all the presents as a thank you."

Rynna's light laughter tinkled through the air, and my chest tightened in stark affection.

I was so happy for her.

For Rex.

That he'd found the love of his life after everything he'd been through.

Rex was one of Ollie's best friends, and I'd known him my whole life. Rex and Kale had become members of our pack somewhere in our childhood, with us nearly as much as Ollie, Sydney, and me had been together.

Rynna had adopted Rex's little girl, Frankie Leigh. Rex and Rynna had a little boy named Ryland who was a year and a half old.

I'd stepped into the role of honorary auntie faster than the doctor could say "one more push."

I adored those babies, my heart overflowing every time I got to be in their space.

Of course, that rule applied to the newest member of our extended family—Evan.

Sweetness didn't come close to describing that little thing. He'd been born completely deaf and had required a heart transplant as an infant.

The thing about him? The child was pure joy, just like his mom, Hope. Honestly, sometimes when I saw Hope and Kale together, I was the deepest shade of jealous a person could be.

I didn't mean to be.

Didn't want to be.

But sometimes it was hard to watch all the things you wanted most, feel them burn inside of you, and have the deep-lying fear that they would never become a reality.

Rynna flicked on the switches right inside the door. Bright lights burst to life in the darkened space.

We all blinked, adjusting to it.

The echo of pots and pans clanged from the very back of the kitchen where Kevin, the head cook, would have already been working for the last two hours preparing for the morning rush.

"Morning, Kevin," Rynna hollered, moving around the counter to start the coffee.

Priorities and all.

His voice was barely heard when he shouted back, "Mornin'."

Lillith slid onto one of the swiveling stools.

"So, what were you doing with Ollie this morning?" Lillith asked, point blank.

Did I really think she'd let it go?

I sucked in a breath, already knowing the riot my response was going to cause.

But there was no hiding this.

"Someone broke into my apartment last night."

Rynna's hand flew to her mouth. "Oh my God."

Lillith flew to her feet. "What?" she demanded while Rynna moved toward me, her hand reaching to grip my forearm, her eyes searching as she whispered, "Are you okay?"

I knew that wasn't going to go over well. But I did my best to downplay it, to shake off just how truly shaken up I was.

Shrugging a shoulder, I leaned against the counter and did my best to sound convincing.

"Seth was the one who responded to the call. He thinks it was just kids running around being punks the way they love to be. They're lucky I didn't catch them. A little ass kickin' would have ensued. Or maybe I would have grabbed them by the ear and dragged them back to their mamas the way my grandma used to do when I was getting unruly. Death by humiliation. I'm pretty sure that's all they need to teach them a lesson. I mean, seriously? Doesn't the world have enough douchebags? Here I'd been crossing my fingers it might skip this new generation."

"This isn't funny, Nikki." A shiver rocked Lillith's entire body as if she'd just been slammed with visions of every single horrible thing that could have happened. "Kids aren't the same as they used to be."

As if I hadn't noticed the downward spiral of decency.

Distress rolled the length of her throat. "They can be dangerous and mean, and they don't think twice about taking someone out if they think it will get them something they want or cover something up to keep them out of trouble."

I deflated.

Because it wasn't a joke.

Not at all.

Deep down in my gut, I knew I'd been targeted. That it was personal, the way Ollie had said.

Brenna and Kyle's faces flashed through my mind.

They were worth it, and I'd learned a long time ago fighting for what was right wasn't always easy.

I rubbed my palms over my arms. "I know. And I promise I'm not being careless. Which is why I went to Ollie's place."

I could fight with the man about going back to his loft until I was blue in the face. But the truth of the matter was, I was thankful. Thankful that he'd somehow known I needed him.

Rynna moved back to the counter. She pressed brew on the coffee machine before she turned around and propped her hip on the counter. "So, you called Ollie, and he came running?"

"Something like that."

Lily's brow arched. "What do you mean, something like that?"

I sighed.

It wasn't like I was surprised that she'd insist on pushing the issue.

I searched for an explanation that wouldn't cause an uproar. "He . . . he'd stopped by just as I was getting home after the meeting, so he was there when I discovered it."

Surprise and speculation slashed a bunch of lines across her forehead. I could almost see the cogs turning in that analytical brain of hers. "He just happened to stop by?"

An uncomfortable chuckle rumbled in my chest. "He said he was worried . . . you know . . . since you went and told him I'd bailed on you for drinks when you knew I just needed to study," I tossed out.

The traitor.

She probably thought she was doing me favors.

The problem was, she didn't have the first clue she was throwing me to the wolves.

Her brows lifted. "Um . . . maybe I was worried, too. Since when do you pass up an awesome bottle of wine on my balcony with your best friend?"

"Since I decided to do something with my life."

"Hey, managing Pepper's is doing something with your life," Rynna pouted through a tease.

A light chuckle rumbled out. "Of course, it is." Turning back to Lily, I cleared my throat. "Correction. Since I decided to do something *different* with my life."

Lily pursed her lips "Uh-huh. Okay. So, you're busy. I get it. That still doesn't explain Ollie showing up at your place. Are you sure there isn't anything you want to tell us?" she pushed.

I shook my head. "There's nothing to tell."

"You have to admit, things have been super weird between the two of you for the last year."

She pointed at me to stop me from speaking when my mouth started to flap with another flimsy excuse.

Because things had been incredibly weird between Ollie and I over the last year.

Worse than ever.

I just hadn't thought she'd noticed.

"Yeah. He showed up, stayed while I dealt with the cops, and then kind of demanded I go home with him since my door was busted in. He said it wasn't safe for me to stay alone."

"Since when do you do anything someone tells you to do?"

Since an overbearing, brute of a man decided he wanted to be my defender.

"Have you met Ollie?" I figured that answer would suffice.

"A sleepover at Ollie's. Sounds to me like you're begging for trouble." Rynna's observation blazed into the air. "There isn't a whole lot that is simple when it comes to that man."

My attention darted to her. A sea of unease lapped and churned in my belly. "Ollie and I are old friends."

Why'd it have to come out sounding like a confession of guilt?

Rynna blushed with whatever thought went racing through her mind, and Lily was looking at me as if she were chipping pieces of me away and labeling each one as evidence.

"That's all you have to say about it? After you've been gushing about that man for all of forever? Dish the goods, lady. God knows you always demand them of me."

I had gushed.

Telling Lillith I thought Ollie was hot and if I got the chance, I would chew him up and spit him out. At the time, it had seemed like the best way to explain away the longing looks that lasted just a little too long.

Play it off.

Pretend.

It was what I'd done to make it through.

"Believe me, if I had goods to dish, I'd be spilling because that would indeed be a fun story to tell." I lumbered through the lie.

At least I got it out.

"The one where he picked me up and dumped me in his guest room, where I slept alone, and then brought me here this morning? Not so much."

I left out all the million other things that made the situation complicated and so very messy. How I'd woken to hearing him having a nightmare and begging Sydney's name. How I'd wanted to go to him.

Comfort him.

He'd only made it worse when he'd stumbled out of his room, rumpled from sleep, looking so sexy, I'd wanted to toss every single promise I'd made about him right out the window.

Lillith pointed at me. "Um . . . I call bullshit. I know that salacious mind of yours just went to dirty, dirty places. I demand a confession."

I shrugged. "The man's hot, and he was sleeping in the room next to me. Don't blame me for a fantasy or two."

Worry pursed Rynna's mouth. "What do you do now? I'm not sure I like the idea of you going back to your apartment by yourself."

Lily nodded. "Me, neither. The second you told me what side of town you were moving to, I knew it had trouble written all over it."

"Okay, Miss Money Bags," I shot at her.

Her mouth dropped open in offense. "Um, hello. You do remember I had to have Addelaine take me in when I had no place to live. It's not like I haven't been penniless before."

"I'm going to have Rex start looking around for a house that his crew can fix up. It isn't right that you're living in that dump by yourself," Rynna piped in.

And here I thought Lillith was going to be the problem.

Adamantly, my head shook. "There is no way I'm letting you two buy a house for me."

Rynna carried on as if I hadn't said a thing. "We've been talking about getting some investment properties. Really, it would be a favor to us."

"Not a chance, Rynna. I'm no charity case. You know me better than that."

She shook her head as she flipped on the heat lamps in the window. "I do . . . and I know you slave away here at my little restaurant for meager pay. If anyone's getting charity, it's me."

"I think it's a great idea," Lillith agreed a little too eagerly. "Maybe Brody can fund it, and together we can get another rejuvenation project going in Gingham Lakes. There are quite a few old neighborhoods that would benefit from one. It's good for everyone—the community, the economy, the investors. It's a win-win, really."

Excitement bounced between the two of them.

"That would be amazing, Rex and Broderick back on a project together."

"Y'all are out of your minds," I said with a flippant wave of my hand, turning to start filling the little creamer pitchers. "When I said gimme all the presents, I was thinking along the lines of a gift certificate to A Drop of Hope, or maybe a nice Vicky's Secret bra, you know, the push-up kind since my boobs are basically non-existent? I didn't mean a house."

Lily pursed her lips. "Well, you can't go back to that hole, and it isn't like you can stay with Ollie forever. God knows I love him, but that man is a moody bear. He'll eat you alive."

That was exactly what I was worried about. I didn't respond.

"Or has that been your plan all along? Tell me you didn't go into some dark alley and pay some sketchy-looking guy to bust in your door just so you could sleep in the same house as Ollie."

"You got me," I told her, the words scratchy with dry sarcasm.

"Hey, when a woman gets desperate . . ."

She had no idea.

I spun back around and leaned on the far counter, arms across my chest. "I'm not desperate. He's the one insisting I go back over there tonight. That he doesn't want me stayin' alone."

Lillith widened her eyes. "Are you surprised?"

"I guess I am."

Shocked.

Floored.

Stupefied.

I figured the last thing Ollie wanted was to be in close quarters with me.

"He cares about you," Rynna said as if it were as plain as the coming day lighting up on the bank of windows that faced the street.

I shook my head. "No. The only thing Ollie cares about is being a savior."

"Isn't that the same thing?"

No. Not when it was going to destroy me in the end.

ten

Ollie

"Seth, it's Ollie."

He blew out a breath on the other end of the line. "Hey, man. Was wondering if you were going to call."

"You think I wouldn't?"

I paced the concrete floors of my loft in front of the big bay of windows that overlooked my balcony and the city beyond. I had a view of the river twisting through the buildings as it cut through Gingham Lakes.

My loft took up the entire third floor of the building, Olive's existing in the bottom two floors besides for the small bit at the back that was my garage.

The main room was open, decorated in dark woods and even darker leathers.

The entire vibe echoed peace.

Too bad I felt none of it.

Seth chuckled a bit, but there wasn't a whole lot of amusement to it. "Nah. I knew you would. Especially with the way you looked like you were going to lose your mind last night."

That was the problem.

That was exactly what was happening.

I was losing my mind.

"You want to tell me about this line of bullshit you were feeding Nikki about it being a bunch of kids breaking into her place? Because it sure didn't look that way to me."

He sighed, and I could almost see him rocking forward in his office chair at the station to lean his elbows on his desk. "That's exactly what it could be, Ollie. We see cases like this all the time. But there was something about it that felt purposed. Like someone was trying to send a message."

My hand curled tighter around my phone. "And what kind of message would that be?"

The sound he made was strained. Like he didn't know what to offer me. "A warning."

Anger tightened around me. Chains. Constricting tighter.

"That doesn't mean that's what it was. It's only a hunch." Silence spun for a second before he continued, "Has she made any enemies lately? Maybe broken up with somebody?"

My teeth gritted.

Because I should know. Should know everything about her. Hold her secrets. Her dreams. Her joy.

I was the one who'd crushed every single one of them.

And I sure as shit shouldn't be pissed by the idea of there even *being* someone for her to break up with.

"Not sure. But she's been interning with a psychologist, helping her run some meetings. She was texting someone last night from there on the ride back to my place. Gut tells me it has something to do with that."

He exhaled heavily. "Anything happening there is going to be confidential. You can't get in the middle of that."

"If it means Nikki's safety, I can."

"Ollie," he warned. "I had you call me because I want you to know what's going on. To watch for anything out of the ordinary. Not for you to take off hunting like . . ."

He trailed off.

Leaving the rest suspended in the distance between us.

My mind filled in the blank.

Like Sydney.
I'd hounded that station for fourteen years.
They'd labeled it a cold case.
And I'd labeled that bullshit.
If they wouldn't hunt? I sure as hell would.
"I won't let anything happen to her, Seth."
It was my own warning.
A promise.
Because whoever this fucker was?
He was gonna learn I had a message to send, too.

I heard the bedroom door snap open. Hell, I probably didn't even hear it. More likely, I felt it, the presence stepping out from the far end of the apartment.

That aura she wore was like an additional layer of her skin.

Glittering diamonds and glimmering golds reflecting off the sun.

Swore, I could feel that girl from a mile away.

Bare feet padded on the concrete floor.

That feeling grew stronger and stronger with each step. It'd covered me whole by the time she made her way out into the main living area.

"What are you doing?" she asked.

That sweet voice hit me from ten feet behind. With the way chills went skating across my skin, she might as well have been whispering it in my ear.

I stirred the ground beef I was browning in the skillet, giving her a quick glance over my shoulder, trying not to get wrapped up in her.

Fresh out of the shower after I'd picked her up from work an hour ago and took her back to her apartment to pick up her car.

Now the girl stood there.
Hair wet.
Skin damp.
Expression confused.

Spirit fierce.

That was what always got me more than anything. The way she glowed this unassuming, timid belief, all wrapped up in a wide, bright smile.

"What's it look like I'm doing?"

"Cooking." It was pure, horrified concern.

I chuckled a little. "Seems like we're on the same page then."

Curiosity drawing her forward, she rounded the tall table surrounded by stools that acted as a partition of the kitchen and living area.

Or maybe it was just me.

Because I could feel the tether.

Pulling, pulling, pulling.

"The question is, why are you cooking? Aren't you supposed to be downstairs working?"

"Probably."

She popped her hip on the counter and crossed her arms over her chest.

The stance pushed up her tiny tits, soft mounds of flesh swelling over the neckline of her tight tank. Her olive skin warm, and her innocent face soft, those freckles running across her nose.

No chance could I keep my gaze from dipping from her mouth to that cleft.

My cock stirred and my chest squeezed painfully.

What the hell had I gotten myself into?

Felt like I'd parachuted right behind enemy lines.

Problem was, I had no idea if it was Nikki I was stealing in to rescue or if it was this girl who was going to kill me in the end.

"So why are you up here then?"

"Thought you might be hungry after a long day's work."

Or maybe I felt like shit after being such an asshole this morning.

It was a toss up.

Her brow rose, and she tightened her hold across her chest. "I'm a big girl. I think I can feed myself. If I'm staying here, I can't be interfering with your job. That bar means the world to you."

So do you.

The thought pierced me like an arrow, sheering straight through me.

I hiked what I hoped looked like an indifferent shoulder, trying to fight off this bullshit feeling I couldn't shake.

Couldn't stop the inundation in my mind, though. The idea of what might have happened had she gone back to her place earlier and gotten in the mix of whoever had been there.

My insides clutched.

In pain.

In dread.

Couldn't stop the assault of images. The horror of someone hurting her.

Stealing her away, too.

I wouldn't let it happen.

Not again.

Not to her.

And my call with Seth was not sitting well.

"Was hungry and didn't feel like eating bar food tonight. Thought you might be, too. That's all. Don't always get down there first thing. Perks of being the boss." I shot her a wink with the last, and she was fighting the smile that was twitching across her lips.

"Must be nice," she said, shifting away and opening the fridge.

She dipped down to peer inside.

My eyes landed on her ass, the girl wearing these tiny black shorts that barely covered her cheeks.

Yeah, so, so nice.

Unbearably nice.

Sweat beaded on my brow, and I beat the attraction back, remembered my mission. Why she was here.

"Want a beer?" she asked, digging through my stash.

"Sure."

She straightened, two beers in hand. She twisted the cap off the first one, handed it to me, and then opened her own before tilting it toward me.

"Truce?"

Unease wound through me as I stared at her standing in my kitchen.

"Never knew we were at war."

She laughed a low sound, shaking her head as she glanced at her feet before she peeked up at me. "Don't pretend we haven't been fighting something for a long, long time, Ollie."

I scrubbed a palm over my face and down my beard, searching for an explanation.

Searching for a valid reason for shutting her out.

The truth of why I broke her heart.

Without revealing the part of myself I couldn't let her have. Not when it belonged to Sydney. Not when I couldn't be trusted.

"Think we both know you are better off without me."

A little scoff bled from her mouth. "I couldn't decide that for myself?"

"You really think so?" It was hard to meet her eyes, but I forced myself to, bringing attention to what I'd done for the first time.

Like a dirty secret kept between us.

"Look what happened the last time I came to you."

Pain lanced across her face.

I felt it right at the center of me.

Lash. Lash. Lash.

Ones my selfishness had inflicted.

But that was what it always was, wasn't it?

Selfishness.

Refused to be that way anymore.

For a beat, she looked away, chewing on her bottom lip before she let out a small breath and asked, "Did you need me or were you just using me?"

Hurt leeched out in every word.

Unable to stop myself, I closed the distance between us and took her face between my palms, my voice grit. "I've always fucking needed you."

She jarred, shocked by my sudden movement, and blinked up

at me with those eyes that twisted me in two.

I loosened my hold, and my words quieted. "But just because I need you doesn't mean I get to keep you."

For a minute, I just got lost there. Looking at her.

Before I ripped myself away from her and turned all of my attention back to fixing dinner.

Guessed I might as well add foolish to that list of fucked-up qualities.

Because that was maybe the dumbest thing I could have given her. But for once, she deserved it.

A little bit of the truth.

She wasn't looking at me as she fidgeted, those fingers moving out to fiddle with a dishtowel sitting on the counter. "I'm not sure how to move on from that night," she admitted.

Sorrow had taken me whole when I looked over at her. "Which one?"

That was the crux of things. We had no way to move on. Both of us stuck, and I'd only made it worse.

Leaving her when she was sixteen and running back to her a year ago.

"Truce?" I mumbled, reiterating what she'd said.

Light laughter fell from under her breath. "Feels like a shaky one."

I gave a tight nod. No question it was.

Shaky.

But she'd been my friend long before she'd been anything else.

So, I searched for some kind of lightness, the easy yet profound way we'd once been. "Probably. Just hold on to something when you move. One look at me, and you won't be able to remain standing."

It was all a tease with a tip of my lips.

She choked out a laugh. "Wow . . . someone really is full of himself."

"Just keeping things real."

Amusement danced across her pretty face.

So damned pretty.

Painfully pretty.

She was all smiles when she tipped the neck of her beer my direction. "To poor girls who can't keep their heads on straight when they're in your presence. May they forever see through the BS."

I clinked my beer against hers and then lifted it in the air. "Believe me, baby, the outside looks way better than the inside."

I let a little of the cold, hard truth sneak into my ribbing.

She took a sip of her beer before she tucked it up close to her chest as she stared at me, her voice close to a whisper. "I think you sell yourself short, Ollie. I've always been pretty fond of what's on the inside."

I tossed a tortilla onto the griddle I'd had heating with oil. It sizzled and hissed, and I focused on evening it out with the spatula.

"That's an ugly place, Nikki. Believe me, you don't want to get anywhere close to that. Not anymore."

"What if I've just always wanted you for your body?"

Could feel her words take to the air, light and playful, the way we'd spent thirteen years. Acting like we didn't really know each other.

Our interactions nothing more than a breezy tease when the wind that gusted beneath them threatened to be a dust storm.

She was all taunting smirks when I looked over at her.

Little Tease.

Probably the last thing I should do, but I went with it.

"Think I'm more than you can handle."

A sexy twist of her lips had me stumbling. "Well, if that's how you feel."

She nodded, and a flash of sadness twined through her demeanor before she tipped her beer my direction. "Friends."

I picked mine back up and clinked it to hers. "Friends."

Problem was, having to remain friends with Nikki Walters was the hardest thing I'd ever had to do.

A half hour later, the girl's contagious laughter was bouncing against the walls.

She popped the last bit of her taco into her mouth, wiped her hands with her napkin, and rocked back on the high-backed stool. "You're such a liar. That was totally your fault."

My laughter was low, way too amused, barriers down that'd been there for so many years. I shook my head as I sopped up a few pieces of meat that'd fallen from my taco, glancing up at her with a grin when I did.

"My fault? Are you kiddin' me? Every bad idea I ever had was because of you. Tying that rope to that tree included. I said it wasn't gonna hold me . . . and what did you say?"

Guilt twitched all over her flirty mouth. "I don't remember."

A rumble of amusement rolled around in my chest. "Think it went something like, 'Ollie thinks he's the shit, but he's really nothin' but a chicken shit.' On repeat, of course."

"No." Her head shook in vigorous denial, but she was doing her best not to bust up in outright confession. Indigo eyes full of old affection.

The same kind gripped at my chest. Claws wanting to take hold.

I shook it off and focused on being *friends*.

"Yes. You were always the instigator, whispering in my ear, making me think I wasn't a man if I didn't go through with whatever you'd concocted."

I wiped my hands and tossed my napkin onto the table, slinging my arm over the stool back, grinning at her. "Took it on myself to prove to you just what kind of man I was."

Mischief moved across her face, honeyed locks of hair swishing across her cheeks, those freckles so fuckin' sweet.

Had the intense urge to lean out and lick them.

Taste her.

That mouth and those lips and every inch of smooth, soft skin.

"Hey, it isn't my fault you thought you had to be such a badass. Sounds like a personal problem to me."

"More like I had my own, personal troublemaker."

"And look who I was trying to keep up with. If anyone was the troublemaker, it was you."

"And look who I was trying to impress."

A blush kissed across her chest, rising with the energy that danced. Slowly. Quietly. Though just as intense.

Her tone turned wistful. "At least Kale discovered his true calling that day. He got really serious about setting your ankle."

"That shit hurt like hell, too," I told her through a chuckle.

Memories hit me hard.

One after one.

Like they were so close, I could take a step and tumble into them.

They called them the good old days.

For us?

They really were.

She bit her lip. Nikki wasn't shy. She was just real. "I really am sorry you broke your ankle."

I didn't know what I was thinking, but I reached out and let my fingertips trail the defined curve of her cheek.

She trembled, and for a moment, she leaned into my touch before she pulled away.

Like she was just then realizing she needed to stay away from me.

That I was dangerous.

I shook the heaviness off and climbed back into the tease, pretending I wasn't treading choppy waters.

"Oh, sure you are. Who was it standing over me, laughing her ass off, holding her stomach, saying she wished she had a video camera so she could send it in to *America's Funniest Home Videos* . . . thought you were gonna get rich off me."

She tried to hold back a giggle. "Hey, I would have shared."

Couldn't keep my eyes from tracing her face.

Every inch.

I'd *managed* for so long.

Keeping her at a distance while still keeping her close.

It's your fault.

I trusted you.

You were supposed to take care of her.

You promised, you'd take care of her.

Voices resonated from the cold valley planed out inside me.

I swallowed around the grief that thickened my throat, welcoming the reminder.

I couldn't be trusted.

God, I knew I needed to get the fuck out of there, but there was something about being with her this way that made me want to stay.

Just for a little bit.

A few moments of the relief she brought all heaped with a load of torment.

I angled my head toward the television. "You want to catch a show before I head downstairs?"

"Are you sure you have time?"

"Why not? Cece doesn't mind running things."

"You know she's just waiting to oust you from your position, right?" she said as she slipped off the stool, her suggestion a bit of a tease, though I thought maybe there was a true question behind it.

"Nah, Cece might look like a viper, but she's harmless."

"Harmless?" She let out a little laugh. "She doesn't look harmless to me. She basically looks like she could annihilate the bar in one fell swoop."

I plopped onto the couch. "You jealous?"

Nikki dropped down on the opposite end with an incredulous shake of her head. "Of the fact she's stunning and scary and basically can command the bar with a single look? Hell, yes."

Cece oozed sex and radiated intimidation. Men flocked to the bar, salivating and begging for a bone. Her attention the prize, the woman had the power to drop the poor suckers right to their knees.

So maybe she wasn't entirely harmless. She just didn't pose any threat to me.

"I'll be sure to tell her that," I told her with a lift of my brow.

"Don't you dare. Women like that eat girls like me for dinner."

"I think you're safe. As far as I know, she likes men."

Disgust made her scowl. "Tell me you don't know that because you've slept with her. She's your employee. That's just all kinds of wrong, Oliver Preston."

She tried to make it come out as nonchalant, like she was giving a friend advice. But I heard the way the idea of it scraped from her throat. Hurting her.

Always, always hurting her.

I looked at her, hooking up a small smile. "Don't worry your pretty little head, Nikki Walters. I don't sleep with my employees. But you know Kale got a taste of that before he met Hope."

Her eyes went wide with the scandal.

"No," she wheezed.

Had no idea if I was breaking bro code by letting her in on that little bit, but somehow, I couldn't make myself shut the hell up, needing this connection with her, hungry for it. Or maybe I was just trying to shift the attention from myself.

"Yup."

"Freaking Kale . . . he's lucky I love him so much."

"Nah . . . he was just doing his thing . . . biding his time until the right girl came into his life."

She blinked these wide blinks at that, that feeling pulsing at my chest, thrumming in the space between us. "So you really never slept with her?"

"No. Not even close."

Her eyes narrowed for a beat, like she was searching me for the truth, before she relaxed against the arm of the couch and pulled her legs up so she could hug her knees. "Good. You're forgiven. For now."

This time, it was my brows riding high. "And just what are you forgiving me for?"

"Being a gorgeous, brainless, womanizing man." She said it with a jut of her chin. Playful even though I could feel the undertone of severity. The two of us broaching a subject we'd never trusted ourselves to touch before.

An incredulous chuckle rolled out. "Womanizing, huh? Now who's making assumptions about the other?"

Her amusement shifted and fell into something somber. "Oh, come on, Ollie. You don't need to pretend for me. You think I don't see those girls?"

Regret clamped down on my chest. I grabbed the remote and aimed it at the television that sat on the console, voice a little lower than it needed to be. "Those girls don't mean anything."

Her voice was softer. "Everyone means something, Ollie. Feels something. Whether you want to take it into account or not."

This girl.

I turned up the volume. Like it might have the power to mute every mistake I'd ever made.

She was right.

Everyone mattered.

Her the most.

And I'd gone and treated her the same goddamned way I treated everyone else.

Needing a diversion, I flipped through some channels.

A grin took over when I found what I was looking for.

Could feel her amusement ripple from her spirit, the way her mouth twisted up as she attempted to keep herself from laughing. She stretched out her leg and gave me a little kick to the thigh.

"AFV? Are you kidding me?"

My eyes glided up her bare leg.

For a beat, my attention locked on the frayed, braided bracelet made of red thread she still wore around her ankle, the worn metal charm in the middle stamped with the words, "Fly."

I had one to match hidden in my room, unable to bear wearing it.

Seeing it.

The third piece was missing forever.

My guts ached.

I shoved off the thoughts and let feigned innocence lift both my shoulders to my ears. "What? I thought it was your favorite show?"

"Stupid boys," she muttered for what had to have been for the millionth time since I'd known her.

The thing about it?

It was the first time she'd said it in fourteen years.

I pretended I didn't feel contentment go sinking all the way to my bones.

She shifted and groaned a little as she tried to get comfortable on my couch.

Totally should have ignored that sound, considering it spoke directly to my dick, but the question was sliding free before I could stop it. "What's wrong?"

"Legs just get tired from running around the diner for nine hours a day. Feels good to lie down. This couch is heaven. Seriously, Ollie, when I leave, I'm taking it with me. No need to report a robbery. You know where it'll be."

I let loose a fake gasp. "After all my kindness, you'd go and steal from me?"

She peeked over at me with a sweet grin that slid right through me. "For this couch? Absolutely."

"Here." Reaching out, I dragged both her feet onto my lap and angled to the side a bit so I was facing her better.

Such a bad, bad idea.

She was right.

Stupid boys.

So damned stupid when I took one of her feet into my hands and kneaded my fingers into her heel.

Nikki's gasp was real.

Hitting the air like a motherfucking drug.

Just a moan from her tongue a spell.

For a moment, she hesitated. Clearly, the girl knew this was a bad idea, too. Because she stilled before she relented.

The anxiety firing through her body went lax, and she rolled onto her back to grant me better access.

She emitted another one of those groans.

Throatier this time.

"Don't make me steal this couch and you, too. A girl could get used to this," she murmured.

I had to suck for air because my lungs squeezed.

Constricted with a rush of lust.

Like a dumbass, I continued to massage her foot, my thumbs pressing deeper into her heel before I moved to the arch.

Wishing I was closer.

Needing more.

A sigh pulled from between those pink lips, and the air shifted.

Sizzled and lit.

That'd always been the problem with Nikki.

She was heat and light. A spark and a flame.

Sunshine.

I thought I just might lose my mind because I swore I could see that aura she wore gather between us.

Colors.

Reds and purples and blues.

They thrummed and lapped. It made it impossible to breathe.

I moved to the ball of her foot and then to her toes, which were tiny and somehow delicate, the nails short and painted the same shimmery pink color of her lips.

Did it make me a sick fucker that I wanted to suck one into my mouth? That I wanted to lick up her bare leg? Nibble at the inside of her thigh?

She squirmed, and my breaths came harder.

Harsher.

While hers turned shallow.

She arched from the couch.

Need and pleasure.

I wondered if a girl could go off from a foot massage alone.

Because I thought maybe I could from giving one.

My cock strained painfully as I moved to her other foot.

"Ollie," she whimpered. "That feels so good."

Visions slammed me.

Clearly.

The girl bare.

Laid out under me.

An offering.

Nikki. Nikki. Nikki.

I dropped her foot like a rock and launched to my feet.

Erratically, my chest heaved as lust careened through my body. I roughed both my hands through my hair, trying to calm the fuck down.

Get myself together.

You can't be trusted. You can't be trusted.

Shocked out of the trace, Nikki shot up to sitting. Her eyes blazed as she stared across at me.

With desire and regret.

With the realization she should be protecting herself from me.

She clutched the couch like it was a life raft she was getting ready to get tossed from.

This was stupid.

So stupid.

"Need to get downstairs," I told her, voice rough.

She nodded.

For the first time since I'd known this girl, no smart reply came from her mouth. I didn't wait for her to form one.

I flew for the door.

My own life raft.

Because I was right.

This girl was a wave getting ready to take me under.

And I didn't think she'd ever let me up for air.

eleven

Nikki

It was close to five p.m. when I bounded down the three flights of stairs and out the big metal door into the back-parking lot.

Humidity smacked me in the face, and I was hit with the overpowering scent of honeysuckle that wafted through the dense air.

I jogged across the lot to where I'd parked my car after Ollie had taken me back to my apartment to pick it up yesterday afternoon.

I knew I shouldn't find comfort in staying with him. But I wouldn't lie to myself.

I did.

I wouldn't have been able to sleep last night had I been staying at my apartment, fearful Caleb might return.

All I wanted was to lie low.

Hide out.

Just for a little while.

Until things between him and Brenna cooled down.

Of course, I had to admit I hadn't slept all that well knowing Ollie was once again just a room away.

A wall and a million miles separating us.

But after the evening we'd spent together, it'd felt as if part of that chasm was being erased.

Drawn.

That magnet that would live forever pulling us together.

It was a bad idea to get close to him. I knew it. Of course, I knew it. But sometimes life made it hard to pretend he hadn't once been the most important person in my life.

Anxious to head to my sister's house, I clicked the fob and started to pull open the driver's side door.

Then I froze.

My stomach plummeted to the ground.

The hairs at the nape of my neck lifted on end, and the sweat that was already threatening to gather beaded across my forehead and neck, trickling down my back in a slow slide of dread.

Another note.

It was folded neatly and tucked beneath the wiper.

He'd found me.

Oh God, he'd found me.

I gulped around the rush of terror that glided through my body.

Followed me more likely.

From Brenna's description, he was manipulative in the worst of ways. Yanking her one direction then the other until she thought she was going insane.

Warily, my attention darted around the area, searching beneath the towering trees that lifted to the blue, blue sky, across the line of cars that were parked next to mine since this area was reserved parking for Olive's employees.

Nothing.

Just the whisper of the leaves and the sound of the busy street echoing from the other side of the building.

"Shit," I mumbled. All I wanted was to run right back upstairs. Maybe curl up in the bed Ollie had told me to consider mine.

Maybe curl up in his.

Damn it.

I could not let my brain go down that train of thought.

But it seemed almost impossible.

Not with the way he'd always made me feel safe.

Not with the way he'd touched me last night.

I wanted to fall into Ollie's strong arms and beg him to take it away.

But I wasn't that girl.

One to be frightened away.

Threatened until I backed down so some jerk could have his way.

Brenna deserved so much better than that.

Taking one last glance around the lot, I snagged the note and hopped into my car, quick to slam the door and press the lock.

Heart a riot in my chest, I carefully unfolded it.

Fear slicked across the surface of my flesh.

A cold, cold dread.

You think you can get away so easily? He can't keep you from what's coming.

Thunder.

It rumbled through my being. A warning. A siren that screamed. Pulse a deafening pound, pound, pound as it echoed in my ears.

I squeezed my eyes closed against the shackle of terror that gripped me.

I'd always known working for the program would require sacrifice.

That it might not always be easy.

Maybe I'd known I was getting in too deep.

I'd just never expected it might make me feel like I was going to drown.

I hoisted myself onto my little sister's kitchen counter.

Sammie gave me a scowl. "Were you born in a barn?"

Playfully, I rolled my eyes at her and tossed another grape into my mouth. "Um, if I was born in a barn, then I'm pretty sure you were, too. Next thing you know, you'll be makin' yo mama jokes. Tryin' to cut me down to size when you're really just cutting yourself off at the knees."

She swatted at me. "Pssh . . . if I wanted to cut you down to size, I wouldn't need to look to our mother. Think I've got plenty to work with just with you sittin' there. We could start with that face."

"Ouch," I said, grinning wide. Funny how neither of us were feeling the love unless we were razzing the other.

Old habits die hard and all that.

"Before you start going down that road, you should probably take a gander in the mirror," I told her.

She laughed. "Oh, God . . . now don't you go talking about how much we look alike. A couple days ago, I was at that little market over by grandma's. Remember her neighbor, Margo? I was loading my groceries onto the conveyor belt when I heard someone shoutin', 'Nikki, Nikki, is that you?' I don't know why she even bothered asking the question when she refused to believe I was your sister and not actually you."

"You say this as if looking like me is a bad thing."

She laughed as she flitted around her cozy country kitchen, preparing dinner, the smell of a roast simmering on the stove making my stomach growl.

Her face really was so much like mine that it felt as if I was looking in a mirror.

A few years younger and a tiny bit rounder from the few pounds she was still clinging to after giving birth to my sweet niece two months ago.

"Did you show up at my door diggin' for compliments?"

"Um, no, I didn't show up at your door diggin' for compliments. I showed up at your door diggin' for dinner."

That, and I needed a distraction.

I had to tell Seth about the notes I'd found on my car. I knew I did. But I needed to work myself up to it. Figure out exactly what information I could give without betraying confidence, knowing I didn't have proof.

But my gut?

It was sure.

On top of that? I'd needed to get out of Ollie's loft. Clear my head. Decide exactly what I was going to say to him.

I couldn't just stay there and keep him in the dark about what was happening.

But God knew, I was terrified of letting him in on this.

He wasn't exactly rational when it came to a threat.

Plus, I had to be careful before I lost my heart all over again.

No doubt, that was the most dangerous position I could get myself into.

Sammie pulled out a cutting board and set a head of broccoli on it. "Well, I guess you came to the right place, then, didn't you? Just expecting your married sister was gonna be slaving away in the kitchen for her husband."

"Isn't that what you're doing?" I teased, eyeing the spread she was preparing.

Chuckling, she shook her head. "I do it because I want to do it, not because I'm obligated."

I nudged her with my shoe. "You think I don't know that? And there is not a thing wrong with you wanting to take care of your family."

She glanced over at me. Something about her expression was wistful and sad. "I never really thought it was what I'd want to do. I always envisioned myself in a big skyscraper in an even bigger city, working my way up the corporate ladder, and now all I want to do is spend the day rockin' that baby."

"You always dreamed of getting away from Gingham Lakes, didn't you?"

Her head shook a bit. "Sometimes you think it's the place you need to escape when really it's just your situation."

I stilled at that, something unsettling about her statement. I searched her face. "What does that mean?"

Her posture stiffened, and she pinned on a smile. "Nothing. Just means I thought there might be better things out there waiting for me in the world."

"Why's that?"

She inhaled deeply, biting her bottom lip as she continued chopping. "It's nothing. Just never quite felt comfortable in my own skin."

I shifted to the side so I could see her better. "I don't get that, Sammie. You were always the happiest of us all."

She puffed a little sound. "Not even. You and Sydney and those boys. You were always running free, leaving your poor baby sister behind."

A chuckle rippled out, and I reached over and grabbed another handful of grapes from the bowl. "Ha. Every time I tried to take you anywhere, you didn't want to walk. How many times did Ollie have to carry you home on his back?"

She laughed low and tossed the florets of broccoli she'd just cut into the pot of water boiling on the stove. "Good thing that boy was always the size of a bear, always having to carry all the poor, pathetic girls around."

She grinned. "Of course, you were probably just faking being tired so you could get yourself one of those rides. Anything to get your arms around that man."

Nostalgia moved through me. Joy chased by sorrow. I couldn't stop the sad smile.

She sobered a bit. "You know, I always thought the two of you would end up together."

My head shook. "No. We have too much in common. Too much history to ever make that work."

"Isn't that what makes a good relationship?"

"Not when all that history is filled with pain."

She nodded slowly, quick to change the subject. "So, how are your classes?"

"Good. I'm so close to being finished. I can't believe it."

"I'm really proud of you, you know?"

Light laughter escaped. "It's about time, isn't it? Here I am thirty, and barely figuring out what I want to do with my life."

Funny how things were supposed to be coming together and every piece of me felt as if it were descending into disorder.

The apartment.

Brenna.

The internship.

And somehow staying with Ollie felt just as big as all of that.

Maybe bigger.

This was Ollie, we were talking about.

My great big world.

He taken that world from me for so long, and now I felt as if I was stumbling through it in the darkness.

I chose not to tell my sister any of those things. She didn't need to be fretting over me when she had her family to care for. To worry for.

The important things in life.

She glanced over at me as she started to make gravy in a skillet. I wasn't joking when I said I'd come around here diggin' up dinner. My baby sister knew how to cook. "Mama is so happy you're getting ready to graduate."

My chest tightened with a smidge of pride. "She's always worrying about me. I think she keeps forgetting I'm thirty."

Sammie laughed under her breath. "That's because Mama thinks *she's* still thirty."

Standing at the stove, she looked back at me, concern in her eyes. "I'm worried about how she's handling Gramma falling ill, moving in with her to be her full-time caretaker. That's gotta be hard, seeing her own mama like that."

So many emotions raced through me at the thought, I didn't know how to make sense of them.

My grandma who'd always been so alive and strong.

The summers we'd spent running in and out of her house, the screen door slamming shut as we came and went.

"It has to be the hardest thing any of us ever go through, watching our mother's fall ill. God, I can't stand seeing it with Gramma. Every time I go over there, it breaks my heart a little more."

She nodded through the somberness of it. That cycle of life we'd give anything to stop but never could. It didn't matter how old my gramma was, my mama, my sister. There'd never be a time when I didn't want to cling to them forever.

"At least Uncle Todd is back in town to help around the house. That will hopefully take away some of the stress," I said.

From behind, Sammie's spine stiffened, and I could have sworn I saw her knees sway, losing balance.

"Sammie . . . you okay?"

She nodded. "Of course. Just . . . hate the thought of Gramma being sick."

Just then, the speaker on the baby monitor crackled. A tiny, rattling cry came through, and I slid off the counter. "Let me get her."

"That'd be nice," Sammie said with a gracious smile, though I couldn't shake the feeling something was suddenly off.

I headed down the hall and eased open the door to Penelope's room, which was adorable with its hearts and elephants everywhere.

My chest filled.

So full.

Almost too full.

The feeling only came stronger as I looked down at my niece, who was flailing one fist while trying to shove the other into her tiny mouth. Somehow, she had kicked free of the blanket and was wiggling around, making the sweetest sounds.

I couldn't help but echo them back. "Hey, Angel," I whispered, scooping her into my arms. "How's my sweet, sweet girl? Auntie Nik has been missing you."

I hugged her to my chest and kissed the top of her head, whispering against her crown. "So much."

She cooed, scratched her sharp little nails in my chin as she fisted at my skin.

Was it wrong the little thing made me ache?

It wasn't like I was *old*. But I still felt that time slipping away. A piece of me missing that I'd always assumed would just be there one day.

I could swill wine with my friends and laugh all my nights away. Give back the best I could, live and embrace who I was.

I'd be happy.

That didn't mean something wouldn't be missing.

Maybe it only seemed fitting it was tucked right down in that place with all those pieces that'd gone missing long ago.

"Nik?"

I startled with my sister's voice coming from behind me.

I spun around to find her standing in the doorway. There was something mournful in her expression. As if she'd just heard every single one of my thoughts as if I'd said them aloud.

Or maybe I just saw it projected back, her face like a picture of mine.

I pasted on a thin smile. "She's so beautiful, Sammie. If I were you, I'd want to sit and rock her all day, too."

Sammie gazed at her daughter. "It's funny, just looking at her makes me believe the world could be a better place."

Hugging the tiny thing to me, I kissed her temple.

And I believed it, too.

Outside of my sister's house, I sat in the driver's side seat of my car in the darkness, holding the card Seth had given me between my fingers. With a shaky hand, I dialed the number.

Two rings later, a scratchy voice came on the line. "Hello?"

"Seth . . . it's Nikki."

"Are you okay?" he rushed.

I sucked in a breath, eyes darting through the windows, searching the shadows.

The feeling of being watched sent chills crawling across my skin.

No question, I was being paranoid, but I couldn't seem to stop the dread clinging to me.

I just couldn't take the risk.

"Yeah. I'm fine. I just . . . I have something I need to tell you, but I need you to promise you won't tell Ollie."

twelve

Ollie

I snapped open the door to my turquoise blue nineteen fifties Chevy truck to the sticky summer air.

Birds flitted across the sky that was painted a bright, brilliant blue, and the lush, towering trees rustled in the gentle breeze blowing through.

I stepped out onto the sidewalk and shut the door to the old truck, which was basically my prized possession.

When I found it, it'd been rotting at the back of this old guy's land, swallowed by weeds and pretty much rusted down to the metal bones.

It was kind of my thing. Taking the dilapidated—the neglected and the failing—and doing my own sort of restoration.

It was where I found my joy.

Taking something that had been left for ruin and giving it a new life. A second chance when I wasn't ever going to get one for myself.

A certain sort of retribution. Like I was desperate to find something good buried in the rubble.

My first love was my bar. Taking it from the ruin it'd been

and breathing a new life into it.

I took just as much pride in the cars I had restored at a local shop, Roke's restorations, a garage I'd invested some money into when it had been threatened with going under.

Hell, I'd invested in a few failing businesses around Gingham Lakes, wanting to see something good rise out of the dust.

But the cars . . .

I loved watching them going from completely rotted to immaculate.

From a heap of junk to a priceless treasure.

Guessed it was a whole lot easier to fall for material things than things made up of flesh and blood and spirit.

Safer.

But sometimes not falling proved itself impossible.

Which was precisely the reason I was there today, driving this specific truck when I had five others to choose from in my garage.

Because . . . Evan.

The first time Kale had brought him to my place, the little boy had run through that garage like he'd gotten a lifetime pass to Disneyland and couldn't wait to visit it every day.

His big ol' bug eyes had been nothing but excitement behind his thick-rimmed glasses as he'd gone from car to car. His fingertips had traced the metal, and he'd sat behind the steering wheel of each car, pretending like he was flying down a racetrack.

Kale hadn't even protested when I'd let Evan climb onto one of my motorcycles.

But this truck?

It was his favorite.

He'd claimed it as his on that big spiral-bound notebook he always carried around, jumping up and down as he'd shoved it toward my face to tell me just how much he loved it.

Then he'd gone and left that ripped-out piece of paper on my coffee table so I wouldn't forget.

A light chuckle rippled out as I thought back to that day, to the way the kid had gotten right under my skin like he'd belonged there all along.

The same way Frankie Leigh and Ryland had done.

So, there I was, locking the door of that truck and reaching into the bed to snag the football I'd tossed back there for my little adventure to the park that sat smack-dab in the middle of our small city.

Meeting up for a motherfucking play date.

Talk about being a third wheel.

Out of place.

A damned fish out of water when this was the very pond I grew up in.

Kale, Rex, and I had spent many an afternoon running the fields as kids, kicking up dirt, causing trouble the way we'd always liked to do.

A couple of hours ago, I'd gotten a text from Rex to meet them there. I hadn't even hesitated. I needed to get the hell out of my loft.

Nikki's scent had been stalking me like a fucking drug since the second I'd woken up.

I could feel the fractures and splinters getting deeper and deeper. Cracking me open wide.

My thoughts dangerous.

My need dark.

The last four days, we'd basically avoided each other, me grunting hellos and her offering timid, unsure smiles as she high-tailed it out the door as quickly as she could, spending as little time within the walls of my apartment as possible.

She'd be gone before I even woke in the morning and already fast asleep by the time I made it back upstairs after closing the bar.

You'd think with the little amount I actually saw her, it wouldn't be all that bad.

Not true.

I was constantly on edge. Need gliding across my flesh like the sharp edge of a knife.

Lust and regret a bottomless pit in the well of my stomach.

Worry this constant thud that banged inside of me.

Seth still had no word on who might have broken into her

apartment, and until he did? I wasn't about to let her leave.

Guessed a little fresh air would do me some good.

I rounded the front of the truck and headed for the park.

Fields and playgrounds went on for what had to be a mile, all closed in by massive, ancient trees.

The second she saw me, Frankie Leigh came running in my direction. Long, brown hair flew behind her like a cape, wild and uncontained.

Grinning, I moved a little faster to meet her.

Like I said.

Sometimes it was impossible not to fall.

I dropped the football just in time to use her momentum to grab her under the arms and spin her around and around.

She howled with laughter, shouting, "Come on, Uncle, can't you go any higher?"

She was a wild one, that was for sure, so damned happy and full of life there was no way you could be around her and not smile.

She reminded me a little of Nikki in that way, the way Nikki had been at her age, so eager to experience life; though, Nikki had done it with a tiny bit more fear.

Doses of hesitation coming on.

Careful.

It had always been Sydney who'd spur her on. Telling her to run. Jump. That she could do it.

I wondered when Nikki had decided to get so reckless.

Brave.

Which fucking sucked because the last thing I wanted was for her to be brave, constantly having to worry about the position she might be putting herself in. Stepping up when she thought it might right a wrong.

Make someone's life better.

Even if it was just a conversation with a lonely old guy living on the street.

I beat back the direction my thoughts were going and instead focused on Frankie who I was still spinning.

Her squeals of joy hit the air, and it didn't take too long

before I decided she had to have had enough and slowed to set her on her feet. Wasn't surprised in the least when she went stumbling back toward the rest of the group, veering to the right, totally dizzy and off-kilter.

Had to admit, I felt a bit of that spin, too.

"She starts puking, and that's on you. Hope you have a rag or two in your truck," Rex shot in my direction as a smug grin tugged on his mouth.

He stood behind his tiny son, Ryland, who was facing out, both of the one-year-old boy's hands in Rex's as Rex helped him balance.

The little thing was doing his best to kick a soccer ball with his foot. Not moving it more than an inch but having a grand time doing it.

That shit was cute, that was for sure, the kid like a tiny version of his dad.

Sometimes it still fucked with my head to see Rex this way. Guy'd been one of my closest friends for pretty much all of my life.

He'd taken it about as hard as I had after Sydney had disappeared. Angry at the whole damned world because ours had been rocked, none of us able to make sense of something so brutal actually taking place.

Shocked.

Traumatized.

It'd taken that sweet little girl being born for his hardened pieces to start chipping away, meeting Rynna stripping the rest to the ground.

Disquiet tumbled through me. A rumble in that dark space. Sometimes it was hard to watch. Time moving on. People moving on. Sometimes, I wished that I could, too.

Didn't matter if I wished for it or not. Knew I'd forever be a captive of that day.

I shoved the thoughts down and snatched up the ball where I'd dropped it and pointed it his direction. "You wish, man. Puke duty is not a part of my repertoire."

Kale, who had been kneeling in front of Evan, pushed to

standing and threw me a grin as he jumped into the conversation. "This from the guy who owns a bar and his sole purpose in life is to get people tanked. I'm pretty sure Olive's has played host to a hurl or two."

Kale was our opposite. All clean-cut lines and cleaner jaw, his title of pediatrician fitting him to a tee.

"Not a chance, man. Olive's is the classiest of establishments. Assholes get trashed, and they're out on their asses. Now you want to talk about what goes down on the front sidewalk in the middle of the night? That's an entirely different story."

"Language, man," Rex said, angling his head to the side. Knew the look on his face. If we'd been fifteen, that would have been delivered with a punch.

"Sorry."

Kale laughed. "Leave it to the bachelor not to be able to figure out how to act around kids."

He glanced down when Evan reached up and tugged him by the hand to get his attention.

Evan's hands flew through the air, quickly signing something I couldn't read.

Kale smiled like a damned fool and signed back.

My chest tightened like the yank of a belt.

Evan's adoption had just gone through. I wasn't sure I'd ever seen the guy happier than that day.

Not that he needed the paper. Pretty sure the guy felt that way from moment one.

Loved seeing my crew happy. Finding love after all the bullshit that'd been tossed our way through the years.

Brutal blow after fucking brutal blow.

Two of them had always had my back, stood beside me during the toughest time of my life.

Both of them had handled it differently.

Rex had fallen into that anger and grief right along with me. Like he'd wanted to take some of it on, shoulder some of the burden like he might be able to grant me some relief, ridden with a dark empathy when I didn't think he really had the first clue what I was going through.

Sydney hadn't been his responsibility. Hadn't been the one who was supposed to watch after her. Keep her safe.

Kale had stood up and become the rock and had been the one to eventually encourage me to move on. To find the bright side when my entire life had gone dark.

I waved back, moving Evan's direction and leaning down in front of him. I ruffled a hand through his red hair.

"Hey, little man," I told him, knowing he'd be able to read my lips. "Did you see what I brought?"

He dropped to his knees with that pad he used for communication, scribbled something quick. He turned it for me to see what he'd written, excitement streaking across the mass of freckles that dotted his pale face.

You brought my truck? I'm saving all my money from my chores so I can buy it when I get my license. I've got twenty dollars. Is that almost enough?

I chuckled under my breath when I read what he'd written.

"You're gettin' close, buddy. Real close. What do you say for now, we play for a bit and then we take it for a drive?"

His eyes went wide, and he mouthed, *Really?*

"Really," I told him, touching his chin.

Yep.

Impossible not to fall.

I stood and gave the football a small toss into the air. "Who's the next Gingham Lakes High wide receiver? Is his name Evan Bryant?"

His eyes lit up behind his thick-rimmed glasses, and he gave me an emphatic nod of his head.

I gave it a soft pitch in his direction, and he fumbled along for the ball.

Kale watched him like a goddamned hawk.

Always wary of the kid's heart.

Couldn't imagine having to carry that weight. But neither he nor Hope would let their own fears get in the way of the kid living a full life. Just because he was born with a genetic defect that had almost taken his young life, his parents weren't going to hold him back.

And man, did the kid live a full life. He was so full of it he shined.

He caught the ball against his chest, and Frankie went flying his way. Arms stretched out like she was soaring.

"Here, Evan. Throw it to me! I wanna catch it!"

Kinda made me sad that her adorable lisp had all but disappeared.

Guess time didn't stop spinning, no matter how badly I might want it to.

Didn't think it was possible, but Evan's face lit up even more when he looked at Frankie, and he threw it with all his might, sending it soaring.

You know, about ten feet in the air.

Fucking cute.

"You've got a visitor, man, three o'clock," Rex warned, and I turned in time to find Ryland toddling my way.

His arms were thrown up over his head, and he was giggling as he tottered over, anticipating that I was going to scoop him up.

I did.

It sent a tremor rolling through me.

Truth was, kids terrified me.

Terrified me in a way that wasn't healthy.

Didn't mean these three hadn't melted through the hard places at the center of me. Worked their way in, my care fierce.

Would do absolutely everything in my power to keep them safe.

Ryland yanked at my beard with his chubby fingers, his grin so wide as he flashed me a row of four teeth on the top and two on the bottom.

He grunted hard like he was talking to me.

"Ouch, dude," I chuckled, trying to unwind his death grip. "That hurts."

Kid laughed like it was the funniest thing in the world.

So did his dad.

Like I said, his dad's mini-me.

I scowled in Rex's direction. "And this is funny, why?"

"Uh, how about because you're holding my one-year-old like a backpack that might contain a bomb."

It was just then I was realizing I had him under the arms, holding him out and away from me. My beard was just out of reach of his flailing arms. "Self-preservation, man. Kid's about to tear me limb from limb."

Such a pussy, Rex mouthed, smirk on his face as he came to collect his kid.

Such an asshole, I mouthed back.

Evan was all of a sudden in my line of sight, his hand going over his mouth like he was trying to shield himself from my corruption.

Awesome.

Turns out, Kale was totally right. I had no idea how to act around kids.

"Such a bad influence. You're hopeless," Kale taunted from behind, picking up the football and hurling it my direction.

Just like the old days.

I ran back, caught it with an *oomph*, and sent it sailing right back.

"Not sure what you expect. Don't run into a lot of kids in my line of work. Sorry I'm not a kiddie doc who always knows the right thing to say."

Catching it, he lifted his arms out to the side. "Has nothing to do with my profession. It's just the natural charm."

I shook my head with a laugh. "Charm? More like constant flow of BS. People just pretend like they tolerate you."

"Which is why you show up to the *park* to hang out with me."

Kale threw the football to Rex.

"Pretty pathetic, if you ask me." Rex. Giving me shit just like the fucker always did.

Without a whole lot of effort, he reached out and caught the spiraling ball.

The look I shot him would have seared a lesser man in two.

"Says the guy who said he would come drag my ass here if I didn't show. Now tell me who the pathetic one is? Just felt sorry for you suckers, that's all."

Rex grinned as he stepped back to hurl the ball. "You're just jealous our lives are filled with parks and diaper bags and spit-up rags. Super glamorous, right?"

"Jealous?" I tossed out, spinning on my heel to run, because Rex had an arm, that was for damned sure. The ball flew high and far.

Finally got out in front of it, and I caught it in both hands.

"Totally jealous," Kale piped in. "Dude doesn't have it in him to admit we have it right, and he's the one missing out."

"Right for you, man, right for you."

Truth was, I knew they had it *right*. Saw it on their faces. They were living for the good in life. But that was the kind of good there was no chance I could stomach.

Because I couldn't be trusted with the *good* things in life.

It's your fault.

I trusted you.

You were supposed to take care of her.

You promised, you'd take care of her.

An echo of those words assaulted me, and I could almost feel the fists beating against my chest as my mother screamed in agony, her anguish its own phantom that would haunt me the rest of my life.

I threw the ball with everything I had, like it might take the sorrow with it. Peel it from my skin. Or maybe take me back to that time. Where I could change it. Make it right.

Kale grunted when he caught the blistering spiral. His eyes narrowed in awareness. The guy knew me well enough to latch on to exactly where my mind had gone.

"Seriously, Ollie. Joking aside. You belong here, man. With our kids. Our families. Don't ever question that."

That was what they'd become. Didn't mean I didn't continually feel like an outsider. The leech who had nothing but was desperate for something, latching on, the whole time praying I didn't bleed them dry.

My voice went hoarse. "Love them like my family," I forced out, my gaze moving to the kids, who were playing so free.

"That's because they are your family. Think we all know well enough blood isn't necessary to make that bond." Rex's words were low.

Emphatic.

Like he needed me to know.

Like he was reminding me of the way it'd been when we were kids. And truthfully, the way we were then. Could trust both of them with anything.

Rex began moving my way, angling his head at Kale to follow.

We met in the middle, moving away from the kids a bit. Clearly moving out of earshot.

"So, what's this bullshit about Nikki's place getting broken into? Any idea who it might have been?"

My head shook, unease tying up my guts. "No. She's being tight-lipped about it."

"Stubborn," Kale said, almost offering a smile.

I huffed out a frustrated sound. "Tell me about it. Pretty sure it has something to do with that meeting she's helping to run. She goes quiet the second I bring it up. Think she's protecting someone."

A fresh round of fury pulsed through my veins.

The acute need to protect Nikki.

The urge to hunt.

Problem was, I wasn't sure what I'd do if I found the fucker who thought it'd be a good idea to mess with her.

"I called Seth this morning, and he said they still don't have any leads."

Couldn't stand the thought that he was still out there.

"I don't like this whole situation. Something just doesn't sit right."

That feeling continued to grow. Coming on stronger. An itchy awareness of an approaching storm. Something wicked wound with the wind.

"She's still staying at your place?" Kale asked.

"Yeah."

As much as it was driving me straight out of my mind, I wasn't letting her go anywhere.

Rex dipped his head quickly, happy with that answer. "Rynna is seriously messed up over it. Keeps bringing it up every night, worried about Nikki and what she's going to do. You know Nikki . . . she tried to play it off like it wasn't a big deal, but Rynna didn't buy it. She suggested we find a house to flip and have Nikki rent it so she's in a safer neighborhood."

In contemplation, he looked away before bringing his attention back to me. "There was a building that went up for sale by the river. One of the deserted warehouses down on Row."

Kale whistled. "Took a drive down that dirt road a few weeks back after we had a picnic at the lake. It's like a fucking ghost town out there."

Rex nodded. "Yup. Place is just about as dilapidated as they come . . . junkies using it as a drug house and God knows what else . . . but the location is mint. And you know Broderick, he's always thinking big. He wants in. Luxury condos right on the river. He's envisioning developing the area into a destination spot with stores and restaurants and maybe another hotel in the future. Think I'm gonna keep a couple units for investment, make it affordable for Nikki. She can stay there as long as she wants until she decides on a permanent place."

With me.

The thought struck me from out of nowhere.

Fuck.

No.

Not from out of nowhere.

I knew exactly which direction it hit me from. Where it lived. In that deep, deep space that would always fucking belong to that girl. The piece of me she would always hold in the palm of her hand.

The only girl I'd ever loved. The one I wanted but couldn't keep.

Throat lined with razors, I swallowed hard. "Sounds like a solid plan."

"Thought so, too. Stand to make a lot of money, so it isn't gonna hurt us a bit to keep one of the units for Nik, even though I know she's gonna be all up in arms about it. We're going to have to ease her into the idea."

"I agree."

He eyed me. "Not sure what she's going to do in the meantime. It's going to take us at least a year to get the first condos ready, but I don't like the idea of her staying at that apartment."

I rubbed my hand over my mouth, my small laugh incredulous. "Think it's safe to say that makes two of us." I sucked in a breath. "She's just going to have to stay with me until then."

Kale's brows shot to the sky. "And you think Nikki is going to go for that?"

"Hell, no," I said. "I'll just have to convince her."

Kale grinned. "Really?"

"Yup."

Rex laughed low, rubbing a hand on his chin. "That sounds like . . ."

Torture?

Torment?

I'd be ruined by then. Didn't matter.

"Fun," Rex finished with a smirk.

I wanted to smack the smirk off his face. "Fun?"

"What?" He was all wide-eyed innocence. "Nikki is all kinds of fun."

Asshole.

I punched at him.

Laughing, he jumped back, blocking himself. "Hey, don't get mad at me because she's . . . fun."

Kale chuckled. "Oh yeah, I bet she's all kinds of fun. Now you get to have *fun* with Nikki for a whole year."

"She's a pain in my ass, is what she is."

"Right . . ." Rex drew out. "You just keep telling yourself that. But if you do, make sure you don't break her heart while you do it."

Suddenly agitated, I scraped a hand through my beard. "Not gonna break her heart."

Not again.

Rex sobered. "That girl's been in love with you for as long as I can remember. Followed you around like a puppy all through school. You've got to be careful with that, man."

Wondered if he really had no clue that it'd been more than Nikki following me around. That it'd grown into something it shouldn't have before it became responsible for the single greatest regret of my life.

How even after I'd shut it down, cut her loose, it'd still festered and grown until it'd consumed me, and I'd found myself a pathetic beggar at her door.

Unable to stop myself from going to her.

Needing her.

Knowing I was just going to hurt her all over in the end.

"Just . . . get that building done. I'll take care of Nikki until it's finished. Barely see her, anyway, since we have opposite schedules."

"All right, then. It's a plan."

I nodded.

It was a plan.

A plan that left me completely screwed and somehow satisfied.

Needing a distraction, I pulled away from the guys and shifted to holler toward the kids, "Who wants to get ice cream with Uncle Ollie?"

Frankie Leigh tapped Evan's shoulder, the little girl signing to her best friend.

In a second flat, both of them were beelining toward me. "Me! Me! Me!" Frankie shouted as she and Evan raced my direction. "I want to ride with you, too!"

Rex laughed under his breath and scratched at the scruff on his chin. "Apparently, I'm going to need to have a talk with Frankie Leigh about ditching her little brother. Literally left my little man in the dust."

I chuckled under my breath. "Don't give her too hard of a

time. She knows you never take your eye off him."

Frankie grabbed me by a hand, and Evan slipped his hand into the other, both of them grinning up at me like I was maybe the coolest person in the world.

I gulped down any unease and tightened my hold on their hands, leading them over to my truck parked on the curb.

I unlocked the passenger door and both of them clambered onto the seat, Evan first considering the truck was so his thing. He was running his palms over the leather dash, the steering wheel, checking out every detail.

I shut the door behind them and rounded the front, climbed inside, turning my face toward him so he could see. "Still your favorite, Buddy?"

He gave me a thumbs-up and a smile that was nothing but bright shiny teeth. I ruffled a hand through his hair. "You have good taste, that I can tell you."

He nodded like crazy as he buckled in before he was grabbing Frankie's hand and weaving his fingers through hers.

I chuckled under my breath.

Oh, so that was how it was.

Little player.

He didn't even blush when he realized I'd caught him, my eyebrows lifting in question. He just gave me a look that told me she was his to watch over.

She missed the whole exchange, too busy vigorously rolling down the window.

"Start her up, Uncle Ollie," she shouted, and I did, the two of them laughing as I quickly flipped a U and headed in the direction of the ice cream parlor that wasn't even up the road a block.

Kale and Rex would walk, but I'd promised Evan a ride, and he was gonna get his ride.

I glanced over at the two of them sitting on the bench seat, so fucking cute, so sweet, so perfect.

Frankie Leigh's hair blown by the whipping wind, her little hand out the window, gliding up and down like she was riding a wave.

Evan's attention was wrapped up in the truck, the dials and gauges and the gear stick I shifted that climbed from the floor and basically stuck up right between his knobby knees.

Their hands?

Still linked together.

I needed to downshift to pull to the curb in front of the parlor, so I grabbed his free hand and wrapped it around the knob, guiding him through the motion.

He made this thrilled, scuffing sound that twisted my spirit like it'd been wrung up by a tornado. Seemed it was the simplest of things that made this kid insanely happy, and damn it, if that didn't make me happy, too.

I let him help me take it out of gear and put on the brake as we parallel parked on the street, and I told them to wait as I jumped out and headed around to the passenger side that butted the sidewalk.

By the time I was helping them out, Rex and Kale were already approaching, little Ryland taking a ride on his daddy's shoulders.

"You finally made it," I tossed out wryly.

"Whatever. I can walk faster than that old truck," Rex badgered.

Frankie hopped out and bounced over to him. "That was so much fun!"

Rex shook his head. "Why doesn't she go on about my truck?"

Frankie Leigh's mouth twisted with distaste. "Daddy, your truck is a work truck and stinky and dirty. Look how pretty Uncle Ollie's is."

She waved her hand out like she was one of those *The Price is Right* models.

Rex latched on to that real quick. "Ah . . . it is pretty, isn't it? Just like Uncle Ollie. Pretty Boy," he taunted.

If his kid hadn't been standing there nodding and agreeing like it was the truest thing he'd ever said, I would have given him a finger.

Pretty Boy, my ass.

"Come on, you two." I stretched out my hands for Evan and Frankie. "I promised you ice cream, let's get you some ice cream."

"Yay!" Frankie yelled, skipping along at my side.

Evan and Frankie went right for the display, pushing up onto their toes so they could see the different flavors displayed behind the glass.

They ordered sundaes, and Rex ordered a cone for Ryland. We found a place in the corner where the kids dug right in.

Conversation easy, Rex, Ollie, and I chatted, catching up since we didn't get to chill like this nearly enough anymore.

I froze when I felt the hairs at the base of my neck lift. A prickle of awareness. Not in fear.

Or hell.

Maybe that was exactly what it was.

Fear.

Because the weight of her presence was beginning to become terrifying. Affecting me more and more.

I slowly shifted in the hard booth so I could glance over my shoulder, wondering if my mind was just making shit up.

But no.

She was there.

Nikki.

Honeyed locks cascading down her back in a wild, erratic stream. Not curly in the least, but still all over the place.

Her back was to me, but she was sitting at a table sharing ice cream with this young girl who couldn't be more than seventeen or eighteen. At the girl's side, covered in chocolate ice cream, was a little boy who probably wasn't much older than Ryland.

Shoveling the ice cream in like he'd just discovered the Holy Grail.

By the look on his face, he had.

That wasn't what had my insides curling with a crazy sort of worry. Wasn't what had disquiet sinking slow and sure in to that vat at the bowels of my spirit where all the bad shit lived.

Compounding and sharpening.

It was the way the girl's expression held nothing but beaten-down fear.

Debased and degraded and disparaged.

Like she couldn't take a single thing more or she would crack.

Nikki held her hand in the middle of the table, her head dropped low and tipped to the side. Even though she was facing away from me, I could tell just by her posture that she was speaking to her.

Her words low but fast.

Desperate encouragement.

Awareness seeped through me like a parched desert sucking up a summer rain.

The realization that whatever was going on with Nikki had everything to do with this girl.

With that little kid.

Like my spirit just got that Nikki was desperate to stand up and protect both of them the way I would protect her.

Fully.

Wholly.

Without question or fear or any consideration to the consequence.

Because that's what it came down to.

I wanted to protect Nikki. Keep her safe. Not because I wanted a second chance at saving someone.

But because it was the only thing I had left to offer.

An eye and an ear and a ruthless heart that wouldn't think twice about striking down anyone who thought to fuck with her.

And whatever was happening at that table?

That unease climbed my spirit. Clawed and expanded.

Fury flamed. Licks of agitation. Stirs of anxiety.

"Uncle Ollie, Uncle Ollie!" Frankie tugged at my shirt. "Isn't that right?"

Damn it. I didn't have a clue what she'd even said.

"That's right, sweetheart," I mumbled under my breath.

Rex cocked a brow. Gave me a look that said *really?*

Who knew what I'd agreed to. Probably had told her the world was made of cotton candy. For her? I'd give anything to make that statement true. Sunshine and rainbows and everything sweet.

I rocked in the hard booth, rubbed my fingertips over my lips, trying to sit still.

Nope.

Couldn't do it.

"Give me a minute," I told the guys.

No one really even responded when I pushed out of the booth and stalked across the small parlor.

Coming to a stop at the edge of their table, I glowered, hands in fists as I stared at Nikki, who still clutched the girl's hand as she frantically whispered something to her.

My guts that were screaming cried out.

Nikki, what are you doing? What exactly have you gotten yourself into?

Reckless girl.

Because the girl across from her, who was little more than a child, all out shook when she jerked her attention my way and saw me standing there.

Fear.

So much fear.

I recognized it, written all over her.

When Nikki followed the girl's attention and her eyes landed on me, it was horror I saw all over that perfect face. "Ollie," she whispered through her shock.

Those indigo eyes went round, and her teeth clamped down on her lower lip. Behind her, the sun streaked through the window, glowing around her head, circling her like one of those rainbows I'd just been talking about.

Motherfucking sunshine.

"Nikki," I said, voice so hard it basically had to be pried off my tongue.

Energy lashed, something alive and painful between us.

"Give me a minute," she asked me, repeating the exact thing I'd just told my crew.

Both of us asking for time.

But time was something we'd never had.

None of it. Too much of it.

Forever lost.

I glanced at the girl and the little boy, who was still shoveling ice cream into his mouth, and scrubbed a hand over my face. "Yeah. Of course."

I stepped back.

But I refused to walk away.

thirteen

Nikki

I remained locked in a stare with Ollie, my hand still clutching Brenna's while I begged him with my eyes to give us space.

Questions billowed from him as if they were written in the rough, choppy air, concern and this knowing kind of anger that twisted my belly with a rush of anxiety.

My worry wasn't for him or what he would think.

It was fully for Brenna, the girl who was so completely terrified she was shaking and cowering in her seat as she wrapped a protective arm around her son's waist.

Ollie towered there. Appearing hard and intimidating.

Menacing.

A beast ready to charge.

What she didn't know was that, even though the man didn't know her, he would go down in a blaze to protect her. He'd never lift a vicious hand toward her. Not ever.

Or me.

It was his gentle hand that put me in danger.

Reluctantly, Ollie backed away. For a beat, my gaze followed him, my heart leaping into my throat when I spotted who he was there with, with those precious kids.

This was the problem of living in a small city. Their idea of a fun outing for kids was basically mine, too, thinking this would be a great place to keep Kyle entertained while I talked with Brenna.

I swiveled my attention back to her. "I'm sorry about that."

Her eyes warily followed the hulking man as he moved back through the little ice cream shop. "Who was that?" Her voice trembled.

"One of my oldest friends. I grew up with him." I gave her hand a squeeze. "He's a good guy. A great guy, actually. You don't need to be nervous."

Funny how it was too easy to sing Ollie's praises because they were true. The man just came with all kinds of other warnings.

"I'm sorry," she whispered, disgrace clouding her expression. She fiddled with a napkin on the table, looking away when she said, "God, I'm such a mess. I'm so sorry. I can't believe I reacted that way. I think I'm losing my mind."

"You aren't."

It was the vile asshole trying to make her think she was insane. Filling her head with lies, making her believe she was responsible for the way he treated her.

She'd called me this morning, telling me Caleb had been bothering her again. Sending her texts. Demanding to see Kyle.

I'd suggested we meet.

I just needed to see her face-to-face.

Needing the validation that she was really okay.

I was sure Caleb was unstable.

I hadn't told her the information I'd shared with Seth, my suspicion that it was Caleb who'd broken into my apartment and had left the two notes.

He'd advised I not. That I allow him to investigate a bit so we could find some proof to pin him to.

And . . . he'd told me to stay close to Ollie.

That was probably the hardest part of what he'd asked me to do.

"I promise you're not," I told her. "You have absolutely

nothing to be sorry about. Nothing to be ashamed about. Heck, I'm pretty sure grown men cower when they see Ollie coming their way." I let the lightness weave into my tone, hoping it would allow her to relax.

"He's . . . big."

Light laughter filtered free. "Yeah, the man is a bear. A big ol' teddy bear."

So maybe that was a tiny white lie.

The man would tear someone to pieces with his teeth, but that side of him was not something she needed to worry about.

"Is he . . ." I heard the suggestion in her question, the pink that touched her cheeks.

Is he yours?

I was sure there was no way she hadn't sensed that intensity that blazed and burned between us. Heavy and fierce.

Combustible.

Ours was not a pretty sort of chemistry.

I forced a smile. "No. We're just friends."

She frowned as if she didn't believe me. "Doesn't seem that way to me, Miss Nikki."

Was that a tease?

Her attention darted to the man I could still feel from behind me as if he was offering up proof.

His presence overwhelming.

A rush of heat thrashing at my back.

No doubt, he was looking this way.

I cleared my throat. "We've just known each other a long, long time. That's all."

"I should probably head back to my momma's." She grabbed a wipe from the baby bag and began to wipe up Kyle's face and hands.

"No, Mommy. I eat ice cweam." He grinned a chocolate smile.

A soft jolt of affection escaped me. "Was it yummy?" I asked him.

"Yummy, yummy, to my tummy."

"Do you have a happy tummy?"

"Uh-huh."

"Good, then my job is done here."

"You just invited me over to fill my boy with sugar, huh? Seems to me like maybe you should have to watch him run wild for the rest of the day."

I loved it when this side of Brenna came out. When she didn't shrink behind her walls and the girl who wanted to be free peeked out from behind.

"I'll gladly watch him. Any time."

She sobered. "Thank you so much, Nikki. For everything."

Standing, she picked up Kyle and settled him on her hip. I slid out of the booth.

"For being here for Kyle and me," she mumbled as I stood with her.

"You're welcome."

I tickled Kyle's neck, and he giggled, burying his face in the fall of her hair while still peeking out.

Affection swelled in my chest.

The little thing was so adorable.

So sweet and innocent that it expanded that place inside of me that somehow kept feeling more and more hollow. I wanted to take him into my arms, feel his weight, breathe him in.

God.

What was wrong with me?

"See you soon, sweet thing," I said, trying to keep my craziness in check.

He wrapped his little arms around his mom's neck and grinned.

I shifted my attention to Brenna before leaning closer to her, my words a hushed whisper, "Remember . . . you *are* strong. You have control of your life. You have control of your body. You have the right."

Her head bobbed along, her lips barely moving as she repeated the support group's mantra.

I moved in and hugged her tight, my mouth at her ear. "Believe it."

Stepping back, she swiped a tear from her cheek. "I do.

Thank you."

For a beat, she looked over my shoulder at the people I could feel staring at me. Giving me space while invading it all at the same time.

I could hear Frankie Leigh jabbering the way she loved to do, and Rex and Kale added little things in. But it was Ollie's silence that was most notable.

"I'll see you Tuesday night?" It was an affirmation and encouragement all in one.

She had to make the commitment even if Caleb was making it hard for her.

"I will . . . I promise."

"Okay, then. I'll see you Tuesday, but if you need anything in the meantime, you know to call me. Don't hesitate."

"I won't."

A desperate sort of a plea wound its way into my tone. "Please . . . Be careful."

She blinked at me as if she were searching for the things I couldn't say. "I will. I promise."

For a moment, we both stared at each other before I gave her an encouraging nod toward the door. "I'll see you soon."

With a timid smile, she turned and made her way through the shop and out into the summer heat.

I just stood there, hoping beyond hope that she would stay strong as she ducked her head and headed down the sidewalk.

The whole time, I was contending with the shivers racing across my flesh.

The awareness that slipped and sped.

I ran my hands up my arms, trying to chase the overwhelming feeling away.

Pinning on a smile, I shifted around and headed in the direction of my friends.

Ollie had remained standing, leaning against the wall with his arms crossed over his massive chest, watching me as if I'd committed some sort of mortal sin.

I did my best to ignore it, the tumble of nerves that worked through my body just at the sight of him standing there.

So wickedly gorgeous.

Jeans and a fitted tee.

The man a wall of muscle.

I turned toward the table. "What are you guys doing here?"

Frankie Leigh squealed just as she was digging a big spoon into the ridiculous concoction she had in her sundae glass.

"We're eatin' ice cream!"

"Is that so?" A warm giggle slipped free.

Frankie started to ramble, staring up at me while she spooned ice cream into her mouth, "I've been missin' you, Auntie Nik! Where you been? Workin' at Pepper's Pies? Did you know my mommy made a brand-new kind of pie? Blueberry. I helped. I think I wanna name it Blueberry Blast. Will you write it on the chalkboard for me?"

"Of course, I will," I told her. "First thing Monday morning when I get back to work."

She grinned. "Did you know my daddy's going to build you a big, big house? Do you think it's going to be bigger than ours? Because my new house is so big . . . so high. But it's not a skyscraper. Nope. It's just two stories, but I have two stairs, one in the kitchen and one in the living room. My momma used to live there with Gramma Corinne. Did you know that?"

Frankie rambled on as if what she'd just let on was no big thing. As if she didn't have my entire being jarring back from the shock.

My attention whipped to Rex. A guilty expression rode on his too-handsome face. "Excuse me, but what did your daughter just say?"

Frankie sighed and lifted her voice. "I SAID, my daddy is gonna build you a new house."

A frown pulled across my brow, one I tipped in Rex's direction. "That's what I thought she said."

Rex scrubbed a hand over his face. "Not like that . . . was gonna talk to you about it once I had some more details."

My frown lifted. "More details? Sounds like there were plenty of details to me."

Kale laughed. "Don't get those knickers all up in a twist, Nik

Nik. Haven't you ever heard not to look a gift horse in the mouth?"

"You mean, punch a gift horse in the mouth?"

He busted up laughing. "Feisty."

Not feisty.

Angry.

They didn't get to go making decisions for me.

I should have known Rynna was gonna say something to him. I knew she meant well, but that didn't mean it didn't make me feel as if they all thought I was helpless.

I turned back to Rex. "We're going to talk about this."

"I figured we would."

"Nothing to talk about." The husky voice hit me from behind.

Shivers raced, and I bit back the irritation that wanted to fly from my tongue. The rest of my friends were just worried about me, even if they were sticking their noses in my business where it didn't belong.

But Ollie . . .

I knew Ollie would be a whole different issue.

I tucked the conversation away for later and pasted on a grin, doing my best to change the subject, the direction of their thoughts so I could figure out a way to get out of there with the least bit of attention aimed at me.

"So, what's with all the hotties at the ice-cream shop with their kids? Breaking a million hearts just by being here. You guys are nothing but a danger to society."

Kale laughed. "Danger to society?"

"Um, yes." I gestured with my chin across the shop to the three women sitting together with their kids.

"The only thing left of those poor women over there is a puddle of drool and a mess of wet panties. It's a sad, sad state of affairs."

"Panties?" Frankie's nose was all scrunched up in confusion.

She was getting way too clever for her own good. I was going to have to watch that.

"Oh, I was just joking," I told her. "Your daddy and your

uncles are just so good-looking, they break hearts without having to say a single word. Good thing, your daddy only has eyes for your mommy."

Evan grabbed the notepad sitting in front of his dad and scribbled across it.

My chest squeezed.

Painful, perfect affection.

My daddy doesn't break hearts. He fixes them.

This kid.

"Of course, your daddy fixes hearts," I told him, wishing I could sign it because it meant so much, Evan's heart now beating strong because Kale had saved him almost two years ago. I could never quite imagine what kind of bond that might forge.

Unshakeable.

At least that I knew.

"Because your daddy is the best."

A rumble of something echoed from Kale's chest. "All right, all right, no need to get carried away. We already know I'm awesome."

"Ish," I told him.

Couldn't let it all go to his head.

He winked at me.

I took a step away, ready to bolt, to get away from the energy that crawled over me from behind. "Well, it was so nice to see you all. Hopefully we can get together soon. I've been missing my little pumpkins. I need some Auntie Nik time."

"Yeah." Chills flashed with the single word. With the rough caress of Ollie's voice. "I was just heading out, too. I'll follow you back to my place."

"I walked," shot from my mouth. If Caleb was keeping tabs on my car? The last thing I wanted was it sitting out front for him to see when I was inside with Brenna.

"Then I'll give you a lift."

My head whipped that way. "I don't think that's necessary."

He stuffed his big hands in his pockets. "Well, I think it is."

I could argue with him right there in front of everyone. What good would it do? It would just prolong the inevitable. But at least that would have bought me some time to figure out what to say.

I said my goodbyes, and Ollie said his. Frankie jumped into his arms and gave him a big hug, peppering his bearded face with little girl kisses that he didn't seem to know how to take yet reveled in at the same time.

The man a twisted dichotomy.

Ollie headed toward the door, and I followed.

Chained to him in some profound, inexplicable way.

Because honestly, I owed him no explanation. But there I was, following right behind him as if I didn't have a choice.

Bound by these zaps of awareness.

Electricity tapped.

Both of us feeding off the other until it became so big we were consumed by it.

We ducked out into the blazing heat. Instantly, we were washed in the overpowering scent of honeysuckle and blazing stars, the air so thick it was almost sweet as it slicked our skin in humidity.

The burly, overbearing man strode for his truck, which was parked at the curb. He opened the passenger door and held it open for me.

"Thank you," I muttered.

Ollie only answered with a tight dip of his head. His entire demeanor was rigid as he climbed into the driver's side and started the old, rambling engine.

I swore, that old truck only shook us up more as we traveled the short distance back to his building.

My lungs squeezed almost painfully when I attempted to draw in a breath.

Everything sharp and too tight.

He pressed the button to open the sliding door that led to his garage. Slowly, we entered into its darkened depths.

The garage door dropped behind us, and it felt as if it closed off the rest of the world.

We disappeared into it.

Into a place that was only Ollie and me.

Anger and attraction and regret.

God. It was so hard sitting at his side and feeling like that was exactly where I was supposed to be and knowing those thoughts were nothing but foolish.

I couldn't allow him to affect me like this.

He parked in the mess of all his metal, his collection of cars and motorcycles just as powerfully beautiful as the man.

He came around and helped me down.

I said nothing, just headed for the old warehouse elevator that had been restored with the rest of the place.

I felt as if I was stepping into a cage as Ollie slid the restored metal gate closed.

Prisoned.

Oh God.

His brutal energy hammered through the confined space, radiating from the walls, slamming back into me. Fed by the flashes of light that blipped through the bars as the elevator clanged and churned and rose.

The elevator jerked as it came to a jolting stop at the top floor, and I stumbled. Ollie's hand darted out to steady me.

Burning on my hip.

Fire flashed.

I sucked in a breath, pinned by that sapphire gaze.

His exhale was close to pained as he opened the gate where it dropped us right at his door. We moved out into the enclosed hall, and he unlocked the door to his loft, stepping in behind me.

Sunlight streaked through the big windows and poured into the rambling space, stretching for all the darkened, shadowy corners.

Anxiety clawed across my chest.

I wasn't ready to answer his questions about Brenna, even though I could feel the weight of them from the harsh pants he exhaled through his nose.

Dropping my head, I started for the hallway that led to the bedrooms.

Needing to escape.

"You gonna tell me who you were sitting with?"

His voice came from right behind me.

Heated chills streaked across my skin. As hot as the sun.

"A friend," I told him.

"A friend?" It was all a challenge, and I whirled on him, ready to put him in his place. Because I didn't owe him a damned thing and he sure as heck didn't have any right to question every single person I spoke to.

Ollie was right there, dipping to get in my face. I swallowed around his blistering potency.

"That girl was terrified of me, Nikki, and I'm pretty sure I know your friends, considering all your friends are mine."

"I don't owe you an explanation."

"Bullshit," he spat. The force of the word pinned my back against the wall. He only backed me further into it by taking another step forward.

Towering over me, his teeth ground as he issued the words a breadth from my lips. "Tell me what the fuck is going on. I know whoever that girl was is linked to what happened at your apartment."

I tipped my head up so I could meet his stare.

Black sapphire. Hard as steel.

"I already told you, there are some things you can't know, Ollie."

He tugged at his hair, agitation thick, eyes pinching before he loosed an uncontained growl as he flew around as if he couldn't stop himself.

A punch landed against the opposite wall.

I shrieked and flinched.

Fear tumbled down my spine.

Not for my physical safety. Just for the sheer ferocity of the man.

Ollie unhinged.

Losing it.

Hanging on by a thread.

He roared and whirled back around before his words

dropped so low they seeped from between clenched teeth. "I know you're hiding something from me. I know it because *I know you*."

He slammed that same fist into his chest, right over his heart. "And I can't protect you if you don't let me in."

I shoved at him, unwilling to allow him to do this. Unwilling to let him look at me as if I was the center of his world.

His gravity.

The only thing that kept him anchored when he continually kept me adrift.

"You don't get every part of me, Ollie. Not anymore." Hurt bled with the words.

I stormed for the bedroom I'd so stupidly begun to think of as my own. I had to get the hell out of there. I couldn't stay a second longer.

Seth had told me to stick close, but I didn't know how to do that, not with Ollie affecting me this way. I had no clue what I was going to do or where I was going to go.

All I knew was I had to leave.

I banged into the door.

The breath jerked from my lungs in another shriek when one of those big hands snatched my wrist and tugged until I was spinning around.

Before I could make sense of it—before I could process it—he had me pressed against the dresser that sat against the wall.

Both of those big hands had me by the face.

A war flashed through his expression. A battle that raged.

It only lasted a second before his mouth crashed against mine.

Crushing.

Devouring.

Overpowering.

And oh God, did it ever feel good.

I whimpered, and my lips parted.

He took it as an invitation.

Or maybe he was just breaking in.

His hot tongue slid against mine, and a ball of want so huge I could barely breathe around it built in my center.

Desire and need.

Old, old love.

If only it wasn't encased in a shell of bitterness. Gelled by bitter, broken hurt.

My hands flew to his wide, wide shoulders, and my fingernails sank in.

I didn't know if I was holding on or pushing him away.

A needy moan escaped my throat, and I clung to him in a way I knew I shouldn't. In a way I couldn't. Yet, there I was, wanting to crawl right inside him. Wanting to stay there forever. Where everything felt perfectly right and there weren't a million things wrong around us.

I felt so small against him, every massive inch of his body covering mine.

Eclipsing everything.

He kissed me as if he'd gone mad.

The man finally undone.

Lost but searching for a way to break out of the labyrinth that held him hostage.

Those big hands spread across my shoulders and rode down my sides until he was palming my bottom and tugging me against his hips. It elicited a pant, and my heart thundered in my chest.

As frantic as his.

I felt the world tremble around me when he rubbed himself between my thighs. His cock so big and hard where it pressed against his jeans. As daunting as the man.

Heat spiraled. A vortex of dark greed. A need I couldn't afford to feel.

But it was there.

I sucked in a desperate breath of desire.

Ollie struggled to get me closer. He rocked and rocked. Creating this friction I could feel sparking between us.

A match and gasoline.

"Nikki . . . sweet girl . . . God. Why do you feel so good? So fucking good."

I could feel his torment slide out with every word. With every wayward thrust of his hips.

I meant to push him away, but my fingers moved to the longer pieces of hair at the top of his head. I fisted two handfuls of it and held on while he consumed my mouth and my knees buckled out from under me.

Hiking me up, he wrapped my legs around his waist, holding me while his lips danced in a delicious push and pull.

Tongue exploring.

Teeth nipping and tugging.

Delirium.

I ripped my mouth from his and prayed it would afford me some good sense, gasping for air as I panted toward the ceiling.

It only made things worse.

Ollie kissed along my chin and across the exposed skin of my throat. He lapped up and down the sensitive flesh, nipping and biting as he continued to grind himself against my center, which throbbed almost painfully.

God.

I wanted him.

I wanted him so badly, but sometimes it was the things we wanted the most that would destroy us in the end.

"Nikki," he rumbled again.

A guttural groan of pleasure all mixed up with agony.

So dark and needy.

"Ollie."

It was a whimper.

Hope and love and everything I'd ever wanted.

He palmed my breast, and he brushed his thumb over my nipple that pebbled with his touch.

I ached.

I glowed.

I pressed deeper into his hold, and he practically growled. "These tits. Fuck, Nikki, you drive me out of my mind. What the fuck am I doin'? What the fuck am I doin'?"

Every fear I had came out with his own reservations that he rumbled across the skin of my neck.

Sliding over me like a slow warning.

Because I knew better. *I knew better.*

I knew this was only going to end with my heart splattered all over the floor, and no one would be there to pick up the pieces because he was the one who'd made the mess in the first place.

Even though it was weak, I nudged at his shoulders.

"Ollie," I cried. Softly. A prayer for him to stop doing this to me.

Pushing and pulling.

Taunting and ruining.

"Nik," he grated, moving back to my mouth. His lips were so plush and soft and smooth, the perfect contrast to the scruff of his beard that scratched at my chin.

The promise of so much pleasure.

Every rush of his hand across my body was fueled by rage.

Softened by affection.

God, this man would be my complete undoing.

My beautiful beast.

He worked his mouth against mine.

Coaxing and demanding.

His presence filled me.

Heart and spirit and lungs.

Toasted vanilla.

Barrels of oak soaked in liquor.

Just his presence was enough to get me drunk. His touch enough to desolate. But this kind of pleasure would only bring pain, and I was so not into that sort of thing.

I pushed again and squeezed my eyes shut when I whispered, "Stop."

It was so low I wasn't sure he could even hear it, but I knew he felt it.

A harsh exhale ripped from his lungs as he set me on my shaky feet. His chest heaved as he reached out and gripped the top of the dresser behind me, locking me in while he pressed his body away.

An earthquake shook, the man a rigid fortress that towered and loomed. Beneath him, my entire being trembled, the quivers starting somewhere in my spirit and rattling out.

Uncontrollable.

Both of us shaking and shaking.

Trying to catch up with what we'd just let happen.

Another mistake tossed in that mounting pile.

I swallowed around the love and need and the hurt. "You don't get to do this to me, Ollie. Not again. I refuse to let you do this to me."

I could feel the erratic boom of his heart, contending with rage and all the things he wouldn't allow me to see.

"Fuck . . . I'm sorry. I'm so goddamned sorry."

He eased back a fraction and shocked me again when he shackled me by the wrists. My hands locked between us, he dropped his forehead to mine. "You can't leave, Nikki. I know what you were getting ready to do, and I can't let you leave."

His voice was grief.

A plea.

He edged back and those blue eyes tangled with mine.

"And I can't let you keep taking pieces of me and discarding the rest. Not again, Ollie. My heart can't take it."

And God, he just kept turning everything upside down because he reached out and cupped one side of my face.

So soft.

So sweet.

His thumb moved across the moisture I didn't even know had seeped onto my cheeks.

"You can hate me all you want. I deserve it. I'm a bastard, and I know it. But I can't stand the thought of you out there by yourself. Can't stand not knowing who broke into your place. Can't stand the thought of knowing you're in trouble and not being able to do anything about it. Please. Don't leave."

"I don't know how to stay here with you. Not when things are like this between us. It hurts too much."

He flinched before all that rippling muscle tightened. Every inch of him hard.

"I need to take care of you. Tell me what's happening with that girl at the ice cream shop."

I started to form the excuse, but he cut me off. "No more

bullshit. I know you're in trouble."

"I can't tell you that." It was the truth. I refused to break Brenna's confidence.

His voice somehow softened, and his head tipped to the side as he looked at me. "What have you gotten yourself into, Nikki?"

For a beat, I hesitated, and then I gave him a little of my truth. "I just want to make the world a better place."

Minutely, his head shook. Anger was clear in the clench of his jaw. "World is nothing but corruption and evil and greed."

Like a fool, I pressed his hand closer to my face, savoring the warmth.

For one more moment, I relished in this brute of a man I had no business taking comfort in.

But he'd always, always been my safe place.

"If I can help one person—just one, Ollie—I made that ugly world better for them."

I wondered how long it'd been since I'd been that honest with him.

Pain struck on his features. Worry and adoration.

The last was always what nearly dropped me to my knees, but there was too much of that corruption piled between us for the last to count.

His soul soiled and brittle and hard.

There was no longer any place for me.

When he looked at me like that, though, it made me want to believe I was wrong.

He blew out a resigned breath. "I need to keep you safe."

I searched his face, my voice quiet but strong. Because for once, I wanted him to be honest with me, too. "You want more than that."

"No. What just happened was a mistake."

He might as well have punched me. That was what his denial felt like.

How many more of them could I take?

A smile wobbled on my face. It was so fake I thought maybe my face might crack. "Then you have to let me go."

"You know that's impossible. I would kill for you, Nikki. Die for you."

Then why wouldn't he live for me?

Devastation crawled across my chest like a disease. Oliver Preston the infection and the cure.

He took a lumbering step back. An agitated, tattooed hand roughed through his hair, which was sticking up everywhere from my desperate hands tugging at it.

"You aren't leaving, Nikki. Someone broke into your place, busted the door, trashed your stuff. You and I both know it wasn't some stupid kids."

My brow pinched in disbelief. "What? Am I your prisoner now?"

"If that's what it comes to."

Tears pricked at my eyes. "You're such an asshole."

He started for the door, mumbling under his breath, "Tell me something I don't know."

A second before he stepped out, he paused and shifted to look back at me.

The severity of it pinned me to the spot. "I'm just asking that you do this one thing for me, Nikki. One thing. All I'm asking is for you to stay."

Without saying another word, he turned and strode out of the room, shutting the door when he went.

How was that fair when the one thing I wanted was the one thing he would never give me?

Not when the only thing I wanted was for him to stop breaking my heart.

fourteen

Nikki
Fourteen Years Old

Nikki's stomach tightened. So tight she wondered how it was possible to breathe.

Grating laughter rolled across the stagnant blaze of summer heat.

She pressed her lips together and focused on plucking at the grasses beneath her that grew thick along the riverbank and not the girl Ollie had his arms around.

They were hanging out under the big shade tree where Ollie, Sydney, and Nikki had played for all their lives along the winding river about a half mile up from the lake.

Sure, Kale and Rex were there, too. They'd become a part of their group a long time ago. They belonged.

But it felt like Meredith was invading it.

Why would Ollie bring her there?

And why did the fact that he had make her feel this way?

It was stupid.

Dumb.

But she couldn't stop the way her insides felt sticky and gross when Ollie picked Meredith up and fell backward with her into the water.

His arms all around her as her screech of surprise ripped through the air.

The two of them were splashing and laughing as they resurfaced before he was kissing her again.

Nausea ran the length of Nikki's throat.

Ugh.

Nikki was gonna throw up.

Boys were so stupid.

Fingers snapped in front of her face, and Sydney's voice broke through the delirium. "Hello? Did you hear a thing I said?"

Nikki's head jerked up. "Yeah, I heard you."

Okay. Not at all. But she wasn't about to admit that.

Sydney's eyes grew round. "So . . ." she drew out.

"So, what?"

Her voice became a hiss beneath her breath. "Did Billie kiss you? I saw you walking with him behind the locker rooms at the park."

Redness flushed to Nikki's cheeks, and her face twisted in disgust. She hugged her knees to her chest a little tighter. "Eww. No way, Sydney. Don't even put that vision in my head. I'm liable to puke right here."

The thought of Billie putting his mouth on her made her want to gag.

Mix that with Ollie kissing Meredith?

She was gonna lose her lunch.

Sydney looked at her as if she was crazy. "Then why'd you go and tell him you'd be his girlfriend? You could have said no, you know? You know you don't have to say yes, right?"

Nikki's bounced her leg. "Of course, I know that. Maybe I said yes because he's the only one who's ever asked me."

Everyone else had a boyfriend. Could anyone blame her for wanting to know what that was like?

"Who asked you what?"

Nikki jumped when the voice hit her from the side. She whipped her head that way. The tiny flush of embarrassment she'd been feeling at confessing it to Sydney bloomed like the red roses in her grandma's garden when she saw Ollie standing there holding Meredith's hand.

He had on no shirt and was dripping wet. Muscles on his arms that hadn't been there before. And his stomach . . .

She had to duck her head when she realized she was staring, her mouth going dry and her stomach that was already in knots making this fluttery feeling that had her thinking she might take flight.

No chance of that when her belly was filled with a pile of boulders that made her feel small and weak.

It was the same thing it kept doing whenever Ollie was around. It made her skin feel hot and her palms get sweaty. Anxious and excited at the same time.

She knew everything she was feeling was just plain stupid.

This was Ollie, she was talking about. Her best friend. The third corner of their triangle, even though that triangle had taken a few new angles since Kale and Rex were always hanging around.

"Ollie . . . don't you know when to mind your own business? We're having an important conversation over here. It's private," Sydney said. She angled her head at Meredith. "Besides, it looks like you have more important things to do."

She said it as if she actually thought it'd make him tuck tail and walk away.

They used to all tell each other everything. Their secrets belonged to the other.

The three of them had since Nikki could remember. Her heart lit in a flurry, wanting to cling to it, for it to always remain.

But she wasn't delusional.

Things had changed.

Ollie, Rex, and Kale had started high school last year, and this fall, she and Sydney would be starting there, too.

They'd all grown.

Changed.

They used to be together constantly, sharing all their time, but their time together was coming less and less.

Plus . . . Ollie had Meredith.

Nikki would be a liar if she said that didn't bother her the most, her chest so heavy when she saw them together she thought it might cave in.

Ollie released Meredith's hand and set both of his on his hips, taking that overbearing stance.

He'd watched them like a hawk for all their days.

Their constant protector.

"No one?" he all but demanded. "I just heard Nikki saying, '*He was the only one who asked her.*' Now I want to know who *he* is and exactly what he asked her."

Embarrassment ripped through Nikki when Meredith giggled at Ollie's side while looking at Nikki as if she was a pitiful little girl.

That's exactly what it felt like.

It didn't help that water dripped from Ollie's hair and down his wide, tanned chest.

Heat blistered across Nikki's face, but she was having the hardest time looking away. Not when he was glowering at her like that.

Sydney made a tsking sound and brushed back her long, sandy-blonde hair. The color almost exactly matched her brother's, the same as their eyes.

Though that was where their similarities ended.

He was a grumbly bear, and she was a curious kitten.

He was brash, and she was delicate.

"We respect your privacy, so you need to respect ours," she said, calm and poised.

While Nikki thought she just might melt into a puddle.

Ollie's brows shot to the sky. "Your privacy? You're my responsibility, Syd. Dad put me in charge, so anything you do is my business. I've got to take care of you. You two get yourselves in trouble, and it's my ass on the line."

His penetrating gaze moved to Nikki. "Now tell me who you're talking about."

A shiver ran the length of Nikki's spine.

"I said it's girl talk," Sydney interrupted the stare down with a rebellious jut of her chin. As if it was gonna put a lid on the topic rather than ripping one off.

"Private," she reiterated.

Meredith laughed. "Aww . . . I think they're talkin' about a boy. Leave 'em alone, Ollie."

Nikki cringed.

"Yep. Private. Clearly code for boy talk," Kale said, shaking his hair out as he climbed from the glistening ripples of water. "Sounds to me like someone's got a crush."

Rex was hoisting himself out right behind him, trudging up the steep embankment. "Who's talking about me? Tell me she's hot."

"Hardly, asshole." Ollie waved an annoyed hand his direction. "You think everyone's talking about you."

"That's because *I'm* hot. Why wouldn't they be talking about me?" Rex grinned as he peeked over at Sydney.

Nikki swore that boy was in love with her, but Sydney swore harder, *not a chance*.

Sydney scowled and crossed her arms over her chest. "You wish, Rex."

Ollie turned back to his sister. "Tell me what you two are whispering about."

"It's none of your business what boy we're talkin' about," she shot back.

Ollie's eyes bugged out of his head.

Sydney had just given him all the confirmation he'd needed.

"Like hell it's not. You're my little sister, and Nikki might as well be. It's my job to watch over you both."

Sister.

Why'd him saying that hurt?

Sydney's pretty face twisted in a scowl.

"Not a chance, Ollie." Defiance blazed from her. "You've been bossin' us forever. You aren't gonna decide who gets to be our boyfriends, too."

"Don't need to pick because no one gets to be your boyfriend." Ollie's attention swept between the two of them. "Not either of you."

A huff dropped Sydney's mouth open while Nikki shifted in discomfort, biting her bottom lip as her attention darted back and forth with the exchange.

"Excuse me? You have a girlfriend standing right beside you, and you think you get to tell us if we get to have a boyfriend or not?" Sydney challenged.

"Uh, yeah, I do. You know Dad said you can't date until you're eighteen, and it's my job to watch out for you. Always has been. Always gonna be. So that means I'm the one who says, and I say no to whoever it is you both are talking about. How's that?"

"That's stupid, that's what it is. Just because I'm a girl, the rules are different? No way."

"Not joking, Syd. You aren't allowed to have a boyfriend. And if I find out you do? Someone's gonna get their ass kicked."

Rex laughed from behind him. "You'd better cover up her boobs if you're gonna make that work."

If Nikki didn't love Sydney so much, she might have been jealous of her. Sydney's boobs were already bigger than her mom's, and Nikki barely needed a bra.

There Sydney was, wearing a pink bikini top and shorts while Nikki was wearing her same white one-piece from two years ago with a pair of cut off shorts to cover up her bottom. Even though they were the same age, Nikki always felt as if she was struggling to keep up.

Nikki peeked at Meredith who was only wearing a bikini, so perfect and pretty and mature. Nikki didn't want to dislike her just because of it, but she couldn't help it.

"It is a stupid rule," Meredith agreed.

"It's not stupid when she has a body like that," Rex shot out.

As soon as Rex said it, Ollie flew around and pushed him hard, right back into the river.

Nikki sucked in a worried breath, and Sydney scrambled to her knees when Rex tumbled backward into the water with a splash. But they should have known Rex would only come up laughing, climbing back to the shore, shoving the flop of hair back that'd fallen in his face.

It wasn't like the three of those boys weren't constantly at each other, always tussling but never mad.

"Temper, temper," Rex said.

"That's my sister you're talkin' about."

"Just sayin' . . . she doesn't look much like a little girl anymore. Just like Nikki doesn't."

She didn't?

She hugged her knees closer.

"Watch it, or the next time I push you into that river, you won't be coming back up," Ollie warned; though, there was laughter running underneath the threat.

"That's right," Ollie started to shout, his voice carrying on the wind as he spun around and shouted, "Let it be known, anyone even thinks of messing with my little sister, and I'll be the one personally taking him down."

Rex shrugged and flicked some of the water from his hair. "It's Nikki with the boyfriend, anyway."

"Stupid boys," Nikki muttered under her breath, wanting to crawl into a hole and disappear.

"Aww, so cute," Meredith sang. Nikki knew she was trying to be nice, but it felt like a dig.

He wasn't looking in Nikki's direction, but she saw it. The way Ollie stiffened and the roll of something angry that shivered along his strong back.

Nikki felt that itchy feeling again. It tingled across her skin—something that felt good and bad and right and wrong. As if she didn't know herself anymore.

Kale ignored the whole exchange and tugged his shirt over his head. "Come on, let's go check out Stillhouse. Haven't been in there since last summer."

"Lucky if it'll still be standing," Rex said.

Nikki chewed her bottom lip. "You know it's not safe to go sneaking around in there."

Rex grinned. "Always so scared, Nik Nik."

"I'm not scared. I'm just not dumb. It's not my fault I hang around with bunch of stupid boys."

"I want to go," Meredith agreed, looking at Ollie with eyes that were begging him to take her along.

Nikki looked at Sydney, praying that she'd get it. That Nikki needed to get away. She didn't think she could handle watching Ollie with Meredith for a second more. "It's a bad idea."

And still, she was climbing to her feet, the same way Sydney was doing, because that was just what they always did, always following the guys around.

Sydney held out her hand to Nikki to help her stand. Excitement blazed in her eyes when she squeezed Nikki's hand and whispered just so she could hear. "Fly, fly, dragonfly."

Nikki sucked in a breath and gave her a nod, following her up the slope to where they'd left their bikes. Kale had already climbed onto his and was taking off down the trail, Rex right behind him, Sydney scrambling to catch up.

Nikki watched them. Rex looked over his shoulder at Sydney like he was challenging her to catch up. Beckoning her to his side. Something special moved through the air between them.

Nikki would bet that something special was something Ollie wouldn't like.

Warily, she moved to pick up her bike, but all her movements felt slowed.

Sluggish.

As if she were trudging through a muddied bog. Held back by that same feeling Ollie radiated like his own special glow.

A brand the boy wore that only she could feel.

She peeked over her shoulder, and he was still there with Meredith, but looking all hard and pissed.

She shook it off. Her private life wasn't any of his concern, and what he did with Meredith was definitely none of hers.

She focused on peddling up the trail, through the weeds that had grown high, the long, floral spines of the purple blazing stars poking up through the spikes of the tall grasses.

As soon as Ollie was out of sight, she peddled harder, faster, thinking she might finally break away. She topped the hill and wound back around the trail toward the abandoned buildings down on Row.

What used to be a dirt road was now an overgrown path that was barely discernable, just like the earth that had grown up around the crumbling, deserted buildings.

They weren't supposed to go in, but they'd been doing it for years. It'd always felt like an adventure.

Thrilling.

A little scary.

A little wrong.

Nikki guessed that was what made it so much fun. What made her stomach still twist with the thought of sneaking inside.

She dropped her bike in front of the three stories of splintered wood and rusted steel.

Inside were old, vacant offices, metal filing cabinets tipped open with the drawers emptied and gaping. Canning facilities with battered, broken-down machines.

When they were younger, it had been a hide-and-seek heaven.

Right then, the only thing Nikki felt like doing was hiding. Because she knew she was stupid for even having these thoughts about Ollie. These feelings that welled so big inside her it made her start to think she was losing her mind.

And she just couldn't stomach the way Ollie had looked at her when she'd taken off.

As if he was angry.

Disappointed.

Just a dumb little girl who couldn't think for herself or decide what she really wanted.

Maybe she really, really was dumb, because what she wanted was him.

Her breaths came short, and her heart raced as she slowly inched toward the hole in the wall they'd always snuck through.

"What, are you scared?" She heard Rex shouting at Kale from inside. A reverberation that left a long echo through the vast stillness.

"Not even, dude. You're the only pussy around here."

Nikki angled to the side and slithered through. Inside the building, it was dark, the dusky space only illuminated by the murky rays of light. They stole through the cracks and the hazed-over windows situated up near the high ceiling that was caved-in on one side.

The urge to escape hit her, and Nikki fumbled for the stairway off to the right, her hands gliding over the splintered walls so she could find her way. Slowly, she edged up the stairs as quietly as she could. No matter how light her footfalls, the aged wood creaked with each movement.

Laughter rang through the cavernous space.

Echoes and joy.

Sydney.

Always so free and brave. Living life the way Nikki had always wanted to.

Nikki made it to the second floor, not even sure where she was going. The only thing she knew was she needed to get there.

The floor moaned when she stepped onto the second-floor landing, and she weaved deeper into the old halls where she'd hidden so many times as a child.

She shrieked when a hand latched on her wrist, and she was suddenly pulled into one of the rooms.

Ollie.

He was there, backing her into a wall, that same look on his face that he was wearing when she'd left him standing down by the river.

"What are you doing?" she demanded.

A glittering beam of light lashed across Ollie's face, one part aglow and the other a shadow. He grinned in that way that made her spirit sing a million songs.

"What does it look like I'm doing," he whispered. "Finding you."

He'd always had an uncanny way of sniffing out her hiding places.

"We're not playing," she managed. She swallowed the big lump that had grown in her throat. Trying to pretend she didn't have that feeling again. "We haven't played that game in years."

Two only.

But that summer felt like a lifetime ago. Before everything got strange and different and better and worse.

She could almost hear the tinkle of Sydney's laughter. *"That's what growing up is. It hurts and it's amazing at the very same time. That's called living, Nik. Don't ever be afraid to live."*

"No? With the way you went running, I sure thought we were." Ollie's voice was a rumble, so much deeper than it'd been.

She shook her head. "I was just looking for everyone."

She tried to shake out of his hold, duck away. The funniest thing about that was he wasn't even touching her.

"Where's Meredith?" she asked, her voice feeling too fragile.

His lips pressed into a thin line that looked like frustration. "Downstairs. She decided she didn't want to come up."

"You should be down there with her."

Nikki didn't know a whole lot about relationships, but at least she knew that. Ditching your girlfriend in a deserted warehouse was not cool.

She could see the shift. As if the lightness he'd found her with had only been a mask, and she stood there watching it be peeled away. Beneath it was confusion. A kind of disorder and anger she hadn't seen him wear before.

Something about it made her shake.

He suddenly reached out and took her by the chin. "Is it true?"

She jarred back a fraction. "What?"

"That you have a boyfriend?"

Her gaze dropped to the side.

"Look at me," he demanded, and her eyes fluttered open, just like the flutter in her belly.

He stared at her, eyes drawing together, teeth gritted. "I don't like it."

A sound scraped from her throat. "You have a girlfriend, but you're telling me you don't like it?"

His jaw clenched, and lines pinched his forehead as if he were trying to make sense of something. "I don't like it. The way it feels. The way it makes me feel."

His eyes moved over her. Nikki felt as if he was looking at her for the first time.

He hesitated, and his tone twisted in confusion. "You make me feel different."

"What's that mean?"

He fiddled with a piece of her hair.

Softly, watching the movement as if he was in awe.

Her knees wobbled. "Ollie." His name was close to a whimper, and if she hadn't had been tied to him in this unseen way, she would have floated through the ceiling.

"It means I want to take care of you."

She tried to clear her head. "You have a girlfriend. Right downstairs. Remember? And I'm not a little girl anymore."

He looked at her in that strange way again. "No. You're not. But that doesn't mean you won't always be mine to protect."

Footsteps clattered up the steps and came their direction. "Hey, assholes," Rex shouted, "We're coming for you."

Ollie jumped back, putting a couple of feet of space between them, looking away from her as if standing that close to her was a sin.

Kale's voice carried, getting closer and closer. "Come on, shit sticks! We're heading to the lake. Cliffs are calling my name. It's hotter than the devil's backside in here. Think we walked right into the pits of hell."

"Alabama is hell. Thought you would have figured that out by now," Ollie shouted back.

"Ollie! Come on. It's hot in here, and this place is super creepy. I want to leave." Meredith's voice echoed through the worn walls, a bit of frustration behind them.

Nikki stumbled away. Confused and somehow hurt. "Just go. I need to go check on my sister, anyway. I promised her I'd take her to the movies today."

Ollie wavered, unsure before they heard Sydney's shouted words filter through with a laugh. "We are three. Forever and ever. You and me."

"Hey, what about me?" Rex's voice echoed.

Sydney laughed. So carefree. "No way."

Ollie gave a last fleeting glance at where Nikki stood trembling against the wall before he relented and headed for the door. "Comin'. Nikki is headin' home."

He was leaving her.

Was it stupid that hurt her, too?

"What?" This from Sydney. Nikki could hear her friend's footsteps growing closer while the guys clanged down the steps.

"Where are you?" Sydney called.

Nikki eased out of the room. Trying to play off whatever had just happened between her and Ollie. It felt so different. So wrong and so right, and Nikki was sure she'd never been so unsure of anything in her whole life.

"Come with us?" Sydney asked, stretching out her hand, head angling, knowing something wasn't right.

"I think I'd better go check on my sister."

"I'll go with you."

"No."

She squeezed Nikki's hand. "We are three. Forever and ever, you and me."

Swallowing hard, she let Sydney guide her out through the motes that floated in the dusky air. The steps creaked and groaned beneath them as they headed down the flight of stairs.

Nikki could feel it, though there was nothing she could do.

The wood giving, splintering beneath her foot.

Nikki screamed as the plank busted, and her leg wedged through the hole.

Sharp arrows of wood cut into her skin. Pain and fear turned her stomach again.

"Oh my God, Nikki!" Sydney cried, and footsteps were bounding again, and Ollie was right there.

His face was twisted in shock and concern.

She didn't want to find comfort in it.

She didn't want to feel as if he made her feel everything would be all right.

But she did.

His touch was gentle as he eased her leg from the hole, careful to wind her ankle and foot free so she wouldn't get any new gouges.

She definitely didn't want the tears that broke free when Ollie pulled her into his arms, but a sob of relief broke free when he held her close and whispered, "I've got you. I won't ever let anything bad happen to you. I promise."

She wound her arms around his neck and buried her face under his jaw. His scent was all around her as she clung tight.

She couldn't make out all the words people were shouting around her.

Because Ollie had her.

And that meant everything in her world was right.

fifteen
Ollie

My phone buzzed in my pocket. I wasn't sure why my damned heart went haywire because of it. Maybe it was because I was praying it was Nikki. Hoping she'd just text to shoot the shit, tell me how her day was going, or maybe ask me about mine.

Hell, I'd settle for a text just to remind me I was an asshole again.

Anything would be better than the two of us acting like the other didn't exist.

Two days of tiptoeing around my house.

We'd been walking on eggshells since I'd brought her there in the first place, just waiting for something to crack.

Come loose.

But now . . . now it was different. A boundary had been crossed. A dam busted. It left me walking through a fucking flood of need.

I was up to my goddamned eyes with it.

Twice, I'd passed her in the hall, and it'd taken every fucking thing I had not to grab her and press her delicate, delicious body up against the wall.

Needing to devour that mouth.

Desperate to take it further.

To slide my hands up her skirt and slip my fingers into her heat.

I'd felt it. How fucking bad she'd wanted me. It was almost as potent as the anger she felt for me.

The fear.

At least she hadn't taken off.

Sucking in a breath, I pulled out my phone and squinted at the text on the screen.

Sage: Got a call. Think I have something you might be interested in.

Sage was one of the guys at the shop I'd invested in where I had all my cars restored.

Disappointment was probably not the reaction he was going for, but I deflated with a heavy exhale as I tapped out a response.

Me: What you got?

Sage: '55 Bel Air. Seller is bringing it by in about 15. Thought you might want dibs.

His offering almost brought on a smile.

Me: Yup. I'll be there.

Sage: Cool.

Tucking my phone into my back pocket, I grabbed my keys and headed out the door, going straight for the elevator and riding it down into the basement. I hopped on one of my bikes, figuring the fresh air would do me some good. Rid me of some of the anxiety and need bottled in my limbs.

Kicking it over, the engine roared to life. Metal vibrated beneath my hands. I took it to the road. Heavy on the throttle.

Weaving through cars as I let the heat blast at my face and beat some of the bullshit away.

Could almost feel it scatter like fall leaves blowing away to reveal what they concealed.

Damp earth.

Darkness.

Blood.

Bones.

Dirt.

That date loomed. Right around the corner. A reminder that Sydney was what I was fighting for.

Ten minutes later, I took a left and then a right, winding down into the industrial section of Gingham Lakes. I passed by warehouses and shops and dingy offices.

Slowing, I made the last right through the big metal gate into Roke's Restorations. I was itching to get my fingers on something good. Something that could be brought back. Something that was safe.

The massive rolling doors of the shop had been lifted. Gliding to a stop, I set my boots out to balance the bike and kicked the stand. I swung off and rushed a hand through my windblown hair as I ducked through the door and into the shop.

Place was in its usual state.

Disarray with the promise of something good. Cars and bikes and parts sitting everywhere in varying states of repair.

When he heard the thud of my boots echoing on the concrete, Sage eased out from under a hood of a classic Pontiac. He lifted his chin, grabbed a rag. "Hey, man, you made it."

"And miss the chance at getting my hands on a Bel Air? Think you know me better than that."

He turned up one of his confident grins. "Which is exactly why I got with you first. Guy said he'd picked it up local and wants to turn it quick."

We both turned when we heard a car rolling into the lot.

"Ready to check this out?"

"Hell yeah."

Side by side, we headed out the garage doors.

Rolling into the lot was a four-door sedan that had to be ten or fifteen years old, beat to shit, and seen better days. But it didn't come anywhere close to looking like the hunk of rusted-out metal being towed in behind it.

How the fuck he even towed it out of whatever dump he'd found it in was beyond me. The tires were flat and rotted, and every inch he moved forward was met with the shrill sound of metal grinding.

Taking a look at the kid behind the wheel of the car, my first thought was desperate times called for desperate measures.

He put it in park and cut the engine. A dude that couldn't have been older than twenty came springing out of the driver's side, scrawny as fuck with ratted out clothes. Cheap ass, second rate, hacked out tattoos littered his arms.

"You Sage?" he asked.

"Nope." I shoved my hands into the pockets of my jeans and rocked back on my heels.

My gut instinct made itself known.

Standing there was something seedy.

I angled my head at Sage, who had to be thinking the same shit. "This is Sage."

The kid nodded at him. "Caleb. We talked on the phone."

Sage extended his hand. "Nice to meet you."

Nervously, the kid looked back at the car. "Well, this is it."

I wandered over to the rusted-out Bel Air. Windshield smashed to oblivion and all the rest of the windows gone, upholstery cracked and ripped with some of the rods and springs poking through.

Resting my hands on the windowsill, I ducked my head inside and peered around at the old gauges and dials in the dash, old style stereo still in its place.

It was gonna need a full overhaul, that was for damned sure.

It was exactly what I'd been looking for. Exactly like I remembered. I pulled my head back and looked his direction.

"Where'd you find her?"

Twitching, he gestured south with his head. "Down on Roddum. A guy is getting rid of some of his mom's old things.

He said he needed to sell it quick because he needs the cash."

I stood, crossed my arms over my chest, and stared at the guy, trying to get a read.

Intuition.

My glare promised him I knew something wasn't quite right.

The punk shifted, about three seconds from pissing his pants.

Knew his type.

Badass until there was someone standing there who was bigger than him.

I ran my fingertips over the hood of the car.

There was something about it that was way too familiar.

Too close.

"What's the guy's name?"

Caleb shrugged. "Todd. Said it wasn't worth anything, and I might as well dump it in the lake."

Awareness pressed down on my chest. Todd. Nikki's uncle.

Maybe I should have recognized the car the second the kid had pulled up. Wasn't like there were all that many of these cars sitting around, which was why I'd been searching for one in the first place.

I'd fallen in love with this very one a long-damned time ago.

Summers spent traipsing in and out of her grandma's house. Playing. Running wild.

We'd sit in this car where it was parked at the back of the lot, turning the wheel and yanking at the gear shift like it might take us to another place.

Fairyland.

Any place we wanted to go.

Todd used to live in a trailer that sat at the very back of Nikki's grandma's land. He had always been out working in the yard and the shed, fixing shit up.

Couldn't even say how long ago it'd been since he'd moved out of town.

Hit with the onslaught of memories, I pressed my palms to the side panel and dropped my head.

Honestly, I wasn't exactly sure of what Nikki would think of me buying this car.

If she'd be pissed or pleased.

Thing was, it was a part of who we were.

On top of that, Nikki's grandma was sick.

Loss was a motherfucking bitch.

What made it worse was I didn't know things were so bad they were needing to sell stuff off.

I looked over at the twitcher who'd probably swindled the car right out from under them. "You said Todd sold you this car?"

"Yeah, dude . . . pretty sure that was his name. Looking to get rid of it fast. I didn't do nothin' wrong, so if you're not interested, let me know and I'm out of here. No big thing."

I roughed a hand through my hair and turned my face up to the strikingly blue sky.

Blowing out a sigh, I looked back at him. "Need to make a call, and I'll let you know. Give me a minute."

Asshole itched, eyes darting around, desperation flooding his tone. "Man, if you're not interested, I'll find someone who is. Don't have time for this bullshit."

I flew at him, getting right in his face.

Off to the side, Sage chuckled, low and dark. Hell, the guy was probably more intimidating than me.

Punk staggered back, and I just backed him closer and closer into the wall until the only way out was through me. "Listen, asshole. I know the owner of that car."

I pointed at it as I said it. "Now give me one fucking minute to figure out if this is legit. Otherwise, I'm gonna take matters into my own hands and make that decision for myself. If you want to leave, be my guest. But you won't be leaving with this car. You got me?"

He shrugged me off, lifting his chin like he thought he was a badass who was going to take me out.

Bring it on.

I'd lay him out in a second flat.

He shook himself out. "Whatever. You have five."

Punk asshole twat. Little fucker needed someone to teach him a lesson.

I gave Sage a warning look.

And he gave me one back.

This shit didn't sit right with either of us.

I pulled out my phone and tapped out a message to Nikki. Hated that she was probably going to cringe when she saw my name come up on the screen.

But this was my job.

To protect her the best way I could.

Me: Hey, is your grandma selling some of her things from her place?

Three of us sat there in silence, waiting for a response. Five minutes passed, then ten.

The asshole smacked his hands out in front of him. "So, are we gonna do this deal or what?"

I groaned out a frustrated sigh. "What are you asking for it?"

"Ten."

I laughed out loud and gave a harsh shake of my head.

With the way he flinched, I was pretty sure it sounded like nothing but a threat.

"I'll give you four."

"What the fuck, man, that's bullshit."

Hands curling in to fists, I edged closer to him, not quite sure why I felt like taking the stain out.

Got the feeling he'd been doing plenty of shady shit on his own.

This guy radiated sleaze.

Wasn't about to let him make out on this car. On Nikki's family's pain.

No fucking way.

"You're free to leave here, deal or not. But you're not leaving here with this car."

sixteen

Nikki

"All right, everyone. Have a seat, and we'll get started," I called to the group of women who had congregated along the back wall of the secluded basement room, pouring themselves coffee and chatting before the meeting.

Everyone moved to their seats.

I glanced around at their faces. Some familiar, regulars who were there week after week, but there were a few new faces, all of which looked unsure of themselves and what they were doing there.

Their expressions ranged from hopeful to sad.

Their ages, heritage, and economic statuses didn't matter. Each of them was so very different, yet in this setting, they were all the same.

Recovering from one trauma or another.

Abuse.

Loss.

Whatever it may be, it united them in solidarity.

Nerves strained tight across my chest at the anxiety I felt each time I sat in this position. The weight and the burden I was gladly taking on.

Their counselor.

Their encourager.

The chatter quieted as everyone settled into their seats, and Dr. Kathy gave me a nod, giving me the go ahead.

I was leading group tonight.

My stomach dipped as those nerves soared.

My gaze met Brenna's, and she gave me a timid smile.

I smiled back and cleared my throat, letting my attention bounce around the group. "Good evening, everyone. Thank you for being here. It's great to see your faces."

"It's good to be here," echoed back.

"For those of you who may not know me, my name is Nikki Walters, and I'll be leading group tonight. Before we start, I'd like to reiterate that this is our safe place. Everything said within these walls is confidential and won't leave this circle. We won't judge each other, but rather we will hold each other up."

Agreement rippled around the circle.

"Let's start this off with our group mantra. Our prayer. We'll remember it with everything that is shared tonight."

I strengthened my voice and began to recite, "I am strong. I have control of my life. I have control of my body. I have the right."

Some of the women chanted it loudly, claiming it, while others merely mumbled it under their breaths.

That was okay.

The only thing that mattered was that each of them would hear it again and again until they believed it.

"Okay . . . tonight I would like us to talk about some of the emotions you experienced when you decided it was time to make a change. No doubt, standing up for what we deserve when we might be in a bad situation is met with a gamut of emotions. Fear and joy and conviction and doubt, just to name a few. Let's look at those and how they impacted your decisions to make a change. Who would like to start?"

Lynetta raised her hand. She was good about sharing first. Getting the words flowing, instilling trust and comfort in the rest of the women who might be nervous and on edge. Exuding her own kind of peace in the way she shared the memories of her abuse as a child.

She wasn't ashamed to admit she still dealt with the scars every day. But that didn't mean she hadn't overcome it and found joy in her life.

"I remember the very moment I'd had enough, and I couldn't take any—"

She stopped speaking when timid footsteps echoed from the stairwell as someone made their way down.

It was very typical for a new member.

Many times, they came in late as if they weren't sure they should be there at all, needing to convince themselves to take that step.

I put a welcoming smile on my face and shifted to look over my shoulder toward the stairwell.

My heart froze in my chest when my eyes landed on the figure standing on the last step.

Ice slicked down my spine.

Horror.

Dread.

Worry.

They twined through me like the roots of a tree breaking through the foundation of a home.

Destructive.

Unseen until the damage was already done.

That was what it felt like, sitting there staring at my little sister and having no idea why she could be there.

Her face was so much like mine.

It felt as if I was looking in a mirror.

Only her eyes widened in shame and disgrace and mine widened with questions.

Why are you here?
What happened?
Why didn't you tell me?
I didn't know. I'm so sorry. I didn't know.

My lips parted on a soft cry while dread pumped through me

with so much force I could feel the thunder of it in my ears. The hardest part was the impact I felt in my spirit.

As if a hammer had cracked me wide open, and everything I'd held true spilled out.

Knees shaking, I climbed to my feet. Metal screeched as the chair slid when I reached out to hold on to the back for support.

I slowly turned all the way around to face my little sister.

That was all it took for her to spin around and bolt.

Footsteps echoed on the concrete as she pounded upstairs. The sound of her escape was what finally shot me into action.

"Nikki." Kathy hissed the warning, trying to stop whatever line she thought I was crossing.

I ignored her and shoved the chair out of my way. It toppled over. The reverberation of it hitting the ground echoed against the walls.

The sound only seemed to gather strength.

Distraught, I stumbled around it.

Everything felt as if it had been set to slow motion, my own steps slackened as I tried to process what was happening.

Because this felt like a nightmare. Like I'd wake up and realize it'd only been brought on by worry. By the reminder that the anniversary of Sydney's disappearance was approaching so fast.

Too fast.

It always made everything raw and new.

But my eyes were wide open.

Too wide.

My spirit screamed that I'd been blind all along.

"Sammie," I cried, chasing her up the stairs. I gathered the hem of my dress with one hand and clung to the railing with the other so I could make it up faster. "Sammie. Sammie, please. Wait."

Tears stung my eyes. A knot grew in my throat, so big that I choked over it.

I couldn't breathe.

"Sammie!" I shouted, her name strangled as it ripped free.

She was already shoving open the glass doors by the time I made it to the first level.

I raced after her and caught the door just before it closed, clamoring after her.

Her brown ponytail swished madly at her back as she rushed for her car that was parked on the street.

"Sammie," I begged, scrambling that way, pleading with her to stop.

To look at me.

To tell me what was happening.

My fingers brushed down her back. She flew around as if she was terrified of me.

Tears soaked her face, but it didn't do anything to conceal the grief.

"No," she rasped. She put out her hand to stop me from coming any closer. "No. This . . . this was supposed to be confidential. Private."

Angrily, she swatted at her tears. "Why are you here? You aren't supposed to be here."

Guilt blazed a path through me.

Clearly, she felt trapped.

Ambushed.

More tears streaked free, and she choked around the words, "It was supposed to be confidential. You . . . you aren't finished with school yet. Why are you here?"

"Sammie," I attempted again, my voice cracking. "I'm sorry. I'm interning here."

I guessed when I'd told her I was almost finished, she hadn't realized that I was actually overseeing a group. That I'd stepped out beyond the online classes to learn the things I could only learn by interacting with people.

I struggled to find the words to give her comfort when I felt so lost.

Bewildered and crushed.

Clearly, my baby sister had kept me in the dark about something awful.

I could feel it, radiating from her in waves of shame.

"Whatever is going on, whatever reason you're here, I'm here for you. It isn't your fault."

She blinked and backed away. "You don't know anything."

Steadily, she kept inching toward her car. She opened the door. "Please . . . just . . . forget you saw me here."

Then she turned, jumped inside, and drove away.

I stood there on the sidewalk as the streetlamps slowly blinked to life.

Stricken.

Broken and not having the answer as to why but knowing there was no chance I could ever forget.

Drained, I snapped open the door and was met by the silence of Ollie's loft radiating back at me.

I didn't really want to be alone, but I didn't have anywhere else to go. No one to turn to. No one to talk to.

Maybe this load really was too heavy. All I'd wanted was to make a difference. Pour goodness into a cruel world. In some small way, make it better.

Now, everything felt so wrong.

It'd taken every single ounce of willpower I had not to jump in my car and chase after Sammie.

She needed time, and my pressing her for answers wouldn't be doing her any favors.

I had to give her space.

It left me feeling mashed up inside. As if I'd been beaten and left for dead.

Wounds bleeding out when I didn't have the first clue how they'd been inflicted.

The vibration of the band playing downstairs at Olive's seeped through the floors and trembled the walls with revelry.

Voices carrying.

Laughter riding.

I'd never felt so brutally alone.

Heavy, sluggish beats drummed in my aching chest as I stepped into the space and let my purse drop to the middle of the floor. Not even caring where it landed.

I felt . . . stunned.

Dazed.

As if another piece of my world had broken loose.

I was happy, wasn't I?

So was my sister. We were close.

I'd always believed it.

Where had things gone wrong?

My gaze was drawn to the bank of windows that overlooked the city below.

My sluggish heart drummed a wayward beat, a thrum of adrenaline through my veins.

It had nothing to do with the view and everything to do with the man sitting on one of the oversized loungers on the balcony.

He faced out, just his head and the expanse of his massive, bare shoulders in my view.

A shiver rolled, and I felt as if my spirit crawled right out of me to make its way to him.

There was nothing I could do. It didn't matter what had happened on Saturday. How much I wanted to protect my heart.

I moved.

Drawn.

The way I'd always been.

Toward him had always felt like the only direction I could go.

And tonight, that feeling was overpowering.

Helplessness streamed through me like an out-of-control current that was getting ready to go right over the edge.

A free fall into nothingness.

I kept my footsteps subdued as I inched across the floor, my motions measured as I slowly opened the glass-plate slider.

Ollie stiffened in the cushioned chair, but he didn't say anything as I stepped out onto the balcony.

Distorted music floated through the muggy air, and that chill scattered. Binding deeper as I eased over to the ornate wrought-iron railing. I wrapped my hands around it and held on tight.

As if it might keep everything from splintering away.

His presence slammed into me from behind. Beat after beat.

Fierce.

Intense.

"Shouldn't you be downstairs working?"

"Was worried about you," he finally grated, blowing out a long breath toward the sky.

"I told you, you don't need to worry about me."

"Tell me how the fuck I'm supposed to do that when the only thing on my mind is you."

His words were delivered quietly, though his voice somehow boomed in the dense, thickened air.

"Texted you earlier. Never heard a thing. Then when I came up to talk to you, you never showed. Went as far as calling Lillith to find out if she'd talked to you after your meeting tonight."

He inhaled a deep breath. "Your meeting ended two hours ago, Nikki. No one's heard from you since, some asshole broke into your apartment during last week's meeting, and you want me *not* to worry about you? Think you know me better than that. I was about five seconds from starting a door-to-door search."

There was a confession to his words. The depth of his worry and the lengths he would go.

I lifted my face to the mild breeze that blew through.

Cars accelerated below with small bleeps of their horns, and cicadas buzzed in the towering trees that reached to our level.

I wanted to dip my fingertips into it. To find the peace it seemed to offer.

But I felt as if I'd completely lost ground. Everything I'd been fighting for somehow felt like a sham.

Warily, I peeked back at him. The man sat in the chair, looking like the king of his own city sprawled out below him.

A conqueror.

A warrior.

Chest bare and abdomen rippling.

Eyes keen.

The longer pieces of his hair whipped around him like a flaming crown, the sides cropped, making the man look every bit the beast that he was.

Yet, there was something about him that remained so unbearably lost.

Sapphire eyes so soft I could fall right inside.

It took about everything I had not to drop at his feet.

I wanted to remain strong. Push him away. Remember how being this close to him only hurt me time and again.

But right then, the only thing I felt was weak.

A tremor rolled through my being.

Or maybe it wasn't weakness.

Maybe I really just needed the one person who could fully understand.

My hands cinched tighter around the metal. "Do you ever wonder where our lives went wrong? Where we changed course or if we were just heading this direction all along?" I hedged, trying to find the best way to invite him into my heart.

Into my grief.

He huffed out a strained breath. "Every day, Nikki. I think about this shit every day. I think we both know exactly where it went wrong."

I glimpsed him from the corner of my eye. He lifted a tumbler to his mouth, a half-empty bottle of amber fluid sitting on the table next to him. He took a long drink.

"It only gets worse when the date gets nearer," he reluctantly added.

Yet to me, it felt like a gift. His words, his *heart*, something he had refused to offer me over all these years.

"Fourteen years," I agreed. "I can't believe that much time has passed. I can't believe it's been so long since our foundation was ripped out from under us. It shaped us into different people," I offered, praying he'd get it.

That I needed him to listen.

That I needed him to be there.

For me.

His grating words filled the distance that separated us. "It doesn't matter how many years go by, it feels like it was yesterday. Feels like I'm stuck there, and I'm never gonna get out."

His confession was hardened with regret.

Muted in sorrow.

"I was there with you. But you wouldn't let me be there for you. You wouldn't let me stay." My voice was a whisper that got swept up in the wind. It felt as if Sydney was caught in it, a ghost howling as she blew through.

I felt him flinch. The man hit by the weight of the reality, even when I knew he never wanted to face it.

"Couldn't let you stay there because you didn't need to be in the middle of my mess."

I looked at him from over my shoulder. My breath hitched.

My beautiful beast, who was so angry at the world, angry at himself, sitting there with his chin lifted and his nostrils flaring.

I knew he would charge into the distance and change it all if he was given the chance.

I knew he would be willing to sacrifice everything.

"If it was your fault, then it was my fault, too."

"Don't ever say that," he spat, jumping to his feet.

Fire and rage.

They lit like a fury inside of him.

My head slowly shook. "You know it's true, Ollie. You can't erase the fact that I was there with you. That we were together. That I'm every bit as responsible as you."

"No. I was responsible for her. Just the same as I am for you."

Those eyes blazed as he took a step forward, and he fisted his hand over his heart. "I was the one who fucked it up. I was the one who pushed things between us when I knew I was crossing lines I wasn't allowed to cross. I was the one who sent her away."

Grief lined his voice.

Emotion tingled my throat, and my eyes stung.

Part of me wanted to stop it.

Walk away and pretend all of this wasn't crashing over me, threatening to bury me alive. The other part wanted to hang on to every second.

It was the first time in years Ollie had opened up to me. A door opened when it'd forever been closed.

"She would have understood," I told him, knowing with all of me that she would have.

He turned his head, looking to the far corner of the balcony. "We had a pact."

The memory it shivered around us. A reel playing in sync in our minds. The vow we'd made before we'd understood that one day we would grow and change and things would no longer look the same.

If I focused hard enough, I could still feel the cut Ollie had made on my palm.

"We were eight years old, Ollie. You were nine. Kids," I told him. "We grew up. All of us changed."

Slowly, he swiveled his attention back. Every muscle in his body was held in restraint. "And you know exactly what happened when we did."

Grief pulsed through the silence that raged between us. So many things left unsaid for so many years. It tickled our ears and hammered our hearts as we finally brought our truths out into the light.

Tears stung my eyes, and I swallowed Ollie's intensity and forced myself to speak. "Fourteen years ago, did I leave everyone else behind, too?" I whispered, the words a tremor.

A plea.

A confession.

"Was I so consumed by that grief, by that loss, that I let everything and everyone else fade into the background?"

Ollie's face pinched, and he was moving closer. "What are you talking about?"

"I missed it. I failed to see what was right in front of my eyes, Ollie."

He was at my side. The magnitude of his presence nearly knocked me from my feet.

"What are you saying?"

"My sister." The words broke on my tongue.

In that moment, I felt something crack.

Chip away.

Secrets slayed.

And all I wanted was this man to hold all of them.

seventeen

Ollie

"My sister." Her confession carried on the wind.

Like a never-ending echo of horror that would ride on the soundwaves forever.

Regret.

The kind I knew all too well.

Grief clustered in my chest as I looked down at her.

Tears streaking down her defined cheeks.

Nikki. Fucking. Walters.

The bane of my existence.

The one who drove me right out of my mind. Left me clinging to the edge of sanity. Made me weak in the damned knees and hard everywhere else.

She was a carrot dangled in front of me like a tease. Always right there, always just out of reach. A connection I couldn't keep but wanted more than my next breath.

Because that was what she was.

Breath.

Life.

The goodness and light in the middle of my dark, dark world.

I wanted to lean in, press my nose to her delicate neck, and suck her down like a sweet, satisfying drink.

Sunshine and lemonade.

In the breeze, locks of that honeyed hair whipped around her head. A few errant pieces stuck to her face, those eyes so wide and innocent, and that mouth so goddamned deliciously pink.

It made her look like the girl I'd fallen so hard for.

She'd driven me crazy then, just like she was driving me crazy now.

Swore to God, the burn of that kiss from the other day was still flames on my lips.

"What do you mean, your sister?" My words were guarded. Careful.

Fuck. Maybe I didn't want to know.

Because a sob tore from Nikki's throat.

"I think someone hurt her."

Rage. It was instant. The fury that banged through my being. It struck in the air.

As deadly as a thunderbolt.

I grabbed her and pulled her all the way around so I could fully see her. "Who?"

She stared up at me. Indigo eyes flashing in the night. Agony wheezed out on her words when she reached up and pressed both her hands to my chest. "I don't know. She . . . she came into the meeting tonight. Neither of us were expecting the other. She saw me . . ."

She choked.

In a flash, I had both my arms around her waist, pulling her up tight against me as I tried to process what that meant. "What was she there for?"

"She ran off before I could get any answers. I . . . I chased after her. Called her name. And she ran, Ollie. She ran from me as if she was scared of me. Like . . . like she didn't trust me."

That description all wrong.

That role was one reserved for me.

My mind spun with a shit-ton of horrible possibilities. There was nothing I could do but gather this girl closer, rocking her slowly, knowing I'd give absolutely anything to take this away. "She didn't know you would be there?"

Burying her face against my chest, she shook her head. "No. I don't think she realized that my internship meant I would be working in the field."

I kissed her crown and ran my fingers through her hair, praying it would soothe her. "You know it wasn't because she was scared of you or didn't trust you, Nik. You know better than that. She just didn't know what to do with exposing her own secret. You took her by surprise."

Hot tears landed on my bare chest, and the girl's lips moved across the flesh. "I don't know what I'm supposed to do."

I was such a twisted fuck.

Depraved.

Because just that touch had my mind going where it couldn't go.

Laying this girl out.

Taking her.

At the same time, I wanted to wrap her up.

Protect her and take every drop of her despair away. Shield her from all the bad shit that ran rampant in this vile world.

I tried to rein in the stampeding need.

"You'll figure it out, sweet girl. Sammie knows you. She's just got to deal with whatever she's going through before she's ready to confide in you."

"I can't stand the thought of someone hurting her. Of her being in pain."

A shudder raked down my spine, spreading out beneath the surface of my skin.

Rage and grief.

I hugged her closer at the same time as she pressed tighter against me, those sweet arms bent and pinned between us as I wrapped her whole. "I know. I'm so fucking sorry. So fucking sorry."

There'd never been truer words.

She pulled back. Just a fraction. Enough that those mesmerizing eyes were gazing up at me.

Casting their spell.

Sucking me under.

"I need you," she whispered, ducking down and placing gentle kisses all over my chest as her fingertips ran down my abdomen.

My muscles tensed beneath the assault.

Her perfect, perfect assault.

I grabbed her by the wrists, voice a warning. "Nikki."

"Please," she whimpered. "I need you. I need you. Take it away."

My mind flashed to a year ago. I could almost hear my own words echo through my spirit. My pleas when I'd needed her in a way no one else could offer.

Like she needed me now.

The two of us knew each other better than anyone else.

Trusted in a way we shouldn't.

"Nikki," I said again, another warning that only sounded like giving in.

"Please." She pressed the word right against my heart that thundered and roared and sent an earthquake through me.

Protection and greed.

"You are so much better than what I've got to offer. I'm messed up."

"What if I want to be messed up with you?"

A low chuckle rumbled out, and my fingertips were tracing across her lips.

Everything coming closer.

Closer and closer.

"It's my job to protect you, remember? Even if that means protecting you from me."

The smallest smile pulled across her sexy mouth, a tease barely winding into the words. "I guess I like your brand of pain, don't I?"

Lust flickered low. Right where it'd always burned for her.

Embers and ash.

An aching, smoldering glow. "Don't want to hurt you, Nikki, and I'm pretty damned sure you don't want me to hurt you, either."

She blinked up at me. No reservations when she should be running for her life. "Then don't."

"Not sure I know anything else."

Need flickered through those bewitching features, and I brushed my fingers through the wild pieces of her hair, holding her by the side of the head.

"If I could, I'd do anything for you. Give you anything."

Her nails scratched over the cross etched right at the center of my chest.

Right over the boom of my heart. It pulsed my blood harder and harder, every thrum winding me higher.

Lust bottled in the air. Wobbling. Teetering as everything threatened to spill.

Stark vulnerability seeped into her words, a line pulling into a scowl across her brow. "Please, Ollie. Touch me."

Need tied my guts into a thousand knots, and I gripped her as we swayed. To the beat of the music that filtered up from below.

The bar alive.

Nikki and I elevated above it.

Removed.

Two strangers who knew each other better than anyone else who'd landed in a realm where they shouldn't be.

My thumb traced along her cheek. Right over those freckles that made her appear so sweet and a little untamed.

She was.

But she was more. So much more.

She was beauty and belief and the sun.

Made up of her own mistakes and her own regrets.

She was fear and challenge and perseverance.

She was the girl I'd thought I would spend my life with until I'd lost it the day I'd lost Sydney. "I will ruin you, Nik. We both know it."

Nails scratched across my skin, searching for a place to sink in. "You ruined me a long time ago."

My nose brushed across hers. "Nikki." Her name was a moan. A plea. It was giving in. "What do you need?"

"You."

A groan rumbled deep in my chest, and I swept her off her feet, one arm under her back and the other under her knees. That was right as my mouth was slanting over hers.

Possessively.

Protectively.

My tongue plundered that smart, delicious mouth.

Deprived of the taste of her for far too long. For too many fucking years. After the tease I'd gotten the other day, I was desperate for more.

Damn the consequences.

A whimper pulled from her, and she murmured, "Ollie," on a needy breath of surrender.

For a moment, both of us were giving in.

Her arms wound around my neck as I moved across the balcony. I owned that mouth the whole way, Nikki clinging to me the entire time.

Kissing me back.

Just as hungry.

Desperate and needy.

Needy for me.

Heaviness stretched my chest taut, everything I'd ever held for this girl swelling.

Getting bigger.

Consuming in a way that I knew would never let me go.

Angling to the side, I slid open the door with my elbow.

Shadows played across the floor and walls of my loft, and I carried her across the dusky, dimly-lit room. When I laid her on the couch, a surprised breath gushed from between her lips.

I swallowed it.

Made it my own.

Wanting more. So much more. Wanting it all.

Fuck.

I had to focus. Focus on this girl, who was squirming on the dark leather, wearing this ridiculous short floral dress and boots.

Those legs bent as her hips bucked from the couch, begging for me. That dress slinked up to reveal the silky skin of her thighs. It gave me a peek of the black lace covering her underneath.

Desire clutched every cell.

Heart and mind and body.

There was nothing I could do. All I wanted was to take her away from there. To a reality where it was us and nothing else.

I stood staring down at her through the darkness.

Eyes tracing every slender curve of her mouthwatering body.

"You are so fucking gorgeous."

She tucked her bottom lip between her teeth, and her chin lifted as her back arched. She pressed her hands to her belly and squirmed.

Unable to sit still.

So needy.

Hot.

Her flames licked out. A spark against my body.

My cock twitched and strained against my jeans. I was blasted by thoughts of how easy it would be to rip all of our clothing away and sink inside.

Get lost in her heat and her sighs and her support.

Forever.

Use her up the way I'd done before and didn't even have the decency to remember.

Motherfucker.

I wasn't about to go there.

This was about her.

Nikki.

I reached out and trailed a single finger down her arm, running from her shoulder to her wrist. "Just have to look at you and another piece of me falls. Breaks away. You were every fantasy I ever had. Teenaged kid dying to get inside you. Knew it'd be heaven."

"Ollie," she whispered, spreading her hands across her dress that had ridden all the way up to her waist, her hands running the length of her thighs of her bent legs. "You were always more than a fantasy to me. You were everything that was real."

God damn it.

She was going to wreck me.

Destroy every ounce of self-control I had. I'd done it once. Lost it. Let her wreck me. Didn't think she could afford for me to lose it again.

So, I kept myself in check, careful as I let my index finger explore, running over the fabric of that dress and riding up her thigh. I palmed the inside of it and dipped down to kiss across her knee.

Shivers rolled through her, running her spine and crashing into me.

Those hypnotic eyes watched me through the pale, muted light, knowing me too well. Seeing too much.

Each movement measured, I slowly crawled over her, bracing, keeping some distance between us while she fought to get closer.

God only knew what would happen if I plastered myself against the shape of her.

A sigh filtered from between her pink lips that were swollen and plump and damp from the force of my kiss.

So damned sexy.

I planted my hands on either side of her head, gaze moving over that unforgettable face. "You are real, Nikki. Don't ever mistake that. You were the most real thing I ever had."

Her fingertips brushed down my chest. "I'm still yours," she whispered.

I slammed my eyes shut and jerked my head to the side like it might protect me from the impact of her confession.

Inhaling deeply, I let my forehead drop to hers, our breaths mingling and our noses grazing.

Both of us hanging at a precipice.

A breath. A pant. A heated second.

Bated, suspended.

Then the band holding me back snapped.

Our lips met in a collision of greed.

Taking and giving.

My lips closed over hers.

Top.

Bottom.
Sucking.
Releasing.
Tugging.
Again and again.

A perfected dance that wasn't close to being slow.

I pressed up higher on my hands, and my head dipped down as I swept my tongue into the wet welcome of her mouth.

Thought I might die right there.

It was met with a whimper at the back of her throat and a tangle of her tongue with mine.

Her fingers scruffed through my beard, and then her hands were fisting in my hair.

Begging for more.

Her body lifting to meet mine as our tongues coiled in a desperate play to get closer to the other.

I took her by the inside of her thigh, making myself room, rocking my cock against her pussy.

Her cry was quiet and needy. A plea lighting in the combustible air. "Ollie. I need you. I need you."

A groan rambled through my spirit, and I tore my mouth from hers. This was not about me.

I'd taken enough.

I plucked at her bottom lip with both of mine before I was kissing a path down her chin, her jaw.

Fingernails scraped my shoulders.

I sucked and licked along the delicate column of her slender throat and to those fucking collarbones that drove me straight out of my mind.

Delirium.

My head spun, and I was kissing across her chest, down over her heart that drummed violently.

Pound, pound, pound.

I felt it beating.

Desperate in its bid to meet with mine.

As if it could catch up to the bolting thunder that raged within the confines of my ribs. Thrashing at my insides.

Seeking a way out.

I sucked in a breath and fought back that feeling. That feeling that she was mine and she was always gonna be.

I kissed across the neckline of her dress, right over the fabric to the swell of those tiny tits.

Fuck.

Why was that so sexy?

So damned sexy that I was yanking the neckline down, exposing her dark, peaked nipple. My tongued licked across the tip before I sucked it into my mouth. One hand came up, palming the bit of flesh, bringing it deeper into my mouth.

Nikki bucked, rubbing her center against my dick that begged at my jeans. She moaned, and her hands were everywhere.

My hair, my face, my shoulders.

Raking down my back, eliciting the most tortuous, pleasured kind of pain. "Ollie. Oh God. That feels so good. You feel so good. I need you. I need you so much."

Her panted words lifted into the dense air, and I sat back on my knees. I grabbed her by the waist, cinching my hands around her. "You want me to make you feel good, sweet girl?"

Her head rocked back on the pillow. I swore, the girl was so damned pretty it hurt to look at her. A punch right to the center of my chest.

"Yes," she drew out, tongue darting out to swipe across her lips. "Please. I need you. I never stopped needing you."

I beat back the guilt. I had no clue about the way I'd treated her last year. But I knew full well the way I'd left her when she was sixteen.

My hands slid up the top of her thighs.

Shivers raced beneath my palms, the girl quivering and shaking like she was seconds from falling apart, and I hadn't even touched her.

I let my hands glide around to her back, lifting her a little as I palmed her ass, her knees dropping open wide when I did. "This ass, baby."

And I was wondering if anyone had been in it. Who'd been in her, taking this sweet body.

Aggression I didn't have any fucking right to feel curled through my being. A dark, violent sickness.

I wanted to possess her.

Every part.

Every inch.

She was supposed to be mine.

I kneaded her cheeks and let my fingers run down her cleft.

"Ollie. What are you doing to me?" Those indigo eyes met with mine as she sucked frantic breaths into her lungs. "You make me crazy."

A low chuckle of warning escaped my mouth. "Safe to say it's the other way around, Sunshine. You make me insane. That mouth, and this body. I want to fuck you wild, Nikki. Mark you. Keep you."

I was saying things I shouldn't be saying. But I couldn't stop the words from scraping from my mouth.

Her dress was bunched all the way up to below her tits, the one I'd been sucking on peeking out the top, nipple still hard and wet from my licks.

Her hands spread out across her flat, naked belly. "Please."

And I knew she'd let me. Knew that she'd let me use her. Maybe . . . maybe she'd use me, too.

The passion roiling in her eyes was untamed. Fierce and savage.

She wanted to get reckless with me.

I snagged my fingers in the edges of her underwear and began to peel them down.

"Shit," I hissed. The ground quaked beneath me as I revealed what was waiting underneath.

Totally un-fucking-prepared for seeing her this way.

Spread out for me.

Pussy wet and glistening.

Lifting her legs between us, I unwound the lace from her ankles and dropped her underwear to the floor, setting one of her ankles on my shoulder as I barely dragged just the tips of my fingers through her slit.

I almost went off right then.

I'd been wanting this girl for far, far too long.

Just that little touch had her hips hiking up, pressing from the couch.

"You want me to touch you, sweet girl? Is that what you want?" The words rumbled from me as I shifted, planting a single hand next to her head.

Caging her in.

She nodded, hair swishing across my couch. "Don't tease me, Ollie. My heart can't take it tonight."

My chest tightened, and I had the wayward thought that there'd be plenty of time for that later.

Teasing and playing.

I knew better than to let my thoughts go wandering that direction. I forced myself back to her in this moment.

To the girl who was shaking on my couch. Desperate for relief.

I slicked my fingers through her pussy, watching the way her lips parted, tasting the sigh that slipped from her tongue when I tucked a single finger into the tight clutch of her body.

Her hands flew to my shoulders and held on. "Ollie."

I drew back, added another. I drove them in slowly.

"Like that?" I murmured at her mouth, teasing her a little.

She swallowed hard, searching for air. "More."

"That's what I thought," I rumbled, nipping at her chin. "I'm gonna take care of you. Sweetness. Sunshine," I rumbled, lips moving across her cheek.

A little moan jetted from her mouth, and I edged back, pulling my fingers free.

Protest had her loosing a tiny groan, and I gave her a lopsided grin. "I've got you. Trust me . . . I've got you."

Those words were out before I could stop them.

Trust.

I deserved none of that.

But she could count on me to give her this.

I spread my hands wide and slipped them up the insides of her thighs, spreading her wide. Hands going back to her bottom, I lifted her from the couch when I leaned down and licked.

She yelped, and those needy little hands flew into my hair.

I turned, kissed the inside of her thigh, whispering against the flesh. "Is this okay, sweet girl?"

Sweet, fucking, delicious girl.

"If you stop, I will stab you, Oliver Preston."

There she was. My smart-mouthed Nikki.

A smile pulled free, one I hid against her skin before I buried my face back in her heat.

Kissing her cunt like I had kissed her mouth.

Laps and licks against her lips, tongue driving between. I licked back to the tight pucker of her ass before I moved to lave at her clit.

Swollen and red.

I rolled my tongue around it.

Sucked.

Licked.

I pressed my hand to her belly, pushing down as I pressed two fingers into her pussy.

Her walls clenched around me, and she gasped, arching and begging and rubbing herself on my face.

Going a little wild the way I knew she would.

My dick pressed painfully at my jeans, so goddamned hard I was pretty sure I was gonna lose my mind if I didn't get inside her. That was all right because this girl had always driven me insane.

After tonight, I feared I would never come back down.

Feared I was never going to be the same.

Guessed I hadn't been since the first time I'd kissed her.

It was Nikki who'd marked me. Written herself on me. Hers when I could never belong.

I fucked her with my fingers, slow and hard while I ate her frantically.

Matching the frenzied beat that hammered my heart.

Driving her mad the way I knew I could. Wishing I could say screw it all and fuck her right.

"Ollie . . ."

She started chanting my name. Lifting her hips and begging

me for more.

I could feel it coming.

Pleasure winding her tight.

So tight she was gonna take me with her.

I sucked and licked and drove my fingers into her tight body.

Everything lifted.

Her body.

My spirit.

She cried out as her entire body arched and bowed. Her stomach flexed, rippled with her sexy little six-pack, and her head rocked back, pressing into the pillow.

Bliss streaked through her and slammed into me.

Swells of pleasure.

A full-body glow.

So fucking gorgeous.

I wanted to sink inside her so bad I couldn't see.

Wanted to disappear in her.

Get lost.

Or maybe find my way back.

Because I didn't think I'd ever felt so close to home than I did while I was holding her like this.

As I led her through her orgasm, I climbed back over her and swallowed every one of her pants like they might be able to sustain me. The girl my breath.

"Ollie," she whimpered as she came down, her hands going back to my bare chest, sliding down my quivering stomach.

She went for my fly.

Quickly, I reached between us and snatched her by the wrists. I pinned both of them over her head. "Told you I was gonna take care of you, Nikki. I meant it."

Hurt washed across her face, and I leaned down and kissed it away.

She sighed into my mouth.

I eased back, grabbed her underwear from the floor, and helped her back into them before I resituated her dress.

Something about it felt so damned intimate.

Like I hadn't been closer to her than right then.

Her eyes tenderly watched me.

"Now, you rest," I told her.

I scooped her up the same way as I'd carried her inside.

Though this time, I carried her to my bed.

I laid her in the middle of it and stood at the side staring at her through the faint light that filtered in from the hall.

It left her nothing but a silhouette.

Still, laid out across my bed, that spellbinding girl was the most gorgeous thing I'd ever seen.

Magic.

Doing something crazy in me.

"So beautiful," I murmured, my damned hand shaking when I reached out and ran my knuckle from her temple to her chin.

She lifted to it, relishing in the touch, her voice a whisper in the night. "You, Ollie. It's you who's beautiful. You just don't see yourself the same way as I do."

I didn't say anything, I just moved to my dresser and pulled out a tee, helped her from her dress, and tugged my shirt over her head.

It swallowed her, and I couldn't help but grin.

I shrugged out of my jeans, leaving myself just in my underwear.

Could feel the fever in her gaze.

A smirk pulled to my mouth. "Told you, one look and you wouldn't be able to think straight."

"I can't see you that well . . . why don't you turn on the light?" The tease spun through the air, and I chuckled, climbed into my bed, and tucked her back against my chest.

So maybe it was stupid, but I pressed my hard cock to her ass. "Then we'd really be in trouble."

She snuggled deeper into my hold. "Don't pretend like we haven't always been."

Somberness moved between us, that awareness that had always been ours.

Magnetic.

I wrapped an arm around her waist and pulled her closer, all distance erased, my mouth at her ear. "I've resisted you for so long."

She danced her fingertips over the mourning blazing stars on my forearm. "Until last year."

My eyes closed, and I pulled in a deep breath.

It was like inhaling life.

"I can't tell you how fucking sorry I am that I did that, Nikki. I . . . lost myself that night. Instead of getting easier, it seems to get more difficult every year. I needed you."

Even though my mind didn't process it, remember it, my soul had sought her out.

"And tonight?" she quietly asked, a million questions in the two tiny words.

What did we just do?
What does this mean?
How long until you hurt me again?

I nuzzled my nose into the locks of her honeyed hair, comfort gliding through me like a balm. "And tonight, you needed me."

I paused for a second, gathering my thoughts, my words. They trembled with the quiet truth. "Stayin' away from you is getting harder to do."

She weaved her fingers through mine and pulled our entwined hands to the thunder of her heart, so loud it ricocheted through my room. "Things are changing, Ollie. I can feel it."

What terrified me most was that I felt them changing, too.

eighteen

Ollie
Sixteen Years Old

The sound of water crashing below them filled their ears, the spray of the falls cooling their skin as they stood at the edge of the cliffs with the sun beating down above them.

"Hey, pussies, are you coming, or what?" Rex hollered from the lake below, his head bobbing as he treaded water, moving out of the way so the three of them could jump.

Kale was already swimming back toward the beach so he could climb back up to jump again.

"Don't be an asshole, Rex," Sydney shouted.

He laughed, swiping his hand across the top of the water to make a wave. Like it could possibly fly all the way up to splash her.

Ollie chuckled under his breath. Sydney was right. Rex was an asshole. Constantly throwing jabs and gibes, Kale and Ollie throwing them right back.

Didn't mean Ollie liked him any less.

They'd just gotten back from football camp. Third year they'd gone. All of them would be starters on the varsity team this year.

It'd been . . . exhilarating. Pushing himself, testing his limits.

But fuck.

He'd missed home.

He'd missed this.

He glanced to the girl, to her trembling hand wound in his.

He'd missed *her*.

Nikki Walters.

The girl who was supposed to be his best friend.

His second sister.

In that second, it slammed him.

The admission no longer something he could deny.

He'd missed her.

More than that, he wanted her.

Wanted her in a way he wasn't supposed to, but with the way he'd been feeling at night in the dark—hell . . . with the way he'd been feeling in light of day—it was getting harder and harder to ignore.

She'd had a boyfriend all last year, even though he'd told her he didn't like it.

Not *liking* it was a damned disrespect to the way he actually felt.

He hated it. Abhorred it. It made his insides feel like they were shriveling up and disintegrating.

Not that he could say a whole lot since he'd gone through at least ten different girls in that time. But not one of them made him feel like Nikki.

Sweet, timid Nikki who was shaking in her floral bikini that showed off her rail-thin body, the girl nothing but skin and bone.

Didn't matter. His body reacted no matter how fucking bad he begged it not to. There was just . . . something about her that twisted him all up inside.

"Come on," Sydney urged, angling her head. "You can do it."

He could feel his sister squeezing Nikki's opposite hand.

There they were. Teenagers. Close to grown. Three of them holding hands the same way as they'd done since they were little kids.

Best friends never leaving the others' sides.

Call it lame.

Hell, Rex constantly razzed him about it, giving him shit that he liked the girls better than him.

He did.

His crew was cool. His friends the type of guys he could count on for anything. Guys who would always have his back and he'd have theirs. No matter the circumstances.

But not like this. He didn't care that the rest of them didn't understand. Ollie's entire world was watching over these two. Protecting them.

Problem was, that protectiveness for Nikki had grown into something new.

Nikki nervously peeked over the edge. She sucked in a staggered breath and started backing away, shaking her head as she tugged her hands from theirs. "You guys go ahead. I'll take the trail back down."

Sydney turned to face her, wearing her own bikini. That made him angry, too.

He'd kill whoever looked at her the wrong way.

The last year, he'd gotten into trouble twice for fighting some dipshit who thought he could mess with his sister.

One he'd overheard talking about her in the locker room, saying how easily he could get in her pants. The other had the audacity to think Ollie would actually turn a blind eye when he'd found them making out in the back of the senior's car at a party.

Fuck no.

"No way, Nik Nik," Sydney said. "We aren't going without you."

"Really. It's fine."

Sydney perched a hand on her hip. "No, it's not fine. It's fun. I promise. You don't want to miss this."

Nikki shook her head, timid the way she'd always been. "I've never done it before."

A giggle lifted from Sydney, and she bounced forward, taking Nikki by the hand. "That's the whole point. It's the experience. About living. You know this. Every day counts, every moment matters. Don't ever forget it."

Ollie reached out and gathered back up Nikki's hand. "Yeah."
Every moment mattered.

"Come on, you can do it," Sydney reassured again. "You don't have anything to be scared of. Ollie and I are right here. We'll be with you the whole time."

All three of them squeezed hands and inched up to the edge of the cliff.

The roar of the waterfalls pouring into the lake a few yards away filled their ears, loud and stirring. Nikki drew in a deep breath, and Sydney peeked around her, his sister's gaze bouncing between the two of them in her soft kind of encouragement.

Then she whispered it, the words no longer a shout but just as loud. "Fly, fly, dragonfly."

They jumped.

Hand in hand.

Nikki screamed, and Sydney shrieked through her laughter.

Joy.

Always joy.

Ollie shouted as they plunged downward.

Loving it.

The feel of just . . . falling.

Falling.

He was falling.

He knew it then.

They hit the water. It split, swallowing them whole, sucking them down deep.

The three of them floated beneath the surface, surrounded by gushing bubbles and the streaks of light that penetrated the cool blue waters. Sound was distorted against his ears, and his heart beat harder in his chest as he used up all his air.

Or maybe it was Nikki who was doing it.

Stealing his breath.

She started to kick her legs through the water, and her foot scraped his upper leg as she propelled herself upward.

Just that graze rushed through him as if she'd raked her nails down his back.

The three of them broke the surface, laughing and gasping

for air.

Nikki giggled the way she always did when she overcame a fear. After she'd tried something new that she wouldn't have done without the two of them.

The roar of the waterfall was almost deafening as he looked across at Nikki with her head kicked back toward the sun.

Everything was so loud and silent at the same time as he stared.

Freckles and olive skin and honey hair.

He wanted to put his mouth on her so badly it hurt.

Sydney was already swimming for the shore, splashing with Rex as they drifted off in the distance, the two of them throwing barbs the way they did.

Ollie ducked under the water. He came up right in front of Nikki.

She gasped in surprise, then her mouth dropped open with more when he wrapped an arm around her waist and started to paddle them toward a cove in the cliffs.

"What are you doing, Ollie, you brute?" she asked, but it was a whisper.

All breathy from exertion.

Or maybe she felt the same way touching him as he did when touching her.

Like it meant something.

Like it meant everything.

Because she wrapped her arms around his neck and clung to him. Her scent was all around him, his thoughts going haywire with having her like this.

"If you dunk me under that waterfall, you're gonna pay for it," she warned, trying to put lightness in her tone.

But there was no missing the way it came raspy from her throat.

Ollie tugged her into one of the secluded recesses carved out in the cliffs. A small vein of the waterfall dumped water into the lake from the rock protruding above their heads, making the cove completely secluded from the shore.

His feet barely touched, and she floated where he still held her around the waist.

"Ollie, what's going on?" she whispered again, so low it was swallowed by the thunder of the waterfall.

He only wavered for a second before he threaded his fingers through her hair and murmured, "This."

He dipped in and brushed his lips against hers.

Softly.

Barely there.

It didn't matter. It was the most powerful thing he'd ever felt.

Intense and overwhelming.

Nikki gasped, but her hands went to the back of his head to pull him closer.

His tongue swept across her lips, prodding, praying she'd want to kiss him back.

Thank God. She did.

Her lips parted, and she plastered her body against his, her tiny boobs pressed against his bare chest.

Ollie grunted, overcome.

Was this really happening?

Their tongues danced.

Carefully.

Cautiously.

Her breaths soft, and his pants hard.

She pulled back, something like awe and confusion in her features. Exactly what he felt.

Confused.

Awed.

He ran the pad of his thumb across her bottom lip. "I've been wanting to do that for the longest time."

A shy smile pulled across her mouth. "I've been wanting you to do that for the longest time, too."

"Yeah?"

She bit at her lip. "Yeah."

Her gaze traveled over his shoulder. Worry climbed to her face. He knew where her mind had gone.

"This is just between us, Nikki. You and me. It's not anyone else's business."

"What about Sydney?" Guilt and more of that worry filled her words.

"Don't think we should tell her." He brushed back her hair, needing to touch her. He didn't ever want to stop. "Not yet. One day . . . just . . . not yet. I don't want her to get upset."

We are three. Forever and ever, you and me.

Their pact swam through his mind. He shoved it down. For right then, he didn't want to contemplate they might be doing something wrong. Leaving his sister when she'd been the one who'd brought them together in the first place.

Warily, Nikki looked back at him like she'd just thought all the same thoughts. "Okay. You and me."

Then Ollie . . . he kissed her again.

And he knew he didn't ever want to stop.

nineteen

Nikki

I snuggled deeper into the massive arms locked around me, and contentment left me on a sigh as I relished in the steady thrum of his heart at my back.

I couldn't believe I was lying there with Ollie wrapped around me like a blanket.

A big, gorgeous, burly blanket.

Heaven.

That's what it was. Even when so much felt unstable and wrong, this felt . . . right.

In the dark recesses of the night, I let my eyes drift back closed, only for them to fly open again when I heard what must have pulled me from sleep in the first place.

Ringing.

Ringing from down the hall.

Shit.

I'd left my phone in my purse where I'd dumped it when I'd come through the door.

Trying not to disturb Ollie, I carefully peeled his arm from me and slid out from his hold, keeping my footsteps quieted as I tiptoed across the floor and out the door.

Once I clicked the door shut behind me, I quickened my pace, rushing for my phone that was ringing again. Both praying and terrified that it would be my sister.

Dropping to my knees, I fumbled through my purse, hands shaking when I grabbed it and spun it around to find the number on the screen.

Not Sammie.

Brenna.

"Shit, shit, shit," I muttered, quick to accept the call and press it to my ear. "Brenna, what's happening?"

My attention darted to the kitchen so I could look at the time on the microwave.

Three twenty-seven a.m.

Not good.

Panicked cries echoed from the other end of the line, and she rambled something I couldn't make out.

"Brenna, calm down. Tell me what's happening."

Staggered breaths ripped from her. She tried to suck them down. Keep them contained. "Caleb . . . he keeps texting me. Telling me he's going to take Kyle from me if I don't go back to his place."

That little asshole.

"I think he might be outside," she all but whispered, as if he could hear her.

I pushed down the anger that surged and gave it my all to remain professional, searching inside myself for the right advice. "You need to hang up and call 9-1-1. Right now. I'll be over as fast as I can. Don't go outside."

There I was. Crossing more lines that weren't supposed to be crossed. But what was I supposed to do?

"Okay," she agreed, and the line went dead.

I started to push back to my feet when I felt the surge of energy blast me from behind.

Potent.

Intense.

That power alone was enough to shift me around to face him.

A magnet.

"Ollie."

"Who was that?" he grated.

I'd realized earlier I wanted this man to hold all of me. Have all of me. My body and my secrets and my heart.

Even if it was foolish. Filled with risk and danger and peril.

But I refused to be the girl who was too scared to live her life.

I needed him.

Wanted him.

And I was taking this chance.

"That was Brenna. The girl you saw me with at the ice-cream shop the other day. Her ex-boyfriend keeps texting her and threatening to take their little boy if she doesn't cave to him."

Ollie's hands clenched. "Piece of shit."

Ollie had it spot on.

For a moment, I wavered before I lowered my voice. "I think he might be the one who broke into my apartment. I was with her the first time she called the cops on him. He was angry. Called me a bitch. There were two notes left on the windshield of my car over the last week that basically said the same thing."

Rage blistered across his handsome face. "What? Someone's been following you? Fuck, Nikki. Why didn't you tell me?"

"I didn't have proof, and I didn't know what you would do."

His jaw clenched, and those sapphire eyes flashed. "I think you knew exactly what I would do."

It was true.

It was exactly why I was afraid to tell him.

I nodded, then started toward him so I could move down the hall. "You're right. I was afraid of what you might do and what that might mean. We can talk about that later. But right now, Brenna needs me, and I need to get over there."

I let my fingertips brush across his bare abdomen as I passed.

He shuddered.

Fire rippled and danced.

I'd almost made it to the guest bedroom when his voice boomed in the enclosed hall, and I froze in the doorway. "I'm coming with you."

Of course, he was. I wasn't even going to argue it. I glanced at him from over my shoulder and gave him a nod before I rushed inside and pulled on some jeans and a tee and slipped my feet into some shoes.

Five minutes later, we were flying down the road in Ollie's Mustang, taking the corners fast.

Intensity bound the air. Worry and fear and fury.

I felt it radiating from Ollie's flesh. Dripping from his pores.

His protection of me. Maybe the protection of a girl he didn't even know.

"Take a right here," I told him.

The tires squealed as he took a sharp turn.

Two seconds later, Brenna's mother's house came into view.

My stomach dropped to the floorboards.

Caleb was in the driveway, shouting at Brenna who was cowering against the back of her car.

Dread spiraled through my senses. "Oh my God, I told her to stay inside."

Quick to release the seatbelt, I sat forward, hand already on the doorlatch as Ollie screeched to a stop.

"What the fuck?" Ollie growled. "It's that little fucker who sold me the car." His arm flew out in front of my chest, his body ridged in hard lines, muscles bristling as he took in the scene. "Don't move out of that seat, Nikki."

His door flew open, voice low. "I mean it."

I didn't pause.

Didn't listen.

I jumped out of the car.

Caleb whirled around when he felt me approaching him. "You, bitch. You're responsible for all of this. Telling her not to be with me."

No, Caleb. You're responsible. You twat.

I didn't say it.

Not wanting to incite him more.

It didn't matter because he started for me as if this time he was going to take his anger out on me.

His warnings never so glaring than right then.

A tremble of fear rocked through me as I prepared for him to hit me.

A blur of movements had me taking a shocked step back.

Before I could process it, Ollie had an arm hooked around Caleb's neck from behind, his hold cinched tight.

No fear.

No reservation.

Brenna shrieked, and Ollie wrangled Caleb who clawed at his arm, flailed and kicked and shouted as if he might wrestle out of his hold.

I doubted it took a whole lot of exertion on Ollie's part to keep Caleb restrained. Ollie had the scrawny kid in a lock that there was no chance he could break free of.

Once he knew he had him contained, Ollie sent me an angry glare. "Told you to stay in the car."

"Since when do you get to tell me what to do?" I shot at him.

He scoffed and pretty much rolled his eyes while he kept a tight hold on Caleb who continued to flail and kick. "And you say I'm impossible," he said.

"You, asshole. Let me go, you piece of shit. You're gonna regret it," Caleb ranted.

Ollie tightened his hold. "Pretty sure it's not gonna be me who's feelin' the regret, fucker. You really think I was gonna let you play us all? Is that what you thought? You thought wrong."

Confusion wound through my mind, Ollie's words making absolutely no sense. But my only concern right then was Brenna. Brenna who started sobbing when I pulled her into my arms.

She clutched me and buried her face in my shirt. "Nikki . . . you're here."

"I've got you. I'm right here."

Sirens rode on the night, a quiet toll that grew closer and closer with every second that passed. "The police are on their way. You're safe. You're safe."

Her fingers curled in my shirt. "I'm so sorry. I'm so sorry. But he was trying to get inside to take Kyle. I couldn't let him take him. I won't let him take him."

"Shh . . . I know. I know. It's okay."

Kyle's cries lifted on the dense air, fearful and distraught, and I peeked over to where Brenna's mother was holding him, her wary attention darting between all of us.

"That's my son," Caleb shouted. "My girlfriend. You can't keep them from me. They're my family."

He thrashed against Ollie's restraint, and Ollie was hauling him further back, out into the street.

Away.

But I could hear him. The low warning he uttered at Caleb's ear. "Shut the fuck up, asshole. You don't get to claim someone as your family when you threaten them. When you hurt them. That's not what family is. You think you can mess with her? Take advantage of her? I'll end you if you even look at her again. You hear me, asshole?"

Two cruisers rounded the corner, lights reflecting off the darkened sky. I knew neighbors were peering out, could feel the eyes of morbid curiosity, but the only thing I cared about was Brenna.

That she was safe.

Four officers slipped out of their cruisers, their guns drawn. Thank God, one was Seth.

"Don't move," one of them shouted.

"Stand down," Seth ordered, pushing a hand out at the officers as he moved toward Ollie and Caleb, cuffs out.

"On the ground," he told Caleb.

Ollie released him, and Caleb dove to the pavement.

"Motherfucker," he gritted, face in the ground.

"Motherfucker is right," Ollie spat, backing away and letting Seth read Caleb his rights as he cuffed him and patted him down.

Seth hauled him to his feet, looking between Ollie and me. "This him?" he asked me.

I nodded. "That's him."

Ollie roughed an agitated hand through his hair that flashed with the colors of the lights that spun through the night, his face lit up.

So bold and striking I lost more of my breath.

My beast.

"Asshole came into Roke's this afternoon with an old car that used to belong to Nikki's grandparents. Nikki told me about the notes. He has to have been stalking her. Finding out who her family was and trying to get close."

Caleb flailed and tried to jerk free from Seth, the guy so clearly high he looked deranged. "What the fuck are you talking about? That's bullshit, man. I haven't been stalking that stupid bitch. I don't want anything to do with her. That car was on the straight."

"Save it. You can make your statement at the station." Seth led him to the back of one of the cruisers and placed him in the backseat.

Brenna breathed out another cry, but this one was made of relief.

I looked over at Ollie, mouthed, *"Thank you."*

He just stared back as if he was promising he wouldn't be anywhere else.

Inside, Seth took both Brenna and her mother's statements. First and foremost, Caleb had violated his restraining order. More charges might be coming. One's related to me and my apartment.

They were still waiting for prints to come back.

Seth was going to put a rush on them, hoping we got something to substantiate our suspicions.

Seth left promising he'd be calling soon.

"Thank you so much," Brenna told him as she showed him to the door.

"Take care of yourself," he told her. "Unfortunately, he'll probably make bail in the morning since he didn't cause any bodily harm. It'd be good for you to have someone with you at all times."

Slipping out, he let his eyes move to Ollie and me in some kind of warning before he disappeared down the walk.

From behind, we watched as Brenna tremored with a fresh round of fear.

Ollie stood.

Gruff and rugged but his voice was soft. "Think it'd be good for you to come to my place tonight until we get this sorted out?"

Brenna turned around, her fingertips pressed to her mouth. "You'd do that for me?"

Ollie rocked in discomfort. I saw it for what it was. The way he wanted to protect the world from horrible people. From the type of man we were sure had stolen Sydney from us.

He dropped his gaze when he finally said, "Don't have a lot to offer people, Brenna . . . but if I can offer this? Take care of you and your son for a little bit?" He looked up. "There's nothing I'd want more."

"I can't tell you how much I appreciate what you did tonight." Brenna spread her hand over the comforter in the guest bedroom, clearly needing something to busy herself.

"You keep telling me that," I told her with a soft smile where I sat next to her with my knees hugged to my chest.

"But I really mean it." Carefully, she peeked up at me. "You know when he started texting me, the first person I thought to call was you. You have a way of making me feel safe."

"I want you to both feel it and live it, Brenna. You don't have to live in fear. We'll make sure of that."

Silence moved through the space, and I could feel her reservations, a new kind of heaviness moving through her heart. "You really think he did that to your apartment?"

I studied her face. "You don't?" I asked carefully.

She lifted a shoulder. "The drugs changed him. He was so sweet to me when we first started dating."

Her voice had turned wistful. Filled with longing of that time. She shook her head. "He's just fine when he's not using, but when he does? He becomes rash and impulsive, and a lot of times it translates to aggression."

She blinked at me. "It's hard for me to imagine him thinking to go to your place to scare you that way. Leaving those notes."

I set my hand on her knee. "People do crazy things when

they're desperate, Brenna. It's part of the problem. The spiral. They dig themselves deeper and deeper until they can't see a way out, and then they're doing everything they can to fight it—change it—all the while they're making the worst choices all over again."

"I just wish he'd go back to bein' the person he was when he asked me to the dance in ninth grade." Her bottom lip trembled. "I know you think it's stupid. That we're young. But there was a time when he really loved me and I loved him. We messed up. Did things too young. It got away from us. But we did love each other."

I took her hand and squeezed it. "I don't think it's stupid. Not at all. Don't ever let someone tell you young love isn't real. But sometimes things change. Things we can't control. All we can control is the here and now—and right now—you and that little boy deserve so much more than what Caleb has been giving you."

"I know that."

"Good." I blew out the strain that weighed heavily and stood. "What do you say I go get your little cutie so you two can get some rest?"

"Tell me that man of yours didn't feed him sugar," she said, voice turning wry.

"Man of mine?" I challenged, lifting my brow with a smirk. "I already told you he was a friend."

"Oh, come on, Miss Nikki. You pretty much have drool dripping from the corner of your mouth every time you look his way."

"Is that so?"

"Uh-huh. And every time he looks at you, I'm pretty sure he's picturing ripping off your clothes with his teeth." She grinned and wiggled her brows. "I have to say, with a man who looks like that? I wouldn't mind all that much having him fantasizing about me, either."

My mouth dropped open. "Hey, don't go making any moves on my man."

She laughed. "See, told you so."

A giggle slipped out. It should have been impossible with everything that'd happened tonight.

But I thought maybe . . . maybe some *good* things were finally coming together.

"I'll be right back," I told her before I eased out the door and down the hall.

Ollie had insisted he would get Kyle a snack while I helped Brenna get settled in the guest room. I'd left them with Kyle sitting on one of the high-backed stools, babbling something Ollie was clearly pretending he understood.

Now I slowed, inching forward when I noticed all the lights had been doused, the open living space only illuminated by the lights that poured in from the windows.

I peeked my head out at the end of the hall.

My chest squeezed and my heart expanded.

Oh God.

This man.

He was absolutely undoing me.

He was sitting on the couch, Kyle fast asleep in his arms. The little boy's thumb was in his mouth and his cheek was pressed to Ollie's chest as Ollie softly patted his back, tattooed arms wrapped so protectively around Kyle's tiny body.

Tears pricked at the back of my eyes, and that old, old love burst free.

No longer held.

No longer bottled.

"Hey," I whispered as I inched out, keeping quiet so as not to startle Kyle.

Ollie's eyes popped open.

And he smiled.

He smiled the softest smile and it moved right through the center of me.

"Hey," he said. "He started to get fussy, so I walked him a bit before he fell asleep."

I nodded at him, unable to speak around the lump that formed in my throat. I moved that way and carefully pulled Kyle from his arms.

Ollie stood behind me, and I walked down the hall, my knock quiet before I pushed open the door and took Kyle to Brenna who was fixing a spot for him to sleep.

I passed him to her. She gazed down at him, adoration on her face.

And I felt it all around me.

Adoration.

Love.

"Sleep well," I told her.

She just nodded, and I moved back out, Ollie waiting for me right on the other side of the door.

He took my hand, and I followed him back to his room.

He flipped on the bedside lamp, and I went directly into his bathroom. I washed my face, peeled off my jeans, and moved back out to where he lay on the bed.

Wearing only his underwear.

His big body sculpted of muscle. Covered in ink.

But those eyes. They pierced me from across the room.

I started for him, only to falter a step when my attention caught on what was on the other side of his room.

A wall covered in pictures.

Not just any pictures.

It was pictures and newspaper articles and prints tacked everywhere.

Layer upon layer.

Sucking in a ragged breath, my eyes narrowed as I inched that way.

Horrified.

And somehow in awe.

Sydney's smiling face beamed from all of the pictures, her expression so free and full of belief.

The way she'd always lived. What she'd always been so patient to instill in me when I'd always been the timid one itching to shed my sticky skin.

There were a ton of pictures of the three of us. Playing. Laughing. Arms hooked over each other's shoulders.

Inseparable.

But it was the newspaper articles that gutted me.

So many of them were about her from the time when she'd gone missing.

More of other girls.

Cold cases.

Kidnappings.

Rapes.

Murders.

Strings were attached between some of them and notes jotted across others.

Clues.

Questions.

A chill slicked down my spine and spread across my skin.

Warily, I looked back at him. He'd sat up on the edge of the bed, his legs flung over the side, raking a nervous hand through his hair.

"You've been looking for her this whole time?"

He looked up at me, his voice quieted so Brenna wouldn't hear. "What else could I possibly do? Forget? Give up like the detectives? Looking for her is the only thing I've ever had, Nikki. I can't give up the hope that maybe, just maybe, one day I might find her."

My stomach twisted.

A coil of misery and desire and affection.

I looked back to the things that he had tacked to the wall. My fingertips reached out to flutter over the red woven bracelet with the charm inscribed with *'fly'*.

It exactly matched the one I still wore around my ankle.

Ollie's piece.

The third one would be forever missing.

They say heartbreak isn't physical.

I believed it was a lie.

Because I could feel it. Could feel his. Just as I could feel the same crack running right down the center of me. Everything adding up and becoming this weight I didn't know how to bear.

It was a rending of my chest.

A splintering of my soul.

Cautiously, I moved toward him.

The space between us coming alive.

Shimmering.

Streaks of color.

Flashes of light.

Chemistry.

Ours had been ugly for so long. Like a shadow hanging over us.

Now, I waded through it like the gift it always should have been. I got down on my knees in front of him and pressed my hand to the side of his face.

"Ollie," I whispered.

Like praise.

Did he know? Could he possibly understand what I felt for him? What I always had? Part of me hated him for not seeing it. Or maybe it was just that I knew he saw it, felt it, and he'd rejected it, anyway.

Most of me understood it fully. The guilt he bore. His own bitter cross. The one marked over his heart that would forever bleed for his sister.

In the dim light, those sapphire eyes captured mine.

Emotion brimming over.

So many questions. All the reservations and walls that were still there.

The hurt laid out between us, and the love that had been the base of it all.

He weaved his fingers through my hair. "Nikki."

My name was a breath.

I smoothed my hands up his strong thighs.

A ripple of need trembled through him. "Nikki."

This time it was a warning.

I edged up and pressed a bunch of kisses across his wide, wide chest.

"What are you doing?" It was a low grumble.

"Taking care of you the way you took care of me."

His fingers sank into my hair, taking fistfuls as he tugged me back. "Don't think that's a good idea."

"And why's that?" I whispered, letting my kisses glide down his abdomen.

Cut and carved.

Perfection.

His muscles twitched beneath my touch, and I felt him grow hard in his briefs.

Earlier on the couch, I'd wanted him to take me. Desperate to feel him inside me again. That greedy place within lighting up with his touch.

Wanting more.

Wanting it all.

But this?

This was for him.

"Because I don't get this. I don't get you," he said, holding on tighter as if he wanted to push me away, but couldn't let me go.

I edged up on my knees and pressed my mouth under his jaw. His short beard tickled my face, and there was nothing I could do but inhale, fill myself with this man.

His pulse boomed, a thunder against my lips. I kissed down his throat and across his pecs, the massive muscles straining as he arched.

Yearning to get closer, to receive it, while his broken spirit believed the only thing he deserved was to suffer this alone.

"You already have me, Ollie. You always did. Did you feel me all that time?" I murmured across his hot flesh, my tongue licking out to taste. "I was right there. All along."

He grunted, and his hands fisted tighter in my hair, words grating as they hit the air. "I fucked it all up. I'm fucked up, Nikki. You deserve much more than what I've got to offer you."

"No, Ollie. You're wrong. You don't see yourself clearly. You don't realize how amazing you are. You don't realize the guy I see when I look at you. The guy I saw tonight."

The man who would have given it all for any of us.

He was a masterpiece. Sculpted and carved and chiseled. Massive. Bigger than life.

I wanted him to see he belonged in my life. The way he always had.

Desire twisted my insides, and I caressed my mouth lower, over the fabric of his underwear where the head of his dick begged for me.

"Nikki." This time it was confusion. My name hanging like a precipice.

So close to letting go.

"It's me, Ollie. Me. Lose yourself in me. I want to take care of you." I peeked up at him and let a small smirk work to my face. "I think it's only fair since I let you take care of me, don't you?"

A dark chuckle resonated in his chest, filled with restraint and lust. He brushed his fingers down the side of my face. "Think the only thing unfair right now is the way you're looking at me."

My tongue darted out to wet my lips. "And how am I looking at you?"

"Like I mean something."

I kissed across the definition of his hip, burying my nose in his skin as I muttered the words, "You mean everything."

He groaned, and he reached down and took me by the sides of the head, lifting me to look at him.

Gently.

So gently it shouldn't have been possible for a hulking man like him.

Beast.

Old memories spun, and a wistful smile swam on my mouth when I took one of his hands and urged him to standing.

The power of his need shook the walls. I could feel it radiating and crashing.

I looked up at him, and he cupped my cheek. "Sweet girl," he murmured, tracing his thumb under my eye. "I don't want to hurt you."

He kept looping back to that. Didn't he know the only way he could hurt me was by letting me go?

"I know, Ollie, I know."

I dipped my fingers in the waistband of his tight black briefs and began to peel them down. My heart raced, and my skin caught fire.

Because his cock jumped free, bouncing in front of me.

Every bit as intimidatingly beautiful as the man.

Every previous encounter with Ollie had been a fumble in the dark. Teens sneaking around and the disaster at my apartment last year.

This . . . this was Ollie and me. Both of us here. Present. No one to tell us we were doing anything wrong except for the guilt we both wore like a shroud.

I saw when he flipped. When he stopped trying to resist *this*. Or maybe he just couldn't any longer.

Blue eyes blazed down at me with a lusty, harsh sort of desire.

He gave a demanding tug at the back of my hair, voice muted, meant only for me. "You gonna let me have that mouth, Sunshine?"

My heart beat frantically. Madly. Every cell in my body was swept up in the intensity.

Stomach trembling, my tongue darted out and licked across his engorged head.

He jerked, gritting his teeth as he tightened his hold in my hair. "Little Tease. Been teasing me all these years. Coming in my bar acting like we didn't know each other. Talking to your friends like I might just be another conquest."

"It was the only thing I could do not to fall at your feet."

"Wanted to kill every guy I ever saw you with."

Hands running up his hips, I whispered, "You managed to chase them all away anyway."

He ran a thumb over my lip. "Couldn't stand the thought of another man with you."

I didn't think he understood the way I felt every time I saw him with another girl. As fleeting as they were, every time, it was the stab of a knife. Bleeding me dry.

I took him in my hand. The velvet flesh was smooth on my palm, such a contradiction to the heavy, hard length that begged for release underneath. "I never wanted anyone else."

A shudder rocked him as I stroked him once. "Fuck."

I wrapped my other hand around him. Both hands running his rigid length as I pumped him, lightly at first, gathering the glistening bead at his throbbing head before I tightened and began to stroke him.

"Nikki . . . you're gonna kill me. Shit . . ."

I peeked up at him as I wound him higher.

Magnificent.

His jaw clenched as he stared down at me, his chest wide, beard full on his immaculate face.

All man.

The man I held in my hands.

Stroking him greedily, my breaths became pants. Need welled in me like the swill of the rising river.

Higher and higher.

Threatening to overflow.

I squeezed my thighs together while his shook.

Splintering control.

"Feels so good," he grunted. "Those sweet hands, Nik . . . they've always been so sweet. You always hid it with that smart mouth . . . but I knew. I knew."

His words were grit. Lined with a tenderness I felt brushing across my flesh like a lover's caress.

I leaned in and pressed a gentle kiss to the tip of his cock. I tasted the salty manliness of him. The intensity of who he was.

My oldest friend.

My first love.

My only love.

His fists were a petition where they wound in my hair. "Please, Nikki. Sweet girl. Take me. Suck me. Need to feel you."

Desperation spun, riding that tether that kept us tied. Binding.

I pressed my tongue to his engorged, fattened tip before I sucked the crown into my mouth.

"Yes," he rumbled, jutting forward, urging me to take him. I laved at the purpled flesh, squeezing his fat base with my hands before I began to take him deeper.

A course groan pressed between his lips. "I have always loved that mouth."

My heart squeezed.

Love.

It was so strong.

So strong it made it hard to see.

Deeper and deeper, I took him, my hands working the base, the feel of him overwhelming.

Moans ripped from his mouth, low and guttural.

Needy in a way I'd never heard this man be. "Yes, baby. Fuck. You feel so good. So damned good."

His hips began to snap, and I was nothing but an offering on my knees in front of him.

Lost.

Lost in him where he was lost in me.

His hands moved to my cheeks, and I relished the feel of them as he started to rock and jut. Harder and deeper.

Slow and measured before he picked up a rigorous pace.

His grunts struck the air, and that energy crackled, licked at my skin, stirred the need into something potent.

Compulsive and seductive.

Inescapable.

"Can you take it?" A question and a warning spoken in a low growl. I answered by moving my hands to his ass and hanging on.

At his mercy.

"Yes," he groaned, fingers spread out wide, holding all of me he could.

Then he fucked my mouth.

Mercilessly.

Wildly.

Madly.

Every thrust raw.

Every rock needy.

Possessive.

Consuming me in a way I'd never before been consumed.

I opened to him and took him as far as I could, my lips stretched thin around his hard, imposing length, jaw burning and my spirit soaring.

"You . . . Nikki . . . You."

The words tumbled from him, jumbled and rushed and as

clear as I'd ever heard him.

My eyes welled with tears as I swallowed around him, taking him to the back of my throat.

"Fuck . . . yes," he hissed, and his hips snapped savagely.

Frenzied.

Succumbing.

Just like me.

Energy flashed.

Colors painting the room.

A river of emotion.

A stream of lust.

His teeth ground to hold back a roar when he came, pouring into my mouth, his gorgeous body bowed as he shivered and jerked.

My beautiful, beautiful beast.

I swallowed, wanting to drown in him, reveling in the sheer bliss etched in his expression.

Streaks of pleasure tore through every tremoring muscle of his body.

The man a mountain.

A rock who'd just crumbled in my hands.

Slowly, he pulled back, still holding my face, and he tenderly ran the pad of his thumb across my bottom lip.

I was almost nervous, having no idea what direction we were going, terrified he would send me crashing into another brick wall until a smirk took hold of one side of his mouth.

"Guess you really are the orgasm fairy," he murmured, lifting me from under the arms and scooping me back into the safety of his hold.

I tried to hold back the shock of surprised laughter. "I told all of you I was. No one believes me. I know a good match when I see one."

Chemistry.

Ours pulsed through the air. Fierce and unrelenting.

He climbed onto his bed and pulled me onto his chest.

Oh God. And he thought I was going to ruin him?

He gentled his fingers through my hair. "Hmm . . . guess I

shouldn't complain about getting on the receiving end of that, now, should I?"

My teeth raked over my bottom lip, warmth heating my cheeks, loving that this lost boy wanted to play. "Definitely not. There are some gifts that should never be shoved in a closet or returned."

I began to casually tick them off. "Heirloom jewelry. Children's handprints set in plaster. Orgasms. Orgasms should never, ever be considered anything less than the gift they are," I said, the quiet tease playing from my tongue.

A thrill of shock vibrated through me. It felt like a dream that I was with him like this. Closer than we'd been in so many years.

My fingertips trailed over his chest. "Well, unless you give one to yourself," I ribbed. "No orgasm fairy required. My services are rendered totally useless."

That was like buying yourself a fake engagement ring.

He grabbed my hand and brought it to his lips. "Don't doubt that you caused a few of those, too, Nikki. All these years, thinking about you . . . wishing it was you."

Chills.

They flashed across my skin. My voice quieted, and I scratched at the beard on the side of his face, "I wanted it to be you, too."

He pushed his fingers into my hair, somberness stealing into his expression as he stared up at me. "What if I hurt you?"

My tongue swept across my bottom lip. In hesitation or need, I wasn't sure. "You keep sayin' that, Ollie, and I'm just gonna keep tellin' you not to. Treating someone the way they deserve to be treated is as simple as making the choice to."

His head minimally shook on his pillow, and he tightened his hold on me.

I didn't want him to ever let go.

"Sometimes life doesn't give us the choice. Sometimes it takes from us. We have no control over that. No say no matter what we give up to change it."

My voice softened, close to a plea. "And sometimes it's as simple as how you handle what life gives you. How you treat the people around you. How you treat *yourself*."

"You deserve better than me, sweet girl. Don't you see that yet?"

Scooting up, I pressed both my hands to either side of his head and stared down at him, hoping he could see. Hoping he could feel what I'd always felt for him.

"You're right, Ollie. I deserve to be loved. To be held and cherished. To have the family I've always wanted. I deserve everything this life has to offer. To make the most of each day. And you . . ."

The words became a wisp from my lips. "You just have to see that you deserve all that, too. That you deserve to be loved and held and cherished. To live life for all it's worth. Every single day. Whether that's with me or not."

Silence swam between us. As heavy as when we'd lay by the lake at night and stare at the sky. When we'd felt so small and still so incredibly brave. Stars strewn out across the black canvas, promising there was more out there than a vast expanse of nothingness.

He trailed his fingers down my cheek. "I want to be that guy, Nikki. Just not sure who you see is real. Think he went missing the day his sister did."

Old grief whipped through my spirit. "I know, Ollie," I said, affection thick. "That guy got lost. But I know he's real. That he's right here."

I reached down and set my palm flat against his hammering heart. "You just have to find him."

He pressed my hand tighter. "We need to stop doing this until I do. Until I know I won't hurt you again. Because I do *cherish* you, Nikki. Don't ever doubt that. I cherish you, but I'm still not sure I deserve to keep you."

His words slashed and cut and healed.

A searing hurt and the sweetest solace.

I gently pressed my lips to his.

Tenderly.

With all I had to give. "Let me help you discover him."

He shocked me with his slight nod, our lips gently brushing.

"I need you to be patient with me because I refuse to be the guy who hurts you again."

Then he pulled back, eyes going hard as he gripped me by both sides of the face. "Need you to stop keeping secrets from me. I have to figure out how to be the guy you really deserve, but more than that, I need to know you're safe. Keep you safe. And I can't do that if you don't let me in."

"I told you where I was going tonight for a reason, Ollie. Because I trust you. Because I want you in my life."

He grimaced, but didn't reject it, before he continued, "How did that punk get your grandpa's old car?"

A sad, slow sickness rolled through me. My grandma was sick, and I wasn't sure how to deal with that.

My mama was worn out.

And my sister . . .

I tucked the thoughts down and focused on what Ollie was saying. "I don't know."

Contemplation rode heavily on the exhale from his nose. "He said your uncle was selling off some stuff . . . they needed money quick."

Unease slithered through my consciousness.

Ollie's voice hardened. "Tried to get in touch with you to make sure it was legit. Needed to know this kid wasn't trying to pull some shit over on us. Bought it either way. Too many memories in that heap for it to go anywhere else."

Heat bloomed at the center of me, a welling of memories. "I'm glad you did."

He caressed his thumb beneath the hollow of my eye. "Yeah . . . me, too."

My head shook. "I'm not sure exactly what's goin' on over at my grandma's. What I know is things . . . aren't good. They could very well be selling stuff off, although I'm not sure how Caleb got involved."

Sorrow took over that confession.

"I'm so sorry. I had no idea."

"I know . . . it's really hard." I paused for a beat before I continued, "I'll go over there this week and find out the details of what they're planning. All's I know is after my grandpa passed, Grandma went through what was left of their savings pretty fast. Wouldn't surprise me if they're needing to get rid of a few of her things to pay for some of the expenses. Mama said it's been a struggle. But I'll find out. You don't need to worry about that. I doubt it's a big deal."

"Everything's a big deal when it comes to you, Nikki. I'm sorry if I ever made it seem like it wasn't. Like I didn't care."

I forced a grin onto my mouth. "Oh, I knew you cared. No mistaking it when a big, overbearing brute constantly puts his nose in your business."

He grunted like he was exactly that.

A beast.

"That's because you are my business."

I traced my fingertips along the swishes of color written across his chest. "Thank you so much for being there tonight. For being there for Brenna and Kyle. Being there for me."

"I promised you, I'd always take care of you. Right?"

I nodded. "Yeah."

I was okay with that.

He tugged me all the way on top of him.

On all things holy, he was not helping things. A tiny moan escaped my throat at the feel of his bare body beneath mine. Strength bristling as our hearts mended.

Going back to not being able to touch him was just plain cruel.

Pretending again.

But this man was worth the wait.

He *deserved* patience.

Understanding.

He *deserved* me.

And God, every part of me knew I deserved him.

twenty
Ollie

I woke with a start.

Un-fucking-prepared to find the girl nestled in my arms.

Unprepared for the way my heart took off racing, drumming with satisfaction.

Unprepared for that voice inside of me that shouted that this was the way it was supposed to be.

Hell, only a moron would think waking up next to Nikki Walters was anything less than paradise.

Didn't mean I wasn't assaulted with a ton of images flying through my brain.

Sydney.
Sydney.
Sydney.

The weight of my debt.

The truth of what we'd done.

I blew it out on a harsh breath and strained to listen to the voices that filtered through the walls.

Brenna was quietly talking to her son who was blabbering back.

So damned cute.

My insides twisted with a swell of protection.

I jerked with the shrill sound of my phone ringing from my nightstand. Reaching behind me, I swatted for it, trying to silence it before it woke up Nikki, considering we'd gotten all of three hours' sleep.

The second I saw who it was, I peeled myself away from Nikki's body and sat up on the edge of the bed. "Seth."

"Hey, man, I've got good news."

Relief gusted from me. "Yeah?"

"Caleb was in front of the judge this morning for his intake hearing. He willingly accepted the offer to go to inhouse rehab for ninety days, plus anger management and parenting classes. In exchange, the restraining order violation charges will be dropped. We still don't have proof of the break-in, so none of that was taken into consideration."

My guts curled.

That little fucker was getting off.

Still couldn't stomach the idea that he'd been in Nikki's apartment. Trashing it. Following her and putting notes on her car.

That he might hurt Brenna and Kyle again.

"Is that supposed to be good news?" It was close to a growl.

Seth chuckled like he was fully expecting what I was going to say. "A whole ton better than him hitting the streets this morning, don't you think?"

I scrubbed a palm over my face, glancing back at Nikki who'd rolled over in my bed, looking like the fucking best thing when her eyes fluttered open.

She smiled at me.

Sunshine.

"Yeah, man. You're right. Just hope it makes a difference."

twenty-one
Nikki

I pulled up in front of the small house. Even though I felt a huge amount of relief that Brenna and Kyle were safe, anxiety still held me captive.

My hands clammy.

Heart racing.

Stomach twisting with the kind of nausea I felt all the way into my soul.

Twilight held fast to the sky, a purpled gray that hugged the earth. The hurricane lamp hanging on the wall at the side of the front door welcomed the approaching night with a soft glow.

A single, mammoth tree stood proud in the yard. Broad branches stretched out as if they were arms of protection. Leaves green and dense and full.

Sucking in a deep breath, I cut the engine and stepped out onto the sidewalk, trying to keep my feet steady underneath me. Still, I wobbled as I headed up the sidewalk and climbed the steps leading to the porch.

Through the walls of the small house, I could hear the distorted sound of Penelope crying, the echo of movement around the house.

Quietly, I rapped at the door. Praying the gentle sound would let my sister know I wasn't there to hurt her, but there was no chance I could respect her petition for me to turn a blind eye.

To pretend as if I hadn't seen her at that meeting.

For the moment, it might have made it easier on her.

But in the end, I knew it'd be nothing less than a disservice.

Shuffling resonated from the other side of the door, the little cries getting louder the closer the footsteps came. A sheer drape covering the long, vertical window that ran the side of her door rustled. I could feel the way she froze.

Hesitated.

Debated.

The longest second passed. I knew that was all it was. But in it, all my sister's reservations and fears pummeled me.

Stone after stone.

I was gasping by the time metal slid, the lock gave, and my sister peeked out the crack in the door.

She didn't ask what I was doing there. She already knew.

"Sammie," I whispered.

A tear leaked from her eye, and I could see that she was bouncing Penelope, holding her tight while the little thing fussed.

"I asked you not to come here like this. I can't do this with you."

A lump grew thick at the base of my throat. I tried to swallow around it, but still, the words stuck. "How could I ignore it? Ignore you?"

Old wounds lashed across her face. She seemed almost frantic as she dipped down and pressed a bunch of kisses to Penelope's forehead, the tiny girl's fussing increasing to an all-out squall, obviously hungry, little fists reaching for her mama.

Sammie bounced her a little more. "I'm not ready yet, Nikki. I'm not ready. Not yet."

"But you went to that meeting looking for help. The last thing I want is to get in the way of that."

A tremble ran through her, and my chest ached. God, I wanted to reach out and take it away. Hunt someone down. The hardest part was not knowing who or what I would be looking for.

I dug out the business card I'd tucked in the back pocket of my jeans and held it out for her. "Take this. Her name is Kathy. She's been my mentor. She's amazing. You can trust her, and I promise you that she won't tell me a thing. Just . . . call her."

With a shaky hand, Sammie reached out and took it, and then she wrapped her arm right back around her baby, card still in her hand.

Relief surged.

I took a step back. "I'm sorry . . . for whatever is going on. For whatever happened. But I want you to know whatever it is? I'm here for you whenever you're ready to talk about it. You don't ever have to be ashamed. And that is not the counselor talking . . . that is your sister, who will always, always be here for you. No matter what."

Tears soaked her face. "Thank you."

I nodded quickly and took a step back, letting her know I was giving her space, but that she wasn't alone. "I'm . . . I'm just gonna go check on Mama and Grandma. It's been too long since I stopped by there."

Sammie blanched, but nodded.

I started for the steps before I paused to look at her over my shoulder. "Call her, Sammie. Please."

"Soon," she murmured, hugging her daughter close, eyes meeting mine intensely before she stepped back and snapped the door shut.

Leaving me standing there wanting to break through that wall of wood to find her. Fight for her. Hold her up.

All I could do was pray the little nudge I'd given her would be enough.

Headlights cast a dingy illumination on the secluded area as I wound down the bumpy dirt road. It was only a half-mile outside of town, but it felt like a million miles and another world away.

Trees lined the path on both sides and reached for the heavens where they had been planted along the barbed-wire fences that marked the property boundaries. It isolated the entire ten-acres from the country road that ran along the river and closed it off from the neighbors that sat on either side of the land that had been in my family for as long as anyone could remember.

Oh, my grandma could tell some stories about that. I never knew what was true or exaggerated or plain made up. What I did know was I'd spent what felt like half my childhood listening to her go on about them while my little sister and I baked and sewed and ran the property.

So many of our summers had been spent here.

Sydney and Ollie always in the midst.

How many times had we raced our bikes down this lane, shouting that the last one there was a rotten egg?

Apparently, I stunk, considering I always came up short.

Funny how I'd always had a smile on my face while doing it.

Nostalgia rippled around me like the small waves that lapped at the shore of the lake as I made it to the clearing and pulled up in front of the old house.

The historic structure oozed a vintage charm, even though it was rundown and needed a whole ton of TLC.

The porch planks were warped and worn and the paint peeling, not to mention all the junk that sat around the property—broken down cars and machines and sheds filled with who knew what.

No wonder they were wanting to unload some of this crap.

Turning off the ignition, the headlights cut and the interior light glowed as I snapped open my car door. I climbed out and was smacked in the face with the overwhelming scent of honeysuckle and the river and decaying earth.

The dirt was rich and heavy, as heavy as the air and the overhead canopy of the darkened sky that was smattered with twinkling stars.

In the distance, a dog barked and bugs thrilled in the trees.

Inhaling deeply, I held the warm familiarity of it all in my lungs and ambled up the creaking steps and onto the porch.

I didn't knock at the door, I just turned the knob and poked my head inside. "Hello, anyone home?"

My mother appeared at the top of the stairs. "Nikki. What on earth are you doin' here?"

"Thought I'd stop by and check in."

"Well, it's about time. Think it's been an age since the last time I saw you. I don't even recognize you."

Light laughter filtered free.

This was exactly the reason I'd come here.

For the warmth.

After everything that had been happening, I just needed to see my mama and grandma. The two women who had been there for me through thick and thin.

There had been so much upheaval in my life.

I started for the wide set of stairs. I slid my hand along the railing as I climbed. "Now, don't go exaggerating. It's been a whole two weeks since you've seen me. Not all that much has changed."

That was a lie.

It felt like everything had changed. Ollie and my sister and my world. I was struggling to make sense of it.

She sent a playful smile my way. "Two weeks is like an eternity when it comes to your kids."

"So, you're saying you missed me?" I teased as I mounted the last step. "Guess people really just can't get enough of me. I am kind of amazing, aren't I? My being around just makes everything better."

I leaned in and dropped a kiss to her cheek.

She reached out and cupped mine. "Totally amazing." Then she hitched up a grin. "You are my daughter, after all."

I laughed. "My, my. Someone is full of herself."

She swatted at me. "Just tellin' it like it is, just like you. No reason to be coy when everyone knows it anyway."

My heart squeezed. Love overflowing.

The truth was, my mama was *amazing*.

Through and through.

And she was a load of fun, too, always laughing and joking and teasing.

Taking life by the reins and leading it where she wanted it to go.

But Ollie was right about some things.

Sometimes, life didn't give us the choice, and tonight, there was no missing the strain that lined my mother's face.

"How's Grandma?" I whispered.

Mama smiled. "Ornery as ever. Why don't you go see for yourself?"

Buoyed, I grinned and moved down the narrow passageway for the master bedroom at the end of the hall. The door was open, and the television blared as it blipped and threw colors across the room.

Affection pulled tight across my chest, thick with nostalgia. Pausing in the doorway, I tapped at the wood. "Hey, Grandma," I called.

She snapped her head my direction. She was sitting propped against a bunch of pillows in her bed. Frailer than she'd once been, but all that vigor still glinted in her eyes. She grabbed the remote and lowered the television volume. "Well, there's my knockout of a granddaughter."

I made a scoffing sound. "Which granddaughter is that you're talkin' about?"

A wide grin pulled across her wrinkled face. "What? You think I'm senile and blind like the rest of this bunch does? Don't go writing this old lady off just yet."

I crossed the room and sat on the edge of the bed. I kissed her forehead. "Never."

She wrapped her hand around mine. "As if I wouldn't recognize you. Tell me you've been tearing up the town and bringing all those boys to their knees."

A soft giggle slipped out. "Oh, you know that I am. None of them know what hit them."

Her eyes narrowed. "And how's *the* boy?"

A quiver rolled down my spine, belly tipping and my pulse giving an extra kick. "I have no idea what boy you're talking about," I said, just as innocently as I could.

Probably about as innocently as the day Ollie'd brought over a bunch of firecrackers and we'd accidentally set the back lot on fire.

"I think you know exactly what boy I'm talkin' about. *Your* boy, trouble maker that he is." She reached up and cupped my cheek. "Tell me he hasn't been causing trouble in your world."

Well hell.

Was it written all over me?

Guessed it must have been because heat went rushing across my flesh and rising to meet with the hand she held on my face.

"Who, Ollie? No," I defended a little too quickly.

Amusement danced across her face. "Think he's always been the one causing all your troubles, hasn't he?"

I attempted to suck down the emotion that followed the blush and painted a big smile on my face. "No, Grandma. He's just a friend. That's all he's ever been."

She patted my cheek. "It's always the one who causes the biggest commotion inside us who leaves the biggest mark. Isn't that right, Megs?" She turned to look at my mom, who was watching us just inside the room.

She started our way. "Sure is. And that boy has been nothing but a commotion since the day Nikki met him."

I waved them off. "You two are ridiculous. He wasn't anything of the sort."

"Ha," Mama said, starting to clear up Grandma's dinner things that were on a tray. "You were the shyest thing in the world, then those Preston's came in and shook you up."

I frowned, and she continued, "Now don't go looking at me like I said that was a bad thing. Those two had you soaring. Not a lot of us get to say we had friendships like that."

"That they did," Grandma agreed before she lowered her voice conspiratorially, "Bet that boy sends you soaring now."

She winked.

I swatted at her. "Grandma."

Mischief sparkled in her eyes. "What?" she defended as if I was crazy. "Have you seen him lately? Whoo-ee. Now that's one fine-looking boy."

On all things holy.

How did I stumble down this rabbit hole?

"Grandma," I scolded again. "That's my friend you're talking about like he's a piece of meat."

As if I hadn't ogled him like he was every time I watched him slinging drinks behind his bar.

So sexy.

Powerful.

Beautiful.

Hell, I'd straight told Lillith I wanted to eat him up at least ten-thousand times.

But this was my grandma we were talking about.

"Besides, he's not a boy."

Memories from last night flashed behind my eyes. Hitting me hard and fast and hot. Heat gathered in my belly, pulsing low.

I inhaled a sharp breath.

He was all man.

Grandma grinned like she'd just won the lottery. "That's what I thought. And the fact he's no longer a boy just means it's time to make him your man."

"I don't need a man to make me happy, Grandma."

I just . . . wanted this one.

To fall into his safety and care because I knew I'd always belonged there.

She waved me off as if I was silly. "I know, I know, you modern women livin' it up by yourselves. Bet that gets lonely after a bit," she said, eyeing me from the corner of her eye, knowing she was hitting it just right.

Dishes clinked as my mama picked up the tray and set it on the desk by the window. "Now, now, Mama, think our Nikki here knows what she needs. Don't give her too hard of a time."

A huff left Grandma's mouth. "Is it too much to ask for another great grandbaby before this old girl rides off into the sunset? That sweet Penelope could use a cousin to run around and get in trouble with. Nothing would make me happier than seeing a new generation taking over before this one blinks out."

I brushed my fingers through her hair. "Don't talk like that."

"You know it's true . . . not gonna be around forever."

Somberness moved through the room, and Grandma patted my hand. Not the teasing way she'd done my cheek. But with such tenderness is brought moisture to my eyes.

"I'm just playin' with you, girl. Not about to pressure you into something you don't want. But I sure would be happy to kick your tail in the direction that you actually want to go."

Sydney's voice moved through my mind like the softest breeze.

"I think it's the things that hurt the worst that mean the most, don't you? Good or bad. That's what's gonna shape us. Make us into who we are. Guide us on the path to what we want the most I think we'll know it when there's no other direction we can go. And I'm not going to be afraid of walking it anymore."

"Some things are just worth the wait, Grandma."

I felt compelled to at least give her that.

She smiled. "Mm-hmm . . . just don't let him drag his feet too long."

I wondered if she could possibly know how complicated our lives had been. What the tragedy of losing Sydney had done to both of us.

She sighed and settled deeper into the pillows, and I adjusted the blanket higher on her chest. "So, Grandma, I wanted to ask you . . . did you sell Grandpa's old Bel Air?"

A small smile lit at the corner of her mouth. "Yeah. Todd came back to take care of me the way your mama has been doing. He's cleaning up this place, getting it back into shape. Lord knows, I've let it go to rot these last few years. Gave him the go ahead to sell whatever he wants since he dropped his job to come out here and fix up the house."

I smiled at her. "It's good he's here. How long's he gonna be staying?"

Her lids drifted closed. "Probably as long as I last. As long as it takes him and your mom to get rid of this place."

Grief.

Stark and quiet and resounding.

It echoed through the room, from the clench of my heart to the flinch of my mama where she fiddled with something across the room, her back to us as if she was giving us privacy.

"Did you go through that box with your sister yet?" Grandma asked, her words starting to jumble, her pain medicine surely kicking in. "Wasn't ever rich, but everything I've ever had worth anything I put in there where I kept it in the attic."

I cringed, unable to confess someone had taken it. I didn't know what would be worse. Admitting that or the fact my apartment had been broken into in the first place.

I smiled softly. "Not yet. We will soon."

The lie fell so easily.

I just didn't know what else to say.

"Want you and your sister to do it soon. See what you might like."

She peeked an eye open at me. "As long as it doesn't lead to the two of you getting in one of those fist fights like you used to have over those dolls. No hair pullin', now."

A light chuckle rippled free. "Nah, I'm pretty sure we can handle ourselves. Unless you have something extra awesome in there."

I winked at her, and she laughed, the sound hitching when she began to cough.

"You two . . . find the important stuff. Keep it. That would make me happier than you know."

I couldn't bring myself to respond. Instead, I eased forward and kissed her cheek. I pulled back a fraction. "I'll let you rest."

She gave a small nod before she was already drifting off.

Reluctantly, I stood, watching over her as she got swept away into a deep sleep. I turned to face my mama who was watching me. Slowly, I approached her and wrapped my arms around her.

She stuttered through a deep breath, doing her best to quiet a sob that clawed at her throat. I just . . . held her while she cried, knowing there were no words that would make it better.

"I'm sorry," she whispered in my ear after a minute.

My head shook. "Nothing to be sorry for, Mama."

She nodded, and I held her out by the arms, voice serious. "If you need to rest, call me. I'll be happy to sit with her."

Regretfully, she looked at her mother before turning back to me. "I think I'll take all the minutes I have. They'll be plenty of time for rest later."

Quiet sorrow moved between us. "Okay," I said, wiping the tear that escaped my eye. "Just . . . promise you'll call if you need me."

"I will."

"I'll be back soon."

My worry for my sister was right there, hovering in my spirit, wanting to be released.

No matter how heavily it weighed, I wouldn't break my sister's trust that way. I had to let her come to me—to us—on her own time.

"I love you, Sunshine," she said, and I almost blushed at the way Ollie's nickname for me had spilled over and clung to the rest of my family.

"I love you more," I told her, backing away.

"Not a chance."

We smiled at each other as I edged across the groaning planks before I turned in the doorway and bounded back downstairs.

I shrieked when the door suddenly burst open just as I was reaching for the latch, my hand flying up to cover the thunder that was suddenly pounding my heart. I stepped back, still rattled. "Uncle Todd," I said, trying to force down the nerves that spiked in my body.

I hated I was still on edge after everything that had happened.

"Well, if it isn't Nikki Lou."

He stood there, years older than I remembered, looking so much different. Lines creased his face, and a few more pounds were around his middle.

But the oil and grease staining his hands wasn't new.

"It's nice to see you," I said.

"Good to see you, too. It's been way too long."

"It has."

Awkwardness spun around us, and I hesitated before I said, "I just wanted you to know my friend bought that old Bel Air. I'm glad it's going to someone we know."

A frown pulled across his brow. "The Bel Air?"

I smiled at him. "It's fine. Grandma told me she is having you sell off some stuff since you left your job to come here and help out. It's good you're here for her."

Unease moved around him, and he nodded, as if he wasn't sure he wanted to take the praise. "It's not a problem."

I gestured for the door. "Well, I was just leaving. We'll have to catch up more soon."

I sidestepped around him.

From behind, I could feel him swivel around to look at me. "Which friend was that?" he asked.

I peeked back at him. "Ollie."

He grimaced then gave a tight nod. Without another word, I ducked out into the night, wondering why it was that I felt so off-kilter.

twenty-two

Ollie
Seventeen Years Old

A pebble pinged against the window. When it got no response, he picked up another and did it again, feeling impatient and antsy as he stood outside of Nikki's grandma's house in the middle of the night.

Heart in his throat, he picked up another and did it again. This time the pebble he picked up was a whole lot closer to being a rock. He cringed when it clanged against the glass, then breathed out in relief when Nikki's face appeared in front of the drape.

There was confusion in her expression before a smile pulled to her face when she saw him standing beneath a big tree. She ducked away, and he was sure it was his pulse that would wake the entire house with the way it boomed, excitement and want filling him so full he thought he just might burst.

Not pretty.

But it was the truth.

This girl drove him right out of his mind.

He was already moving her direction by the time she slipped

out the front door and silently snapped it shut behind her. She padded across the porch and down the stairs as he jogged her way.

They met in the middle, and he lifted her a couple of inches from the ground so he could feel her weight, spinning her around as he buried his face in the sweetness of her skin.

Honey and light.

She giggled and clung to him, her voice quieted to a whisper. "What are you doing here?"

"I needed to see you."

"And what if it had been your sister you woke up instead of me?"

He shrugged a little and settled Nikki back on her feet. "Then I'd tell her I was here to check on you two. Pretty much the truth, anyway."

Nikki stepped back and bit her bottom lip. She took his hand in hers, swaying lightly, spinning around, peeking back at him as she danced them off into the secluded cover of the towering trees. "Is that all you're here for, Oliver Preston? To check on us?"

There was a tease to her voice, and every inch of his body reacted.

He followed.

Where else was he going to go?

He was enraptured.

Enchanted.

This girl magic.

He rushed her, scooping her up from behind. Her feet kicked into the air as she squealed quietly, her back to his chest and his mouth at her ear. "You know why I'm here."

"And why's that?" she played along when he set her back down. She swung back around to face him.

He rushed his fingers through the softness of her hair. "For you."

"And now that you're here, what are you going to do with me?"

In a second flat, he had her pressed against the old car her grandpa still drove where it was parked behind a shed at least a hundred yards from the house. Where no one could see them. "First off, I'm going to kiss you."

He did. He took her face in his hands and he kissed her. Slow and long. He felt like he was standing in the middle of the river, taken by the current, unable to stand.

She sighed, and he hummed as he dropped his forehead to hers. "I was going nuts not getting to do that all day."

Rex and Sydney were around the whole time, and he hadn't gotten to sneak a second alone with Nikki.

Hiding this was getting harder and harder, but somehow, finally telling everyone after all this time felt harder to do, too. They'd been doing it for so long, it was beginning to feel like a lie.

A sin.

"You're driving me crazy, Nik," he whispered at her mouth. "Don't know what I'm supposed to do. The second I'm away from you, all I can think about is the next time I get to be with you. You've got me so spun up inside."

Her hands fisted in his shirt. "And the second you walk away, I feel a piece of myself go missing."

A breath left him, and he ran his lips up her cheek and whispered at her temple, "Sunshine."

"Beast," she teased quietly.

He fumbled with the door latch behind her, and Nikki was giggling as he angled her around to open the door. He fell into the seat and took her with him. She was quick to straddle his lap, hands on his shoulders, rocking against him.

If he didn't get to feel all of her soon, he might die.

He was sure of it.

Because her rubbing on him like that was nothing but torture.

The best kind of torture.

He just didn't know how much more of it he could take.

His hands went to her waist. "What if we stole the keys to this car and just drove away?"

She was kissing him, murmuring at his mouth, "Where would we go?"

"Anywhere . . . everywhere . . ." he rumbled. "Just so long as we're together. Can't wait until it's just us. You and me . . . my girl riding at my side in my badass car."

She giggled. The sound of it vibrated right through the center of him. "Mmm . . . you want an old car like this?"

Their hands were everywhere. Touching and exploring.

He groaned. "Hell, yes."

"Hot rod, huh?" she whispered.

"You know it. Nothing cooler than that. Gonna have one by the time I'm eighteen. Just wait. Then it's just you and me. No more hiding."

"Are you going to wait that long to take me?"

He stilled at her question. Because her voice had gone different. Something needy. No longer a tease.

He pulled back and looked at her through the milky light of the moon. Trusting eyes and freckled skin and heated body. "You want that?"

Didn't matter it was dark, he could feel the warmth rise to her cheeks. "Yes."

He swallowed around the lump that almost strangled him.

Nerves and excitement and lust.

He stared up at her, watching her expression when he said, "Next weekend . . . there's a big bonfire at the lake. Supposed to camp with a bunch of people from school. Tell your mom you're spending the night with Sydney."

Her head angled to the side, that same worry they had over his sister taking over her features. "And what am I supposed to tell Sydney?"

A sigh pilfered free. He didn't want to be annoyed. Irritated that they were sneaking around because they were afraid they might offend her or hurt her.

"We'll . . . figure it out, okay? We'll make it work. I just want to be with you."

She wound her arms around his neck. "I just want to be with you, too."

twenty-three
Ollie

Traditions.

It was hard to pinpoint exactly how they were formed. How they came into existence. It was like a slow slide of habits that gathered and merged until they stuck. Most people viewed them as a good thing.

Holidays and family and celebration.
Cherished memories repeated again and again.
This tradition?
It was nothing less than masochistic.
Hot blades cutting into my skin.
Needlessly, considering the scars were already there. Etched in me so deeply they could never be erased.

Kale and Rex both inclined back on different pieces of furniture in the back office at Olive's, Rex with the bottle this year, pouring it into the shooters. "Seems crazy this date has come up again. Years going by faster than I can make sense of them."

A sorrowful, wistful sound filtered from Kale. "Yeah. Time just keeps rolling, things changing so quickly, and still I can close my eyes, and I swear, I'm back there at the lake that night."

Shivers scraped across the surface of my skin.

Agony.

Rex peered over at me. "You sure you want to do this again?"

"What's changed?" My voice was grit, even though the words were feeling more and more like a lie.

The first time we'd gathered on the anniversary of this night? We'd been eighteen. They'd found me at the lake.

Alone.

Looking at the water like it might conjure her existence on the glassy, darkened surface.

They'd climbed down on either side of me.

Kale with all his quiet understanding and support. Rex wearing some sort of unfathomable grief on his face.

He'd pulled out this massive bottle of cheap whiskey, twisted the cap, and handed it to me.

I'd chugged what had to have been half of it until I'd choked on the burning liquid that'd pooled in my empty gut, then the three of us had sat there for hours, passing it back and forth until it was empty and the sun was coming up.

Two of them swimming in my loss. Keeping me from drowning.

I'd pushed Nikki away. Hadn't seen more of her that unbearable year than stolen glances that had damned near destroyed the last bit of me.

Cutting her out of my life had hurt like a fucking bitch. But how could I have her when the cost of wanting her was my sister?

I couldn't.

And I'd hated and hated and hated, and that feeling had built for so many years until it suffocated me. Until I could no longer see straight, which was how I'd ended up at Nikki's door a year ago tonight.

Nothing but a selfish bastard.

Taking her.

Of course, I couldn't even remember how I'd gotten there since I'd been so messed up that my rational mind could no longer convince my spirit that I wasn't allowed to have her.

It was like finding peace in the darkest night.

Then, like a piece of shit, I'd slipped from her bed before dawn, fucking wrecked, leaving her lying there naked where I'd been tangled with her.

The whole time wanting to climb right back into her arms.

To wrap her up and never let her go.

But I'd left her there because I'd had to.

What other choice did I have?

Didn't think I'd ever been so torn about anything.

I had been wrong.

Tonight, I felt like I was being shredded in two. Never so caught up in right and wrong. The girl once again a secret.

My best secret.

One I wanted to keep.

Just didn't know what kind of person that made me if I did.

Rex handed Kale a shot glass and then gave one to me. The three of us met in the middle of the small office. We lifted the shots above our heads. "To Sydney. We'll never forget."

Glasses clinked, and we tossed back the shots. I swallowed it down. Heat blistered my stomach and crawled through my senses. This date would haunt me forever—but I could feel something . . . something changing.

Kale clapped me on the back. "You okay, man?"

A huff left my nose, and I scrubbed a palm over my face. "Not sure that's the right description. Okay would mean forgetting."

He looked at me seriously. "Not sure there's any chance of that. Don't think you're ever going to forget. And I don't think you'd want to."

He started to move around me to head for the door. All the girls and Broderick would be waiting, probably wondering where the hell we'd slipped off to.

He paused when he was right at my side, both of us facing opposite directions. He reached out and squeezed my shoulder, his attention cast to the ground. "But it's been fourteen years, Ollie. If I knew Sydney at all? She's looking down on you, wishing you'd finally let her go. Wishing that you'd finally let yourself live."

I didn't say anything, and he opened the door and stepped out into the bar, the muted thrum of the band playing tonight growing loud as he did. Without looking back, he snapped it shut, closing Rex and me in, the beat once again distorted, faint and vibrating through the walls.

Warily, I looked up to meet Rex's piercing gaze. Something about it was unsettling. Remorseful but strong. "He's right, man." The words caught in his throat. "It's time."

I looked to the floor, hand running down my beard. "Not sure that's possible. Not until I find her."

He winced, eyes slamming closed and hands turning to fists. "You're hung up on an impossibility, Ollie. It's time you admitted that."

Part of me wanted to lash out at him. Tell him to fuck off because he couldn't understand. This was my sister we were talking about. They'd barely even been friends, only knowing each other because he and I hung out.

The other part knew he was right.

Fourteen years, I'd been searching. Cutting out every fucking news article about her that had ever been written, comparing it against other cases, sure that, if I was patient enough, I would notice something. Piece together a clue that had been missed.

Hell, that'd been part of the reason I'd opened this bar in the first place. Figuring one day, someone would slip, say something they shouldn't. Or maybe someone would say something they didn't know was important in the first place.

I felt that hope slipping away.

What scared me most was I didn't know where that left me.

Rex hesitated, the words almost a groan when he released them. "I miss her, too, man. You think if I could go back, I wouldn't do things differently?"

I looked up, trying to gauge where he was coming from, what he was trying to get at.

He sighed, shook whatever thoughts he was having off. "Everyone's out there. Together. The people who care about you most. Don't neglect that. You're gonna regret it if you do. Time goes by so fast, Ollie. So damned fast. You've got to treasure the days you're given."

An echo of my mother's screams filled my ear, the impact of them thrashing in my spirit, her fists a phantom pain on my chest.

It's your fault.
I trusted you.
You were supposed to take care of her.
You promised, you'd take care of her.

"Not sure I even deserve to be out there with them."

Rex strode for the door, pausing with it open as he turned, his words pointed. "Don't you?"

For twenty minutes, I sat alone with only my thoughts and the sounds of the bar seeping through the walls to keep me company.

Processing.

Sifting through my thoughts and my worries.

The deep-seated need to cling to this day—to the memory of Sydney—to give her the devotion that she'd deserved.

The other part was all fucked up over Nikki.

Nikki. Fucking. Walters.

Invading my life when I didn't know how to keep her there.

How to make her fit.

The girl so fucking wrong. So fucking right.

Like I said, I'd never been so torn.

Finally, I forced myself to get it together, got behind my bar, and went to work.

Seemed impossible, but the smile tacked to my face wasn't all that hard to find, considering I was surrounded by the group of people who had gathered directly across from me.

Laughing and treasuring and *cherishing*.

Most of all . . . Nikki was right there.

Safe.

I poured Lillith a glass of chilled white wine, whipped up a pitcher of margaritas for Rynna, Hope, and Jenna. After that, I handed a beer to Rex, filled a tumbler of whiskey for Kale, and passed a glass of red wine to Broderick.

I went to work on Nikki's drink, listening to my friends carrying on, having a great time.

Their laughter rang free, blending with the beat of the band where they'd taken up residence at the bar like they owned the place.

Their voices were loud and their mood a little bit rowdy.

From across the bar, Nikki met my eyes.

Tentatively.

Tenderly.

The girl sending me her soft encouragement. Aware and sweet and filled with all that light I'd taken for granted for all these years.

I sent her a covert smile back as I slid her pink cosmo across the gleaming wood in her direction.

Telling her I saw her. That I felt her. That I knew this day wasn't easy on her either.

That she had just as much on her mind as me.

Maybe more.

I was grateful there was a smile on her face, too.

That she was acting like her normal self.

Her old self.

Laughing and teasing and playing with her friends.

Jenna who was Hope's best friend, squealed, jerking my attention away from Nikki's hypnotizing stare. "I knew there was a reason I loved you."

She wrapped both hands around the margarita glass rimmed with salt, bringing it to her nose and inhaling like it was some kind of rose or some shit.

My brows pitched high. "That's the reason you love me? My bar?" I razzed, shaking my head like I was completely outraged.

Jenna's brown hair swished around her face. "You've got to admit that having a friend who owns a bar is filled with all kinds of perks. I wish I would have known you earlier. A girl could use a guy like you right about the time she turns twenty-one. I have major catching up to do."

"I take offense to that."

Rex waved his beer in the air. "Why do you think I still put up with your sorry ass?"

I lifted my arms out to the sides. "Uh . . . because I'm awesome. That's why."

This was always just our way, going from heavy to light in a second flat, giving each other shit as if they hadn't just been right there, coming beside me when they always knew I needed them most.

Kale laughed. "Sure, sure, man, you just go on thinking that."

Hope swatted at his chest. "Leave Ollie alone." She turned her attention to me, her eyes wide with playful sympathy. "I know you're awesome. Ignore these monsters."

Incredulous, Kale snorted. "Monsters?"

"Monsters," I agreed, giving Hope a smile.

Kale pointed at me with his index finger, the rest of his hand still wrapped around the glass. "If anyone looks like a monster around here, it's you. Seriously, I've seen grown men shudder in their damned boots at the sight of you. Little do they know, you're nothing but a pansy under all that muscle. What a damned waste."

A smile threatened at the edge of my mouth.

Assholes.

All of them.

"Keep dreaming. Nothing wasted here." I flexed like one of those fuckers showing off on Venice Beach. "Guys piss their pants when they see me because they know I'm not to be fucked with. Unlike you." Was doing my best to keep a straight face and not bust out laughing as I played along.

Kale puffed out his chest. "Oh, come on, Ollie. You know I could take you."

I laughed under my breath.

"You think so, huh?"

"Yup. Remember that time in fourth grade behind the swing sets? Totally whooped your ass, my friend."

My brow lifted. "That's because I let you win."

Nikki widened playful eyes, her attention bouncing around the group, that mesmerizing color so pretty where they glinted under the lights.

"I can now attest to the fact that Ollie is, in fact, a monster. A bear. Or maybe an ogre. I'm concerned for my safety. The man actually growls in his sleep."

The last week had been nothing but cruel.

Being with her and not being able to touch her.

Trying to keep that promise that I needed to figure my shit out before I hurt her again.

She draped an arm around Jenna's shoulders. Swore, two of them might have been twins separated at birth.

Lillith's hawk eyes darted between us. Swore she could spot a rat from a hundred miles away. "So, how is the whole roommate thing going? Should I thank you for not killing my best friend yet?"

I glanced at Nikki for a flash before I set my palms on the bar and leaned toward Lillith. "*Yet* being the operative word."

Rynna giggled. "Tell me she's not as messy at your place as she is at Pepper's Pies. I swear to goodness, that whirlwind leaves a trail of crumbs everywhere she goes like she's leaving behind a distress call."

Nikki's mouth dropped open. "What in the world are you talkin' about, Rynna? I bus those tables faster than all those kids you hired combined. I run circles around them."

"Oh, so that explains the crop circles of bread crumbs scattered around the floor."

"That's it, I quit."

Nikki was fighting a grin behind her overexaggerated pout. But there was no missing the way her sexy mouth twisted with affection.

"I'm just playing!" Rynna cried, rushing her friend and taking up her other side. "Don't leave me yet. I might up and die. Don't know what I'm going to do without you. Crumbs and all."

"We'll find someone awesome to take my place, don't worry. I mean, hello, *not* as awesome, because we all know that would be totally impossible, but someone who will make do."

Rynna pouted. "But I love you best."

"I'm feeling totally left out here." Hope pursed her lips where she was tucked against Kale.

Nikki reached out and waved her in. "Well, get in here then . . . we aren't complete without you and Lillith."

Hope didn't even hesitate. She rushed into the circle.

Lillith rolled her eyes. "Are we seriously group-hugging in the middle of the bar?"

Nikki's brows shot to the ceiling. "You know what they say, how are your friends going to know you love them if you're not drunk at two a.m. on a Saturday night?"

Lillith glanced at the glittering diamond watch wrapped around her wrist, a gift from Broderick for her birthday. "Its nine, Nikki. Nine."

"Semantics. Get your ass over here."

From behind, Broderick gave her a tiny shove, his grin wolfish when she looked back at him. "Go on, baby. Get a little of that group love. That's enough fantasies for an entire week."

Nikki pointed at him. "Eww, Brody. Just no. Don't you dare go there."

Yeah. Don't go there. And here I'd thought I liked the guy.

But Rex was shaking his head, Kale was chuckling, and the girls were standing and hugging and jumping and laughing as they swayed in this big huddle, and there was nothing I could do but grin right the hell along.

My chest tightened.

Sweet agony.

Because a piece was missing, and I'd give fucking anything for Sydney to be there. My mind flashed with what she might look like now.

Fourteen years gone.

Where she'd be in her life. If she'd be married. Have kids.

Or if she'd be living in some faraway city, chasing down a dream.

"Hey, boss," Cece called from the other end of the bar, breaking into the thoughts that cut me down at the knees.

I jerked my attention that way.

So maybe Nikki had a few things right about Cece.

My head bartender was nothing short of a tattooed sex

goddess.

Long, jet-black hair, the scraps she wore screaming seduction, almost as loud as the red painted on her lips.

Maybe it wasn't so strange for Nikki to make assumptions about us. People would probably take one look at Cece and think her my perfect match.

Two of us cut from the same cloth.

Or maybe chipped from the same stone.

Truth was, I had never even had the urge.

Didn't mean it didn't bug the hell out of me that Nikki had brought it up. I hated the idea that she had ever felt an ounce of what I'd felt when I'd had to stomach looking at her with another man.

Wanted to dig my nails into my mind and claw all those images from my consciousness.

"What's up?" I hollered, grateful for the distraction.

She cocked a wry grin, and the poor asshole sitting at the bar across from her was nothing but a puddle at her feet.

"Could use backup. Pack of f-boys, eleven o'clock."

I laughed under my breath.

Only Cece.

Fuckboy.

Fratboy.

As far as she was concerned, that title was as interchangeable as the guy's that held it were abhorrent. She slapped them with a "douche" label across their pretty-boy foreheads before they even had a chance to make it through rush week.

I rapped my fist on the counter, pointed at my friends. "Be right back."

I moved to the opposite end of the bar, sliding in beside Cece to help her fill the beers for the rowdy table that was up close to the band.

Did my best not to cringe when I saw the guy who walked through the door.

Talk about a douche.

Matt Walker.

Asshole we'd all known since high school. Something about

him festered right below my skin.

Oh, that was right.

Fucker had wanted to get his grimy hands on Nikki for just as long as I had known him.

Didn't matter that he was all fitted, posh business suits and shiny fucking shoes to match his shiny fucking smile.

Asshole was slimy as fuck.

A weasel.

"You good?" I asked Cece when I'd finished helping her fill the huge order. Could feel the tether pulling me back that way. Toward Nikki who I knew would be the prick's target.

Time and again.

She'd left with him once, a few years ago, and I'd about damned lost my mind.

Thought of it happening again had panic laying siege to my veins.

"Yep. Think we have it under control now. Let's just hope they don't eff up the rest of my night."

The girl smirked, hip tossed out to the side.

My laugh was wry.

Wouldn't want to tangle with that one.

I booked it back to my post.

Lillith had already spotted Matt, and she bumped her hip into Nikki's to get her attention. "Oh, look who just walked in. It's Make-Out Matt," she sang like she didn't know she was basically crushing me beneath her red-soled shoe.

Nikki's gaze flashed to me.

Remorse and awareness and a lifetime of unanswered questions.

Where do we go from here?
Who are we?
Do I belong to you?
Most importantly, do you belong to me?

I gulped under the force of them, wanting nothing more than to reach out, touch her face. Maybe climb right the hell over this bar, take her in my arms, and kiss her in front of all our friends.

Claim her as mine.

She'd been a secret for so damned long. Problem was, I still didn't know if I deserved to stand in her light.

Possession tearing through my senses, I watched as the prick made his way through the crowd like he had no real destination, no care in the world.

Still, it was obvious as hell he knew exactly what direction he was heading.

Lillith nudged Nikki with her elbow. "You should totally give him a chance, Nikki. That poor man has been salivating over you since the day he joined the track team your senior year just so he could watch your tits bounce when you ran."

Nikki visibly pushed back the discomfort that surged between us and pinned one of those faked smiles on her mouth.

"Pssh . . ." Nikki stepped back and gestured at her chest.

I wiped my brow.

Why the fuck wasn't the air conditioner on? Was dying in there.

"What tits? I'm as flat as Kansas," she said, laughing and joking the way she'd done for all these years.

Images rushed. The girl on my couch. Her tit in my mouth. My hands on her body.

Need spun and licked and teased.

She had no fucking clue just how perfect they were, peaking below that satiny material. Nikki's own personal form of harassment.

"Matt seems to be just fine with that." Rynna nodded emphatically.

Great. That was all I needed.

Nikki had yet another meddler urging her along, not that Rynna could have a clue.

I glared between Rex and Kale.

Where was my crew when I needed them most?

Did they not see this bullshit?

I mean, I know I'd taken responsibility for Nikki's well-being. But there were times when good friends should step in.

Like when a douche tried to make his way into territory he didn't belong.

Fuck that.

Rex met my eyes, narrowing his, studying me as he took a swig of his beer.

Did he have any idea? All that time Nikki and I had been sneaking around, hiding away, hoping Rex and Kale would be enough of a distraction that Sydney wouldn't notice. Guess I hadn't given it all that much thought as to if they had.

Hope landed a bunch of excited smacks against Nikki's arm, her eyes wide and her lips barely moving, like she thought she was telling a secret that she was actually issuing to the world. "Oh, oh, don't look behind you . . . but he's coming this way. Oh, wow, he really is good-looking."

"Hey," Kale defended.

Now the asshole had something to say.

She looked up at her husband, her red hair moving over her shoulders. "Oh, Cowboy . . . I was talking about for Nikki. Don't get your britches in a twist."

He leaned down, rubbing his nose against hers. "Cowboy? I'm your king, baby."

Had to resist from balling up a dish rag and throwing it against the side of his face.

Yeah, this was not gonna end well.

Because my guts were churning when Matt, the fucker, came up to the bar just behind where Nikki stood.

He grinned at me like we were the oldest of mates. "Hey, man." Still standing, he leaned his forearms on the bar. "How's it going?"

Fan-fucking-tastic, that's how.

"Good," I rumbled. I tossed a napkin down in front of him. "What can I get you?"

How about the door?

"Whatever's on tap."

Everything's on tap, asshole.

But I didn't say anything, I just filled up a chilled mug with a light.

Figured that was all the pussy could handle.

I smiled at him when I slid it across the bar.

All teeth.

"Thanks, brother," he said like he didn't even notice I was five seconds from ripping him to shreds.

He lifted it in the air before he took a big swallow.

"Sure thing."

He was grinning when he moved into the circle, going right for her. "Hey, Nikki. It's good to see you."

She peeked my way.

A flash of indigo.

A glimpse of the freckles on her defined cheeks.

My chest tightened.

She offered him a small smile. "Hi, Matt. How have you been?"

"Good, good," he said. "Work's busy, but other than that, I can't complain. You?"

"Same here."

Seemed like so many lies fell from her mouth with that simple statement.

Like all this bullshit wasn't going down in her life.

This was brutal, watching them chat like every word wasn't killing me.

I was a hot second from losing my cool. Turned out it was Nikki who was getting ready to do all the shredding, and the girl didn't even have to lift a finger.

Our friends had turned to each other, talking quietly, giving them space, while I scrubbed at the bar with a rag and tried to pretend like it wasn't any of my business.

Didn't matter.

The turn in Nikki and Matt's conversation hit me like a loudspeaker screaming in my ear.

"Band's good tonight. You want to dance?" Matt asked.

Of course, that was when Lillith found it fit to pipe in. She all but shoved Nikki his direction. "Sure, she does."

There was no missing the resistance that lined Nikki's posture when Lily pushed her that way, the way her shoulders went up and her shoes slid across the floor.

An inch, and then two.

Enough to make my mind tip to the side. Axis creaking. Threatening to crack.

Nikki peeked back at me.

Was that an apology or her own anger and frustration, her spirit screaming out that I was responsible for this?

I'd known all along that one day . . . one day she'd move on.

Find joy.

A husband and a family and a load of kids, exactly what she deserved.

The way she'd dreamed about growing up.

How many kids are we gonna have?" she'd whispered when she was just fifteen, laying on a bed of blazing stars, nestled on my chest as we'd looked up at the night sky.

"Three. One little girl with your eyes and two boys just like me."

She giggled. "I don't think I could handle three of you."

It was what I'd wanted for her even though the thought destroyed something in me.

Of her finding that with someone other than me.

Then I'd gone and ruined every chance she'd had. Chased off every guy. Certain they weren't good enough for her.

Amusement was suddenly in her smile, wry as her gaze moved across all the girls, then she turned back to Matt. "Actually, all my friends would like to dance."

Another warning in her expression when she looked back at them. "Wouldn't they?"

She spun around, facing them as she backed away and waved for them to follow. The girl was wearing this short, frilly skirt and a silky tank, heels on her feet making her legs look like they were a mile long.

Everything about her was exotic and still as comfortable and down to earth as a home-cooked meal.

Yeah.

I wanted to fucking eat her.

Devour every inch.

Jenna clapped in excitement, while Hope passed her drink off to Kale, pecking him on the lips before she rushed to join them.

Lillith? Lillith hit me with a smirk as she let go of Broderick's hand and then followed Hope.

Swore to God, the world was against me.

Cursed.

They edged into the thick, pushing through the raving throng. Bodies surged and swayed and pulsed. They all made their way to the dance floor at the base of the elevated stage.

Nearly choked when Matt edged up to Nikki from behind and tugged her against his chest.

In the roiling crowd, she was facing me when he splayed his hand across her belly.

From across the space, those mesmerizing eyes, so odd of a color you could vanish in the depths, tangled with mine.

Hypnotizing.

A motherfucking spell.

Black fucking magic.

That was what she was.

Rage blew in like a bleak, black storm.

Rex looked that way before he turned back to me with a grumbled laugh. "You're so fucked, dude."

I wiped at the bar, so hard I was pretty sure it was rubbing off the glossy stain.

Stripping it down to bare bones.

That was exactly what I felt like.

Bare bones.

"What's that supposed to mean?" I gritted.

He shared a look with Kale before he turned back to me. "If you saw your face right now, you'd know exactly what that means."

"Don't know what you're talking about."

"You still gonna stand there and deny it after all this time?"

Unease rippled through me. Maybe he really had had a clue. "Deny what?"

Disappointment came out with the shake of his head before he tipped back his beer and drained the bottle. He stood and slammed the empty on the bar. "Think I'm gonna go claim my girl before some poor, unknowing bastard has to die trying. Someone else here might want to do the same."

And he wasn't looking at Kale or Broderick when he said it.

twenty-four
Nikki

Chaos drummed through the air. I felt caught up in it.

Elevated and lost.

My feet not quite touching the ground. Held by the sapphire gaze that ravaged me from across the space.

Intense, fierce, and blistering.

Torment and need and possession.

Crash after crash.

Matt slipped his hand around my waist and pulled me flush against his body.

A shudder ripped free of my lungs. It wasn't even close to being elicited by Matt's touch. It was because the only thing I could feel was Ollie covering me.

I didn't even have to close my eyes to imagine the man was touching me everywhere, the sensation of his hands from last weekend still alive and vibrant.

Sizzling across my flesh.

Turmoil played across Ollie's striking face.

It was possessive and wild, and still, incredibly sad.

Unable to remain upright under the severity of it, I tore

myself out of Matt's hold and whirled around to face him, turning my back to Ollie because I no longer knew how to stand beneath it all.

The sorrow and the regret and the need.

In the throbbing crush, I struggled to maintain balance where my friends danced around me as if they couldn't feel the quake of the earth that rocked beneath my feet.

Dim lights were at one with the smoky fog that twisted and twined in the air, the bar nothing but a dizzying haze.

Bodies pulsed, a mass that toiled in the hypnotic beat.

Matt slanted me a smile, what he thought was seduction carved out on his face, and my stomach turned.

I didn't want this.

Not tonight.

Not when I wanted to turn around, go to Ollie, and tell him I wasn't going anywhere.

Promise him I'd stay.

Matt edged forward again. This time, he placed both his hands to my hips in a bid to bring us closer.

I set my hands on his chest, intending to tell him I was sorry but I couldn't do this. Even if it was just a dance, it felt wrong.

But my mouth went dry, and my tongue got stuck on the roof of my mouth when I felt the energy surge over me from behind. At the same time, the waters parting as the air rushed and whirled.

I didn't even have time to process it before Ollie was there.

Towering next to where Matt attempted to bring us together.

The man so big.

Savage and fierce.

Hands fisted at his sides and something like anger in his expression.

There was no chance I could breathe through the impact.

He turned all that intimidation on Matt. "Sorry, *brother*, but I'm gonna have to cut in."

His tone was a low threat.

Irritated, Matt's attention flicked to Ollie.

For a second, I thought he was going to refuse. Maybe he

Lead Me Home

hadn't known who it was before he'd looked, or maybe it hadn't been until then that he'd caught on to the possessive indignation that radiated from Ollie's flesh.

But Matt jolted and started to slowly back away. Eyes darting between us for a beat, annoyed and off-put before he seemed to give and disappeared into the fray.

Then Ollie looped a massive arm around my waist as he wound the other hand into my hair.

A gasp burst from my lungs.

Never, ever had Ollie touched me in public. Not like this.

He pulled me flush against his heat and strength and battering heart.

His forehead dropped to mine, and our bodies began to sway, to move in time to the beat, our hips rocking as we fell into the dance.

People throbbed around us, and he held me tighter. He bent down, wedging his knee between my thighs.

One hand gripped me by the waist, that thumb running dizzying circles on my hipbone.

"Nikki," he murmured. My name sounded fragile and unsure where he released it an inch from my mouth. "I'm going to lose my mind, looking at you on this floor, another man touching you."

My hands fisted in his shirt, desperate to get him closer.

"Ollie," I whispered, close to begging.

What is this?

I can't handle being this close to you, and you push me away again.

His nose brushed mine, and his expression verged on pained as he drew in a ragged breath.

Trembling with need.

We rocked in hesitation, and his mouth was in my hair, at my temple, running tenderly down my cheek.

Fire on my skin.

Then he brushed his lips across mine.

Once.

Twice.

So sweet.

Lightheadedness swept through me like a slow dream.

Then he crushed his mouth to mine.

Indecision erased. The man consuming me in a way he'd never done.

Openly.

It felt like a claiming.

His hand moved to the back of my head as he angled me just right. His tongue demanding all of me right out in the middle of the dance floor.

My heart took off at a sprint, racing for his that hammered in the air.

And we spun.

Kissing.

Kissing and kissing and kissing.

Desire flashed.

Ollie groaned.

I burned—every cell in my body coming alive under his touch.

He suddenly pulled away, and I was blinking, trying to find my senses. But the only thing I could see was this man.

Peering down at me, something so different in his gaze.

Powerful and unending.

My knees shook, and he took me by the hand, and that was when I noticed that all of our friends were frozen in the middle of the floor.

Shocked, every single one of them stared back at us.

Rex cracked a grin in Ollie's direction, and Ollie just gave him a finger as he began to haul me back through the crowd.

Heat flushed my body, my cheeks.

Not because I was embarrassed or ashamed but because, for the first time ever, it felt like I was finally right, and I had no idea how long this feeling would remain.

I struggled to keep up on my heels as Ollie wound through the groups packed around the high-top tables, the man on a mission as he beelined for the darkened hall.

The second we were in it, he had me pinned, my back against the wall and my legs around his waist. He ground himself against my center.

Pleasure sparked.

He groaned, the man plundering my mouth as he did.

"Nikki," he muttered, hands running the outside of my bare thighs. "Nikki."

Without setting me on my feet, he jerked me from the wall, never ceasing that frenzied kiss as he carried me the rest of the way down the hall and started up the zigzagging stairwell.

We banged up the steps, the man spinning and pressing and clamoring, his hands everywhere.

Needy.

As needy as his mouth that consumed mine.

As needy as my pleas that whispered from my soul.

My hands threaded in his hair, and my body rocked against his.

Every brush spurred me higher.

"Ollie. Ollie," I whimpered, swept away in his madness. Willing to float away forever if it meant getting to be with him.

He stumbled up the three flights of stairs. The music from downstairs became a dull, vibrating hum, our hearts becoming louder as he made it through the door to his loft.

He didn't stop before he pinned me to the wall right outside his bedroom door. He pulled back, his cock straining against his jeans, pressed hot against my panties.

The man panted as he stared down at me with crazed, hungry eyes.

I searched for air. The only thing it accomplished was inhaling him. Taking on more.

Reaching out a trembling hand, I ran it slowly—tenderly—through the longer pieces of his hair. My head angled with the plea that cracked at the back of my throat. "I want this, Ollie. I want you. But I need to know this is what you want. I can't allow you to trample my heart all over again. If you take me in that room, there's no going back for me."

twenty-five
Ollie

Her words blasted through my consciousness. A reminder of all the mistakes I'd made. The continuous hurt I'd inflicted.

Forcing myself to slow down, I spread my hand out across the side of her face. Wishing I could hold all of her.

Wishing I could tell her I'd love her forever.

Instead, a confession was falling from my mouth. "This date . . . it nearly ruins me every time it comes around. But this . . . this isn't about Sydney. This is about you. This is about us. This is about finding what we lost."

My words grew low and fast. "You make everything feel different. Always have, Nikki. Like I'm someone else when I get near you. Like I'm someone better."

Those indigo eyes moved over my face. Searching and memorizing. Drinking me in. Remembering this moment for what it always should have been.

"When I went to you last year . . . I was so fucked up. But I know now, I couldn't go anywhere else. Because you made everything right when it was so fucking wrong."

"Ollie . . ."

I pulled her from the wall, the girl still in my arms, my face buried in her hair. "I need you. I need you in a way I never thought possible," I muttered, praying she'd get it.

That it was different than when I went to her a year before telling her the same thing.

This was a promise.

This time, when I moved, it wasn't frenzied or panicked like it'd been when I'd carried her upstairs. It was cautious and slow. Holding her the way she'd always deserved to be.

Tenderly.

The girl precious.

I'd always wanted to wrap her up.

Protect her.

All these years, it'd made me crazy, and I'd wished for a way to scrape it from my psyche, from who I was. It'd taken until tonight to realize she'd only driven me mad because I refused to allow her where she was always meant to be.

With me.

Mine.

I laid her out across my bed. Slowly, I crawled over her. Hovering. Staring down at her through the milky glow of the moon that spread over the room and set her aglow.

Light.

"No more, Nikki. Can't go on pretending that I don't want you. That I don't need you. I want to try to be the kind of guy you deserve."

Grief fisted my heart.

Thoughts of my sister running rampant.

If I was gonna be with Nikki, it was time I ripped myself open wide. My eyes squeezed closed, and my teeth ground together as I forced out the words. "I'm so lost, and I don't know if that vacant feeling is ever going to go away. Only thing I know is when I'm with you, it doesn't feel so vast."

Hands caressed both sides of my face, and my eyes eased open to see the girl staring up at me. Her breaths short, so much evident in her adoring gaze. Words I wasn't ready to hear. Really didn't matter if she said them aloud, anyway, because I felt them when I dipped down and kissed her.

Slow and tender, the softest kind of adoration on her tongue.

Her fingertips slipped through my beard and found their way into our kiss, running over my lips. "I'm right here, Ollie. I've always been. Waiting for you. I can't take it away, but we can hold each other through the middle of it."

I edged back, sitting up on my knees and bringing her with me. She straddled me where I knelt on the bed, this gorgeous girl wrapped around my lap.

My dick strained, and my muscles ticked.

I wanted to devour her.

Inch by inch.

I held her by the side of the neck, her pulse going wild against my palm. "Want to be right for you. Good for you."

The hint of a smile played across her lips. The girl so sexy.

Olive skin and honeyed hair and freckled cheeks.

Sunshine.

She slipped down my body until she was resting on her knees. Our bodies swayed. A breadth apart.

Her fingertips fluttered out, running down my shirt.

Need raced my veins.

She gathered the hem and began to drag it up, peeking at my face as she did. "You've always been right for me. You just need to accept that you are. That none of us are perfect. That the world is cruel, but it's also given us the greatest gift."

She dragged the shirt over my head and dropped it at her side.

A shudder ripped through me.

Lashes of fire.

That feeling again.

Energy.

"It gave us this," she murmured so softly, hands tender as they pressed to the thunder at my chest. "*Us.*"

A moan climbed my throat, and that was all I could take, and I was pulling that silky tank over her head.

No bra.

Those tiny tits perky. Nipples pebbled and hard.

God. She would be my undoing.

That moan turned to a growl, and I pushed her onto her back.

She bounced on the bed and a giggle slipped from between her lips.

"Beast," she teased.

My entire chest squeezed.

Warmth and fire and need.

My mouth went for the flat planes of her belly, kissing across the satiny skin, my hands winding in the hem of her skirt. "Don't even know if I can bring myself to get you out of this skirt. Do you have any clue what you were doing to me all night? Looking like this?" I grumbled at her stomach.

Vibrations of low laughter shook beneath my lips, and her fingers were winding in my hair. "I thought you told me the way I dressed was ridiculous."

"It is ridiculous. It's ridiculous how hard it makes me. Ridiculous how much it makes me want you. Ridiculous how much time I've spent fantasizing about peeling you out of those clothes."

Her laughter turned into a needy gasp as I started dragging off her skirt. I took her underwear with it.

Sliding the fabric down those long, slender legs until every inch of her was laid bare.

"Shit . . . ridiculous," I hissed, letting a smirk climb to my mouth. "Ridiculous how gorgeous you are."

She trembled, and her hips arched just from the heat of my stare. "Ollie, I need you."

And I knew . . . I knew that I needed her more than she could ever need me, and that was kind of fucked up, but I couldn't go on for one more second without her.

She was everything. *Everything.*

"So gorgeous," I told her, the tip of my index finger running the center of her chest, riding down, across her trembling belly.

I eased off the bed, standing beside it, watching her in the night as I shrugged out of my boots and jeans and underwear.

Her lips parted and her gaze swept over me. Want darkened

those indigo eyes.

Lust and desire and something that was so much bigger than that.

"You are what's beautiful, Ollie. So beautiful. All these years, it's been hard to look at you because I missed you so much."

Sadness tinted the words, and I knew it came from that hurt I'd inflicted. Years of rejecting us both.

I reached in the drawer, quick to cover my cock, which was pointing for the sky, begging for her, before I was crawling back over her, between her thighs.

Desire brimmed and boiled, threatening to blow.

I cradled one side of her face in my hand.

"Sunshine," I whispered.

Emotion thick, her face pinched, and her chest heaved with each shallow breath.

I wanted to swallow every single one of them down. Keep them tucked away as a reminder of the way I felt at this moment. So I'd never forget.

"Are you mine, Ollie?" whispered from her swollen, damp lips.

My mouth brushed hers, tasting the words. "I've always been."

"Then take me." She wound her arms around my neck. "Keep me."

A thunder lit up my heart, pulse raging as it careened through my veins, our bodies catching as I nestled deeper between her thighs.

Her pussy slick and wet, my cock hard and ready.

That beast she was always all too pleased to remind me I was wanted to devour her. Take her fast and wild and hard.

There'd be plenty of time for that later.

Tonight, I wrapped her up and nuzzled my face in her hair. My murmur climbed into the dense air. "You owned me from the first day that I met you."

She hooked her arm around my head, her perfect tits pressed to my chest, her body arching, begging for mine. "I had no idea that day that you'd become the focus of my life. The one I longed for. My whole life, all it took was a glance from you, and I knew I was exactly where I was supposed to be."

Emotion clutched and clenched. I eased back a fraction, rubbing against the slick heat that burned between her thighs.

The tip of my cock caught.

Our breaths hitched, and our gazes tangled.

For the flash of a second, it was like I felt everything snapping into place.

Worlds aligning and spirits syncing.

Us.

She was right.

Exactly the way it was supposed to be.

She stared at me through the shadows, her lips parting as I pressed just the tip of my dick in to the silky welcome of her body.

"Tell me this is what you want," I grunted, holding back.

"I want you more than you could ever know." Her words struck me like arrows, and that was all I needed.

I nudged deeper into her warmth.

The girl so damned tiny that she was gasping and my jaw was clenching as I slowly spread her.

Felt so much like the first time I'd taken her, when she'd cried out from the pain and begged me for more, and I'd held her and whispered that I'd love her forever.

Didn't matter that I'd only been a kid. Seventeen. I knew I'd never be given a greater gift than that.

And somehow, this felt just as big.

Because the girl?

The girl was giving her trust.

Even when I knew I didn't deserve it. That I hadn't *earned* it. But fuck . . . I was gonna try.

"Shit, Nikki," I wheezed as I took her by the caps of her delicate shoulders, trying to hold myself in check when this girl had always made me lose all control.

She panted, her legs dropping wide, jagged gasps from her mouth as she adjusted to me again. Nails sank into my shoulders, and we both held tight until I fully buried myself in her body.

Nothing had ever felt so right.

"Are you okay?" I managed, propping myself up on an elbow so I could look down at her.

Need prowled my spine, begging me to move.

To take her right.

Those eyes met mine, so intense, that feeling gripping, sinking all the way inside.

She looked up at me like maybe I might be her sun, the way she was mine, her voice scratchy when she said, "You always take my breath away."

My forehead dropped to hers. "Fuck . . . Nikki . . . Sunshine."

She splayed her hands out wide across my back, and I was gathering her in my arms, getting her as close as I could get her. I began to move, measured rocks of my hips as I took her.

Stroke after stroke.

Friction and gravity.

Her whimpers struck the air, and I held her, took her slow and deep while I kissed her like the treasure she was.

While I cherished and adored.

Because Rex was right.

We never knew how many days we'd be given, and I'd already wasted too many.

Her breaths came harder. "Please." It was a prayer from her mouth.

I shifted back to kneeling, taking her with me, and the girl began to ride me like that was what she'd been made to do.

Motherfucker, if it wasn't the most magical thing.

Her body stretched out like a sensuous band, head tipped back, her tits in my face.

Desperate hands yanked at my hair. I licked at one of those dark nipples, swirling it with my tongue and sucking it in to my mouth.

I pressed my thumb to her clit, winding her up.

She whimpered, "Yes."

It was like the girl cast a single-word spell.

Yes.

She went off, an orgasm streaking through every cell of her

body. Energy and light.

She writhed on me, walls clutching my dick so damned perfectly.

Taking every inch of me hostage.

Held by this girl.

The way I'd always been.

Yes.

Bliss.

It exploded, splintering out.

Blinding my eyes and battering my senses.

I came with a shout that I released right at the center of that giving heart.

She sagged her sweat-slicked body against mine, and I burrowed my face in the sweet essence that radiated from her neck.

Nikki sighed, my name her breath.

Couldn't believe that I was holding her like this. I tightened my arms around her waist and held her as we drifted on that energy that swam around us.

Soft, lulling waves.

Comfort and all things right.

Light.

Yes.

Yes.

I'd give this girl my life.

twenty-six
Ollie

"Someone has some explaining to do."

Couldn't stop the roll of my eyes as I climbed into Rex's huge-ass work truck.

"You think I could at least get in before you start riding my ass? Might be just as easy to roll down your window and shout it at me where I'm standing on the sidewalk."

Drive-by style.

When I'd gotten his texts at the ass crack of dawn, claiming that he needed my help with a project, I knew I was in trouble. Wasn't like I wasn't asking for it, mauling Nikki on the dance floor right in front of our friends before I'd dragged her off like some kind of madman.

I just couldn't hold it back a second longer.

That band had stretched too thin before it had finally snapped.

Rex kicked up a smirk that he punted my direction. "Pretty sure it's not me doing the whole ass riding."

Punk had the nerve to waggle his brows.

I shook my head, but there was no stopping my grin as I

hopped inside his truck and snapped the seat belt into place.

Rex pulled away from Olive's, the diesel engine loud as he accelerated down the road.

From the side, I looked at him. "So, did you actually need help this morning or did you just need to say I told you so to my face, sooner rather than later?"

Low laughter escaped him. Totally at my expense. "Little of both, man, a little of both."

We headed out of town toward the old buildings on Row that he and Broderick would be turning into luxury condos and God knew what else.

It still impressed the hell out of me that my best friend, who had been little more than a handyman, had taken the small construction company and built it into a massive enterprise.

Each project got bigger and more complicated. Dude was leaving his stamp all over this small city.

"You don't have a crew for this shit? It's barely nine in the morning, on a Sunday, mind you."

He kneaded the steering wheel as he made a right, hitting the two-lane road that led out of the north end of town. Taking another right up about half a mile would lead to the lower lake where we'd spent all our time as kids, and the old warehouses that lined the river up on Row were about a mile up from that.

"Yeah, yeah. I know, your lazy ass always wants to sleep half the day away."

That was not the case this morning.

This morning, the only thing I'd wanted to do was stay wrapped up in Nikki instead of leaving her naked and twisted in my sheets. The girl so damned gorgeous, all lit up in the emerging morning light.

Rex leered over at me like the punk he was, pure suggestion bleeding from his words. "You do look a little tired this morning. Didn't get a whole lot of sleep last night?"

I chuckled under my breath.

Asshole.

"Nah . . . didn't get a whole lot of sleep last night," I admitted, fingers scraping at the seam of my jeans, needing to do something with my hands. Agitation and residual need clamored through me, leaving my insides scrambled.

My mind was still trying to catch up with what had gone down last night.

Thing was, my heart was already there.

The girl inevitable.

Should have known it all along.

After we'd finally given in?

It was on.

Nikki and I had gone at it again and again. Hard and rough and tender and soft and every-fucking-thing between.

We'd collapse in each other's arms, drifting off for a half hour or so before one of us would once again be seeking the other in the night.

Had taken all I had to peel myself away from her sleeping form when my phone had lit up with a string of texts, Rex prodding me out of that place that had become a sanctuary.

"About time, man," he said with a harsh shake of his head.

Didn't even know if I should deny it or play dumb.

He was right.

It was about time.

"So, what changed?" he attempted, stealing a glimpse at me before he looked back out through the windshield.

Trees hugged the narrow road, whooshing by as he wound deeper into the area where the woods became dense, giving way to the tall, thin, spindly trees that made up the forest that surrounded the lake and river.

"Not sure what you mean."

Deflecting.

Sometimes that was all I had because I didn't think I had an answer for that.

"Are you kidding me?" Rex laughed an incredulous sound and gave a harsh shake of his head. "You've been tiptoeing around this thing with Nikki for years. Don't act like you haven't wanted her all this time. Second she'd walked into the room, your spine would go stiff. Willing to put down bets your dick did, too."

I rubbed my hand down my beard, taunting him. "Looking at my dick now?"

"You wish, asshole. They don't make glasses that thick."

"Now who's wishing?" I tossed back.

Both of us laughed for a second before we fell into silence.

"Seriously," he prodded, "what changed?"

Could feel him pushing, edging me a direction I wasn't sure I was ready to go.

I blinked through the protective anger that wound back through me when I really evaluated it.

Yeah.

I'd felt something coming.

Something wicked and dark.

But there'd been a tipping point.

"Finding her apartment that way . . . knowing she could have been in danger . . . that someone might have hurt her?"

My teeth ground so hard I could hear my jaw popping in my ears. "It . . . brought everything crashing down. Turns out the punk had been leaving notes on her car, too. Just the idea of someone hurting her made me want to hunt down any fucker who even looked at her wrong and silence that threat forever. I guess that was the moment I realized I could no longer stand the thought of her being anywhere else than with me."

He blew out a strained breath. "So, this wasn't you pulling any of that one-night bullshit? You know Nikki doesn't deserve that, and you know she wants more than that."

He slowed and took a right onto the bumpy dirt road that wound down the hill.

The glittering river stretched out below us, trees reaching for the sky like they were offering up prayers to the sun.

In the distance, the roofs of the old buildings jutted up through the cover of the branches, a reminder that this area had once not been so desolate.

My chest clutched when we wound around a corner that opened to a field of purple blazing stars that swayed in the breeze. A million memories slammed me. One after one.

"This way."

"Follow me."

"We'll be together forever."

Sydney's sweet voice as she'd run and explored and looked at the world with so much wonder in her eyes. Nikki and I in tow.

I pushed out a sigh. "Why do you think I've been ignoring it for so long? Last thing I want to do is hurt her. Makes me insane to hold something so precious and know that, chances are, in the end, I'm going to crush it in my hands."

"And why would you do that?" Wasn't so much of a question as a challenge.

I looked out over the landscape. "Men are prone to destroying beautiful things."

He swallowed hard. "Maybe. Unless they finally open their damned eyes and see that beauty for what it's worth. Make the choice to build it up. Protect it and keep it."

Unease wound through me, and I swore my throat was closing tight.

Didn't want to go there.

But Nikki deserved for me to.

To stop fucking hiding.

"What happens when you want to protect it and fail anyway?" It was a wheeze I forced out. My inadequacy a glaring defeat.

Rex came to a stop in a small clearing that had been made.

Equipment and machinery had already been delivered and was set up within a temporary chain-link fence as they prepared for construction.

He hesitated for a moment, squeezing the wheel, staring out the windshield to the splintered wood and crumbling stone of the weathered building. "We do our best, Ollie. We live and we love. We cherish and we hold."

He killed the engine, set his hand on the latch, and looked over at me. "We fight with everything we have, even when we know we might lose."

He clicked open the door. "We do it because we can't do anything else. Because we love so hard, loving is the only thing we can do. Rynna and my kids? I love them so damned much, Ollie. With every single thing I have. Never thought I'd get that chance, and I'd be nothing but a bastard and a fool not to recognize it."

His message slammed me on all sides. Pointed and demanding. Forcing me to evaluate the way I'd been living.

He climbed out and moved toward the bank of the river, staring out over it. I got out and followed.

"Do you remember playing here? Growing up? Running wild?" There was something somber in his tone.

"Of course, I remember."

Pretty much had spent the last fourteen years living in the past.

"We were all close."

I glanced at him, no clue what had climbed into the tone of his voice.

"Yeah. Not many people get lucky enough to grow up the way we did. Remain friends the way we have."

Saw the way the muscles in his arms twitched and bunched, apprehension in his stance. "I need you to know you aren't alone in the regrets, either, man. That you don't shoulder that alone."

A gust of doubt rustled through, my nerve endings zapping with unease.

"You're wrong, Rex. She was my sister. My responsibility."

Wasn't trying to be a dick. It was just the cold, bitter truth.

His eyes flashed in a kind of grief I didn't quite understand. "It was my fault, too. I was there that night. Remember? You think I don't wish I could go back and change everything? I'd give anything to. But I can't. And neither can you. Both of us have to accept that."

"I was responsible for her." My words were a low, harsh rasp.

He dropped his head, his hands landing on his hips as he struggled with what to say as he stared at the ground. "Ollie—"

"Just don't, Rex." Shooting my hand out between us, I cut him off before he could get whatever bullshit he was going out of his mouth. Didn't need another person to tell me it wasn't my fault when I knew full well that it was. "I don't need a therapist. I need a friend. That's it."

Something moved through his eyes.

Regret and . . . guilt.

Glaring guilt.

I tried to process it.

He blew out a breath toward his boots. "Fine. Just forget it."

Good damned idea.

Yesterday was hard enough without Rex trying to make it more difficult. The worry about Nikki had only compounded it.

Now that the threat was gone, I just wanted to forget it all.

Push it into the past where it all belonged.

Question was if I was capable of that.

I forced some lightness into my words. "Ready to tell me why you had to go and drag me out of my bed when I'd finally gotten Nikki into it?"

He laughed a little, shooting me a grin. "Sorry about that."

"Not cool, man. You owe me big."

"Maybe this will suffice."

"What's that?"

With his chin, he gestured toward the row of run-down buildings. They'd been near falling down when we'd played in them, and time sure hadn't improved them. They were covered in graffiti, there was garbage everywhere, and the frames were sagging toward the ground like they didn't have the will to stand for much longer.

"Back building will become upscale condos, one of which will go to Nikki. First two will be what becomes the hotel and shops."

He looked down the riverbank before he eyed me carefully. "Plan to put in a couple of restaurants and a bar. Broderick and I want you to open a second Olive's here."

Stunned, I stared at him, minutes or an hour passing, waiting for the punch line. "You're serious," I finally managed when he didn't say anything.

"Hell, yeah, I'm serious. You know Olive's is the best bar in Gingham Lakes. Brody plans to make this a destination. Only the best. So, of course, it only makes sense to add the best bar to the list of attractions. He's funding the upfront costs, but you'll have shares in the entire development."

"You want me to partner with you and Brody?" Still wasn't making sense of it, shock lurching through my senses.

"It's not like we weren't partnered on Olive's to begin with."

"Yeah . . . but I hired RG Construction to redo the building."

No risk on his end.

He looked over at me. "You act like you haven't been investing in this city. Taking failing businesses and breathing new life in to them."

"But it's always been my money on the line."

If I failed, it was on me.

It's your fault.

I trusted you.

You were supposed to take care of her.

You promised, you'd take care of her.

It should have been me. It should have been me.

In silence, we both stood there while I contemplated. Warred with all the reasons I shouldn't do this.

I inhaled sharply, filling my lungs with the scent of the river and damp earth and possibility. "You guys really trust me to be a partner?"

"Wouldn't ask you if we didn't." Rex started back for the truck before he paused to look at me from over his shoulder. "Think maybe the only person you need to prove to that you can be trusted is yourself."

I stood there, staring at him as he hopped back into the truck.

Business done.

My attention darted between him and the old buildings, imagining what this place would look like one day, while Rex just sat in the truck, giving me time.

Finally, I hefted out a breath and strode back for the truck. I hopped inside, slamming the door shut as I said, "I'm in."

He started the engine. "Good."

I scrubbed a sweaty palm on the thigh of my jeans. "And don't count on Nikki needing that condo."

Rex laughed, loud and with a grin. "Had a feeling you might say that."

twenty-seven
Ollie

The low grumble of my bike filled my ears as I eased into one of the parking spaces in front of Pepper's Pies. The damned grin plastered on my face was so big, there was no chance I could wipe it off.

Inside, heads turned at the sound of my rumbling bike, but the only one that mattered was the girl who stood in front of one of the booths right by the window, her head jerking up and those eyes meeting with mine through the glass.

My chest tightened.

That feeling hitting me hard.

So intense, I could feel it riding through my veins. Itching through me. Same way as I was itching to get my girl on the back of my bike and those long legs wrapped around my waist.

Kicking the stand and killing the engine, I swung my leg over the side just as Nikki was peeking her head outside.

A smile danced on her pretty face. "What are you doing here?"

I glanced at my watch. "You get off at two."

"And?" It was a playful challenge.

"And I missed you. You have a problem with that?" I all but growled, stalking her way, looping an arm around her waist and tugging her against me as she stepped all the way out onto the sidewalk.

Hands clutching my shoulders, she bent back, swaying as she smiled up at me. "No, Beast. I definitely don't have a problem with that."

"Good," I told her. "Go get your stuff."

"Bossy," she tossed back as she started toward the door.

I swatted her sweet ass. "You have no idea."

She yelped, and then giggled. "Why do I get the feeling you're going to take all kinds of pleasure in educating me on that fact?"

A smirk caught on one side of my mouth. "Maybe you do have an idea."

Her laugh was low.

Sexy.

"Oh, Ollie. We're gonna have so much fun."

My smile went soft.

Yeah.

We were. And we'd wasted too much time, and I was so over that. "Hurry up and get that sweet body back to me."

"I need to change," she said as she was stepping back inside.

"I'll wait."

Those pink lips twisted in a teasing pout. "You'd better."

Like I was going anywhere.

Not without her.

Five minutes later, she was bursting back out the door, pretty much skipping her way over to me where I was waiting by my bike.

She looked so young when she was like this.

Free and excited.

"Come here," I told her, taking her hand and guiding her to stand between my knees. I situated the helmet I'd brought for her on her head, tucking some of those warm, honeyed locks back away from her face.

The girl's breaths came shorter just from that simple touch.

And that's what this felt like.

Simple.

Simple and complicated and perfect.

Like it'd been coming all along.

Or maybe it'd just been set to pause, and we had to pick up where we'd left off, even though I knew it couldn't be as *simple* as forgetting all those hurtful years stuck in the middle of us.

Only thing I could do now was make up for them.

"Where are we going?" she asked, eyes glinting with a thrill.

"You'll see," I told her, moving to straddle my bike and taking her with me.

"Ah, come on, Ollie. That's totally not fair. I want to know." Her voice was filled with laughter.

She slid in behind me, the insides of her thighs pressing to the outsides of mine.

Electricity.

It zinged and shook.

A chuckle rumbled free as she wrapped those arms around me. I patted her hands that locked to my stomach. "Don't you trust me?"

I could feel the draw of her breath, the way she snuggled as close as she could get, holding on tight.

Her words dropped so low I could barely hear them. "Yes, Ollie. I trust you. I trust you more than anyone else."

Trust.

It was the first time I wanted her to give me hers.

Swallowing any heaviness down, I kicked over the engine, rolled my bike back, my feet guiding us, before I hit the street.

I kept our speed low.

Controlled.

Careful of my girl who was hugging me from behind. Her heart beating into my back. Hard and wild and drumming with passion.

Washing me in that warmth.

We headed through town, taking a couple of turns, before I hit the road that led out toward the river and lakes. The air shifted as we left the traffic behind, full, lush trees growing up at the sides of the two-lane road and closing us in.

It felt like an embrace.

A welcome back to the place where we always should have been. I passed by the turn-off to the lake.

We'd go there one day. To our sacred place. But this felt too raw and new to dive so deeply into the past.

I'd give us time. Time to adjust.

My bike glided around a swooping curve in the road.

Swore, it felt like we were flying.

Nothing but the feel of the wind and the sound of my bike and the aura of us to fill our senses.

Suspended.

Taken.

Funny because I'd never felt so close to home.

I slowed when the dirt road approached, and I could feel her shiver of excitement that zipped through her body when I began to wind down toward the river.

We curved and wound, rounding a corner, and that same endless expanse of purple blazing stars came into view where they grew along the riverbank.

Instead of continuing on to the old buildings were Rex and Broderick would be developing—where I'd be opening up a second bar, which still blew my mind—I took a right on what was nothing more than an overgrown, bumpy trail down toward the river. It rippled a glittering blue.

I eased to a stop beneath the big tree where we used to play.

Its thick branches were stretched out like protection.

A canopy of security.

The old rope swing we'd swung from a thousand times as kids was now frayed where it hung from one of the branches that reached over the river, swaying in the light breeze, in time with the spikey blazing stars that poked up through the high grasses.

I cut the engine.

Peace covered us.

The only sounds were the gurgling river and the thunder of our hearts.

For a few minutes, we just sat there. Taking it in.

Finally, I took her hand, and a shiver of nervous anticipation rolled through her. Like she wasn't quite sure why we were there or what my intentions were.

I started to walk backward, tugging her along. "Come here, I want to show you something."

A giggle slipped from between those flirty lips.

So easy and sweet.

Carrying on the wind. "You do, huh?" she teased. "What exactly do you want to show me? I know your style of show and tell, Oliver Preston."

Laughter rumbled in my chest. "I'll show you plenty of that later, sweet girl, but right now, I had something else in mind."

Her brows rose. "Really? You have something else in mind? Tell me why I don't believe you. I don't even know how I'm walkin' right now. You might as well keep me tied to your bed."

Lust twisted through me.

Hard.

Fast.

Couldn't even come close to stopping the visions that assaulted me with just the thought of getting inside this girl again.

Over the last week, I'd taken her over and over. Every second I could get her.

"That sounds like a great idea. I knew you were a smart one."

Another giggle. "Smart? I call it needy."

"I like you needy and begging my name."

"Is that so?" She was stumbling along as I hauled her toward the tree, a smile written on every inch of her face.

Hell.

I could see it written all over her body.

That rail-thin body I'd had to pretend wasn't close to my taste so I could try to rid her from my mind for all those years. Going after girls who were exactly her opposite. Praying when I closed my eyes, I wouldn't see her face.

Impossible.

She was the only thing I'd ever seen.

"That's so. I promise to make you beg it a little bit later, but right now, I want you to sit right here."

I took her by the outside of her shoulders and led her to the exact spot, urging her to sit down.

"What are you doing?" she laughed through the words, shaking her head by following along.

She settled on the small incline under the shade of the tree.

I took a step back, my attention rapt.

"Perfect," I said.

She rocked her knees that were bent, tucking her bottom lip between her teeth like she was both shy and relishing the way I was looking at her.

Without a doubt, I looked like a starving man. All I wanted was to eat her all over again.

Consume and devour.

I backed up a few more steps so I could better take her in.

"What are you looking at?" she finally asked, her voice breathy from that connection that sizzled through the heated air.

Two of us alive in the other.

How the hell had I lived without this?

Without her?

"You."

"I know you're *looking* at me, but why?"

A grin pulled at one side of my mouth.

"That's exactly where you were. Right there."

I could never forget it.

She frowned. "Ollie, what in the world are you talking about?"

I pointed at her. "That's where you were the day I finally admitted it."

Her brows drew closer, and she minimally shook her head in question.

I took a slow step back her direction. "When I admitted to myself that you were something more than my best friend. When I realized you made me feel different."

I turned my gaze away, lifting it toward the wind as I let some of the memories pummel me. Hit me and slam me.

Instead of hating them, I welcomed them.

Finally, I looked back at her. "You were whispering with Sydney. She said something about a guy, and I just knew it.

Knew it. That you had a boyfriend or someone had kissed you."

I took another step forward, and she sucked in a shivered breath.

Energy pulsed.

"I'll never forget the way that felt, Nikki. The way my stomach balled up in a fist and it felt like my heart was gonna bust right out of my chest. I played it off that I was just looking out for you, but it was more."

One step closer, and I dropped to my knees in front of her, my hands going to her knees. I palmed them, dipped my head in closer, my mouth an inch from hers "You were more."

She reached out and cupped the side of my face, tenderness moving through her expression as she studied me. Her thumb traced along the hollow of my eye, and her head tipped in emphasis. "I think you were always more. I just didn't know what that meant yet."

I lunged at her, tackling her to the soft earth. She gasped and yelped, and then laughed.

That sweet, sweet sound floated on the wind.

Twisted through me.

I pushed up onto my hands and stared down at her. The girl who'd always been my forever.

There she was, all laid out on a bed of blazing stars.

Purple a halo around her head.

I reached out and plucked one, twirled the stem between my thumb and index finger. I brushed the tip down her cheek.

Softly.

Her lips parted on a sigh.

"Did you know the first time I saw you, what I noticed was your eyes? I thought they were the exact same color as these flowers, but like they were floatin' through the air. Transparent. Like I could see right inside of you. I won't ever forget that moment, either."

Her fingertips scratched through my beard. "I don't think I could ever forget a moment with you, Oliver Preston."

I kissed at the tips of her fingers, wanting to take in every bit of her.

The movement was almost playful, but my words were somber. "We've got a lot of bad memories, Nikki."

She nodded slow. "Yeah. But we have a lot of good ones, too. That's what makes up life. The good and the bad. We couldn't have one without the other. We couldn't share a life without experiencing both sides of it."

"That what you want? To share a life with me?" My voice was gruff.

"I always wanted that."

"Good," I said, making her squeal when I suddenly reached around her and flipped our positions. She straddled me at the waist, her hands on my chest, all that hair blowing around her, whipped by the wind.

Stirring our spirits.

I tightened my hold. "Don't think you could get rid of me if you tried."

She grinned. "And why would I want to go and do something like that? Not when all my matchmaking skills have finally started to work in my favor."

"Oh, you think you're responsible for this, too, huh?"

She widened her eyes. "Um, hello, I am the Orgasm Fairy."

"And who's the one giving them?" I teased. "Guess I'll have to stop handing them out like they're candy and then we can decide who's really responsible."

Nikki dipped down, pressing her mouth to mine.

All kinds of possessive.

Just the way I wanted her.

Then I could feel the weight of her grin. "Don't you dare. You owe me all the orgasms. All. Of. Them. Forever."

"Greedy girl."

"Accept it. You created a monster."

"I thought you said I was the monster. Ogre, to be correct."

"I told you . . . you're my beast. Get used to it."

I laughed.

A laugh that came from my belly, but I was pretty sure it originated in the depths of me. In that dark place that was somehow feeling a fraction lighter.

Like maybe I was finally letting a little of me go.

Didn't mean I wouldn't still battle demons.

But what Nikki and I had going?

Maybe it was stronger.

That's what I wanted to be.

Strong for her.

Right for her.

I brushed my knuckles down the defined curve of her face, and she leaned into my touch. "Everything I have, I want to give to you. I belong to you, Nikki."

And I wasn't going to let anything get in the way of that.

An hour later, I weaved back into town, Nikki clinging to me where she sat on the back of my bike.

Wasn't sure anything had ever felt so right.

I rumbled to a stop in front of the old market that we used to come to all the time as kids, saving up coins so we could go in to buy ice cream or candy or sodas.

The second I stopped, Nikki was climbing off and going through the buckle of the helmet, grinning back at me as she headed for the entrance since she'd said she would just run in really quick to grab something to make for us for dinner tonight.

I hopped off, stalking right behind her.

She'd barely made it onto the sidewalk when I snagged her wrist, spun her around, and pinned her to the wall.

Plastered myself against that sweet body.

I kissed her hard.

Tongue gliding against hers.

My hands wrapped up in that honeyed hair.

She released a tiny moan, and I rubbed myself against her, and she was moaning again before she was laughing and pushing me back. "What are you doing, Ollie? You're gonna get us arrested for indecency."

"The only think indecent around here is how hot you look."

"Ollie," she admonished, a flush lighting up those cheeks.

Sunshine.

"What? My girlfriend is smoking hot."

Her eyes went wide.

So yeah, it was the first time I'd said it in what felt like a hundred years.

I'd said it before.

But I'd never gotten to claim it.

I grabbed her hand and started leading her toward the entrance, my voice lifting a little louder than it probably needed to be.

Strike that.

It was completely, one-hundred percent necessary.

"My girlfriend is hot!" I shouted.

"Ollie."

Nikki's head whipped around, wondering what attention we'd gathered, but she was giggling under her breath. She struggled to keep up as I hauled her inside and grabbed a cart.

I started pushing it down the first aisle.

"I thought I was just running in by myself?" she asked.

"What, I just wanted to be near my girlfriend."

Yep, the words were elevated again.

A woman who was probably only a handful of years older than us cut us a glance.

I totally ignored it. "What are we having for dinner? I'm going to need to hang down in the bar for a few hours to make sure things are running smoothly, but I won't stay too long"

"Chicken and potatoes. And you don't have to take off more time, Ollie. You've barely been down there all week."

"What? I just want to be with my girlfriend." The last I all but shouted.

An old lady blushed, peeking our way, her husband grinning wide.

"My girlfriend is gorgeous, isn't she?" I asked them as they ambled by. I swept an arm at Nikki like she was a prize.

That's exactly what she was.

"Sure is," the old guy agreed, "almost as pretty as mine."

His wife shushed him with a blush, and I was grinning so

fucking hard I thought I was gonna break my face.

Nikki's smile was just about as big, but she was shaking her head, tugging at my hand like she needed to get me out of there before I caused any more of a scene. "Are you insane? You're going to get us kicked out of here."

"Wouldn't be the first time," I told her.

"Uh, yeah, and the last time I had to have my mama come pick me up at the station because you and Rex had knocked that whole display over playing chase. Whole wall of glass mayonnaise jars smashed on the ground. It wasn't pretty."

"But you're pretty," I shot at her.

"Ollie." She was smiling as she searched my eyes, clearly wondering what had gotten into me.

She had.

She so absolutely had.

I yanked her close to me. "I want everyone to know it, Nikki. That you're mine. No more hiding."

She set both of those hands on my face and hiked up on her tiptoes. She pressed the gentlest kiss to my lips. "No more hiding."

"C'mere," I told her, voice going soft as I wound her in front of me, wrapping my arms around her and taking the cart again.

She giggled and sank against my chest, my mouth planting kisses along the side of her jaw as we wandered down the aisle. "Mine," I whispered against her temple.

"Nikki?"

The voice stopped both of us in our tracks, and our attention jerked to the source.

There was Sammie coming the other direction, a baby sleeping in her arms and her husband pushing a cart beside her.

Bottled rage rumbled in that ugly, dark space inside of me. I knew it wasn't gone. There were some things that didn't just go away.

Like the fury I felt that some asshole had hurt her in some way.

Nikki had confessed to me a few days ago that she was having trouble sleeping because she was so worried about her sister. That her sister hadn't called her or come to her, and Nikki was fearing she wouldn't be able to sit idle for much longer.

Worried her sister might be in trouble.

Surprise streaked across Sammie's face as she took in the two of us.

Nikki was still caged between the cart and me, my head barely angling toward them, two of us about as close as we could get in a public place.

I could feel the strain return to Nikki, and she unwound herself from my hold and cleared her throat.

Sammie actually grinned.

Wry and knowing.

Eyes so close to the same as Nikki's were locked on me for a beat before she turned her attention to Nikki. "Looks like we have some catching up to do."

A nervous giggle escaped from Nikki, and she fidgeted with her hair, trying to straighten it which was impossible after the ride on the bike. She peeked back at me. "Yeah, we definitely have some catching up to do."

Nikki seemed to shake the surprise off and stepped toward her sister, lowering her voice. "How have you been?"

Awareness moved through Sammie's expression, and my eyes were locked on her husband.

Studying.

Searching.

Watching for any sort of reaction that might be off.

Sammie glanced over at her husband.

There was no warning for her to keep quiet. No hardness. Just a soft understanding in his eyes.

The anger that threatened to boil inside of me eased back into a simmer. I was pretty sure this guy wasn't the one responsible for whatever Sammie was going through.

Sammie turned back to Nikki. "I've been good."

Swore, a thousand unsaid words were offered between the two of them.

Nikki suddenly reached out. "Gimme that baby."

Light laughter filtered from Sammie. "Bossy."

"I'm your big sister. It's your job to listen to me."

"You wish," Sammie tossed back at her, but she was passing a sleeping bundle off to Nikki.

Nikki took the baby, a soft sound leaving her mouth as she shifted the tiny thing and set her against her chest. The little girl's head turned to the side, still sleeping, face scrunched up as she snuggled against Nikki's warmth.

Nikki bounced her.

Sometimes it was a little too much when your connection to someone was so intense.

Because I could feel her spirit doing some crazy thing. Making the air seem too thin.

She looked up at me with those indigo eyes.

Adoring.

Hugging the baby to her chest, she whispered up at me. "Ollie . . . this is my niece, Penelope. Isn't she incredible?"

Her smile was so soft I felt it cut right through the center of me.

Tentatively, I reached out and ran my knuckle down the baby's soft, plump cheek. "She's beautiful."

Nikki looked back down, her voice not intended for me. "She's the most beautiful thing I've ever seen."

I stepped back, watching her as she rocked and cooed and pressed kisses to the crown of Penelope's head before she reluctantly passed her back to Sammie.

The sisters embraced with the baby between them, the two of them whispering words, ones I knew were of encouragement.

Because that was Nikki.

Spreading her light.

Giving.

Doing her best to pour a little good into this wicked world.

twenty-eight
Nikki

I stood at the wall of windows that looked out on the city spread out below me. It was nothing but a maze of twinkling lights—streets and neighborhoods and cars.

Behind me, the door creaked open.

At the sound, my spirit jumped into a frenzy, instant and eager as it stretched out for him.

Slowly, I shifted to look at Ollie who had frozen in the doorway.

My breath hitched.

Caught up in his potency.

He stood stock still. I thought maybe he couldn't believe I was standing there any more than I could, unable to fathom he was coming home.

And he was coming home to me.

"Are you already finished?" I asked, flashing him a smile as I turned the rest of the way around and moved into the kitchen. "I thought you decided you needed to stay a little longer tonight?"

He stepped into the loft and clicked the door shut behind him. "Think I was missin' someone."

"Is that so?" I went to the stove where I was making a lemon garlic chicken and roasted potatoes. I peeked over at him, lifting a shoulder as I did. "And just who was it you were missin'?"

So what if I put a little flirt in it? This was my man we were talking about.

He stalked across the space, coming right up behind me.

Towering.

Eclipsing.

He was all too quick to tug me against that wall of muscle. The man was so big, I could wear him like a blanket.

He gathered up my hair in one hand so he could run his mouth along the sensitive flesh of my neck. "You," he murmured.

Chills flashed. Streaking across my skin. That feeling took a dive directly in that pool of desire that had taken up permanent residence low in my belly.

"Mmm, that's good," I whispered, bringing the wooden spoon to my mouth to test the sauce. "Because I was thinking about you."

"You'd better be." I could feel his smile at the side of my neck.

"Like I ever stop. How was it downstairs?" I asked.

"Busy."

"And you're here?"

"It's where you are, isn't it?"

Butterflies.

They should have been impossible after all this time. After everything we'd been through. Yet, there I stood, feeling like that fifteen-year-old girl who'd been kissed for the first time under a waterfall.

"Besides, I was pretty sure I could smell you making dinner all the way down there. Stomach was growling."

He kissed up and down my neck. "Among other things."

"Insatiable."

"I thought you told me earlier that you wanted all the orgasms?"

It plucked a laugh free. "You have me there."

"See, we're completely on the same page. Think we totally have what it takes to make this work."

I could feel the tease tinting every single one of his words.

Today had been bliss.

It just kept getting better and better.

"Want a taste?" I asked, spooning some sauce onto a spoon and lifting it to his mouth.

He groaned when it touched those full, full lips, framed by that beard that turned me on more than should be possible.

Everything about him was sexy.

That monstrous body and those knowing eyes and those demanding hands.

And God . . . that sound he was making at the back of his throat when he tasted the sauce.

"That's it, you're tryin' to ruin me, aren't you? Knowing my girl is up here, waiting on me while I'm downstairs working. Then I show up, and you're wearing *this*."

He flattened his palms on the short slip of a nightgown I was wearing. Silky and trimmed in lace, slits up the sides that were entirely unnecessary considering it barely covered my bottom in the first place.

I knew Ollie would love it.

His teeth nipped at my earlobe. Catching and releasing.

Didn't mean I wasn't completely ensnared.

I peeked back at him, unable to stop the grin that pulled to one side of my mouth. "Someone once told me the way to a man's heart was through his stomach. Well . . . that and rough, sweaty, amazing sex."

I bumped back into him and had to stifle a groan.

He was already hard and needy for me.

Was it wrong that I loved it?

That I reveled in the fact that one brush of a hand, one look, and we were both laid bare?

A rumble rolled from his chest and slid through me like a caress. "I like this someone. Tell them I approve."

I giggled. "You can thank my grandma."

Easy laughter rippled from his lips. "Oh God . . . your

grandma is really gonna want to kick my ass now, isn't she? God knows she always wanted to back in the day. She'd see me coming up the road, and the first thing I would hear was her shouting from the porch that she was watching me."

"That's because you were nothin' but trouble."

Those massive arms tightened around my waist, and he nuzzled his face under my jaw. "Gave her plenty of ammunition to hate me."

I tsked quietly, loving the feel of his mouth where he was kissing on the cap of my shoulder. "She loved you."

Obviously, she still did.

"Hardly."

I stilled a little, hoping he'd hear the truth of my words. "You have it all wrong again, Ollie. You're impossible not to love."

His hands slipped down to the fronts of my thighs, riding up. "Could use a little of that lovin' right now."

I shivered and tried not to moan. "Think we better start on the stomach part before we get too distracted."

He ran his nose through my hair.

Chills scattered.

"This kind of distraction is worth it, don't you think, Sunshine?"

My knees went weak when he spread his hands out across my belly, the feel of him and the silky fabric gliding through the center of me.

"I think you're gonna need your strength," I breathed.

Another growl.

"You're in so much trouble, Nikki Walters. So much trouble."

"I can't wait," I told him.

Peeling himself away, he pulled two plates from the cabinet and poured a glass of wine for me and a scotch for himself. We plated our food and moved to the long high-top table that took up most of his kitchen space.

The view breathtaking.

The city and the night and the man sitting angled right next to me.

We ate and laughed.

We drank and reminisced.

Old bonds strengthening and new ones forming.

We tiptoed around the mention of Sydney, ignoring how it seemed as if she was right there in the middle of us. I couldn't help but feel she kept coming closer and closer. Filling up the space between us and forcing us to look at the things that might be a true threat.

The things that would rip us apart.

I'd never been so sure of it than when Ollie suddenly palmed my knee under the table.

Though this time, it was different than the flirty, playful touches. A current of severity moved through it, and his voice went hoarse. "I missed you, Nikki."

"You said that," I teased, going back to what he'd said when he'd come upstairs.

He shook his head, refusing the lightness, and I knew he was stepping into the rough terrain we'd avoided.

Both of us knowing it was there.

Underfoot.

Unsure if we could navigate it.

"No, Nikki. I *missed* you. All these years, I *missed* you. So bad that I could physically feel another piece of myself missing."

His words shivered through me like the warmest breeze, and he reached over and cupped the side of my face in one of his big, protective hands.

"I think that's what missing someone means. They're missing from you, not just from your life, but from your heart. And nothing, no matter how hard you try, really works or fully functions because you're missing that piece."

Moisture gathered in my eyes, and emotion rushed to thicken at the base of my throat. I covered his hand with mine and pressed him closer.

Wanting to erase everything between us.

Space and time and questions.

"I know, Ollie. I know exactly what you're saying. Because I was missing that piece, too."

He swallowed hard, his throat bobbing beneath his beard. I could feel the switch. The way every muscle in his body tightened.

Edged in grief and radiating with hope. "And Sydney . . ."

Her name struck the air like a sword. A whirring slice right down the middle, cutting us in two.

"She's always gonna be missing from me, Nikki. There's always gonna be that piece that isn't entirely whole. I've got to accept that I'm never going to know what happened to her. Accept that part and try to let it go the best that I can. Because I want to be whole for you."

Trembling, I set my hand on his face. "I would never ask you to let her go. All I can ask you to do is love me in the middle of it. Forgive yourself. Forgive me. Forgive *us*. Because I know Sydney would have forgiven us for falling in love. All she wanted was to experience life. All of us. She would never ask you to give that up."

His entire body flinched, and his eyes slammed closed. "I'm trying, Nikki. I'm trying to believe that."

"I don't want to be your sin."

Draining the rest of his third scotch, he looked away from me and out over the city.

Turmoil rolled through him.

A blackout.

He turned that sapphire gaze back on me. "I saw the look on your face today."

I blinked, unsure of what he was getting at.

His tongue darted out to wet his lips. "When you were holding Penelope."

My spirit thrashed in its confines.

"You still want that? A family? Three kids and a husband and a little house?" His voice cracked when he said it.

Pain breaking free.

My eyes could no longer hold back. A tear slipped down my cheek. "I do. Someday, if I get lucky enough, I want that."

I wouldn't lie.

Not to him.

His forehead dropped to mine, and I reached out and held him by both sides of the face, my voice a quiet whisper, "But I would never push that on you."

His breaths came shorter, panted into my mouth. "I . . . don't know if I can give you that, Nikki. I don't know what kind of father I would be. If I could be trusted to be the kind of man that a kid would deserve."

My heart broke a little more, overflowing from the crack.

This man.

I pressed my lips to his.

Gently.

"You are the best man I know."

His head shook against my forehead. "Not even close, but I'm going to try. I'm going to try to be right. To protect you and take care of you. I want to be enough."

"All I want is for you to love me."

He didn't tell me that he did.

I knew he wasn't ready for that.

All of this would take time.

I wasn't fool enough to think that gulf that had roiled between us for years would suddenly evaporate.

He needed to learn to trust himself before he could fully give himself to me.

He pulled me to straddle his lap.

Energy flashed.

A bright light through the swimming darkness.

My heart raced, a thudding drum, drum, drum, a match to his.

He watched me in the shadows, as if I might disappear. He pulled the bottle of scotch from the table and chugged from it, that stare never leaving mine.

His gaze hot.

Feral.

Verging on wild.

So different than when he'd been so carefree earlier today. As if him seeing me with Penelope had unlocked something inside of him.

Slammed him directly into our reality.

I guess I'd felt a little of that shift, too.

Holding my niece with him looking at me, my sister there with her secret that had brimmed so fiercely between us I could taste it.

Riding on her tongue.

Desperate to be set free and held back by her shame.

I could only pray she would open up to me so she could heal.

The way I wanted Ollie to heal.

Not to forget.

But to live whole and free in the middle of it.

Right then, he seemed compelled to live in this moment.

Those sapphire eyes intense. Staring at me as if he were racing through time to meet with me.

A shiver rolled through my body.

He tipped the bottle up to me, and I drank from it.

The amber fluid lit a path down my throat and landed directly in that pit of desire that lapped in my belly.

A few droplets trickled out the side of my lips.

Ollie leaned in and licked them clean.

"Ollie," I moaned, the man my seduction.

"What do you need, Sunshine?"

"You . . . I always need you."

Hot hands landed on my bottom, and he squeezed and tucked me against his hard cock.

He nipped at my bottom lip, dragging it between his teeth in a pleasured sort of pain. From the look that took over his expression, I knew he was gonna make good on his warning.

Tonight, I was in so much trouble.

I knew it the second his tongue stroked into my mouth, deep and demanding and desperate.

I fell in, consumed by his presence.

My senses filled with him, the man washing me through, claiming every crevice.

Toasted almonds.

Barrels of oak.

Liquor kisses.

They were dizzying.

Drugging.
Maddening as the intensity increased.
Our energy flared.
Licking out to touch me everywhere.

His fingers sank into my sides as he pushed to his feet, taking me with him. He didn't go far. He settled me on my feet behind the couch that overlooked the city.

I gasped when he planted my hands on the back of the couch.

"Hold on, Sunshine." It was a whisper of warning in my ear, and my knees went weak when those hands were gliding up my thighs, dragging the silky material up and over my bottom.

"Little Tease," he muttered.

Words grit.

He squeezed my bottom in both hands.

"Do you have any idea what you did to me when I came through the door and saw you dressed in this?"

I pressed back into his hold. "I want you to look at me and never forget it."

He groaned a needy sound. "You think that's even possible? Forgetting you?"

His hands swept up my sides, taking the material with them, making me shiver as he ripped it over my head.

He left me bare, save for the scrap of my underwear.

"One look, and I was yours." He curved himself over my body, pushing my chest to the couch.

His mouth was at my ear, heat across my skin. "One touch, and you owned my soul."

I gripped at the cushions, trying to stay standing, to maintain sanity.

But it was far too late.

I'd already completely lost myself in this man.

I could feel him taking pieces of me.

Bit by bit.

Until he held every part of me in the palm of his hand.

Magnetic.

Gravity.

"Don't move," he demanded.

I shook.

I could feel him undressing behind me while I stood there chained by his potency.

A breath ripped from my lungs when he was suddenly on his knees, his nose pressing against the fabric that covered my center.

"You have the sweetest cunt. Pure fucking honey."

My knees knocked, and he held them apart, tongue teasing at the fabric.

"Ollie."

He ripped my underwear free, his hands and fingers spreading my cheeks, his tongue licking up my center.

I gasped, taken by the sensation that assaulted me before I pressed back.

Begging for more.

With Ollie, I wanted it all.

He licked and stroked with his tongue, his hands moving all over my body.

Hands on my stomach.

My breasts.

Running down my thighs.

As if he needed all of me, too.

He sucked at my clit, dragging back, his big fingers finding me.

Pressing deep.

It felt like a claiming.

Like something had changed.

Like Ollie was dropping another brick from the walls he'd built around his hardened heart.

He kissed my bottom, teeth raking the skin.

Chills scattered while his fingers drove me higher.

Right up to the edge.

"Ollie," I pled.

"What is it, sweet girl?"

"I'm so close." My fingers curled into the cushion. "I need you."

"You have me."

You have me. You have me.

His words tumbled through my spirit.

He was suddenly right there, plastered to my back, his cock nudging at my folds.

"And I want all of you," he said.

I cried out when he took me in a possessive stroke.

He gave me no warning.

No time to adjust.

One hand was wound up in a knot in my hair and his other hand was pressed flat to my lower belly as he began to fuck me.

Fuck me hard and fast and deep.

Our pants filled the dense air.

Needy rasps.

"You . . . you feel so good . . . nothing is better than this . . . you are mine. Mine, Nikki. I'm not ever letting you go."

Ollie's words spun and lifted, floating out as our bodies slapped, the sound matching his grunts.

He filled me.

Again and again.

Touching me everywhere.

Heart. Spirit. Soul.

I met his fierce gaze through the reflection of the window. The man behind me. Taking me. Owning me.

While I offered him everything.

All of me.

Nothing left to hide.

He tugged at my hair, pulling my head against his shoulder, his cheek on mine.

"Look at you," he demanded.

My body was stretched out against his, bowed back, my breasts pointed, tingling with the flickers of pleasure that grew more intense.

Every nerve ending alive. Zaps and pulses and zings.

It gathered fast as Ollie took me deeper and harder and higher.

He spread me with his fingers, stroking my clit.

A match tossed on kindling and gasoline.

Incinerated.

I'd never felt anything like it.

The fire that engulfed me.

Burning and singeing and scarring.

My body arched with the orgasm, and Ollie held me tighter, an arm around my waist as he drove deep.

So full I couldn't see.

His hips snapped.

Frenzied.

His groan guttural.

Teeth sank into my shoulder when he came, his body going rigid as he grunted through his release.

My beast.

My mind tilted, the floor going missing from under me as we both struggled to come back down.

"Fuck," he muttered as we both gasped for the nonexistent air.

"Fuck," he whispered again, almost frantically.

Fuck.

Another shiver rolled, and he held me up. Keeping me from falling.

His mouth was at my ear. "I just want to be the one to give you everything."

I wanted to believe that he was ready to take that leap. But there was no missing the desperation that bled through his words.

Fueled by an urgent desire to tighten the tether he feared might break.

I stood right there, at that edge, ready to jump.

I just prayed Ollie wouldn't let me fall alone.

twenty-nine
Ollie

I pressed my cell to my ear. "Sage, man, what's up. How's it coming?"

I hadn't heard from him in a couple of weeks, which wasn't uncommon for restorations. It took a shit ton of time to get anything accomplished. The search for replacement parts could take months, not to mention the actual work that needed to be done.

He hesitated on the other end of the line.

"What's going on?"

He blew out a sigh. "Not sure, man. There's just some weird shit with this car."

Only thing I heard was Sage shouting dollar signs.

"That car's special to me. Doesn't matter what it costs."

He inhaled, stalled, and an odd sensation gathered in my chest while I waited for him to fill me in.

"No. This isn't about money. There's some . . . shit in the trunk that doesn't sit right."

"What's that mean?"

I could hear him pacing on the concrete floors. "There's

some rope. A torn shirt that looks like it's splattered with blood."

Unease moved through me, silence falling over us as Sage let me catch up to what he was implying.

I sucked for a breath, teeth gritting as I spoke through the anger that lit inside of me. "That kid Caleb . . . he . . . who knows what the fuck he was mixed up in. Knew he was trouble the second I saw him."

"That's what I was worried about. And it might not be anything. Someone could have just as easily cut themselves and tossed the shirt in there. Just have to verify it before we gut this thing and start on the actual work."

I was always quick to jump to conclusions.

Sage was just taking the steps needed to get things done.

I shoved down the swelling rage.

"Of course."

"Honestly, the more I think about it, I'm sure it's nothing, but it's gonna nag if I don't call it in."

"Do what you've got to do, man. Can't blame you for that. Just let me know when you get started."

He was right. It was probably nothing, and if that punk had been up to something shadier than we'd thought, at least he was in rehab. If he did try to leave, he'd land his scrawny ass in a jail cell.

I couldn't worry about it right then.

Because my girl was peeling off her panties and grinning at me as she climbed into my bed.

And no matter how awesome that old car turned out, it wouldn't ever come as close to looking as good as that.

thirty
Nikki

My phone buzzed in my hand, and I was already grinning when I slid my finger across the plate.

Then my heart . . . it pattered when I saw the text that had come through. Was that normal? I was thirty, for God's sake.

But it did.

My eyes traced across the screen.

Ollie: Pretty please.

It probably wasn't the words that got me so much as the picture that he had sent along with it that had my pulse skipping a beat. My teeth tucked my bottom lip between them as I was hit with a rush of giddiness.

Because there was an up-close selfie of Ollie.

He was leaning against the bar downstairs at Olive's. An arm was crossed over his chest, and one of those tatted hands held onto his opposite shoulder.

The man was grinning at the camera, at me. And his eyes? They glinted. Glinted with happiness, and there was no description for how happy that made me.

Walking down the busy sidewalk, I tapped out a response.

Me: Not a chance, playboy.

I hadn't made it two steps before my phone buzzed again.

Ollie: Come on, gorgeous. Show me that face and just a little bit of that body. I'll make it worth your while ☐

There was that patter again.

Six weeks had passed since that fateful night on the dance floor when everything had changed. When the anniversary of Sydney's disappearance had changed us again. Although this time, it had pushed us together.

Closer and closer each day.

Our lives knitting together, so tightly we'd become one.

Easy.

The way it was always supposed to be.

Things had settled.

Caleb was still in the long-term rehab center, hopefully making a real effort to piece his life back together and become the type of man Brenna and Kyle deserved.

I tried not to be skeptical.

Sometimes that was hard because it turned out I was protective, too.

Sammie still hadn't confided in me, but she'd been calling more, asking me over, and I got the feeling she was working herself up to the place where she felt comfortable enough to do it.

I would never push her, even though sometimes I had the itch to beg her to tell me, that part of myself that wanted to make everything better screaming out to do something.

I had to accept I didn't have that kind of control.

All I could do was love and support and be there for her when she was ready.

Two weeks ago, Hope and Kale had announced that they

were expecting, which filled me up with an intense joy for them and also lit a few sparks of jealousy.

I'd pushed those feelings down.

Of course, I ignored all of Lily's ribbing when Ollie and I stepped out as a couple. We'd had a heart to heart, and I'd finally confessed to her that I'd loved him all along.

That it'd always been so much more than a crush.

That it was everything.

That Ollie was everything.

Which was exactly why I was grinning like a fool as I hurried the last few steps down the sidewalk and swung open the door to the old building.

Instead of going right for the basement stairs to set up like I typically would have done, I slipped into a deserted hallway to the left and tucked myself into an alcove where I'd be out of view.

I lifted my phone and snapped a picture, giving the barest hint of the pretty much nonexistent cleavage revealed by my pretty blouse.

Ollie definitely didn't seem to mind.

Me: That's going to have to tide you over until later.

Ollie: Dying.

Ollie: So gorgeous.

Ollie: You're ruining me, baby.

Redness flushed across my skin as I read the words that kept blipping through.

Me: I think you have it all backward. It's you who's ruining me.

Ollie: Hurry up and get that sexy ass home. I'll see you at ten.

Ollie: I miss you.

Me: I miss you, too.

I felt as if I was riding on a cloud, floating down the stairs that led to the basement. I was halfway through setting up the circle of chairs when Ms. Kathy came in, started a pot of coffee, and arranged the donuts she'd picked up on a tray.

"I hear congratulations are in order."

I beamed. I couldn't help it. "I can't believe I'm really finished."

Yesterday, I'd gotten my certificate in the mail from the online college.

I officially had my bachelor's degree. All I needed to do was take the state test, and I would be certified.

"This is when the fun part begins." She winked at me.

"Uh-oh. Tell me that wasn't a warnin'," I said, laughing a little.

She made a humming sound. "Some days will make you feel like a champion and other's will drop you right to your knees. But what you can count on is it will never be dull."

I hesitated for a second, peeking over at her. "Is it worth it?"

She reached out and squeezed my shoulder. "Always."

Fifteen minutes later, the secluded basement was a rumble of voices and screeching chairs as we all gathered around the circle.

I opened the session with our mantra. "I am strong. I have control of my life. I have control of my body. I have the right."

I looked around the group of faces. Even though so many were full of sorrow, it filled me with extreme hope. I did my normal introduction, telling them this was their safe place and completely confidential.

"Tonight, I would like us to talk through how you might look at situations differently since you've been attending this group. How has this changed the way you've reacted? How has it changed the way you handle the hurdles you face? Would anyone like to start?"

I was surprised when Brenna raised her hand. "I'd like to start, Miss Nikki. There's something that's been bothering me, and I want to make sure I'm handling it right."

Over the last few weeks, she'd really come out of her shell, exuding a confidence that had been lacking before.

"Okay, tell us what's happening."

Almost nervously, her attention darted around the group before she began, "Well, Caleb has been in rehab for six weeks now. He's now allowed to make calls. He's called a couple of times and is promising me he is changing. That he's making a real effort. I don't want to walk through life with a chip on my shoulder, but I also don't want to be naïve."

Pride welled inside of me, and I started to speak, but I stilled when tentative footsteps echoed down the stairs.

I paused to look over my shoulder, and like all those weeks ago, my sister appeared in the doorway.

Her eyes met mine.

There was something so broken there that my heart froze in the middle of my chest.

I tried to swallow around the apprehension that climbed to my throat as my little sister moved around the circle and tentatively took an empty seat.

I should have been relieved.

I should have taken solace in the fact she was there.

But I swore, I felt the air go cold.

thirty-one
Ollie

"You want another?"

"You know I do," the old guy said as he drained his fourth beer of the evening.

I filled a chilled glass, foam overflowing down the sides as I cocked him a look. "You better watch yourself, or I'm gonna have to cut you off."

He laughed and waved a flippant hand over his head. "You think this old-timer can't handle his liquor? Couple of cold ones sure aren't gonna hurt me. Why do you think I'm still alive and kickin'?"

Laughing, I slid him the pint glass. I'd been chatting with him all afternoon. He was either telling some tall, tall tales or the old bastard had lived quite the life.

Olive's had been quiet during the dead hours between the lunch rush and the after-work crowd. Evening was setting in, and the place was beginning to fill up.

For so long, my bar had basically been my entire life. Now, I couldn't wait for the night to pass so I could get back upstairs.

Fact I kept looking at my phone was proof enough.

"Who ya got on that phone? You got yourself one of them sassy modern girls? Bet you do."

I chuckled under my breath, setting my phone aside. I had to have looked at Nikki's picture at least a thousand times since she'd sent it an hour ago.

"That I do."

Still blew my mind that I did. That Nikki was mine.

My body rumbled with possession.

Every inch.

"She pretty? Let me see."

Old pervert.

Amusement swimming through me, I started wiping down the bar. "Hell no. Do I look like the kind of guy who shares my girl?"

His laughter was some kind of ridiculous guffaw and he smacked his hand on the wood. "Don't reckon you do. Look like you'd tear a poor sucker limb from limb."

"Sounds about right," I said, grinning when I felt the presence standing across the bar from me.

I looked up.

Seth.

My smile started to widen until I caught the expression on his face.

I straightened. "Seth, man, what are you doing here?"

His voice was quiet, lined with a tremor. "Need to talk to you. In private."

I tossed the rag onto the bar and hollered at Cece, who was manning the opposite end. "Watch things for a bit. I've got to step outside."

"Sure thing, boss."

I wound around the end of the bar and followed Seth. He headed straight down the back hall, passing by the sign that read: Employees Only.

Could feel the disturbance radiating from him, riding on the air that suddenly felt too fucking thick.

My breaths grew hard, and my heart fisted in an unknown sort of pain when he blew out the big metal door and into the vacant back lot.

Only thing back there were the employees' cars and the dumpster the kitchen used.

Humidity slapped me in the face, but it was Rex standing with his back pressed to the brick exterior wall, his head rocking up and down and his fists shoved deep in his pockets, that felt like a punch to the gut.

My attention swung back to Seth. "What's going on?"

His eyes squeezed shut. "I'm breaking a thousand rules by doing this, but I needed to tell you before you heard it somewhere else."

Tension stretched across my chest.

Pulling and pulling.

Any harder and it would rip me right in half.

"What?" I had to force out the word.

Seth hesitated, looking to the ground, inhaling deep. Sympathy shaded his eyes when he looked back up at me. "You know they started excavation down on Row."

I glanced over at Rex, confusion so thick I was having a hard time seeing through it, before I swung my gaze back to Seth. "Yeah, of course, I know. Rex said everything was given the go and the permits had been approved."

Seth blew out a strained breath, a bluster of hesitation coming off of him.

Overwhelming waves.

"Ollie." There was nothing but pity in the word.

Could feel Rex flinch from the side.

Foreboding ridged like ice skating down my spine.

"What the fuck is goin' on, man?"

Seth blinked, and the words came from his mouth like a slow purge. "A body was unearthed at the work site."

My knees gave with the blow, and my hand shot out, catching on the wall. I shoved it down and gritted my teeth. "What's that got to do with me?"

The words might as well have been darts.

Sharp as arrows.

Denial and defense.

Seth's brow twisted, lines distorting his face, and his words were a choked breath. "They're speculating they're Sydney's remains."

"No." My head shook, and my lips pursed as I rejected the idea. "No."

Seth reached out and set his hand on my shoulder. "I'm sorry, Ollie. I know you always hoped for a miracle."

Hoped for a miracle.

Hoped that my sister was still alive.

That someone hadn't buried her like she was trash.

Blood.

Dirt.

Bones.

I gasped for nothing. My lungs no longer functioning.

Seth edged back, and his attention jumped between Rex and me. "God, I'm sorry. This is the last kind of news I want to deliver. I'll give you guys some privacy. If I find out anything, I promise, you'll be the first to know."

He turned, and I stood stock still, watching him jog away.

Frozen.

Brittle.

It only sent a crack running down the middle of me that I knew would shatter me in a million unrecognizable pieces.

Rex groaned a devastated sound. "Fuck, Ollie . . . I—"

I flew around to face him. "It's not her."

Grief blistered across his face, through his red-rimmed eyes. Etched and carved and wrecked. He pushed from the wall, approaching me carefully.

"It was her, man. The foreman . . ." He blinked a bunch of times. Like he couldn't see through the horror wracking my mind. "He called me away from the architect when they uncovered something."

My head shook.

Rejection.

I didn't want to hear it.

I just couldn't make the words from on my tongue.

"I ran over there . . . thinking it was gonna be an old sewer system or something like that and they needed my direction."

He pressed both his hands over his face. His voice cracked on a cry. "The necklace, the one your mom gave her for her sixteenth birthday, it was there with the remains."

"No . . . she must have dropped it there sometime."

His hands dropped, and he took a step forward, getting in my line of sight, misery etched across his face. "She was wearing it that night."

My head shook. "No. She couldn't have been. You don't know that."

A groan ripped from him. "She was wearing it, Ollie. She was."

I pointed at him, trying to put some space between us. Refusing what was trying to suck me under.

Darkness.

Terror.

Hate.

"You don't fucking know that," I grated.

He stared at me, something so raw on his face that my heart slammed against my ribs.

"I do know, Ollie."

"How the fuck would you know that?" I spat, unable to keep the anger out of my words.

"I was with her." It was a raked gasp. Words barely formed.

My brow pinched. "We all were with her."

His hands fisted in front of him. Regret and frustration and something that look too much like guilt. "Fuck. Listen to me, Ollie. I was *with* her."

I blinked. "What?"

"I was with her." It was a shamed whisper.

There was nothing I could do.

The rage that poured free, leaching into my veins.

I shoved him.

Hard.

He flew back against the brick wall.

"What did you say?" I demanded.

"We were together. I told you it wasn't just your fault."

Red blurred my vision, and everything spun.

The sky and the earth and my spirit.

A jumbled chaos that took over inside of me. "You fucked my sister?" The accusation was full of disbelief.

Of disgust.

No words came from his mouth.

But guilt was written all over his face.

Anger burst in my blood. "You fucked my sister?"

Disgust met the roar as I lunged for him. My fist flew. Connected with flesh and bone.

Pain burst in my hand, and Rex just . . . took it. Face pinched up in pain as a trickle of blood dripped from his nose. "I'm sorry," he whispered.

He slid down the wall, hitting the ground with a thud. His head rocked back and he buried his face in his hands. "So fucking sorry."

I backed away.

Gripped by sorrow.

Grief swooping in.

Clouding my mind.

Shutting down my spirit.

My lip curled, and I backed further away. "Sorry's not good enough."

I turned and left him there, unable to see as I stumbled up the three flights of steps in the darkened stairwell.

Everything was blurred.

My eyes and mind.

An altered state of consciousness.

It couldn't be her.

It couldn't.

I had to keep searching. Keep watching. Keep hunting.

I would find her.

She would be safe.

Fly, fly, dragonfly.

Her voice danced all around me, and I choked, a cry ripping free.

It echoed on the enclosed walls.

Bouncing back.

Grief.

Grief.

Grief.

I couldn't stand.

I dropped to my knees, crawled the rest of the way up the last flight.

At the top, I forced myself to standing as I staggered out into the short hall, hands pressed to the wall to keep myself from falling.

Falling.

I'd thought I could live.

That I could see through this.

Past it.

That I could let go.

But this?

It was all I could feel.

All I could feel.

Pain.

Excruciating.

"We are three. Forever and ever, you and me."

I fumbled through the door and into my loft.

Nikki's scent hit me like a blow.

It blasted me back, and a sob ripped free from deep within my chest.

What did we do?

What did we do?

I stumbled to the cupboard and pulled out a brand-new bottle, twisted off the cap.

Anything to dull the feeling of my skin being sheered from my bones.

Flaying me open.

I tipped it up and gulped half of it down, drenching my stomach in morbid heat. Praying for reprieve.

I moved to the couch, and like a fool, I grabbed the remote and flipped on the television.

I slugged back another huge gulp.

Another and another.

Time passed.

A minute. An hour. A day.

I didn't know.

It didn't matter.

My head lolled against the back of the couch as I drifted through the haze.

Darkness spun.

Color blipped and flashed from the television. A slur of voices landed on my ears. Too loud. Too much.

A woman in a purple dress stood in front of the yellow tape that blocked off the old building where investigators swarmed, delivering her news.

A body had been discovered.

Forensics was on the scene.

Speculation.

Speculation.

"Sydney Preston was sixteen years old when she went missing fourteen years ago."

That storm rumbled from the depths of me.

Rising and lifting and consuming.

For months, I'd had the gut-deep intuition that something was coming.

Something wicked.

Ruthless and cruel.

A warning before it'd been overhead.

I'd known it was coming.

I'd known.

Like a fool, I hadn't realized what that'd meant.

It's your fault.

I trusted you.

You were supposed to take care of her.

You promised, you'd take care of her.

It should have been me.

It should have been me.

I'd done this.

Agony sliced through the center of me.

Excruciating, blinding pain.
Gutting and destroying.
My body wept. Bleeding out.
I could feel her spirit whip through the room.
An earthquake.
It spurred a tidal wave that decimated the coastline.
I saw it.
Felt it.
I welcomed it when it crashed over me.
A gulf overhead.
Taking me under.
Suffocating.
Drowning.
Me.
It should have been me.

thirty-two

Ollie
Seventeen Years Old

Flames from the bonfire licked and lapped, jumping toward the canopy of night that covered overhead.

Embers popped and snapped before they broke away like golden ash that floated for the heavens.

A ton of their friends were out there tonight.

More than Ollie had planned. Half the town had caught wind of the lake party, and people had kept showing up.

Wouldn't have been that big of a deal had a bunch of chicks from their class not climbed in the bed of Rex's truck to share the case of beer Rex's older cousin had scored.

Clearly, they thought they were gonna nab a piece of the star quarterback and defensive end as well.

What made it worse was Ollie's sister was there, sitting on the tailgate of the truck with her legs swinging over the edge.

Tonight, she looked pissed and bored and annoyed, and Ollie tried not to be annoyed right back.

He'd given it his best to convince her not to come tonight. He and Nikki had even concocted a story that Nikki wasn't feeling well so she was staying home.

He'd planned to pick her up on the way so Sydney wouldn't know. Guys wouldn't question it since Nikki was always with him, anyway.

Plan was solid.

No harm. No foul.

That was until Sydney had shoved a bunch of stuff in a tote bag and jumped into his car, saying he wasn't leaving without her.

Nikki had *magically* started feeling better.

Now, Nikki sat all the way on the other side of the fire, sitting on the same whitewashed log they'd dragged up from the lake when they'd all first started camping out here in middle school.

Those sweet freckles glimmered like glitter on her face as she watched him through the flames.

Her eyes dropped closed for a second, lashes casting a shadow on her cheeks.

God.

She was pretty.

So damned pretty he was sure he was going to lose his mind.

His insides twisted in a need that was close to painful, and he swore that the condom he'd brought was burning a hole in his back pocket that was as hot as the sparks that flickered from the pit.

Giggles rolled from beside him, and Ollie had to stop himself from rolling his eyes when he glanced that way and saw Jessica straddling Rex's lap.

Sydney's mouth pursed in a prissy way.

God, what was her problem?

She'd gotten so weird lately. She had to be catching on about him and Nikki. It wasn't like she was an idiot.

But he couldn't worry about that tonight.

They were going to tell her soon. This weekend.

After they were together.

All they wanted was this night.

Something special.

Rex laughed, and he set his hands awkwardly on Jessica's

waist.

Dude was such a pansy, acting like he wasn't interested in getting laid. Hell, Ollie could hardly remember the last time Rex had a girlfriend.

He looked Rex's way, grinning wide and covertly blocking Kayla from climbing into a similar position on his lap. "Stop being a pussy, dude. It's about time you saw some action. Get that dick wet before it shrivels up and falls off."

Rex laughed. "The hell? I get plenty of action."

"Yeah. Complements of your hand."

Sydney hopped off the tail, spun around, and crossed her arms over her chest. "You guys are such assholes. Can you stop being pigs for five seconds?"

Anger pinged at his ribs. Sydney had always been right there. He'd never had a minute to himself. To figure out who he was outside of watching over her.

And she thought she could judge them? Call them assholes when he was the one to bring her out there?

The one who'd always taken her everywhere.

"Take me home." She was looking directly at Rex.

Jessica giggled and snuggled closer against his chest.

"Think he'd rather be spending his time kissing Jessica than running you around. Wouldn't you, Rex?"

Ollie lifted his chin at Rex and Jessica. Prodding him.

Rex laughed before he kissed Jessica, so damned clumsily you'd think he'd never kissed a girl before.

But hell, Ollie wasn't joking.

It was about time his best friend saw some action.

Kale was already off with his new girlfriend, and damn, it would be nice if Rex had a distraction, too.

All he needed was to finally get Nikki alone.

"Told you not to come," Ollie told her.

Hurt twisted up Sydney's face, and crap, that was all it took for regret to start tugging at Ollie's conscience. At that place carved out that would forever give up anything for his sister.

She was supposed to be his priority.

His best friend.

It tugged and it tugged.

Only it wasn't as strong as his need for Nikki that pulled at the inside of him.

Two of them tethered and hooked.

Just one night. All he wanted was one night.

He looked at his sister, whose expression was so pinched with betrayal he almost apologized.

He swallowed it back, his voice a little rough when he said, "Go home, Sydney. Told you tonight wasn't for you. Call Mom to come pick you up at the dock."

Wounded disbelief glistened in her eyes as she looked at Ollie then turned her attention to Rex.

A beat passed.

Then two with no one saying anything.

Like she was waiting for someone to change their minds.

To tell her to stay.

Guilt clawed through Ollie, but he forced it down.

One night.

On a choked cry, she finally turned and started to walk away.

Nikki scrambled to her feet to go after her, and Ollie sent her a pleading glance.

Stay.

She blinked between them, torn, before she settled back onto the log.

All of them watched Sydney walk down the dirt road, her receding silhouette getting dimmer and dimmer before she disappeared around a bend.

Ollie breathed out, a loaded sound of frustration and relief. This was so messed up.

He watched as Nikki got up, clearly upset. She headed toward her things she'd left behind in one of the tents.

Pushing to standing, Ollie hopped over the side of the truck, feet landing hard on the dirt. "Got to take a piss."

He skirted around the camp, going around the long way until he found Nikki standing with her head dropped. Without saying anything, he grabbed her hand and the rolled-up pallet he'd made.

Silently, he clutched her hand, guiding her through the maze of spindly trees.

The voices and laughter grew more distant the farther they went, the sound of the waterfalls growing more distinct.

Nikki finally tugged at his hand, and he spun around to face her.

His breath hitched.

Air gone.

It was the exact same thing it did whenever he looked at her.

That feeling sweeping through him with the strength of the falls that crashed into the lake below.

But her voice, it was pained and whispered. "I think we should go after her. This isn't right."

He dropped the pallet to the ground and gathered her face in his hands. "Just tonight, Nikki. I want it to be us. For one night. That's all I'm asking for. Tomorrow, we'll apologize to her. Confess everything. We'll make it right."

Those mesmerizing eyes searched his face. "Why can't we do that right now?"

"Because you know it's going to be a thing. She's going to be upset. It would ruin tonight. It would ruin everything we have planned."

Her gaze drifted, worry written in her expression. "I just hate the idea of her going home angry. Feeling like we don't care."

Nikki fiddled with the red woven bracelet she wore on her wrist. The one that matched Sydney and Ollie's. Like if she touched it, she might be able to touch Sydney through the distance.

"She'll understand. It might take her some time, but she'll understand."

Nikki looked out over the streams that ran over the smooth rocks and tumbled over the cliffs. "I just . . . don't want her to be mad at me. When this comes out, I don't want it to change things between her and me."

He gathered her closer. "Is that what you're so worried about?"

Nikki nodded, eyes dropping when she confessed, "I've been

worried all week. So worried, Ollie. She's been my best friend my whole life. I don't want to ruin that."

Ollie brushed his fingertips across the moisture on her cheek.

Moonlight poured from above, caressing her olive skin, spinning it into silk.

"You don't need to worry. We'll make this right. I promise. But for tonight, it's just you and me." He brushed his nose against hers. "And me and you."

She set her delicate hands on his trembling stomach. "Us."

"Us," he murmured, so softly, a promise that came from his spirit and fell from his lips.

He took her hand again, picked up the pack, and silently wound her the rest of the way to the meadow secreted by a break in the trees.

It was the spot where he'd found her every single time they'd played hide and seek there at the lake.

Where they'd grown and learned and changed.

Where she'd run and hide and wait for him to come for her.

To find her.

He spread out the cushion and blankets, and they both knelt on their knees as he silently, slowly undressed her and she timidly undressed him.

A blush on her skin as she peeked up at him.

Energy roiled between them.

Soft surges.

Gentle prods.

She was shaking when she laid down beneath the covers, but it didn't come close to the quakes that rolled through Ollie as he fumbled to cover himself.

He'd had sex with two other girls.

It hadn't come close to feeling like this.

He was overwhelmed that Nikki trusted him with it.

With her.

He crawled under the covers with her, and he gathered her closer, holding her in a way he never had.

Their noses touched. Their breaths mingled. Their hearts joined.

And Ollie . . . he found her again, in their hidden spot, though this time, they would never be the same.

He knew as they moved beneath the moonlight that he was going to keep her.

That he'd give up anything for her.

Anything.

Anyone.

Protect her with all he had.

If she was lost, he would always find her.

That was what loving someone was all about.

Giving all of yourself.

Completely.

And Nikki Walters owned every part of him.

thirty-three
Nikki

I sucked in a shattered breath as I stumbled to stand, catching myself on the back of the chair.

"What did you just say?"

I'd still been staring at my sister.

Caught up in the fact she was there.

But there was no missing what Maggie had whispered to Nina after she'd looked at something on her phone.

"I'm sorry, Miss Nikki, I wasn't trying to disrupt the group. My mama just texted me three times in a row, and I figured I'd better check to make sure my kids weren't tearing her house down."

I blinked, frantically shook my head, and tried to swallow around the sticky dread that had wrapped me in chains so quickly I was sure I was being strangled. "No . . . tell me what you just said. What you just whispered."

She frowned. "They found a body out by the river near those old, abandoned buildings. News report said they think it's that poor girl Sydney Preston who went missing all those years ago. So sad."

No.

Oh . . . God . . . no.

My hand went to my stomach as my body bent in half, and I tried to draw air in to my lungs. Through that haze of disbelief and sorrow.

I only managed to draw in more.

Shock.

Anguish.

A chatter of uneasy, confused voices sounded, each one hitting me so hard they had to be boxing my ears.

I shoved my chair back, stumbling as I broke out of the circle that was suffocating me. My head spun, faster than the walls that canted and tipped.

At the same time, every evil force in the world pressed down.

I could feel it crush my heart right in the center of my chest.

I didn't know how I made it across the floor, but my hand shot out to keep myself from dropping to my knees when I reached the stairwell, my feet failing beneath me.

Like everything else. My heart and my spirit and my belief.

From behind, an arm looped around my middle, holding me up. My sister's voice was so soft as it moved through the daze. "I've got you, Nik. Oh, God, I'm so sorry. I'm so sorry. I'm right here. I've got you."

She helped me to stand. Eyes the same color as mine searched my face as I sagged against the wall. "I need . . . I need to get to Ollie."

She nodded. "Okay . . . I'll drive you."

I didn't even process the ride over. The grief was too overwhelming. Every single beat of my splintered heart was excruciating.

Rynna had texted me a hundred times, my phone blipping incessantly when I'd fumbled to turn it on where I sat in Sammie's car.

Rynna: Are you okay?

Rynna: Call me.

Rynna: I'm here if you need me.

Texts from Lily had started up right after, a bunch of calls that I couldn't bring myself to answer.

I had to get to Ollie.

My sister kept glancing over at me, kneading the wheel, so much concern and care on her face. "I can't imagine what you're feeling right now."

My head shook, voice barely breaking the air. "I . . . I always knew she was gone. But it'd always felt like her spirit had just been swept away. In my mind, I'd imagined she'd ridden off on the wind to find some new adventure. This . . ."

A gasp pulled from my spirit, and sickness bubbled and churned in that well of grief. That place deep inside that had been shored up and protected. A vat of misery and despair and questions.

That dam had been broken, and every ounce of it surged through me. A devastating flood.

She glanced at me before turning her attention back to the road. "They aren't even sure it's her."

She cringed when she said it.

Because we both knew it was her.

It was Sydney.

Her name begged from the depths of me.

Sammie pulled to the curb in front of Olive's. I jumped out and bolted for the door, flinging it open, gasping as my attention jumped around the space.

Ollie wasn't behind the bar, and Cece lifted one of her defined brows and gave a shrug, but there was concern behind it.

And I knew. I knew, I knew, I knew.

Ollie had already heard.

Dread balled in the pit of my stomach.

I didn't slow as I raced down the hall and up the three flights of stairs to his loft.

My feet had finally found their purpose.

Ollie.

Ollie.

I burst through the door.

Then I skidded to a stop.

Dense darkness echoed back.

So dark it coated my eyes.

Coated my spirit.

Only the blips coming from the television that played illuminated what was stricken on his face.

Torment.

Agony.

Slowly, his gaze lifted to mine, as if he couldn't process that I was there.

Vacant.

I could feel the distance grow so immense between us I had no idea how I would reach him.

Rushing for him, I dropped to my knees in front of him where he sat on the couch.

Unmoving.

"Ollie," I whispered, desperation on my tongue. I lifted onto my knees so I could hold his face.

His beautiful, tortured face.

His eyes dropped closed, and there was nothing but pain on his lips. "Please, don't touch me."

I clung to him tighter. "Ollie . . . I'm so sorry."

As if my words had snapped him out of the daze, he flew to his feet, writhing as if he were being burned alive.

Misery in his eyes and alcohol on his breath. "This can't be happening, Nikki. Tell me it's not happening."

I fumbled to standing, my arms across my middle as I tried to keep myself upright, as if I could physically hold myself together. "I'm so sorry"

What else was I going to say. That it was okay? Because this was most definitely not okay.

"Tell me what I can do," I begged instead.

His brow pinched. "What can you do? You can't *do* anything, Nikki. It's already done. My sister is gone."

Him saying it sent shards of glass blasting through me.

He whirled away, gripping fistfuls of his hair as a groan erupted from his soul.

His entire body clenched, and he harshly shook his head, voice gravel. "I was supposed to save her. I spent my whole life looking for her. Searching for her. Thinking someday, I would make this right. That I'd fix what I'd done. And I can't fix it."

A sob raked from him, and he dropped to his knees and buried his face in his hands.

"My sister is gone. Oh, God. She's dead. She's dead."

Whimpers echoed from him.

A shattered, broken cry.

The man was falling apart in front of my eyes.

I wanted to hold him.

Fix him.

But neither of us were capable of fixing this.

He was right.

It was already done.

The only thing we could do was be there for each other in the middle of it.

Slowly, I inched toward him, kneeling as I set a hand on his arm.

He flinched.

"I'm right here, Ollie."

Under my touch, I could feel the tremor roll through him.

Crushed, he finally turned his potent gaze on me. "I have no idea who the fuck I'm supposed to be."

My mouth quivered, and I searched his face. "You're supposed to be mine."

Sorrow swam.

So thick.

So deep.

Quicksand.

"I don't know how to do that when all I see when I look at you is Sydney standing at your side."

Pain squashed my lungs.

Obliterating air.

I blinked. Wanting to negate it. To tell him we could

overcome it.

"Ollie?" I begged quietly.

Praying he'd refute it.

Say what he'd implied wasn't true.

But his expression shifted.

Hardened.

The walls coming up.

They swore there was no way for us to overcome *this*.

My nod was slow surrender as I pushed back to standing.

"I have to go."

I turned and fumbled for the door.

Barely able to stand.

A new kind of grief cut through me.

Overpowering.

Overbearing.

Too much.

How was I supposed to stand under it all?

"Nik," he suddenly begged. His voice gruff. "Don't just take off."

It only propelled me faster.

I needed to get away.

Run from this grief.

I clamored back out into the hall.

I could feel his presence from behind, a shockwave that banged against the walls.

"Nikki."

His voice sounded like heartbreak.

Like an apology.

Like a goodbye.

I paused to look back at him, barely able to force out the words. "I will always love you, Ollie, but I can't be with you when you don't know how to love me back."

I'd known to guard my heart.

I'd known. I'd known all along.

Oliver Preston was armor and stone.

Bitterness and venom.

Broken fragments.

Shrapnel waiting to bust.

He was the bullet that pierced right through the center of me.

Barely able to see, I ran back down the hall and hit the door that led to the steps. Holding onto the railing, I bounded downstairs.

Sniffling, trying to hold back the sob that bottled in my throat.

At the bottom, I blew out the backdoor and the sob broke free.

It echoed on the night.

Resounding.

A boomerang.

It bounced back, slamming into me, adding to the turmoil that sieged every cell in my body.

Hands shaking, I fumbled into my purse and pulled out my phone, barely able to make the call.

Sammie answered on the first ring. "Are you okay?"

I could hardly speak. "No. I'm not okay."

"Where are you?"

"At the back of Olive's," I begged through another cry.

"Stay right there. I'll be there to get you in five minutes."

"Okay."

I ended the call and hugged my arms across my chest, tears streaking free.

There was no way to stop them.

Solid ground had finally been ripped from beneath our feet.

My heart shattered, pieces scattered.

Verification that we'd lost Sydney in this horrible, horrible way crumbled the last of our foundation.

I guessed it'd been flimsy and unstable, anyway.

But now it was Ollie who was lost beneath the rubble.

Unable to see his way out of it.

Unable to see past what he thought was a failure.

And he'd broken my heart all over again while mine broke *for* him.

I wanted to hold him and make promises I couldn't keep.

That one day it wouldn't hurt so bad.

But I knew that would only be a lie.

Headlights cut into the back-alley road, and Sammie's car came to a stop in front of me.

The front-passenger door flew open, and Sammie jumped out, her husband Lyle in the driver's seat.

I collapsed in her arms and wept.

"I've got you, Nikki. It's going to be okay."

I nodded against her, even though I couldn't bring myself to belief it was true.

Finally, I pried myself away and climbed into the backseat with Penelope, took the little girl's hand, clinging to the comfort she brought.

Looking at her had always made me feel as if the world could be a better place.

I just wished I could still believe that as the truth.

They swung by where I'd left my car outside the building, and Lyle took my keys and said he'd meet us back at the house, doing what he could to lighten some of the load.

As if I'd give my car a second thought.

But he'd always been a doer, and I understood the feeling of being helpless, desperate to find something to do.

Sammie moved into the driver's seat.

I stayed stagnant in the backseat, silent tears running down my face.

They didn't stop or slow when we went inside.

Choked sobs erupted at unexpected times, as if the sorrow would bottle and pressurize and then burst to do it all over again.

Sammie made me a spot on the couch to sleep, and I hugged the blankets around my body as it if might offer comfort.

"Do you want me to sit with you?" Sammie finally asked, fidgeting, her house quiet in the dark hours of the night.

"No, you go on to bed and get some rest. There's nothing you can do."

I needed to be alone.

To process.

To grieve.

She wavered as if she was going to stay anyway. "I want to be here for you, too," she whispered, as if she were trying to cross a bridge.

My eyes blinked open to her.

Bleary and blurry.

Burning from the tears.

Something passed through her expression.

"I know that. Thank you."

She nodded quickly and then ducked her head down the hall, shutting off the last light and casting the entire house in a dreary darkness.

I didn't toss.

I just laid there.

Frozen in the silence.

Tied by sorrow.

Cutting, blinding grief.

I'd felt as if I'd lost both of them all over again.

As if I was taken back to the day when my world went dim.

Because Ollie . . .

He'd always been my great big world.

Finally, I drifted on it, exhaustion taking hold of my consciousness. Horrible dreams just raced in to take its place.

My eyes popped open, a fresh sob on my breath, night still all around me. Disoriented, I blinked through it. I jerked my head when I felt the presence at my side.

"Sammie," I gasped, my eyes going wide when I found my sister sitting on the floor next to me, her knees tucked to her chest as she rocked.

Even in the darkness, I could see the shimmer of tears that stained her cheeks.

"What's wrong?" I whispered fiercely, shooting up to sitting, the worry for her chasing away the weight that wanted to pin me down. "What happened?"

Shivers of pain radiated from her.

"I went to that meetin' last night, thinking I was going to be able to talk to you."

Oh God.

My heart raced.

Banged at my ribs.

"And I'm so sorry this is comin' now . . . when you're going through so much. I just don't think I can keep it inside anymore. Everything feels wrong."

I knew this was her way of opening a door.

Breaching a divide.

Inviting me inside.

I wanted to be there. For her.

Even though I was terrified I might not be strong enough to handle anything else. If my emotions might get the better of me.

"I'm *always* here for you, Sammie. No matter what is happening in my life, I will always be here for you."

"I know that," she mumbled, hugging her knees tighter, her attention darting all over the living room as if she was searching for ghosts among the shadows.

Finally, she turned her tortured gaze back on me, the words forced from her mouth. "He's back."

Confused, I sat forward more as I tried to decipher what she was trying to say. "Who?"

She swiped the back of her hand under her nose. "Uncle Todd."

"What?"

The name rocked me back.

Shocked.

Stunned.

Horrified by the look on Sammie's face.

Sickness turned in my guts, and I was sure I was gonna throw up.

She blinked a bunch of times, as if she were seeing things she didn't want to see. "I . . . I thought I was okay, Nikki. For all these years, I'd convinced myself it was okay because he was gone. All my prayers had been answered because he'd just . . . moved. Was gone. So, I shoved it down and pretended like it didn't exist, and then he came back to help Grandma and . . . and . . . it was all right back there again."

Dread.

It chained and bound.

Everything felt too heavy.

Crushing.

I tried to breathe around it. To convince my heart it was okay to still beat.

I needed to be strong for my sister.

She needed me. She *needed* me, and I needed to be there for her.

"What exactly are you sayin'?" I tried to keep the question soft. Frame it like I would to anyone who came to me for help.

But it felt impossible when my baby sister was the one sitting there looking at me.

"Didn't you think Uncle Todd was a creep?" she almost begged.

Leading me. Trying to get me to a point without her having to say it.

I swallowed hard, my mind reeling through a million memories.

Had I missed it?

Because it hit me.

The way he'd been too attentive.

Too interested in what we were doing.

Always asking me questions.

Where I was going and who I was with.

But at the time, it'd barely blipped on my radar.

"He was . . . odd."

More tears streaked from her eyes, soaking her face. "He wasn't odd, Nikki. He was a monster."

Horror locked up my throat, and my hands went to my chest as if it might shield me from her words.

"He was a creep and a monster, Nikki. Of the worst kind. A vile, disgusting creep who stole my childhood. My innocence. He made me believe I could never trust a man until Lyle came into my life. And . . . and . . . and I just have this sick feeling . . ."

Her grief spun through the room. Hanging on the dense air. Clinging to the walls.

I swore I could feel it crawling across the floor and climbing into me.

My spirit shook, so heavy I could feel the weight of it sagging in the middle of me.

Regret and confusion and anger.

Who knew hate could be such an instant thing?

But I did.

I hated him.

Hated that he could hurt my sister.

"Sammie." Tears flooded down my face. "I'm so sorry I didn't know."

She swiped at the wetness on her face and released a brittle, frustrated sound. "How could you know when I kept it a secret? It was my darkest secret, Nikki, because I couldn't stand the thought of someone knowing. Of someone knowing what he'd done to me."

My eyes squeezed, and I forced out the words, praying she hadn't gone through this alone her whole life. "But Lyle knows?"

She barely nodded. "He knows what happened to me. He doesn't know who. He thinks it was a stranger. I didn't know how to tell him if I didn't want my family to know. God knows what he'd do."

Oh, that made two of us.

Fury bristled through my being, and I thought maybe I could relate to the things Ollie had said. To the way he'd wanted to hunt down whoever had hurt his sister.

The overwhelming need to make something right when you had absolutely no control over it.

But at least in this circumstance, we could still do something.

Sammie suddenly gasped for a breath. "I didn't . . . I didn't want to burden you with this when you are dealing with so much, but I couldn't keep it in any longer. Not with him out there. Not with my baby girl in her room . . . not with other little girls out there. Not after all these years of hiding it. I . . . I—"

A shadow of grief clouded her face. "What if he's hurt someone else? What if I never told anyone and he did it to someone else? I'm responsible for that."

Dropping onto my knees on the carpeted floor, I inched her direction, took her by both of the wrists, and lifted her arms in between us.

They'd been hanging so helplessly at her sides.

I needed her to know she wasn't weak. That she had strength. "No. You can't blame yourself. You were just a little girl."

Conflict pinched her face. "It was still happening when I was fifteen." Her voice clogged with a ragged cry.

"Fifteen, Nikki," she begged, as if it changed things, and she was all of a sudden somehow responsible.

But that's what predators did. They made their victims believe they were somehow to blame. That they should be the one's ashamed, manipulating and filling them with fear.

A panicked disgust clotted in my chest, and I was sure my heart was no longer working. "It's not your fault. It's his. But . . ."

My voice shifted to a quiet plea, praying my sister would find comfort in me. That she would understand she no longer had to be afraid. "We have to report this to the police, Sammie. We can't let him get away with this."

"I know." The words cracked, and a cry ripped from her throat.

It was born of desperation. Of grief and sorrow and shame.

She began to ramble, "I just . . . you have to give me a little time. I've been trying so hard. So hard to get to the point where I could tell you, and I trust you more than anyone."

She squeezed her eyes shut and struggled for a breath. "They're gonna ask for details, Nikki. I know they are, and I don't think I'm ready yet."

I squeezed her hand. "How long was it going on?"

She dropped her attention to the floor, shuttering, her chest heaving with her breaths. "He always . . . made me uncomfortable. The way he used to look at me. The way he'd brush against me. I was twelve the first time he took me to one of those abandoned buildings by the river."

Shock blew me back, and the air sucked into my vacant lungs.

A cloying type of awareness shook through me.

"What did you say?"

She blinked. "The buildings. Down on Row."

Tremors rocked through me.

Full body.

Jolting.

"Oh, God. Oh God."

I couldn't breathe.

No.

No.

It couldn't be. I was making assumptions, anxiety and fear getting out ahead of me.

Dizziness swooped down, making my mind tilt and the room cant.

I tried to get to my feet, but the weakness that had taken hold of my knees nearly dropped me back to the ground. My hand darted out to the couch as I forced myself to stand.

Nausea churned, twisting my stomach in painful knots. I tried to swallow around the bile I could feel crawling up my throat.

"Oh God," I whispered again, looking around as if I were searching for an answer when there wasn't one there.

Sammie pushed to standing, her hand on my arm, worry moving all over her face. "What if it was him?"

My eyes shifted to her.

I knew they poured with sorrow. With speculation.

The same as hers.

It hit me light a freight train.

What she'd been implying all along.

Why she felt compelled to tell me now.

I stumbled back, hand scrubbing over my face in hopes that it might break up the confusion. "I need to go. I need to think."

I stumbled back into the kitchen and grappled for my purse, which I'd left on the little breakfast nook table last night.

I jerked open the door.

A tease of daylight danced on the horizon, cool morning air splashing my face.

It didn't matter.

I felt sticky.

Clammy.

I stumbled down the two steps, unable to move any further

when I lurched forward and puked in the shrubs.

My spirit revolting.

Purging the instinct that had kicked up at the back of my mind.

Sammie was behind me. "Nikki, what are you going to do?"

"I just . . . I need to think. Figure this out."

I didn't even want to contemplate it. Didn't want it to be true.

"He was a monster."

Sammie's confession whipped through my spirit.

"Where are you going?" she begged, clinging to the railing on the steps.

"I don't know. I just . . . I need to go."

I had to make sense of this before I made accusations I couldn't take back. Even though my gut screamed they were real.

"Please, don't do something stupid."

I ran to her and pulled her into my arms, squeezing her so tight I could feel her heart battering against mine. "I'm so sorry, my sweet sister."

Then I turned and rushed away.

thirty-four
Ollie

Footsteps pounded on the damp earth.

Desperate.
Frantic.
Trees rose on all sides, sentries and witnesses, and branches tore into my skin as I ran through the oppressive night.
Searching.
My eyes blurred in the darkness. Muddied by despair. I stumbled through the forest. Gnarled roots twisted, like spindly fingers that had clawed out of hell to hold me back.
Tears burned my cheeks as the wind blasted my face.
Cruel like the laughter I swore I heard before it was swallowed by a gust of air.
I screamed in the middle of it. "Sydney!"
Voice hoarse, throat bleeding with the pain. "Sydney!"
Sydney. Sydney. Sydney.
I dropped to my knees.
Sydney.

I roared, trying to break free of the sheets that were twisted around me like ropes and chains. Sweat slicked my skin, and my heart was busting right through the confines of my ribs.

Panted cries clawed at my raw throat.

Panic and desperation.

I kicked off the sheets and sat up on the edge of my bed.

I blinked through the dusky shadows that leapt through my room, trying to ignore what had pulled me from sleep.

Banging.

A constant pound, pound, pound at my front door.

The room spun like a bitch, that bottle I'd drained sitting in my stomach like a lethal dose of poison.

Or maybe it was just the poison of what I'd done.

Sydney.

Sydney.

I could still hear my screams echoing back from the forest. I'd hunted for days, which had turned to weeks . . . months . . . years.

Listening and waiting, and for all these years the tiniest spark of hope had remained.

The hope that she was out there somewhere, safe and happy but trying to get home.

A fool's dream. A dream that had kept me going.

Moving.

Breathing.

Pain attacked me from all sides.

Knives stabbing deep, driving all the way through.

Piercing. Cutting.

My guts spilled out onto the floor.

I'd wanted to be a better man. Fuck, I'd wanted to be a better man.

"All I want is for you to love me."

Nikki's voice danced through the void of my room.

Taunting. Coaxing. Prodding.

Little Tease.

Little Tease.

I wanted to cling to it. Hold it. Cherish it.

But it hurt too bad.

More pounding echoed from the front door.

"Go away," I shouted, knowing there wasn't a chance in hell they could hear me from my room.

Whoever it was just kept on. Becoming more and more demanding. Harder and harsher with each boom.

Someone wanted to get their ass kicked.

Scrubbing a palm down my face, I glanced at the clock.

Four in the afternoon.

Fuck.

I should have gotten up.

Gone to the station.

Demanded answers.

Hunted more.

Hopelessness wrapped around me.

Chained to bricks and stones that dragged me down into the blackest abyss.

What the fuck good would it do?

I had nothing left to find.

Nothing left to give.

I hadn't checked in downstairs. Had no clue if the shifts were manned. If the bar was running smoothly or if everything had gone to hell.

Thing was, that bar could burn to the ground with me in it, and I wouldn't even blink.

Because I was already in hell.

A brutal, unrelenting hell.

Another round of pounding.

I did my best to keep the rush of fury in check, but my blood was already boiling.

At myself. At the world. At whoever had done this to my sister.

Pain clutched my stomach when I let the idea slink into my mind. Swore that it physically shredded my insides.

Still couldn't process it. Didn't want to.

Couldn't stop it.

It was the only thing I could see.

Blood.

Dirt.
Bones.
A cry raked from my lungs.
More pounding.
I staggered out that way, careening across the floor, ready to tear into any poor fucker who was waiting on the other side.
I peered through the peephole.
Rex.
Motherfucker.
That was a whole new layer I couldn't process.
Couldn't stomach.
A fresh round of hatred went skating through my veins. Boiling over.
"Not sure you want me to let you in here."
"Need to talk to you," rumbled through the wood.
"Not exactly up for chit chat."
Because what the fuck was he going to say?
"Not going anywhere until you open this door, so you might as well open up."
"Then you're going to be there all night."
"God damn it, Ollie, this isn't a fucking game. Open the door. I need to talk to you."
Rage had me twisting the lock and flinging the door open.
"You got something to say?"
Bitterness bled out.
Hurt right behind it.
Rex stood in my doorway.
Dark bags under his eyes. Hair a complete mess.
Like he hadn't slept for a second last night.
Ridden with guilt.
Good.
Warily, he glanced up at me. "Deserve for you to hate me, Ollie. I should have told you a long time ago."
Sharp laughter bounced from the walls. "You should have told me? Told me what? That you were fucking my little sister? That the two of you had something going on that night? That you knew where she went?"

I moved to get in his face, words flying, razors on my tongue. "Is that what you've got to tell me?"

He shoved me.

It was enough to knock me back a foot.

He jabbed his finger against my chest. "You want to blame me, Ollie. Blame me. Fine. If you think I haven't been blaming myself for all these years, you're a fool."

My teeth ground as I got back in his face. "Yeah, you made me a fool. Keeping this from me? Are you kiddin' me, Rex? You were supposed to be my best friend. I trusted you with her, and you were the one I should have been protecting her from."

Rex stalked deeper into my loft, hands ripping at his hair, growls coming from him like he was the one who was about to lose all control instead of me.

He whirled back around. "I fucking loved her, okay?"

He gasped, like saying it was met with gutting relief.

"I loved her, and you made it plenty clear that I couldn't. That any guy who even looked at your sister was getting his ass kicked. Tell me how the fuck we could contend with that?"

His face contorted in anger.

In rage and grief.

"So, we snuck around. Kept it a secret so we wouldn't hurt you. Because your sister didn't want you to be angry with her. Didn't want you to be angry with me. She was keeping the peace the exact same way as you did with Nikki."

I jarred back.

He scoffed. "Don't act like we didn't know. All this time, and you think we didn't know? That she didn't know?"

Shock beat through my blood. "Sydney knew?"

Rex huffed a breath. "Of course, she knew. She was pissed you wouldn't tell her. That you thought you had to keep her out. That you wouldn't let her in."

More regret.

Could I shoulder any more of it? I didn't fucking know how. I could feel it piling on me.

Rubble and rocks and debris.

A fucking bomb.

It'd destroyed any semblance of peace.

Old grief curled through Rex's hard expression, something sour seeping through.

"And I was too big of a pussy to stand up and say something. I should have said something. Instead I—" His words broke off, and Rex gave a harsh shake of his head.

Heartbreak.

I knew exactly what it looked like.

It clutched and clung and tortured.

Slamming him from all sides.

"If I'd have just stood up that day and made a claim, Ollie."

He choked, trying to bite back a sob.

Like it'd come from out of nowhere.

Balled up grief that had simmered for too many years.

His eyes filled with moisture, and my heart was beating out of my fucking chest.

Regret. Confusion. Sympathy.

For a beat, I covered my face with both my hands.

What the fuck was I supposed to think? What was I supposed to feel? Because right then, I was feeling too damned much.

Rex stood up straight. Stretching his arms out wide. "It was my fault. Be pissed off at me, man. Hate me. Blame me. Because it was my fault. She was there that night because that was where I was gonna be. She was pissed *because* of me. She left *because* of me."

With every line of confession, he hit his fist against his chest.

Harder each time.

"Because I kissed that chick because that was what I thought you expected me to do. You were right that night. I *was* a pussy. I was a pussy because I didn't have the guts to tell my best friend I loved his sister." He slammed his fist against his heart again.

"My fault." It was a rasped cry that boomed against my walls.

I blinked at him, trying to see through the daze. To process and add and make sense of what he was saying.

His mouth twisted in agony. "We loved each other. We did. Just like you loved Nikki, and you're a fucking fool if you think that it was any different."

He sucked in a choppy breath. "We're all responsible. All of us . . . a bunch of stupid, ignorant kids who didn't know any better. We made mistakes. Mistakes we didn't have any clue would lead to what they did."

My back hit the wall, and I was searching for air, lungs squeezed tight.

Regret shook Rex's head. "The next morning when we found out she hadn't made it home . . ." He stumbled like he couldn't handle the memory, his voice hoarse and raw when he finally spoke. "I wanted to die. I wanted to curl up and die, Ollie."

Hurt blistered through me.

His.

Mine.

My body rocked.

I didn't know how to stand under it.

"Rex," I attempted. Needing to shut him down. Because I wasn't sure how much more of this I could take.

Torment rushed from him on a torrent.

The guy beaten up and mangled.

In a way I'd never seen him before.

Like maybe there was a chance he felt an ounce of what I was feeling right then.

He held his hand out like he was the one stopping me. "Just fucking listen, man. I've kept this in for so long. For so long, and I can't bear it anymore."

A harsh breath wheezed into his lungs. "I didn't say anything because I didn't know how to admit it. I didn't know how to tell you I was the one to blame. I was fucking terrified and heartbroken, and all I wanted was for it to end."

An exact echo of me.

Rex took another step back my direction. "We fucked up. We fucked up so bad. But I see it clearly now. I get it in a way I couldn't then. Those mistakes weren't malicious. They weren't cruel or intended to hurt. They were mistakes we made as we tried to figure out who we were."

His brow twisted in emphasis. "Figure out how to live and who we were supposed to be. How we'd all fit because every single one of us knew things had changed. No longer kids but not grown, either. All of us were fumbling through."

His entire face pinched.

Agony and grief.

Lifting an arm, he drove his finger toward the door as he chucked the words. "But there is someone out there who *is* cruel. Someone who *is* malicious. Someone out there who did this to her. Someone who hurt her. He's the one to blame, Ollie."

Stumbling back, he bent in two, his hands on his knees as he tried to catch his breath like he'd just been struck in the stomach with a bat. "He *did* this. Not you. Not me."

I could barely form the words, the weight of them so heavy on my tongue. "We sent her out into the night. By herself."

"I know." He angled his face up to look at me. "I know. I've carried that for so many years, just like you. And God, it hurts so bad, thinking about what she might have gone through. But I *knew* Sydney, and so did you."

He seemed to have to force himself to straighten. "And I know you know she wouldn't want this. You know she'd want you to live. To experience and to love and to take this life for all it's worth."

My hands curled into fists, my mind and my heart and my spirit at war.

For a minute, we got lost in it, both of us trying to catch up, before Rex took a step forward, his head angling as he started to speak.

"Rynna? My family? They are *that* life. I didn't think I could love again after Sydney. It took me so many years of hating myself, thinking I deserved to be alone, that I didn't get to find joy because of it. Thinking I deserved to suffer."

Tremors raked down my spine, his words like claws sinking in my skin.

"I know better now. I know that's not what Sydney would have wanted. I got that chance to live, Ollie. I was given it, and I'm not going to reject that gift. I won't waste it. I love Rynna with all of me. Wholly. I was the fool who thought I didn't have anything left to give when really I had everything. Right there.

Waiting for me."

Emotion curled and crushed.

Overwhelming.

Too much.

He shifted away, his hands on his hips, speaking the words toward the wall. "Don't waste your life blaming yourself, Ollie. I've stood aside and watched you in misery for too long. I was a fucking coward who couldn't tell you the truth because I was afraid you'd hate me. I'd convinced myself it'd only hurt you more, knowing about us. But I know better now."

He looked back at me. "It's time for us to both stop making those mistakes. It's time for us to live. To embrace life the way Sydney would have wanted us to. Don't waste that. Don't waste what you and Nikki have. I haven't seen you happy in so goddamned long . . . and these last weeks? That's what you've been. Happy."

Could feel my heart clattering in my chest. My voice shook. "I don't know how to do that . . . how to live knowing she didn't. I've spent my whole life searching for her. I don't know how to accept that she's . . . gone."

Saying it was a blade.

Cutting deep.

Tears blurred my eyes.

Sydney was gone.

He looked back at me, his mouth wobbling with the truth. "You remember who she was."

Fly, fly dragonfly.

We both jerked when the door leading to the outside stairs banged open. I moved to peer out into the hall.

I had to blink to clear my eyes, my spirit soaring at the sight before I realized it wasn't Nikki.

It was Sammie.

Wringing her fingers nervously, attention darting all over the place like she thought she was doing something wrong.

"Sammie," I said, stepping out into the hall. "What are you doing here?"

She gulped and tentatively looked up at me. "I'm worried

about Nikki. She left early this morning, and I can't get in touch with her. I was hoping she was here."

It was instant.

The worry that blasted through me. "She's not here. I haven't talked to her. What do you mean, she left early?"

Sammie's face fell. "I think she's in trouble."

Felt the world crashing down on me when Sammie nervously told me her suspicion of her uncle, and I grabbed my keys, rushing for the door.

Rex told me to go, promising that he would get Sammie home safely.

No one needed to be alone until we were sure.

Sammie didn't want to speculate.

Terrified she was pointing a finger that shouldn't be pointed.

But my guts screamed, my spirit sure.

I didn't wait for the elevator. I took the three flights of stairs faster than I ever had, busting into the garage after I'd punched in the code.

Dread leeched through every inch of me when my sight landed on my turquoise truck.

The windshield was smashed in.

Fury rumbled like a storm.

Coming closer and closer.

My garage was a fucking fortress.

A place not a soul who wasn't welcome should be able to get in to.

I inched forward.

Fear leeched into my flesh when I reached out and plucked the tiny folded note out from under the wiper.

Heart in my throat, I unfolded it, horror eating me up when I found what was written inside.

She can't hide. She's always been mine.

thirty-five
Nikki

It was funny how different it felt being out there alone. When there were no voices to cloud the calm beauty of the scene spread out like a painting in front of me.

The gurgle of the streams and the rush of the water as it gathered strength, rolling over the side of the jagged cliffs and tumbling to the lake far, far below.

I needed it.

Peace.

For hours, I'd driven in search of an answer, and I'd ended up here, seeking a place to process what had become a muddled, chaotic disaster inside me.

One made of sorrow and hurt and an onslaught of overwhelmingly devastating questions.

I lifted my face to the blazing sun that pounded from above, falling through the Alabama sky that was the purest blue.

The sweeping stretch of beauty laid out below was almost a mirror, the blue, expansive lake and the twist of the river that wound around the mountain in the distance.

My spirit throbbed and pulsed, and the prayer silently spilled out into the vast expanse of land below.

Sydney, I'm so sorry. I'm so sorry this happened to you.
I hate it.
I wish I could go back to that day and change it.
Take it back.
Let you know that we loved you. So much. It was the fear of it that had held our tongues. We'd never, ever wanted to sever those bonds.

Yet, those bonds had been severed in the worst, worst way.

And my sister . . .

Hugging my knees to my chest, I rocked where I sat on a dry patch on a smooth stone that had been carved out by the flow of the waters.

Sadness cut through the center of me. I had no idea how to piece it together.

If I was attempting to draw lines that didn't connect, or if I was just praying that they didn't.

A gentle breeze rippled through, swishing through the tops of the trees. I hugged my knees tighter.

I swore, I could feel her brushing across me, a whisper in my ear.

Fly, fly, dragonfly.

A wistful smile tugged at one side of my mouth, and I let my eyes drop closed and relished in her memory.

In her hope and her beauty and the way she had looked at life.

I was almost too lost in the moment to hear the movement behind me. It took me a second before I froze just as the hairs at the nape of my neck prickled in awareness, standing on end.

"They'll be coming for me soon."

The voice swallowed me from behind.

Low and menacing.

Disgust swam with the fear. Lighting my nerves and jumping into my veins.

Todd. He was there.

And I suddenly got the sensation of something I should have known all along.

The way he'd watched.

The comments he'd made.

Always right there, gaze directed at me in ways it shouldn't have been.

Tremors rolled, and I tried to hold them back when I slowly pushed to standing and cautiously swiveled around to face him.

He stood at the edge of the woods that grew up the side of the mountain behind him.

The same mountain where I'd played as a child. Ran and laughed and believed.

"Uncle Todd." I attempted to send him a surprised, welcoming smile as if this was all one big coincidence when all I wanted to do was throw up again.

This was the man who'd hurt my sister.

Inflicted a kind of pain I couldn't comprehend.

My mind flipped back through everything that had happened over the last few months.

My apartment getting broken into.

My grandma's box stolen.

The notes on my windshield.

Caleb shouting at Ollie that he had no clue what he had been talking about.

It wasn't until that second I realized he hadn't been lying.

It wasn't Caleb who had done all those things.

Todd cracked a smile that sent a cold chill skating over me. "Well . . . if it isn't Nikki Lou."

I tried to smile again. All I managed was a grimace with the way he was looking at me. "What are you doing all the way out here?" I asked, going for coy.

As if I were clueless.

A naïve little girl.

That's what he'd always wanted, right?

"Looking for you."

My knees knocked.

Oh, God.

I had to stay strong.

I frowned at him in an innocuous way. "Well, you could have just called. I would have been happy to come out to Grandma's for a visit."

"Think we both know it's too late for that."

My mouth went dry. "I don't know what you're talking about."

It was a lie.

I knew it would be so much better to play dumb with a desperate man.

He laughed. Biting and hard. "Come now, Nikki. You think I don't recognize it in your eyes? You think I don't see the way you're looking at me?"

So badly, I wanted to refute it. To stand my ground. To continue to pretend. But the denial of his claim won out. "You don't know anything about me."

An ominous chuckle rode on the dense, dense air. "I know everything about you, Nikki."

My blood froze.

My heart stuttered.

I tried to remain steady. To draw out time. Studying the best way to beat him.

Fight or flight.

I still wasn't sure.

All I knew was I wouldn't let him win.

His nose curled in some kind of unknown disgust. "I should have known better than to trust someone to do what they're told. Should have known that punk kid would get greedy and not follow directions."

Confusion had me shaking my head. "I honestly have no idea what you're talking about."

It was true.

He was talking in circles.

Unbalanced.

I guessed I'd just missed out on the fact he was deranged.

He made a low sound. Disbelief and outrage. "He was supposed to dump that old car. Should have done it myself, but I figured the farther away I kept myself from it, the better. Hell, should have done it all those years ago, but I figured I'd better get gone."

A disorder shifted through the breeze. Branches lashing as if they felt the tumult.

He took a step forward, coming out of the shade of the trees and into the light.

Depraved darkness standing in the rays.

Brown hair greasy and unkempt, the same way as it'd always been. Clothes a little ratty. Those few extra pounds prominent around his middle. None of those things mattered.

It was the evil in his eyes that made him ugly.

"Never imagined that tweeker would run straight to that asshole who was always watching you like he thought you belonged to him."

Uncertainty moved through me, a niggle at the back of my mind that was quickly adding up.

He was talking about the Bel Air.

Ollie had bought the Bel Air.

"You know Caleb?" I asked.

Keep him talking.

Keep him talking.

"Of course, I know who Caleb is considering you do. Wasn't sure if I should run out and protect you from him that night a couple months back when I followed you to his and that girl's apartment. Had to stay back when the cops showed up a few minutes later."

Dread spiraled.

He'd been following me all this time.

Since the first time Brenna had called me for help.

"About a week later, I found him downtown, all itchy and antsy, and I knew it wouldn't take all that much to convince him to haul it away." Todd smiled as if his thought process was genius.

"He was supposed to dump it in the river or the lake. Should have known, even with all the rust, he'd be seeing dollar signs. Didn't want to get close to it, touch it, dirty it up more."

"Dirty?" Fear blazed. So hot I could feel the bead of sweat slide down my spine.

I took a step back, trying to keep as much distance between

us as possible. "What do you mean by that?"

His voice was nonchalant. "I was watching. Figured it wasn't such a bad thing when they were gonna take it into that garage and fix her up. That might even be better than dumping it in the lake. But the second I saw that pig show up and the police take it away, I knew I had to speed things up. That you and I didn't have that much more time."

He was moving closer, rounding to the side. For every step of his, I took one in the opposite direction.

"And my apartment?" I asked, hating that I had to, but knowing my only chance of getting away from him was understanding his depravity.

"Sorry about that, but I had to get that box. Put some stuff in there for safe keeping 'fore I left. When I heard my ma was starting to sell stuff off, that she was failing, I knew it was time I came back. Been planning it for a while, needing to get back to you. It was a sign when your mama told me on the phone she'd been clearing out the attic. That was my collection, you know?"

Nausea surged and my heart hurt.

God only knew what was in that box.

"Didn't help matters that you had to go and run those classes for women in that basement. Bunch of hens cackling and gossiping and saying things they have no business saying. Your head all filled up with that nonsense."

"How do you know that?" I shouldn't have said anything, shouldn't have bitten, but the scraping words pulled free of my throat.

His chuckle could have been construed as affectionate—soft and warm—if it hadn't skated through me like ice. "Told you, I know everything about you. Been watching you for your whole life. Knew the second I saw you that you were mine. 'Course, I had to stop watching you for a bit when things got messy, and I had to go away."

Messy.
Sydney.
Sydney.
I'm so sorry. I'm so sorry.

Bile prowled my throat, stomach twisting in sickness.

Vomit threatened at my mouth, and I struggled to keep it down. To stay strong.

But I was so close to falling to my knees and weeping.

For my sister.

For my best friend.

For me.

We'd begun to circle. Our footsteps crunched beneath us, his forward, mine back.

I was trying to figure out the best direction to run, the quickest route to help, when the wicked words strummed from his tongue.

"Didn't mean to kill her."

A stifled gasp jerked into my lungs.

The air stifling.

Suffocating.

"Why?" It was a plea. "Why would you hurt her? Hurt my sister?"

Why if he'd always been after me?

He shrugged as if it didn't matter. "Some things you just have to test out."

I choked.

"I had to protect us, Nikki. Everything I've ever done, I've done for you. So we can be together."

My knees wobbled.

"They weren't supposed to find her . . . and that damned car . . . should have burned it." He said it all as if I should feel sorry for him.

As if the world was against him when he was the monster prowling in the midst.

"Now everyone's gonna know. Means we don't have much time.

thirty-six

Sydney
Sixteen Years Old

Tears stung her eyes, and her heart physically hurt. She hugged herself around her middle as she trudged along the side of the curving country road.

She should have called her mama like Ollie had suggested, but she needed to think. Clear her head before she went and said something she would regret.

She tightened her arms around her as a hot wind blew through, her skin sticky from the exertion and her face hot from the tears.

She was so over this. It was as if all four of them were playing a stupid game and none of them were gonna win.

She almost rolled her eyes.

As if she didn't know about Ollie and Nikki.

She'd known for years that there was something extra special about the two of them. That they were more. Their spirits seemed tangled in a way that'd been intended before time existed.

Made for each other.

Did they really think she would consider that a bad thing?

Did they even know her at all?

She just wanted them to embrace it.

Live free.

The same as she wanted for herself and Rex.

And the only thing it felt like was they were clipping her wings.

Cutting little bits of her away as they pushed her further to the outside.

There was no reason for them to be hiding, just like there was no reason for her and Rex to be hiding.

Rex.

At the thought of his name, her chest pulled tight.

Stretched and yearned.

She loved him so much. She didn't think she really knew how much until she'd had to watch him kiss that girl.

And she was the one who got to stay.

The one who was with him.

New tears pricked at her eyes.

He hadn't come after her. Hadn't stood up for her. Instead, he'd just driven a knife into her heart.

No more.

She stumbled to a stop.

No more.

Maybe Rex didn't know what she wanted. That she wanted him to stand up for her. Make a claim.

Fight for her.

She'd just have to do it herself.

She touched the red-woven bracelet that she always wore around her left wrist. The other two matching pieces belonging to Ollie and Nikki.

Her best friends.

But they had to realize her life was changing, too.

All of them had to make room for something new.

She came to a stop.

Realization struck.

She was gonna turn around, go back to that camp, and

demand Rex say it.

Tell Ollie.

She was his and he was hers and no one would have anything bad to say about it.

Because *it* was good.

They were good.

Ollie and Nikki were good.

She started to cross the road but froze when headlights cut into the night and a loud car roared around the corner.

She took a step back away from the road as it flew by before the red brake lights flashed, splashing the color all over the night as the old car skidded to a stop.

Her heart trembled with a dose of anxiety.

She squinted her eyes, relief leaving her on a breath when she realized she recognized that car.

Nikki's grandpa.

He could give her a ride back to the lake.

She jogged that way with a smile on her face, and she saw his silhouette as he leaned over to fling open the passenger door as she approached. She started to duck her head inside to say hello when her knees wobbled beneath her.

Not Nikki's grandpa.

It was Nikki's uncle.

Todd.

He grinned, his teeth stained yellow from cigarettes, his hands still greasy from always working on cars.

There was something about him Sydney had never liked. The way he looked at Nikki. Watched her too close.

"Well, look who it is. Sydney Sue. Where's my Nikki Lou?"

Unease rippled through her consciousness, a cringe rolling through her at the stupid, creepy nicknames he'd give them, as if it was actually their middle names.

"She's at home," Sydney lied. Not sure why.

He frowned. "That so?"

His eyes moved over her, and a cold shiver rippled down her back.

"What are you doin' out here all alone?"

"I'm just heading home," she said, angling back.

"I'll give you a ride."

She backed away. "No, that's okay. My brother should be coming this way in a second, anyway."

She pinned on a smile and hoped he'd fall for the lie.

He wasn't exactly the smartest guy she knew.

His eyes flicked from her face and down to her chest. "You look different than her."

He said it as if she should be ashamed of it. As if it were disappointing.

Then he shrugged. "Guess for tonight, you'll have to do."

thirty-seven
Ollie

"Don't do anything until I get there, Ollie. I'm right behind you."

"No promises, man."

Not when it came to Nikki.

My Nikki.

My girl who'd been desperate to be there through this with me, and I'd been too much of a fool to see it for what it was.

Thinking I forever owed a debt, the girl nothing but a tease, a torment of what I couldn't have.

When in reality?

She'd been a gift, always right there, waiting for me to accept it.

I tossed my cell to the seat beside me and made a sharp right onto the drive that was close to being hidden under a thicket of trees that ran the land.

Engine roaring, I gunned the accelerator. My Mustang bounced on the dirt road, wheels kicking up a cloud of dust as I flew down the narrow lane.

The heart I thought I no longer had thrashed at my chest, my teeth clenched just about as tight as my hands were clenched on the steering wheel.

I barreled around the corner, and the old house came into view.

There were a million memories here. I could get lost in them. Stuck like I'd been.

But I realized when Sammie had stood there in the hall, I couldn't change the past, no matter how fucking badly I wanted to.

I had nothing but this moment and the future.

Nothing but Nikki.

Swinging into the rounded drive at the front of the house, I rammed the brakes and jumped out, not bothering to shut the door when I thundered up the rickety porch steps that had seen far better days.

I pounded on the door and then began to pace, roughing a hand over the top of my head as I waited.

As seconds ticked.

As I felt myself going insane.

I couldn't let this happen.

I couldn't let someone hurt her.

I promised I'd protect her.

That I wasn't ever gonna let anyone hurt her.

I could hear the car coming up the road, and Seth's cruiser rolled into view right when Nikki's mom swung open the door with a smile on her face.

A smile that slid off the second she saw me.

"Oliver Preston." She looked around, spotting the approaching patrol car. Worry took hold of her expression.

"What are you doing here? What's going on? Is Nikki okay?" Each word came faster than the last, panted pleas winding into her tone when she stepped outside.

Anxiety fisted my throat, and I pushed the gritted words through it. "I was hoping you could tell me that. You haven't seen her?"

She shook her head, and there was no missing the glimmers of fear that streaked through her expression when Seth stepped from his car.

Her brow pinched with confusion. "No . . . I haven't seen her for a couple of days. Sammie called a few hours ago, wondering if she'd come by, but she didn't say anything else."

Apprehension trembled her voice, and she reached out and grabbed my arm. "Tell me what's going on."

"I need to find her."

"What's happening?"

"Where's that piece of shit Todd?"

The question knocked her back a step, and her brows twisted into a knot. "I . . . I don't know. Heard him leaving late last night. I don't think he's been back."

Fuck. Fuck. Fuck.

I fisted my hands in my hair, searching for the air. Desperation climbing.

"Does he still stay in the trailer in the back lot?"

Warily, she nodded.

I spun around.

Seth caught me by the arm as he came up to the door. "Where are you going?"

I ripped my arm away. "To find Nikki."

I bounded down the steps and ran for the trailer that sat little more than a quarter mile back from the house.

"Ollie," Seth shouted from behind me. "Wait, man. We need to let the warrant come through."

I didn't even stop to ponder it. I pounded the heel of my fist on the door.

Nothing.

No movement.

Holding on to the railing, I leaned back and lifted my leg.

"Fuck, Ollie, you can't just bust in there."

"Watch me."

There was no way I was sitting idle.

Waiting.

Not when waiting meant we could be running out of time.

I slammed the sole of my boot into the door at the side of the flimsy knob. The old wood splintered and gave. Nothing holding it together.

I wrenched open the door, flying inside.

The place was a disgusting mess. Dishes piled in the sink, garbage everywhere.

Decay and rot.

Silence hung in the air.

Vacant.

Ominous.

A stark emptiness echoing back.

Still, I couldn't stop myself from pushing deeper into the rat hole, rushing down the short hall and throwing open the door to the only bedroom.

The sight bent me in two.

Pictures.

Everywhere.

All of them were of Nikki.

Baby pictures.

Ones of her as a little girl.

A few with Sydney as a teenager.

But it was the current ones that sent panic sloshing through my system.

There were a bunch of Nikki at the diner.

Some outside of Olive's.

One of her walking up the steps to her apartment.

Motherfucker.

Her apartment.

It was him. It was him.

My eyes darted around for anything else, and I started to push out of the room, when my sight snagged on something in the closet.

The sliding door had barely been left open a sliver.

A floral box.

A box.

Anxiety gripped me everywhere, and my movements slowed as I edged forward. Slowly, I slid the closet door open farther. The lock had been broken, the lid ripped off, the contents tossed aside as if someone had frantically dug through it to find what was hidden underneath.

A groan climbed out from my soul.

Agony.

Sydney's bracelet.

It was there in the middle of it as if the asshole had needed to hold it.

Sick and deranged and twisted.

"Oh God," I whimpered, unable to stomach it.

Sickness clawed, and I was clutching my head, trying to see through the web of darkness that spun through me.

Cruelty.

Cruelty.

My sister.

Fuck, my sister.

It hurt. It hurt so damned bad.

The reality.

I'd hunted for so long.

And the proof was right there.

It was like the idiot wanted everyone to know. Or maybe he'd just realized once they'd found Sydney, there was no place left to hide.

I'd die before I let it happen again.

"Shit," Seth whispered in shock from behind me, pulling me back. "Get out of here, Ollie. Don't touch anything. This is evidence."

I blinked at him, seeing nothing but red.

He didn't have to ask me twice.

I was busting back out the door and running for my Mustang.

"What do you think you're doing?" he shouted.

I jumped inside. "I'm going to find Nikki. You go to her apartment . . . he's been there. Call me if you find anything."

"Where are you going?"

"Up the river."

"I can't just let you take off like some kind of vigilante. I'm calling it in, everyone will be looking for them."

"And you can't expect me to stand aside and wait for that to happen. I'll call you if I see anything. Swear, man. I'll call. But you can't expect me to sit here. Go. Find her," I begged him.

He gave me a reluctant nod before he jogged back to his cruiser.

I was throwing my car into first when I met Nikki's mom's stare through the windshield. Her hands were pressed against her chin and tears blanketed her face.

I made her a silent promise.

I'll fight for her.
I'll die for her.
Most of all, I'll live for her.

Twenty minutes later, I'd made it through town. Dusk sat heavily as I wound down the twisty, country road.

My nerves were speeding while I drove like a motherfucking snail, foot itching to hit the gas. But I was looking for a hint of . . . anything. Anything that felt off.

I passed the turn that would lead to the lake and wound around a bend, heading for Row. There were at least a hundred little offshoots of deserted roads, no more than trails carved out between the trees.

Anxiety clawed, the sharpest talons in my flesh.

Flickers of awareness.

Realization and a tease.

Little Tease.

I jammed on the brakes in the middle of the road as a sticky feeling came over me.

Drawn.

Compelled.

Row would still be crawling with investigators.

And Nikki . . . she wouldn't go there.

I knew it.

I knew it all the way into my soul.

Heart taking off at a sprint, I flipped a U-turn in the middle of the road, tires sliding off into the shrubs and dirt. The tail end whipped behind me when I forced the accelerator to the floor, and I righted the car when it skidded.

Two seconds later, I was cutting across the road to make the left.

Praying the whole way that she was there.

That she was alone.

That she was just seeking the solace this place had always given us.

Needing that peace when I'd done the exact thing I promised her I wouldn't.

I'd hurt her.

Shunned her.

Left her.

When she was dealing with the same damned thing.

I was so finished with being this selfish prick. The guy who thought it was his duty to suffer. Only thing that stupidity accomplished was taking the ones he loved down with him.

Again, I was gonna be the beggar. Pleading for forgiveness when I didn't deserve it. Couldn't change that.

All I could do was fucking fight.

Fight for her.

This time, I would make it right.

The lake shone a vibrant pink as the sun sank at the far end of the sky.

Off to the left was the public beach.

I knew that wouldn't be where Nikki would go.

I barreled on to where the road curved at its end, and I took the same worn-out path we'd used for all our lives.

It wound up through the trees and back down again.

My pulse thudded when I caught sight of the glint of metal in the dusky haze. I edged forward until it fully came into view.

Nikki's car.

But it was the beater truck sitting next to it that punched the air from my lungs.

Sent a quiver of stakes through my spirit.

An earthquake.

Hate and fury and devastation.

I wouldn't let this happen.

Hands shaking like a bitch, I dialed Seth.

He answered on the first ring. "You got anything?"

"They're here. At the secluded cove at the far end of the lake.

Both of them. I'm parked behind both their cars."

"Fuck," he shouted. I could hear the siren blip on the other end before it became a full, shrill cry, the sound of his cruiser quickly accelerating. "Do not approach them, Ollie. I'll be there in ten minutes."

"Send help," I told him before tossing my phone back to the seat without taking the time to end the call.

I reached for the glove box and pulled out the handgun I'd taken from the safe before I'd headed for Nikki's grandparents' land.

I jerked open the door, blood pumping so hard I could feel it as it slogged through my body.

Taste it on my tongue.

Rage and desperation.

Fear and hope.

As silently as I could, I edged up the path, terrified of what I was going to find.

If I was too late, I wasn't sure I would survive it this time.

My guts clenched in both relief and misery when I heard the whimper. The rumble of a low voice came out behind it, but the words were indistinguishable.

The threat of night hugged the earth, the day slipping away and stealing the light. Twilight swam through the trees in a dreamlike haze.

Footsteps quieted, I inched all the way up to the spot where we used to jump from the cliffs.

I pressed against a tree, trying not to shout out when they came into view.

In pain.

In vengeance.

In the violence that twisted through me like the blackest storm.

Ravaging.

Annihilating.

Destroying.

Nikki was on her knees, arms twisted behind her back as he stood behind her and shackled her wrists with a thin twine.

The sick fuck had her gagged, the same twine running across the rag he'd stuffed in her mouth and tied behind her head to keep it in place.

But the hardest part was the terror that blazed in her eyes.

I nearly dropped to my knees when I was slammed with the gutting relief that overwhelmed her when she saw me at the line of trees.

Tears spilled out, and she released a gurgled cry as she sagged forward.

And that energy.

It surged.

So intense.

The greatest thing I'd ever felt.

Wave after wave.

Blast after blast.

This girl was everything.

All of me.

"None of that," the vile piece of shit seethed, yanking her back up, and I had no reservations left.

My feet were moving, the gun lifted in the air, boots crunched beneath me.

His head whipped up. "You little fuck. Always hanging around her. Thinking she belonged to you. I never should have waited so long. It needed to be perfect. It needed to be perfect."

The last spiraled in derangement.

I almost laughed, an unhinged sound I felt bubble at the back of my throat. "Let her go. Let her go. Don't think I will hesitate to kill you."

He killed my sister.

He killed my sister.

Oh God.

Bile swam, and every muscle in my body bristled. Flexed with aggression.

With this possessive protection that seethed from the depths of me.

I took another powerful step forward, promising him I wasn't playing games.

He yanked Nikki to standing, and her gaze was on me, mine on her.

Trust me.

Trust me.

It was a silent plea, praying she would feel me. That I wouldn't allow anything bad to happen to her.

That I was there.

I wouldn't ever leave her again.

I choked, stumbling to a stop when I saw the glint of the knife he had pressed to her side.

"I'd rethink that." His voice was all sneer as he dragged her back against his chest.

They were teetering right at the edge of the cliff. The asshole had backed himself right into a corner, nowhere for him to run.

"Let her go," I demanded, trying to keep the tremble from my voice.

I wasn't backing down.

Like I'd let him take her.

"There's nowhere for you to go. Nothing left. The police are already on their way, and they know what you did to my sister. The game is up. Let her go."

He cracked a demented grin. "She and I have a little time, don't we, Nikki?" he whispered in her ear.

She cried out.

Disgust and revulsion rolled through me. Sickness and that hate.

Hate. So much hate.

For so long, I'd pinned it on myself. No more. This was all on him.

He'd hurt my sister. Sammie. Nikki. God knew who else.

No more.

No more.

My head shook, and the bitterness quivered my lips, but my hand was steady. "Wrong, asshole. Time's up."

Somewhere in the distance, sirens blared, riding on the encroaching night. Coming closer and closer.

As soon as he heard it, deranged panic lit in the sick fuck's eyes. Like he actually thought he was going to make it out of there with Nikki.

Saw it the second he let desperation take him over. He jerked Nikki closer and started to run to the side.

Nikki flailed, swinging her shoulders, kicking her feet.

She broke free, stumbling back and away from him.

He whirled back to look at her. Stunned. Like he couldn't believe she would fight him.

Like he was witnessing his own kind of horror.

That was my chance.

I was taking it.

I rushed that way, intent on tackling the fucker to the ground.

His eyes met mine, and I saw the shift. When he realized he had no choice left.

Madness filled his eyes, his vile gaze darting all over, searching for escape.

The piece of shit started running my direction, charging me with the knife drawn.

Thinking I was going to let him get through me.

Disappear in to the forest.

"Stop," I shouted.

He just kept coming, the knife raised above his head.

"Stop," I roared.

He made a sound to match as he rushed me.

Insane.

Crazed.

Unwilling to stop.

Squeezing my eyes shut, I pulled the trigger.

The sound was deafening.

Ricocheting on the cliffs and rocks and moving through me.

He crumpled into a pile at my feet.

My lungs squeezed, and I panted through the haze, everything set to slow as my mind tried to catch up.

Ears ringing, my attention swooped across the space for Nikki.

She teetered at the edge of the cliffs.

Feet sliding out from beneath her. Hands tied behind her and setting her off-balance on the slick, wet surface.

I was running that way as she struggled to regain her footing on the slipping rocks.

Those indigo eyes went wide as one foot gave.

Falling backward.

A shout of agony tore from me as I watched her tip over the side.

My pulse thundered, and my heart screamed as loud as the screams that tore from my mouth.

"Nikki! Nikki. God, no, Nikki!"

I raced for the edge.

I skidded right before I hit the crumbling ledge.

Sucking in a staggered breath.

Blinking as I swore I saw Sydney standing at the cliff, her flowy dress billowing around her, hair soft as it whispered across her face.

Her voice lilted on the breeze. *"You were my protector. My savior. My hero. It's okay, Ollie. It's okay to be hers."*

"Forgive me," I begged, the words so small.

She smiled. The softest smile. *"There was never anything to forgive. Just promise me one thing."*

"Anything." It was my own pleas.

"Never stop going after what makes your heart feel right."

She angled her head toward the edge and lifted her chin.

"Fly, fly, dragonfly."

I blinked, and she was gone.

I was at a flat-out run when I dove over the side.

Falling.

I'd been all along.

I hit the water. It split, swallowing me in a pit of darkness.

I couldn't see anything, and I started flailing, searching the water, my chest burning from the exertion and the loss of oxygen.

And I felt my sister. All around. And I wondered if she'd always been.

I pushed myself harder, a little deeper.

My fingertips just brushed against something.

Didn't matter.
I saw it.
Could feel it.
The flash.
A spark.
Energy.
Light.
The meaning of life.

A half second later, I had an arm around Nikki's waist, and I propelled us up. We broke the surface, and I was gasping for breath, frantic as I freed her of the bonds.

But Nikki.

She wasn't breathing.

And I was crying out, floating on my back as I turned her so her face was out of the water, swimming back toward the shore with one arm.

The sound of the sirens traveled across the water, and swirling lights came into view from the shore, hitting the lake and blinking across the sky like an endless mirror.

"Nikki," I cried, my feet finally hitting the bottom of the lake. I gathered her in my arms and staggered up the rocky beach as officers came rushing down the incline.

I screamed with everything I had. "Help!"

thirty-eight
Ollie

The monitor blipped quietly in the still of the room, the lights muted and her soft, soft breaths filling the air.

Swore, they breathed right back into me.

The sound of her where she slept on the hospital bed.

Olive skin and honeyed hair and freckled cheeks.

Sunshine.

She still hadn't gained consciousness, but they thought she was going to be okay.

Her saturations and pulse ox had been good, but they would be taking her for scans to make sure her lungs were clear.

I leaned forward, taking her hand in mine, bringing it to my lips.

I was swept by an undercurrent of that energy. A sated fire that streamed between us. Our connection quieted but so goddamned bold.

Overwhelming.

I inhaled, and I swore, it felt like I was inhaling the breaking day.

Something fresh and new.

I stared at her, eyes tracing every unforgettable line of her face.

She was so pretty.

So pretty my guts clenched and my heart was drumming its song, the way it did whenever Nikki stepped into a room.

When she took up my space.

"You're going to be just fine," I whispered at her knuckles, praying she could feel my promise. That it was touching that bright, bright spirit.

That she'd know she wasn't alone.

Her mom had been here.

Her sister.

Lillith and Rynna and Hope.

This girl surrounded by love.

Because that's what she was.

Love.

The lightest tap sounded at the door, and I shifted to see Kale popping his head inside.

Thank God for Kale.

Kale, who'd come running when I'd sent out the distress call that we needed him. Even though he was no longer a physician at the ER, there wasn't anyone I trusted more than him to be there, acting as Nikki's intercessor, making sure no stone was left unturned.

"Hey," I said, voice so low it barely broke the air. "Is it time for her to get the scans?"

He grimaced a little as he stepped inside. "Not quite," he told me.

Unease wound through my being, and I couldn't keep the quiver of distress out of my voice. "Did the tests come back?"

"Yeah. Everything looks good. CBC is good, and her O2 sats have been normal."

Relief blew out on the heaviest sigh, and I was nodding, rubbing my face as this feeling came over me. This stunning gratitude that had taken the place of the weight that had been on my shoulders.

Was close to weighing the amount of the love that pressed

through me.

Filling me full.

He studied the readout on one of the monitors. "Has she opened her eyes yet?"

"No . . . but . . . I can feel it. She's gonna be okay. I think she's just sleeping off the trauma."

It wasn't like I was some kind of medical guru.

It was just like I'd said.

I could *feel* it.

He came to stand beside me, looking at Nikki.

"That's what she needs the most. Rest." He angled his attention to me. "And support. Someone to be there for her when she wakes up so she knows she isn't alone."

I shifted in the seat, tightening my hold on her hand. "I'm not going anywhere."

"Are you finished running, Ollie?" he asked, staring at me like he was searching for the truth of my answer. Something hard in his expression.

My gaze traveled back to Nikki.

Nikki. Fucking. Walters.

The girl I'd thought the bane of my existence.

The girl nothing but a tease and a taunt of what I couldn't have.

I'd just been too blind to recognize that she was my *very* existence.

"Yeah, I'm done running," I murmured, more to her than to him.

He cracked a smile. "Good." He gave a pat to my shoulder before he moved for the door. "Oh, and she won't be getting those x-rays."

I shifted in the chair so I could see him. "Why's that?"

He paused to look back at me. "Because she's pregnant."

thirty-nine
Nikki

My eyes fluttered open, the sound of a constant, low beep, beep, beep filling my ears. But my sight, it was filled with Ollie.

Beautiful Ollie who was staring over at me.

The man who had wrecked me.

The one who had saved me.

He'd always been an enigma.

The hardest jaw and the quickest smile.

"Nikki," he murmured as he watched me studying him, and he reached out and set a big hand on the side of my head.

Energy flashed.

The connection so intense that I felt my insides clutch.

"Ollie."

"You're okay. You're okay."

I flinched as all the memories came flooding back.

My sister.

Sydney.

The cliffs.

"What happened?" I rasped, my throat achy and raw and my lungs too tight, but there was no stopping the panic that seized my heart. "What happened to Todd?"

So many things moved through his expression.

Hate.

Worry.

Regret.

Relief.

"He can't hurt you anymore."

"Oh." It was a breath. A strike of realization. The sound of a gunshot ricocheting in my mind.

Ollie brushed his thumb over my cheek. "I'm sorry I didn't get there sooner."

My lips pursed, and I fought the tears that worked in my eyes. "You saved me."

"I told you I would never let anyone hurt you again. Protecting you is my duty."

I could feel the twist of my brow. The sorrow on my heart, and it hurt so much to say the words.

But it was time.

I couldn't do this anymore.

Not after everything.

"I don't want to be your duty, Ollie. I can't be a sin you're trying to make amends for."

Regret streaked across Ollie's handsome face.

Sapphire eyes flashed with intensity as he sat forward, his hold on the side of my head tightening.

Hand spread out as if he wanted to touch me everywhere.

"I've spent my life living in the past, Nikki."

His voice was gruff. Strained as he seemed to struggle with the words. "I spent years searching for something that wasn't there. It'd felt like hope. But I know now, I was trying to pay a debt. That I thought I didn't deserve to live because Sydney hadn't."

Grief billowed from him.

"My mom . . ." His voice broke, and my heart fisted because never in all these years had he mentioned her.

Their relationship severed.

I'd never been privy to the details.

"She blamed me," he whispered as if it hurt too much to say it aloud. He gave a harsh shake of his head. "I'll never forget when the police left after taking my statement, she . . . lost it."

He gulped. "She just . . . started hammering on my chest. I'd barely been able to hear what she was saying, she was crying so hard. But I did, Nikki. She was saying that she'd trusted me . . . that it was my fault . . . that I'd promised I would take care of her. She said I failed her. Failed Sydney."

Sympathy stretched so tight I couldn't breathe.

"Oh, God. Ollie. I didn't know."

He looked at me. Laid bare. "In some way, I did fail, Nikki. We all did. We made mistakes, but none of us meant to hurt her."

He blinked through the dim-lights of the room. "I thought . . . I thought for all these years that I couldn't be trusted. That I didn't deserve to be."

He gathered up my arm and pressed the underside of my wrist to his lips.

A sound hitched in his throat. A guttural cry that I felt move all the way through the center of me.

"I'm always gonna miss her, Nikki. I will miss her every day of my life. I thought that made me a lost soul. That I had no home. But you . . ."

He eased off the chair and moved so he was completely hovering over me, taking both sides of my face in his hands.

He squeezed me tightly. As if he were begging me to hear.

"You, Nikki . . . you are my home. You've been leading me there all along, calling me there, and I was too blind to see that was where I belonged. Too afraid to accept it. Too afraid to believe in it. Too afraid to *trust* in myself."

His throat bobbed when he swallowed, and he edged back to standing. He set one of those tattooed hands over his heart.

"I'm a simple, man, Nikki. If I were Kale, I'd have planned some big thing. Wooed you. Impressed the hell out of you," he said, mouth tweaking into something that resembled a grin before it fell flat again.

"But I'm not . . . I'm just here . . . this lost soul who finally found his home, begging her to open the door and let him in."

Tears rushed to my eyes, and a ball of emotion rolled through my chest.

Pressing and pulling and pleading.

"The door was always open, Ollie. Always. You just had to make the choice to stay."

"Only if you let me stay forever."

I hated the reservations that scrambled to be heard. That wall that wanted to rise up and protect my heart that he'd broken again and again. But they shouted at me not to be a fool.

"What about Sydney, Ollie? The fact that you can't look at me without seeing her? Without thinking of her? I don't want to be the girl standing in her shadow."

He was back to hovering over my hospital bed, this time his nose so close to brushing mine. "How could you stand in the shadows when you are the brightest thing in the room?"

His lips brushed against mine in the softest kiss.

"Sunshine," he murmured like praise. "You are light and life. My life. My everything. Let me be yours."

Tears streaked free, and I lifted my chin, our mouths meeting as I whispered, "I've always been yours."

Our foreheads met, and we shared our breaths.

That energy rippled and danced.

Climbing into the atmosphere.

Colors and light.

Chemistry.

He kissed me again as one of his hands slid down my face, cupping my jaw, my chin, gliding to my heart. "I've got something to tell you."

Nerves tumbled. "What's that?"

His hand kept moving, slipping over my hip until he moved it over my stomach. His hand resting between us. "We're gonna have a baby."

forty
Ollie

"Ollie, I'm not crippled." She swatted at my shoulder.

Playfully.

I had her swept up in my arms, holding her as the elevator clanged for the third floor of my building.

I nuzzled my nose along her jaw, inhaling deep, my lips a soft brush against her cheek. "How about you just let me hold you for a while, yeah?"

Her arms were looped around my neck, and she buried her face in my beard. "If you insist, big boy."

I squeezed her as the elevator jostled to a stop at the top floor, cages sliding open to the hall. "Plan on holding you forever, sweet girl."

She giggled.

God.

Was it possible I got this? Her giggles and her smiles and all her days?

I wanted them. Fuck, I wanted them so bad that I held her a little tighter against me as I carried her down the hall.

"That might get awkward, you know."

"What, you don't think people would approve of me carrying you to work?"

She was chewing on her bottom lip as she looked up at me, a flush on her cheeks that screamed of so much life. "People might get weird ideas about us."

Us.

I grinned. "Let them get all the ideas they want."

I angled to the side so I could fumble with the lock on the front door. I was still carrying her when we got inside.

It was late when she'd been discharged from the hospital this evening.

Her attending doctor had told her the exact thing Kale had told me.

The most important thing she needed was rest. To give her body time to recuperate from the trauma. I took her straight to my bedroom.

Strike that.

Our room.

I laid her on the bed, and she giggled again, just as I was crawling right up with her, unable to leave any distance between us.

Needing her near.

I propped myself on my elbow, making sure to keep my weight off her, and ran my fingers through her hair. "How are you able to keep smiling after everything you just went through?"

It wasn't an accusation.

It was awe.

Pure. Fucking. Awe.

This girl.

Goodness and light.

With a shaky hand, she reached out and ran her fingers through my beard before she let them drift up, moving across my cheeks, my eyebrow, my nose.

Closing my eyes, I sighed and relished the sensation.

Her touching me.

So freely.

"How could I not be?" she whispered.

That aura she wore rolled through the room.

Thunder.

Colors and strobes.

I eased back more so I could look at her.

She caressed along the line of my hair, head tilting as she spoke softly. "My sister is home. Safe with Penelope and her husband."

She stroked across the shell of my ear.

So tender.

So sweet.

It sent a chill trembling through the middle of me. "My mama is safe. My grandma is safe."

Her brow pinched as she moved to trace down my jaw. "I'm here, with you."

Her fingertips plucked at my bottom lip, her words turning to wonder. "And we're gonna have a baby."

One side of my mouth pulled up, twisting into a smile. "I can't believe it."

She searched my face. "I know you question it, Ollie. But I want you to know I *trust* that you are going to be the best daddy this baby could have."

Overcome, I kissed her, long and deep.

Who could blame me?

I was just a man loving on his girl.

I threaded my fingers through her hair, our gazes locked.

I was entranced by that energy.

The girl a spell.

The best kind of magic.

Caging her in, I pushed onto my hands and knees. I dove in to kiss across her bright, bright heart, and then I worked all the way down until I made it to her stomach.

"Thank you, Nikki, for trusting in me," I mumbled at her flat belly.

I sucked in a deep breath and made a promise that I would never, ever break. "This baby will always know that her daddy will be there for her. No matter what. No matter what mistakes she might make. No matter what life throws our way. For all my days."

Nikki's fingers were in my hair, and she was nudging me up. Eyes glistening with adoration in the muted, dancing light. "You want this? With me?"

I finally settled my weight between her thighs.

Carefully.

I wrapped her up.

Held her close.

Because I was never going to let her go.

"There's nothing more I want than to get to have a family with you, Nikki Walters. Nothing I want more than to spend all my days loving you. Nothing that makes me happier than you loving me back. You are my home."

Because I finally got that life was worth living.

It was worth cherishing.

And I had everything to live for.

Nikki stared up at me, her words so soft. "You have it all wrong, Ollie. I always trusted you. You just had to figure out how to trust yourself."

I pulled back and gazed down at her, running my thumb across her temple. "Forever and ever, you and me."

I felt it.

The spirit that fluttered through the air.

And I knew, Sydney would always be there, too.

Free.

Watching over us.

A smile forever on her face.

epilogue

I peeked out into the hall, frantically waving Hope and Jenna in where they had parked in the back lot. "Do you have it?"

Giggling, they both bustled inside, slinking through the big metal door.

"No, Nikki, we totally don't have it," Jenna said with all kinds of sarcasm dripping from her smart mouth as she lifted the huge pink cake box a few inches higher, waving it in my face.

"Stop that," I swatted at her. "I just want this to be perfect. Goodness, I'm nervous."

"You're bein' ridiculous, Nikki. Ollie is gonna love it," Hope told me in her sweet way. She was two months further along than I was.

Excitement blistered through my veins, and my hand was caressing over the tiny mound growing in my stomach, my skinny jeans still fitting but just barely.

Goodness, I couldn't wait to be a mommy. The proof that the world really could be a better place. That good things were still granted.

Blessings and joy.

Jenna let go of a loud laugh. "That, or he's going to go all savage ogre on our asses and kick us to the curb for throwing him a surprise birthday party. I'm not sure which one to put my money on."

"I'm putting all my money on my man," I told her, lifting my brow as they passed by.

"Oh, someone has it bad," Jenna sang as she started down the hall toward the main area of the bar.

"Well, if thinking about someone twenty-four seven and missing him like crazy all day while he's gone is having it bad, then so be it."

I might have it bad.

A damned fever when it came to Oliver Preston.

Rex and Kale were supposed to be keeping him busy today. A guy's fishing trip for his birthday.

It really was just to give me the time to set up.

Streamers and balloons and twinkle lights had been strewn across the entire space, and one big area had been sectioned off just for our friends and family.

The Italian caterer was already setting up at the back of the roped off area.

We rounded the corner, and Cece was setting up the private bar next to the caterer. "Made sure to stock you two some ginger ale," she said with a wink as she tossed a few bottles of it into the big ice bucket.

Turned out, she wasn't so bad after all.

I laughed. "Oh man, I do miss my wine." Tenderly, I ran my hand over my belly. "But she is definitely worth it."

Yep.

She.

Just like Ollie had insisted since the day we found out.

He may have been a bear before, brash and protective and nothing but a brute, but he'd taken it to all kinds of new levels. Watching over us so carefully, love shining so bright in his blue eyes.

Sometimes I still woke wrapped in his arms and thought I was dreaming, having wanted this for so long, tied to a man in such an intrinsic way, that it didn't seem real.

Then he'd tuck me close, and it'd all come rushing back.

He was mine, and I was his.

"Is there a cool place we can put the cake?" Hope asked Cece.

Cece grinned. "Tell me that cake is compliments of A Drop of Hope."

Hope laughed a light sound. "Well, of course it is. As if I'd trust anyone else to make the cake for Ollie's big day. I mean, unless he wanted a pie," she teased.

Sometimes I wondered how there wasn't a baking war going on between Rynna and Hope.

"And it doesn't even have sticks with pictures of Ollie on it." Sadly, Jenna shook her head. "What a shame."

"Don't even remind me of you going and pulling that with Kale. Putting pictures of my man on cupcakes for all the girls to devour. That's sacrilege."

"Um, those cupcakes were delicious," I told her. "Everyone needs a little sex on a stick."

She shooed me. "You've got your own man, Nikki. Don't be licking on mine."

"But I don't have one," Jenna whined.

"Me, neither," Cece called.

"Y'all are ridiculous." Hope was laughing when she took the cake from Jenna as if she no longer trusted her with it. "Where to?"

Cece lifted her chin. "Go through the swinging door there. Cleared a spot in the refrigerator."

"Thank you."

Hope waddled her way back there just as the band was striking up.

Ollie's favorite.

Carolina George.

One of his oldest friends was the guitarist, and it only made sense for me to invite them in.

I rubbed my palms together. "Am I missing anything?"

Cece squeezed my shoulder as she strutted by. "You're good, Nik. Ollie's gonna love it. Relax."

"Thank you."

Didn't mean I wasn't totally nervous. This was his first birthday that we'd really been together, and I wanted him to remember it forever.

What life was like when it really started.

Guests started showing up at a quarter to six. My mama and then my grandma in her wheelchair, which just made my heart sing.

Sammie and her husband were next, Penelope at home with a sitter. Even though we *were* in Alabama, we definitely didn't need any babies hanging out in the bar.

Lily and Broderick waked through the door with Rynna.

Some of Ollie's friends, guys from the bar and the shop that he had a partnership with came as well.

My heart stammered when I saw who warily came through the door, nervous as her gaze jumped around the bar.

Ollie's Mama.

I eased that way. "Margaret, I'm so glad you're here." I gripped both of her hands between mine.

"Thank you for inviting me."

"Of course."

Their relationship had a long way to go, but when Ollie had started counseling to work through his lingering guilt over Sydney, his therapist had urged him to make peace with his mother.

Even if she didn't accept it, he had to seek it.

Come to terms with it.

Forgive himself.

She'd broken down when he'd reached out, also haunted by their separation.

Sometimes forgiveness took time, but they were well on their way.

Ten more minutes passed, and we all gathered together when Hope got a text from Kale that they were almost there.

I held on to Lily and Hope's hands when we saw the guys walking up the sidewalk, laughing and joking, Ollie thinking they were coming in to share a beer before they went on their own way.

They opened the door and stepped inside, and everyone yelled surprise.

But they weren't looking at Ollie.

They had all of a sudden all turned to look at me.

They made a circle around me, a gap at the front as Ollie slowly approached me.

He tipped me up a cocky, gorgeous smile. His beard was a little shorter, hair neat, definitely not wearing the jeans he'd been wearing when he left this morning.

Instead, he wore a fitted button up with the sleeves rolled up his forearms, flashing the ink that danced above his muscle like the beat of the song that was quietly playing.

A tremble of something rippled through the air.

Something so big.

And I didn't know why, but a tear slipped from my eye.

"Ollie," I whispered, looking around at everyone who was grinning.

"Nikki."

He started moving my direction, a grin on his striking face but the world in his eyes.

That's what he was.

My great big world.

"It's your birthday," I whispered like I was issuing some kind of plea, trying to catch up to what was happening.

"You're right, Nikki, today is my birthday. Call me selfish, but I had a certain present in mind."

All the voices had gone quiet, and Carolina George eased out of a song in the middle and struck up another.

The lyrics filtered through the mic.

Richard's voice was so rough when he started playing the cover from Train. It was a song about how forever could never be enough.

My fingertips went to my lips.

Ollie took another step forward. "Nikki . . . you were my first love. My only love. The one who was always supposed to be at my side."

He inched forward and set those big hands on my swelling

belly. "You're the mother of my baby girl. You're my life."

He dropped to both of his knees, pulling the silver box with a black ribbon from his pocket. A present in the palm of his hand. "So, for my birthday, I want you to tell me you'll be my wife. Tell me that forever you'll be my home."

I dropped to my knees with him, tears streaming free, blurring my eyes, but I was sure I'd never seen so clearly.

I saw the future.

I saw joy.

I saw love.

I saw my life.

"Yes. Oh, Ollie . . . yes."

He cocked a smirk. "You haven't even seen the ring yet."

A soggy laugh pilfered free. "Give me that ring, you bear."

"You sure you want it?" Mischief danced around his face.

Happiness. The pure, innocent kind we used to share.

"Yes, Ollie. I am sure. Let me see it."

"Someone's eager."

I swiped under my eyes with the back of my hand.

Yes, yes, someone was eager.

He tugged at the little bow and pulled off the lid.

A gift.

For me.

For us.

The ring appeared antique.

Vintage.

Unique.

Encrusted in diamonds, a purple solitaire in the middle.

I breathed out between the tears that kept streaming down my face, eyes flicking between him and the ring. "It's gorgeous, Ollie."

"It's different, I know. But I saw it, and it reminded me of you. Not close to being traditional, and still so beautiful it stole my breath."

My spirit rumbled, a whisper from the deepest part of me. Where I'd always held this man. Ollie took the ring out of the box. "Marry me, Nikki."

"Yes."

I just caught a glimpse of it. What was etched on the inside of the ring at the base.

A dragonfly.

Everything soared.

Flapped in a flurry of emotion and memories.

And I swore I could hear Sydney's voice echo through the bar.

Whisper in my ear.

"Fly, fly, dragonfly."

Ollie slid the ring onto my finger. It fit so perfectly.

He pulled me into his arms, kissing me wildly, both of us on our knees while our friends and family shouted and cheered.

Carolina George continued to play *Marry Me*. The song so profound.

As if it it'd been written for us.

We finally climbed to standing, and Ollie was holding my hand as everyone came up individually to give us congratulations.

Hope was there, the lid off her cake, congratulations written in curvy letters, a field of purple blazing stars as the decoration.

I choked over a laugh. "You sneak."

"Hey, you were trying to sneak the party in on Ollie. Don't blame me that he one-upped you."

He turned to me before he started backing away, dragging me along with him, right up to that gleaming, carved bar.

He hopped on top of it, staring at me. He lifted his arms up and shouted toward the high ceilings. "Nikki Walters is gonna be my wife!"

Like he needed the world to know.

That he was proclaiming it to the heavens.

My attraction to him was so intense I wondered how he didn't taste it in the air.

Well, I guessed he did. Because he was watching me as if he was lost in it, too.

Bristling and brimming and begging.

Chemistry.

Bigger than life.

Somehow even bigger than the man that was this hulking tower of muscle and brawn and intricately drawn ink.

Every inch of him was rugged and rough and commanding, all dressed up in black fitted pants and a button-up, his body dripping sex.

An enigma.

A veiled mystery.

A cliffhanger waiting to be written.

And we were getting ready to write the rest of our story.

He hopped down and picked me up and spun me around as if I didn't weigh anything at all.

"I love you, Nikki Walters."

"I love you, Oliver Preston."

I love you.

My beautiful beast.

the end

Thank you for reading *Lead Me Home*! Did you love getting to know Ollie and Nikki? Please consider leaving a review!

I invite you to sign up for mobile updates to receive short, but sweet updates on all my latest releases.
Text "aljackson" to 33222
(US Only)
or
Sign up for my newsletter
http://smarturl.it/NewsFromALJackson

Watch for my upcoming series, *Confessions of the Heart*, coming Fall 2018!

Want to know when it's live?
Sign up here: http://smarturl.it/liveonamzn

More From A.L. Jackson

Confessions of the Heart – NEW SERIES COMING SOON
More of You
All of Me
Pieces of Us

Fight for Me
Show Me the Way
Hunt Me Down
Lead Me Home – Spring 2018

Bleeding Stars
A Stone in the Sea
Drowning to Breathe
Where Lightning Strikes
Wait
Stay
Stand

The Regret Series
Lost to You
Take This Regret
If Forever Comes

The Closer to You Series
Come to Me Quietly
Come to Me Softly
Come to Me Recklessly

Stand-Alone Novels
Pulled
When We Collide

A.L. Jackson

Hollywood Chronicles, a collaboration with USA Today Bestselling Author, Rebecca Shea –
One Wild Night
One Wild Ride – Coming Soon

ABOUT THE AUTHOR

A.L. Jackson is the New York Times & USA Today Bestselling author of contemporary romance. She writes emotional, sexy, heart-filled stories about boys who usually like to be a little bit bad.

Her bestselling series include THE REGRET SERIES, CLOSER TO YOU, BLEEDING STARS, as well as the newest FIGHT FOR ME novels.

Watch for her new series, CONFESSIONS OF THE HEART, coming Fall 2018

If she's not writing, you can find her hanging out by the pool with her family, sipping cocktails with her friends, or of course with her nose buried in a book.

Be sure not to miss new releases and sales from A.L. Jackson - Sign up to receive her newsletter http://smarturl.it/NewsFromALJackson or text "aljackson" to 33222 to receive short but sweet updates on all the important news.

Connect with A.L. Jackson online:

Page **http://smarturl.it/ALJacksonPage**
Newsletter **http://smarturl.it/NewsFromALJackson**
Angels **http://smarturl.it/AmysAngelsRock**
Amazon **http://smarturl.it/ALJacksonAmzn**
Book Bub **http://smarturl.it/ALJacksonBookbub**
Text "aljackson" to 33222 to receive short but sweet updates on all the important news.